SAM MILLS was born in 1975. After graduating from Lincoln College, Oxford University, she worked briefly as a chess journalist and publicist before becoming a full-time writer. She has contributed short stories to literary magazines and websites such as *Tomazi* and *3am* and written articles for the *Guardian*. Sam is one of the founding members of the Will Self Club (WSC) and was recently elevated to the position of Sovereign Grand Quiddity Inspector General, the most powerful position in the Selfian hierarchy: www.thewillselfclub.co.uk

THE QUIDDITY OF WILL SELF

SAM MILLS

corsair

Constable & Robinson Ltd
55-56 Russell Square
London WC1B 4HP
www.constablerobinson.com

First published in the UK by Corsair,
an imprint of Constable & Robinson, 2012

PEFC
PEFC/16-33-111
CATG-PEFC-052
www.pefc.org

For L.K.

With all my love

'The reader I seek is a tautology, for he/she is simply exactly the person who wants to read what I have written, and in this sense writing is a paradigm for the greatest of intimacy.'

Will Self, 2007

'It was Cocteau who said that all artists are hermaphroditic.'

Will Self, 1999

Contents

Prologue

Once upon a time in the city of London, a young woman was raped by a dictionary. Nine months later, she gave birth to twins. They were semi-Siamese, joined by their penises, but since their mother was Jewish, a convenient circumcision was the solution that separated them. Sadly, their mother was sickened by the very sight of them: their gurgles and soft, papery hair constantly reminded her of the black tome who had forced himself on her in an alleyway on that dark, doomed night in Soho. She gave them up for adoption, and the couple who cared for them – a pair of kindly, elderly lexicographers – decided to call the boys Will and Self.

Now, some people have a very foolish idea that twins are like two halves of one consciousness. But Will and Self, I am glad to say, disproved this theory. They grew up to be as different as Julian Barnes from Jilly Cooper, and their diversity was epitomized in their attitude towards languages. Self sought relief from the pain of adolescence by burying himself in the works of Roland Barthes, Derrida and other works of modern critical literary theory. He found himself falling orgasmically in love with the theories of Saussure and, most of all, the idea that language is a random tool, that word and form are unrelated: i.e., a rose could be called a table, or a table a rose. Words are merely meaningless interchangeable labels.

But Will . . . ah, Will was a more traditional chap. He loved ancient languages – Latin and Greek, their strict, unforgiving rules of grammar. He spent hours memorizing ninety tables of noun and verb cases; his favourite was the locative present pluperfect. He would taunt his brother by speaking in Sanskrit whenever he telephoned him; for Sanskrit, as we all know, is a purely onomatopoeic language which refutes Saussure's theories. You need only take the first syllable of the *Rik Ved* – and, indeed, Will spent many an hour taking it – to see this is the case. When he read the story of the Great Vowel Shift, describing the way that Old English had mutated into Modern, he wept his heart out and prayed that our beautiful language would slide back down the throat to its original, more guttural sounds.

Self was a subversive chap. He took a vindictive pleasure in seducing young girls from foreign-language schools and peppering his conversation with long words they could not understand, or giving them informal lessons that only left them more confused, in order to prove what a fickle and absurd language English was. (A useful side effect from their cross-purpose conversations was that the girls often slept with him too.) When he wrote articles for the *Guardian*, he regularly slipped in new, made-up words in his efforts to corrupt and mutate the language, like a scientist playing with genetically engineered animals in a laboratory.

And so they both spent their hours locked in their London flats in Chelsea (Self) and Shepherd's Bush (Will), immersing themselves in the study of the English language; one mocked and derided her as a whore, the other worshipped her as a princess. They both disturbed the English language, for she felt alternately loathed and loved in unhealthy measures. She asked them both to stop by way of symbolic dreams but, since neither was superstitious, this had no effect. She became angry and, as a result, she enacted a slow and subtle vengeance on the nation.

At first nobody in London noticed the changes. One or two became aware that they kept forgetting names, but they put it down to old age, stress or pollution. Then people began to realize that a verbal amnesia was slowly seeping through the city. Tourists would visit and stare at a square filled with pigeons and ask passers-by what the square was called, but nobody could quite remember. They mmmed and mused, puffed and panted. 'It begins with T ... it's just on the tip of my tongue ...' The same with the Houses of P— of ... P-p-p— Pickle! No, no, that's not it! I simply can't remember what they're called!' Soon it became an epidemic, worse than Aids or avian flu; people would call offices asking for 'Mr ... er, I can't remember his name', introducing themselves as 'Mr ... er, I can't remember my name', resulting in a muddle of business transactions that plunged the country into a catastrophic economic depression.

A meeting was held. The mayor spoke from a lectern, trying to reassure his people, but this was not easy when the malaise had shrunk his vocabulary to words of one syllable. As words failed him, the crowds jeered and threw stones.

And then, seemingly from nowhere, the most beautiful and buxom woman appeared. She was tall, with blonde tresses, her curves accentuated by a scarlet velvet dress. Instantly the crowd fell silent.

'I am the English language,' she said, in a sultry voice. 'And this crisis will be solved in the following way: I will have sexual intercourse with Will, and sexual intercourse with Self, and whoever pleases me most will dictate the future of the English language.'

Will was the first to go up to the hotel suite in the Hilton and share a bed with the beautiful temptress. He was shaking with nerves. However, his innocence proved useful, as he had no idea of foreplay, and a more experienced man might have been surprised by Ms English Language's actions. First of all, she took a Will Self novel (*How the Dead Live*, to be precise) and ripped out a flurry of pages. Then she threw them over the bed and pulled Will on to it. They made mad, wonderful and passionate love, the pages rippling and crinkling beneath them like the scales of an enormous paper fish, rubbing inky phrases into their flesh. Will was so awed by the power of his orgasm that he found himself struck dumb with love. From that day onwards, he left his books behind and wandered through the city of London, a silent but happy figure, forever cherishing that precious hour he had spent with her.

Next came Self. Self was more of a cynical chap, and Ms English Language could tell at once that he was trouble. She was about to rip open the pages of a Will Self novel, when he grabbed her wrist and stopped her, threatening to rape her if she dared to tear out just one page. Enraged, she cast a spell on him. Self found himself starting to shrink and shrink and shrink and shrink, like something out of a Hollywood black-and-white B-movie. He kept yelling words but, of course, words are not everything and they cannot save you when you are dying. And as he shrank, he found himself being slowly sucked into the Will Self novel until his soul was trapped inside the spine.

'My deed is done,' said Ms English Language. 'The language is now stabilized. However, Self's soul will live on inside every Will Self book that is ever published, and it will silently cry out to every person who reads one, so that they find themselves unable to put his books down, feeling compelled to keep reading and reading and reading, driven by some invisible, insidious force ...'

And so this true story explains why Will Self is one of the most successful writers around today.

Jamie Curren
Extract from *How Will Self Can Change Your Life* © 2006

Part One:
Richard

One

It was quite by accident that I discovered the body of Will Self. I had recently moved into a block of flats in Primrose Hill. They were plush, with white carpets, chandeliers in every hallway, and a guard slumped by the main door, who never raised his eyes from the *Daily Mail*. I was twenty-three years old and fresh out of Durham. Unlike most of my friends, who scurried away their lives in corporate wheels, I did not work. Earlier in the year my grandfather had died, leaving me a large inheritance. I had purchased the flat for the sole purpose of idling away the days until I woke up at some point in my thirties beset by an early mid-life crisis. But idling isn't easy: it requires thoughtful planning and diligent effort. I had no radio yet to lie back and listen to; a TV was still an idea circled in a catalogue; my books were all in boxes. I was tired of staring at white walls. I was tired of staring through the window at my moving painting of middle-class affluence. I was also lonely. And so I decided to knock on the door of the flat downstairs, asking if I might borrow a bowl of salt in an attempt to avoid sugary cliché.

I had seen the girl once, maybe twice. She looked as though she was a similar age to me: tall and slender, with fair hair and a nervous smile. She had muttered a few sweet hellos at me, and last week I had even instigated a conversation. 'Hello?'

'Hi, hi, you're new here . . .'

'Yes, I'm Richard.'

'I'm Sylvie.'

'Well, pleased to meet you.'

'Pleased to meet you. Well. 'Bye then.'

''Bye.' Well, it was a start. The start of what, I could not say. I did not find her particularly attractive. I told myself that I wanted to make her my friend, knowing that such a relationship between opposite sexes is impossible: the see-saw always tips one way or the other. Perhaps I liked the idea of her being in love with me.

As she fumbled with her keys, a card dropped from her handbag on to the floor. I only noticed it when she slammed the door and the gust of wind blew it across the carpet towards my feet. It was black and shiny, and looked as though it belonged in a Cluedo set. But I was certain no game of Cluedo had ever included a character called Mr Rabindarath. I felt a mild disappointment, assuming he was her boyfriend. Upstairs, I examined the card and deduced that it was advertising some sort of London club. The letters *WSC* swirled at the bottom, alongside *15 January 11 p.m.* I could not help suffering a flicker of jealousy; the Grouch instinct rears in us all.

And so the card, coupled with my desperate salt shortage, seemed to coalesce into a good enough excuse to interrupt her life.

Her door was white, the number, 32, nailed in gold. When I knocked, I realized that the door was already open: it swung forth gently.

A triangle of shadow spilled into the bright lobby. In

retrospect, I am certain I felt a chill as I stepped forwards into that darkness.

I remember the sounds I heard as the shadows enveloped me: the monotonous refrigerator hum of the building; the poignant cry of a child playing on the street outside. When I saw the shape slumped on the floor, I told myself that (s)he must be hungover and in need of help. But my subconscious had already computed that the victim was dead: there was a whiff of decay in the air, an aura of gloom around the body.

I stepped closer and saw that it was encased in a black suit. He – for he seemed a he – was lying face down on the floor. There was a wet pool spreading from his ribcage; the colour of red wine. I thought he might be Mr Rabindarath.

'Sylvie?' I called out softly. 'Sylvie?'

I pictured a terrible sequence of domestic scenes involving the now deceased Mr Rabindarath. I stepped backwards, suddenly conscious of fingerprints, hairs, fine fibres of my shoes and clothing. I had no desire to be labelled an accessory.

But something stopped me leaving. I saw that the walls were papered; I felt as though they were watching me. I flicked on the light and then I saw everything.

'Tell me again why you entered the flat?'

A pale light filled the creases in the policeman's hand. His biro smeared against the page and then hovered. He did not impress me. I was at that time rather a fan of crime fiction. I wanted a detective with heavy sideburns and a dirty mackintosh, with intelligence flashing in his dark eyes and a breath sour with whisky and despair. This man looked too soft to understand murder, with his baby curls and triple chin. He would have better suited to a country estate, knocking golf balls about.

Behind him a clock, five minutes fast, ticked loudly on the wall.

'Look, I hardly knew the girl. I just wanted to ask if I could borrow some salt – I mean, sugar . . .'

His eyes flickered.

'I'm new – I've only just moved into the area. I wanted to be her friend.'

'I see. What sort of friend?'

'Her friend. That's all.'

I was terrified that one thoughtless turn of phrase would condemn me. All my life, I have been intimidated by authority. It began at school, when I would never hand in a piece of homework late; I would walk through security arches at airports, convinced that the alarms were testing my conscience; if I pulled up alongside a police car at traffic lights I would give the officer a respectful nod and then fix my stare straight ahead of me. Sitting in this small interrogation room, my body became a physical Catch-22. My nervousness about not appearing nervous prompted a sweat on my forehead, a tic in my knee. I could not even drink the tea he had given me for fear of china rattling against the desk. The fact that I was innocent only made me more fraught; if I had been guilty, I suspect I would have been able to behave in a calm and insolent manner.

'What did you make of the pictures on the walls?'

'I thought they were very – well, odd.'

The pictures. They had surrounded the body like an obituary.

The room was a shrine. From wall to wall, from ceiling to floor, the same face stared down, omnipotent. A man who was both ugly and beautiful, with shrewd eyes, a heavy face and a grimacing smile. There was a huge black-and-white poster of him on the wall opposite, with the name *Will* scrawled in black ink. There were smaller pictures of him, in Andy Warhol strips. There were book covers, cut out and pasted into weird collages. There was a picture of an ape's head sporting glasses, with 'GREAT APES' scribbled in wild red pen across it; another of a woman waving a huge penis as she ran, like Cathy in *Wuthering Heights*, across a technicolour landscape. There were snippets of articles and journalism, all cut up and blown up and swirled together in a psychotic soup of images.

A black-and-white cat had appeared, miaowing, nuzzling against my legs. I had noticed a bloodstain on its nose, variegated on its ear. I had knelt down by the body. My fingers had travelled uneasily to his neck. No pulse, nothing . . . and yet . . . I swear I felt one last ripple of life before he finally passed away. Even now, months later, I sometimes still feel that beat pulsating at the tip of my right forefinger: the sensation spreads up my arm, into my blood, as though that last heartbeat lives on inside me.

Then the shock hit me on a physical level. My knees buckled and I half toppled on to the body, my sleeve soaking in the blood. The body still felt warm, as if hovering between life and death, and later, replaying the scene, I pictured its spirit still lingering in its fleshy shell, slipping out above me, looking down on the room, on the man by its body who clambered up, ran from the room into the hallway, hammered on a door and screamed for help.

'Nobody answered,' I explained. 'It was three o'clock in the afternoon. I guess most people were at work. Then I got myself — my act together. I went to my room, took my mobile and called you. Nine nine nine, I mean.'

He grated his chair. I winced. Since the discovery, my senses had become fine-tuned to a level of shell-shock sensitivity.

'I'd like you to examine these photographs. When you last saw Sylvie Pettersson, did she look like this?'

I was so revolted by them that I did not digest his words for several minutes.

'Sylvie? But the body I found – it – he was a – man.'

The policeman looked surprised, then suspicious. 'She had been dressed up as a man,' he said.

'But it can't have been her – it wasn't . . .'

'The body was Sylvie Pettersson's.'

I began shaking violently. The policeman pushed the tea in my direction. I gulped it down, blinking hard. Caffeine and sugar knifed my clenched stomach. Headlines from all the newspapers I had read idly on tubes and over breakfast tables spliced together to form nightmare visions of what might have happened before he took her life. I saw her mouth twisted into an O; I felt a jolt of revolted sexual pleasure, then shoved it away. I realized that the psycho might have been raping or slicing her as I had been lounging on my bed, examining marks on the ceiling in various shades of boredom. If I had just thought to listen, to be alert, I might have heard a scream, a bang, something.

I pushed the photographs away with shaking hands. The policeman laid his chubby fingers over them and pushed them back.

I stared down at them.

'That's not Sylvie!' I cried. 'Her face – that's just not her . . .'

'I can assure you, this is Sylvie Pettersson,' he insisted.

I lowered my eyes again. The tea threatened to rush back up my throat. The photos were of what could barely be termed a face. It was a puffy, bloated white *thing*, and yet, like a sculpture whose shape is half finished, there were moments of definition: a large nose, a thick jaw, a thin mouth. And beneath these foreign features I saw flashes of her ghost, in the curve of the creature's bruised cheeks, in the dainty flare of its nostrils. The face was not hers and yet hers.

I remembered that when I'd knelt down by the body I had noticed its fine, short blonde hair. The killer must have cut off Sylvie's mane. My mouth became weak with bile.

'So the murderer . . . did this to her . . .'

'You tell me.'

I gave him a look of such despair that he relented. 'No. In actual fact, we doubt it was the work of her killer. We have records of a plastic surgeon she visited several days before the killing. It was actually the second time she'd seen him for additional work on her nose, and it was only just beginning to heal. The killer had ripped the bandages from her face.'

'But why would she want to look like that? It's ridiculous!' My anger that he could have imagined I was the animal who had done this to her now found its channel. 'It's just insane. This doesn't make any sense. I don't want to speak to you any more until I have a lawyer.'

The policeman ignored me and pushed another photograph in my direction. I recognized it at once. It was the same man who had been plastered over her walls. And then I saw what her surgery had been aiming for: the face she sought to mimic. I found myself laughing. The policeman frowned.

'This — this is simply absurd.' I giggled. 'She was a beautiful girl . . . This is—'

'This,' the policeman tapped the photograph, 'this is a photograph of Will Self.'

'Will Self?' The name was familiar. 'He's a—'

'— novelist.' The policeman took a swig of tea. 'He writes novels set in, um, Africa. Romantic thrillers, I think. Terrific yarns. He's quite old but married to a young Oriental girl—'

'You're thinking of Wilbur Smith,' I corrected him. 'Will

Self – he's a serious writer, I think he's even been up for the Man Booker, and he writes about . . . well, about all kinds of challenging and intellectual subjects.'

The policeman did not look pleased. 'So you're saying you've read this man?' he asked suspiciously, as though Will Self clearly had only one reader, who was therefore conclusively Sylvie's murderer.

'No, I haven't,' I said. 'I've just – well, read about him, seen him on telly . . .'

'You're quite sure about that? So this wouldn't mean anything to you?' He drew out a cellophane folder, which carried a crumpled note. In bitter red letters was written:

I won't even win the Nonce Prize

'Did Sylvie leave this?' I didn't recall seeing it in the room.

'I'm asking you if this makes any sense to you.'

'If you're asking me if Sylvie was the type to take her own life, if you're asking me that, then I can't answer – I didn't know her. Like I said, I met her once! Okay? And we spoke for all of five minutes. I just don't know–' My voice broke off and I started shaking again. 'I'm sorry.' I swept my hands over my face.

To my surprise, the policeman reached out and gave my shoulder a quick, gruff rub. 'Have some more tea,' he said.

I was interrogated for another half-hour, my statement was taken and then I was released.

'Do let us know,' the policeman advised, passing me a card, 'if you remember anything else.'

I was just leaving when I remembered it: a crucial detail that I knew I ought to disclose to them. I wavered on the steps of the police station, dreading a return into its claustrophobic heat. Later, I told myself, and began the long walk home . . .

Two

Police cars were parked outside my block of flats, sirens scything the night sky. Residents clustered about, clutching their dinner jackets tightly around them, pearls and frightened eyewhites gleaming in the darkness as they exchanged shocked whispers. The building's exclusive aura had been tainted by the bureaucratic hangover of crime. Inside, I found the guard was no longer reading the *Daily Mail* but being interviewed by one of their reporters. The stairs were carpeted with the mud footprints of officers. I pictured the red tape ribboned across her door. I took the lift.

I sat on my bed for some time, hands nursing a mug. A pill tempted me but I told myself sternly that I was strong enough.

I recalled my journey to the police station: the sense of excitement mingling with the fear. I had assumed that the dead body had belonged to an ex, and hence rewritten Sylvie as a *femme fatale*, repainted her in my mind with fairer, tighter curls and a slash of scarlet across her lips. But now that I knew she was the victim, she took on the fragility of a Dickens heroine. I remembered her pale skin and the fear in her eyes. Her wrists, so slender that I'd felt if I grabbed one too suddenly she might shatter.

Her bizarre attempts at surgery only heightened my desire. I have always been drawn to crazy women. And so, that night, I fell in love with a suicide blonde. If she had lived, I suspect that the reality of our love affair would have been a post-coital exchange of lies, the subsequent dread of my flashing answer-phone and an embarrassed 'let's be friends' conclusion. But my imagination was busy fictionalizing her into an ideal. It was no different from an obituary, whereby the pointless chaos of a person's life is ordered into a beginning, a middle and an end: a story. The incomprehensible riddle of the human spirit is reduced to a series of two-D personality traits. It is, ultimately, a religious exercise, showing life leading towards a goal. And so I spent several poignant hours creating an alternative destiny: a first date; breathless lovemaking; a shared flat; a proposal. Despite our years of growing intimacy, the Sylvie in my mind never grew old: like Monroe and Dean, she was embalmed by eternal, tragic youth. Before I climbed into bed, I noticed that there were still crescents of her blood beneath my nails, which felt strangely comforting as I sank into sleep with her essence lingering about me.

My sleep did not last. I was woken repeatedly by the noises of policemen below. I pictured them going through her private space. Their hands dirty on her sheets, uncorking her bottles of perfume, fingering a diary. At two a.m., I woke again and they had gone, but the silence they left behind was more chilling. I pictured the surgeon's knife plunging into her pretty face. I had read somewhere that you were far more likely to be killed by someone you knew than someone stalking you on the street. *If you think of anything else, let us know.* Mr Raymond from twenty-six had dark, slanting brows and a suspicious face. Did I have a suspicious face? When I was a teenager and never had much luck with girls, I used to trace my reflection in the mirror, searching for an adjective to explain my failure. *Nondescript.* Brown hair, pale eyes, freckles. But what if the police were, at this very moment, discussing the guilt my features implied — *It's always the quiet ones* ... I got up and made myself some tea, eager to type her name into Google. But paranoia, bred from the consumption of too many American movies, prevented me. What if they were watching me? Tracing my trail? Recording each keystroke? I yanked out my cable and shut down.

Morning came. The light brought no relief. I wallowed in bed. My consciousness seemed to spread through the flat until, whether I stood up, bathed or strolled, its fog clung to me. I needed to escape myself. I packed my books and pencils into a battered briefcase. Outside, the air was fresh, but it was the collective consciousness that soothed me. To be swept up the escalators to the ticket machines, to feel my mind coloured by the conversations of others, to feel my tragedies diluted by the stories in newspapers.

At the library, I clicked on Google and typed: 'Sylvie Pettersson'.

I discovered an artist and an actress who shared the same name. And then a hit: she had once attended a luncheon for the Romantic Novelists Association in 2005. A search of Google images revealed a photo of her that made me start. She was at some sort of party, looking unexpectedly sexy, her eyes framed by a scarlet mask studded with silvery gems. In one hand, she held a tall green drink; her other palm was splayed open and in the centre was a small white object, barely larger than a postage stamp. I tried to zoom in on it, but the resolution was too low, and when I tried to discover who had taken the photo, I found the URL was broken.

Someone else was queuing for the computer, so I printed

out the picture and tucked it into my bag to examine later. I sat down at a desk, figuring that I ought to harvest my experience for the novel I was working on. I waited for inspiration to strike. I pictured my glowing reviewers, the champagne parties, my Man Booker Prize acceptance speech, all so vivid, so close – if only I could just write the first sentence! I recalled a piece of advice a friend had given me: 'If you're going to write a crime novel, you must mention the body on the first page.' I had decided crime was my genre – I was drawn to the neatness of a plot constructed like a puzzle. Tiredness began to afflict me; I longed to lay out my arms and sink my head into them. I reprimanded myself and took out a copy of Raymond Chandler's *The Big Sleep*.

> *It was about eleven o'clock in the morning, mid October, with the sun not shining and a look of hard wet rain in the clearness . . .*

I picked up my pen and wrote:

> *It was about eleven o'clock in the morning, mid October, with the sun not shining and a look of hard wet rain in the clearness . . .*

At university, a friend had once caught me preparing for a short-story competition by copying out the first chapter of Martin Amis's *Money*. He had initially been outraged, pointing out that the judges were not imbeciles, they would notice, Amis would sue. I argued back that I was not planning to use his work. I was trying to Amis-train my mind: quite a different thing. After all, I pointed out, an aspiring artist might be encouraged by his tutor to sculpt an imitation of Michelangelo's famous bust of Brutus. Likewise, by filtering Amis's prose through my pen, tiny grains of his genius would be left lingering in my consciousness. My friend was still incensed. 'You ought to aim for originality,' he said. 'You ought to develop *your own literary style*. The more you read, the more you will be in danger of never finding a pure voice; your style will simply become a cocktail of other writers',' he warned, scanning my bookcase darkly – a base of Amis, layers of de Bernières, a dash of Rushdie and a Barnes cherry on the top.

I disagreed. I pointed out that recent scientific research had proven that those who were most successful in life were those who learnt to imitate quickest. A child begins life like a chimp; locked in the zoo of his innocence and ignorance, he is chided by his keepers to learn to walk, to talk, to shit in the right place, to say please and thank you and hello how are you. In school he learns by copying down things from the teacher's blackboard. We live in a multicultural society where all differences are cherished, as long as we don't wear veils or crosses and we all look as uniform as possible. Those who fail to learn the art of imitation are punished, bullied in the playground or locked away in institutions. I concluded my argument by declaring that even God was afraid of being original, since He had made man in His own image. Therefore, it was perfectly natural that I should want to follow the literary herd.

And so I began copying out Chandler. I wondered if he had taken time crafting Marlowe's voice or if Marlowe had been born in his psyche fully formed, like some sort of literary spirit searching for a host. The thought of a voice finding its way into my consciousness, dictating prose, made me uneasy: I was much safer sticking with Chandler. Having copied out two pages, I attempted the opening of my novel. It would begin with a young man, fresh out of Oxford, asking a girl living below him to borrow a bowl of salt.

After a few lines, however, I felt spent. How did Chandler

do it? When he pared down his sentences, they snapped and crackled on the page; mine just seemed dull. Perhaps prose styles were unique snowflakes after all. I wondered if a few more metaphors might save me and spent half an hour trying to think of ways to immortalize Sylvie's hair.

On the tube home, I surreptitiously watched the rest of the carriage, and that familiar feeling seeped through me, so common these days – though I hoped it was due to my extreme tiredness rather than something requiring medication – that everyone else's lives were inherently superior to mine. The pregnant girl reading a magazine and circling her hand over her stomach possessed an unconditional love my heart would never know; the man in the pin-striped suit drove the type of car I would never own; the young black guy with dreads fingering his mobile belonged to a circle of friends I would never be cool enough for. I felt like a stranger walking about among life's satisfied customers, unable to obtain a refund.

I shook myself and spent the rest of the journey staring at the technicolour ads for cheap flights, stress pills and laddish beers, all promising the secrets of everlasting happiness.

On the walk to my flat, I bought a copy of the *Evening Standard* but there was no mention of her death.

Red light, red light. As I turned the key in the door, I pictured it winking. I threw down my books on the bed, took a deep breath, turned. The answerphone was still. My relief that there was no message from the police began to morph into a vague sense of disappointment.

My flat seemed to be shrinking. I sat in the kitchen. Everything was still in boxes. I drank some soup. I examined the passage I had copied. The clock ticked. I washed up. The clock said it was eight thirty. I might as well go to bed now. There was nothing else to do.

In bed, I twitched my hand over my pyjamas but my cock was too bored to respond. I sighed and switched off my light. And then I remembered.

I leapt up, checked the drawer. My God.

I picked up the phone, but on the third nine, I put it back down. I slid the card from the drawer. The detail I had failed to tell the police: the card that had slipped from Sylvie's handbag. Maybe I ought to destroy it.

I examined the card once more.

Mr Rabindarath: an Asian man with a double chin supported by a yellow and green tartan collar. His dark eyebrows beetled over squinty eyes. His expression was smug. Beneath his face, the swirling letters said, '11 p.m., Tuesday, 15 January, Rothwell Towers'.

Tuesday, 15 January was tomorrow night.

Three

I've always liked being stuck in motorway traffic.

I was expecting the WSC to be held in a trendy basement in Soho, but when I typed the postcode into 'streetmap', it turned out to be somewhere in Buckinghamshire. Halfway down the A40, the cars ground to a standstill. Someone looking down on us might have concluded that the gridlock was a festival for a particularly vindictive God taking Tithes of Boredom. I turned my car into a private cathedral, Radio 3 up to full volume, so that Handel's *Messiah* shook the car at heavy-rock decibels. After weeks of idling, I felt utterly alive. I was almost disappointed when the red Ford in front of me picked up pace and the service ended.

I had to focus on the map now, which meant turning *Messiah* down low. At this pitch, it became haunting. I found myself thinking of Sylvie. Where she might be. For a few minutes I allowed myself the indulgence of picturing her soul floating in clouds, hugging ancient relatives, suspended in waves of celestial music. But Sylvie was rotting in a coffin. Being raped by worms. An underground party. Insecticidal glut.

I didn't believe in God. That only led to War. One fewer believer would help contribute to the cause of peace. But, like all cynics, I was an idealist at heart. As a teenager I had under-gone the crisis that everyone suffers at some point in their lives, sooner or later: a sense that life is not as it should be, that some magical ingredient is missing. I turned to Christianity. It was a mistake, for there is a seed of latent fanaticism in my personal-ity that had led to amusing obsessions in my boyhood (killing worms, frying ants, collecting matchboxes) but when planted in religion grew into something rather terrifying. It could not last.

And so I settled for atheism. It was safer. Easier, too. For atheism is, of course, the opium of the individual. Believing in divine punishment, in an afterlife, in karma, forces you con-stantly to face the consequences of your choices. In atheism, your actions are like dominoes that fall without ever strik-ing another piece. Religion was not something I wanted to return to.

Except for Death. Only the loss of people I loved made me yearn once more for Something, Someone to believe in.

By the time I reached Cheddington, I found myself ahead of time. London's dirty air had become purified; here it was sweet with birdsong and hints of an early spring. I pulled up in a coun-try lane and took a short break. I'd brought sandwiches, which I munched while slurping a can of Sprite. I flicked through a copy of the *Daily Telegraph*. Every so often my eyes flicked to the invitation, sitting on the dashboard, and a voice asked, *What are you doing?* in a tone that was sometimes admonitory, sometimes happy, and sometimes claimed that I was doing this for Sylvie.

When I realized that I was lost, I enjoyed having to stop and ask a stranger for directions. As I thanked him, I heard my voice deepen with a Marlowe edge.

I rolled down a country lane, turned left and saw a large pair of iron gates, wrought with elegant ivy curls. A green Jaguar swung up the drive and a guard dressed in black with a cap opened them. I pulled up right behind the car, still observing carefully. The window on the driver's side hummed down. A black-gloved hand was thrust out, proffering a small card. The guard nodded, waved him on. Before I had a chance to prepare, he was knocking on my window. As I rolled it down, the mint of his gum stung my nostrils. His eyes narrowed on my face. I had to steady my hand as I reached for the Cluedo card and passed it over. He held it up to the light, tapped it against his teeth, examined it again and then passed it back with a brusque nod.

'Put your mask on,' he said.

'Oh, sure.' I licked my lips and swallowed. 'Sorry, I forgot — it's in the back. I'll just put it on now.'

I saw doubt in his eyes again, so I quickly wound the window up before he could change his mind.

Mask? I rolled up the driveway, the car bumping over the sweep of gravel. When I saw the mansion, it took my breath away. Perched on a sweep of green hill, it looked as though it had been cut out of a Gothic ghost story, spires piercing the twilight clouds. Two lions growled on stone columns and a thousand windows stared out with dead eyes. It took me a moment to work out why I couldn't see inside: every single one had been boarded up.

The driveway at the front was empty. The gravel split into two paths, one that dipped down the hill and trailed off into a sea of grass, another that wound round the back. Which way, which way? My engine thrummed. Then one of the windows blinked, a sudden flash of yellow iris before it snapped shut again. I began to panic that my erratic behaviour was being noted and turned on to the path that ran down the side of the mansion. Trees formed an arch overhead; a rabbit scampered across my headlights. I quickly braked. Out of the darkness, the Angel of Death suddenly appeared in the periphery of my car's beam. His face swung towards me for a few seconds, in which I realized he was human, dressed in black, and wearing a mask. Then he disappeared into a side door.

I heard voices in the distance and switched off my head-lamps. Two more figures dressed in black strolled by and I ducked down, pretending to be searching for something, my face dangerously naked. Fortunately, they were too engrossed in their conversation to notice me.

'Are you going to Jamie's on Thursday?' His voice startled me with its middle-class banality.

'I don't know . . . I don't know . . .'

'Aw, come on, you have to go . . .'

'Jamie-bloody-Curren . . . I don't know . . .'

'It was Jamie-bloody-Curren who made you a neophyte, so be grateful!'

Then, in a quieter voice: 'Do you have the knife?'

'Who do you think will be chosen to use it tonight?'

They entered the side door and were lost.

I sat there, engine throbbing, suspended in shock. Then I fumbled a pen from my pocket and scrawled on the corner of my newspaper, *Jamie Curren*.

A toot behind me made me jump. In my mirror, I saw a face winged with black silk butterflies. I rolled the car to one side, waving, *move on*, with my palm. Her eyes devoured me before she disappeared round the back.

I reversed and sped up the driveway. The guard folded his arms, a little snigger twisted on to his lips, as though he had known all along that I was an imposter. I rolled down the win-dow and called out — and the panic that had taken possession of me added an authentic trembling to my voice: 'I have to go – it's an emergency – my mother. Please give Jamie Curren my apologies.'

Were 'Jamie Curren' the magic words? Or did he really believe the story about my mother? In any case, he looked apologetic, hastening to the gates and unlocking the padlock. I sped out, swerved around the corner and drove for about fifteen minutes until I found myself in a dark lane and finally felt safe. Finally my heart was still.

Sprite bubbles floated in my stomach. The fluorescent light in my car beamed down on *Daily Telegraph* headlines. A woman had been convicted of shaking her one-year-old baby to death. We were bombing the Middle East once more. In China, a restaurant was now serving Tiger's Penis, charging businessmen three thousand pounds in the belief that it would improve their life energy and virility. For once, the paper's harvesting of the sadness and absurdity of everyday life reassured rather than depressed me. As I turned to the Letters page, my mind drifted, recalled the mansion. In the grip of fear I had been convinced I was in a real-life horror movie involving eerie choreographed dances, haunted halls drowning in blood, and drugged guests lying groaning beneath the flickering light of rusty candelabra as masked surgeons carved apart their faces. Now my embarrassed imagination rewrote the scene as a comedy. No doubt at this very moment – 1.04 a.m., my car clock informed me – the boys and girls were glugging beer, snogging, bopping, masks sagging, cloak hems stained with footprints and sick. Or was I just downplaying the danger to soothe myself? I recalled the knife discussion with a prickle of unease. Perhaps the picture of Sylvie wearing the mask had been taken at one of these parties. Once more, I wondered if I ought to have informed the police.

I had made a pathetic Marlowe.

A light flashed on in the cottage across the lane. An old woman peered through her curtains, eyeing my car suspiciously.

I had started the engine and was just folding up the paper when I saw it. Page nine:

> Police are investigating the murder of Sylvie Pettersson, aged twenty-five, who was found dead in her flat last Friday. She suffered multiple knife wounds to her body and died of excessive bleeding. Friends say that she was in a fraught state before she died, and when her death was first announced, some even assumed that she had committed suicide.

I heard the guard again, warning me to put on my mask. What would he have done if I hadn't – shot me? I laughed out loud. Then my laughter became tears. I thought of Sylvie's shy smile. I kept on driving, pausing to mimic the windscreen wipers and clean my face. It took me several more hours of blurred missed turns to get home.

I pulled into the residents' garage. Outside, the sky was shifting between night and dawn. I felt as though the city had been wiped out by a plague and the only ones left were me, the old man playing Rachmaninov in the flat above and the fighting cats whose yowls scratched the air. Home, sweet home, felt like a dead-end; I would have preferred to be back in my car, driving into the day.

Up in my flat, I walked on tiptoe. I felt her presence: I could not enter a room without first switching on the light. The curtain hiding the shower, and whatever was behind that, hung in crenullations that I was too fraught to twitch. I had thought this past was buried. I had thought these demons had been beaten so small they were beyond atoms. Tonight they had been reincarnated. I heard their laughter as I knelt down before the box, disturbing dust as I pulled out piles of books, napkins, crockery. I knocked back the pills, downed water, then curled up in bed, shivering, as dawn bled round the edges of the curtains and the cats continued to howl.

Four

After the age of thirty, every man is responsible for his own face. A Japanese saying that I had once read in a book, whispered by a woman to her lover. My reflection in the mirror smiled back at me, enjoying its youthful lie. I had a habit of holding my expression taut when I looked into the glass; if I took off my social mask and let it fall slack, my expression was one of deep worry. I forced a smile and whispered, 'Yes, Richard Byam-Cock, how do you do? Yes, I've always been a fan of Jamie's work.' Behind me, the shower curtain had been pulled neatly to the end of the rail, exposing a pristine bath.

I stood on tiptoe – for this square of mirror was the only insight I had into my appearance – and was pleased that I looked the part. Earlier today, I had gone to Hugo Boss and splashed out on a charcoal suit. It wasn't me, but that was part of the joy: normally the prospect of a literary party would have sent me into a flurry of nerves on what to wear and what to say. Particularly one that I had blagged my way into by calling up a Penguin publicist. Because I was adopting a persona I felt no fear; my lines were already written for me.

Drifting out of the bathroom, I picked up the clippings lying on my bed.

Tonight I was determined to find out what the WSC was. I had researched Jamie Curren and discovered that he was actually vaguely famous, the leader of a literary clique that consisted of around half a dozen writers. I had printed off material from the Internet and assembled a little collage of their personalities made up of Amazon reviews, *Guardian* columns, and profiles in the *Face, Dogmatika, 3am* and *Dazed and Confused.*

Jamie had begun his writing career at the tender age of eighteen. His novel, *Pus,* was about a group of bored teenagers who, weary with *ennui* and cynicism, spent much of the novel stealing, shoplifting, joy-riding, having anal-sex orgies and, from time to time, debating the meaning of life. He had received a lot of acclaim and backlash over his long descriptions of drugs – teenagers injecting themselves with heroin, rolling around on Axminsters, throwing up in expensive lavatories and so forth – though on close reading, I suspected that he had probably never smoked much beyond the odd joint. His interviews suggested that he had delighted in all the controversy. They were peppered with phrases such as 'I can't see why everyone is making so much fuss' or 'I just wrote the book without thinking about how anyone might react to it'; he protested just a little too much.

Jamie was now twenty-five, and aside from *Pus,* all he had penned was a Samuel Beckett-style novella about an elderly man, the sole inhabitant of a remote Scottish island, who sits and writes a biography of Wagner and, having got bored halfway through, strolls out and shags a sheep. It hadn't sold many copies. Since then, he had spewed out an impressive deluge of reviews, articles and opinion pieces, and made frequent appearances on TV in late-night debate shows about topics such as 'Do we really need men any more?' In short, he had become more of a media personality than a writer, his image more polished than his prose style.

Another member of Jamie's clique was Tobias, nicknamed Toady. He was publishing a book this autumn, one of those memoirs about abusive childhoods involving horrific beatings and being forced to drink Polyfilla. Zara, Jamie's half-sister, had published a multicultural love story called *Bombay Mix*. And then there was Nicholas, a tall, thin man who wrote stylish crime fiction about London gangsters, *à la* Tarantino. Individually, none of these writers was especially interesting, but as a group they formed an incestuous, exclusive little clique that had caught the attention of the media. Interestingly enough, they were not called the WSC anywhere in public. Instead the gossip columns regularly referred to them as 'Jamie's Boys' or 'The Bright Young Things' or 'The Young Literary Élite'. They were infamous for their bad behaviour: Jamie was being sued for punching a reviewer, they had all been thrown out of the Hilton last month for their debauched partying, and Zara had been arrested for streaking naked across Trafalgar Square (a dare). A lot of critics and chatrooms were devoted to slating them, declaring that they were 'pathetic' and 'media tarts' and 'élitist to the point of Fascism'. While I was in no doubt that this was true, I had to admit that I was already a little in love with all of them, and could hardly wait to make their acquaintance.

Due to a problem on the Northern Line, it was a quarter past eight when I finally reached the Bloomsbury gallery. The guests were already on their second glass of wine and act of conversation.

I passed through a sea of crowds, pausing at exhibits that looked as though they'd washed up from a shipwrecked boat on which Dalí, Cronenberg and Burroughs had been sailing. The central piece was a papier-mâché brain, composed of pages ripped from various books (*The Unbearable Lightness of Being, Decline and Fall, The Heavenly Sisters* among others), with pencils sticking in and out of its wet membrane. I moved into another ante-chamber, where I spotted Jamie standing behind a life-size plastic doll. The doll's limbs were twisted into contortions of pain; every three seconds a giant motorized HB pencil swung and thrust into her vagina and a stream of red ink slithered down her thighs. The plaque beneath it said: *The Rape of the Muses.*

Jamie's laughter overlapped her cries. Admirers surrounded him. Cameras flashed. Reporters pondered. Someone thrust a mike into his face. Though he wasn't nearly as handsome in the flesh as he was in his grainy black-and-white photographs, I was struck by the force of his charisma. There was an arrogance in his face – in the jut of his chin, the snarl of his eyebrows – counterbalanced by a feminine vulnerability in his lips and high cheekbones. The group of journalists around him had struck up a sort of informal press conference and, since I was Richard Byam-Cock from the *Sunday Telegraph*, I joined them.

'Could you give me a soundbite, please? Something to sum up the basis of thought behind this exhibition?'

'I'm fascinated by the manner in which the Berlin walls that have previously separated art, literature and music are finally being dismantled. I think what we're finding at the moment is a kind of synthesis and a synaesthesia of arts. There are comic books, graphic novels, combining amazing storytelling with vivid visual images. And then, of course, there is the great Will Self himself, who is at this moment in time sitting in a Liverpudlian tower block, working on his latest novel, allowing people to view at him at work. An Author who has also fash-ioned himself as a work of Art, who is creating as he allows him-self to be created and shaped by other people's imaginations.

'I wanted each visitor to feel as though they were not enter-ing a gallery but a virtual reality of my subconscious. I wanted this gallery to be a kind of chronology of the growth of a poet's mind – a visual equivalent of *The Prelude*. All the writers, artists and musicians who have influenced me are here, from Jarvis Cocker playing in the gallery to my *Ode to Will Self*.'

Will Self, Will Self. A few weeks ago I had never heard of him; now he seemed omnipotent. I raised a nervous hand and asked, 'Can I ask what sort of influence precisely Will Self has had on you?'

I had intended the question harmlessly; indeed, I had hoped to flatter his ego and catch his attention. But several review-ers tittered and Jamie's expression became decidedly cool. He replied, 'Well, we both use full stops,' which prompted raucous laughter and a spatter of applause.

Jamie curtly concluded that he'd answered enough ques-tions. He pinned his eyes on my face and held me, like a scien-tist with an insect squiggling between his tweezers.

'I –' I began to stutter '– I . . . I only meant . . .' But Jamie had already walked off. The rest of the reviewers shook their heads and gave me unimpressed glances.

Well, I thought, acid burning in my stomach. Suddenly I was Richard Smith again, standing in a suit that didn't suit, as ludi-crous as a child trying on his parent's clothes. I thought: I can't do this – I don't have the skills. I'm a writer, an observer, not a charmer, not a spy.

I became aware that I was being watched. A girl was standing a few feet away, taking sips from a cup and jutting her chin with an air of self-sufficiency while clearly longing for some-one to talk to. She was wearing a pink summer dress and kept tugging at the hem and rearranging the straps and smoothing her hand over the skirt, a display of modesty that was actually rather sexy, drawing attention to her flesh: thin thighs, ice-cream scoop shoulders, lightly freckled arms. She gave me a terse smile. I grimaced back, disliking this mirror of my own social ineptitude, and moved on.

I wanted a drink but I'd taken some more of my old med this morning so instead I decided to get some air. I sat on the chilly steps and broke a six-month smoking fast, my conversation with Jamie going over and over in my head, only each time my replies got wittier until I was the centre of attention and everyone was laughing at him.

Then I felt it. A whisper shivering behind my left ear. I had the curious sensation of a presence again, as though Sylvie had leant over my shoulder and I had felt her hair brush against my skin.

The moment died and I frowned, posthumously attributing it to the wind. I was about to go back in when I was distracted by a large, shiny car pulling up. Out stepped a tall man in his fifties, with magnificent grey hair swept back from his patrician's face. He carried an air of self-importance, like a fur coat draped across his shoulders.

A young woman got out of the other side. As she bent down to wipe an invisible smudge off her black leather boot, I was treated to a glimpse of possibly the largest cleavage I had ever encountered. Then she stood up, flicked back her blonde dreadlocks, looped her arm through his and they marched into the party together. I followed them in at a distance, intrigued by the excitement that rippled through the crowds: 'It's Archie West!'

'Archie, oh, wow!'

'What – here?'

'Yes, here. He represents Jamie now, you know.'

'Sacked his other agent for him.'

'Gets a million for every client.'

'Who on earth is that girl with him?'

I rolled my eyes and downed the rest of my orange juice with a sour burp. Back inside, I passed an exhibit called *Writer's Block on a Bad Day.* A paraplegic in a wheelchair was swiping a fat brush in a tin of red paint and swishing it over the white stretch of wall in clumsy patterns, like a corybantic CAT scan. One young girl started crying, saying that her brother had Down's syndrome and she didn't think it was a laughing matter; the security guard assured her that the paraplegic was enjoying his celebrity status and had got laid for the first time last week.

On a better day, I might have found the whole thing funny. But I was determined to hate Jamie, so I adopted a repulsed expression.

Then I saw it. It was hanging at the back of the exhibition, like an afterthought. A small picture of Sylvie at a party wearing a mask: the same one that I had printed out in the library. The plaque next to it read: *In memory of a dear friend.* This version was much bigger than the one I had; I leant in, examining the small square in her palm. There was a picture on it — of Self's face. Was it a Will Self postage stamp? I squinted in puzzlement, studying it for a good ten minutes, but I still could not come up with any explanation.

I longed to ask Jamie but I had no desire to suffer another whiplash of sarcasm. Then I spotted Toady and Nicholas. They were standing in a corner, seemingly uninterested in the exhibition, chatting quietly. Toady had sandy hair and wore red Christopher Biggins spectacles. He was extremely tall and quite plump, his gestures possessing the apologetic clumsiness of a Dobermann. Nicholas was tall, reedy and dressed in a black polo-neck. Smoke from a little white cigarette curled about his profile; he looked as though he belonged in the back alley of a *film noir*. They seemed marginally more approachable than Jamie.

I sidled up to them, pretending to be interested in an exhibit entitled *Books that have never given me the slightest spark of inspiration*: a pile of chick lit with mounds of stinking shit slopped on to their glossy covers, and the cheerful footnote beneath: 'The faeces were kindly denoted by horses from the London County Shire Stables.'

'I just don't know what the hell Archie is doing,' Toady was saying. 'I mean, how can he concentrate on selling *us* if he's bloody screwing glamour girls? I can't believe he brought that bimbo. I thought Archie had class.'

'Oh, he's not fucking her,' said Nicholas.

'So what is he doing, then? Teaching her to knit?'

'She's publishing a kids' book. Archie agented the deal. Over a million pounds in advances from thirty countries. Some book teaching kids the moral of not eating too much or they grow up obese.'

They burst into inebriated laughter and I found myself chuckling out loud. They noticed me and I smiled at them. They didn't smile back.

'Hi, I'm Richard Byam-Cock.' I mustered up a display of confidence, putting out my hand for them to shake.

They looked even more put out, but Toady had the grace to shake my hand and manage half a grin. Nicholas merely raised an eyebrow and looked over my shoulder.

'Any relation to, er, Jamie?' Toady asked.

'None, I'm afraid,' I said. 'I'm a journalist.'

'Oh.' They looked at me as though I'd just announced I swept the streets for a living.

'Well,' Toady reflected, 'there could be worse professions. Like prostitution.' He giggled, and a smile rippled across Nicholas's thin lips.

'Well, nice chatting to you,' I said tightly, about to move

away, when Toady patted my arm and said, 'Look, I'm sorry – I didn't mean anything. I just have a bit of thing against journalists but, hey, I'm sure some of you are almost human.'

'Do you – do you happen to remember a girl called Sylvie Pettersson?' I asked. 'I noticed there's a picture of her over there.'

Their reaction was marked. Immediately Toady buried his nose in his glass, while Nicholas swallowed hard and stared into the distance.

'She was . . . We liked her very much. She was a good egg,' said Toady, nervously.

'Zara is surrounded by perverts,' Nicholas interrupted, shaking his head and blowing a thin funnel of smoke out of the corner of his mouth. 'Look at them. I don't know what Jamie's playing at. He just wants people to think he's secretly doing her.' He sighed. 'When are we going to get out of here and get to the Sealink?'

'You go and ask Jamie. He hasn't forgiven me still for Saturday night when I beat him at Cluedo.'

'That's because you cheat, Toady.'

'I do *not* cheat . . .'

Their conversation faded away, for I had turned and caught my first glimpse of Zara.

Among the literary shipwreck, she lay washed up like an exhausted siren who has given *un petit mort* to too many a sailor. Naked on the bed; a chessboard of white sheet and black hair.

Muted light softened her curves, covered with a thousand downy gold hairs, like the skin of some fabulous exotic fruit.

I thought of Eliot and *The Love Song of J. R. Prufrock* and, for the first time, words sharpened into reality and I understood what it meant.

There was a sign above her bed that read *My Muses*. Men had gathered round, surreptitiously raping her by eyeball. They stared at her while chatting to their friends, or stared at her while feigning to look at a programme, or stared at her while pretending to drop their programme and do up their shoe-laces; and all hovered around a three-minute threshold, then hurried on reluctantly, fearing anything more would appear obscene. I didn't care. I stood and stared, and came closer, and stared some more. Next to me I overheard a guy whispering loudly whether one could buy tickets for a closer look. I wanted to grab a sword and slash them all to blood and bones, to pick her up and carry her out like a conquering knight.

I kept willing her to look at me, but she stared at the floor. Gradually, I began to spot what everyone else had failed to notice. She was hiding it well, but I could see it in the goose pimples on her arms, the yellow hue lacing her eyewhites, the feverish flush in her cheeks. I was about to go and get her a glass of water when suddenly she looked up at me, then glanced away, without even an attempt at retinal battle.

Suddenly I felt cheap. I looked like just another guy hosing his silent lust all over her. I wanted to say, It's more than that. I wanted to walk up to her and touch her fabulous skin. For one frightening, dazed moment, I actually thought I was going to do it. Then someone shoved past me. Jamie.

He stepped over the red velvet ropes and sat down on the bed next to her. His expression was uncharacteristically tender. He whispered something in her ear, and she nodded, gathering the sheets up around her.

A new flood of people entered the party, led by a small man in Armani with greasy brown hair. Jamie's face tightened and he pushed through the crowds, muttering, 'I can't believe his fucking nerve.'

I'm not quite sure how the fight started. I was too distracted by watching Zara glide across the room, a sheet wrapped round her, and into the dressing rooms. By the time I became aware of the noise and the crowd forming, I'd missed most of the action. I did, however, hear the crack, like a gunshot, a noise that went through me and echoed in the roots of my teeth. I turned to see Jamie throwing a punch at the guy's face. The violence aroused me and I followed the pull of my cock, leaning in closer. I was disappointed when Jamie's friends held him back. 'I told you not to come,' he kept crying, while the other man yelled back, 'All this over a few bloody full stops!' After a little more kerfuffle, Jamie and his friends made for the door.

My heart skipped as Zara emerged from the Ladies. I was disappointed when she ignored my gaze, hurrying past in a flurry of perfume and dark hair. I opened my mouth and fought saliva for a few seconds; by the time I'd called, 'Hello,' she was already ploughing through the crowds, cigarette dangling from her mouth. Jamie put his arm round her and his clique left the building.

The party emptied fast. The injured man (who turned to be a journalist), still holding a handkerchief to his bloody nose, was arguing quietly with a small, dapper man (the gallery owner, I believe) on whether or not it was a matter for the police. People were gossiping and muttering, but their conversation sounded grey. It was as though a flock of peacocks had shown up to flash their plumage and then taken flight, leaving pigeons to peck at the crumbs they'd left behind. The drinks were running out and sticky paper cups lay littered across the floor. I felt washed up and listless; perhaps I'd go and find an Oddbins, then head home and drink until I passed out.

I was collecting my coat from the cloakroom when the dark-haired girl in the pink dress I had noticed earlier appeared behind me. She was burrowing in her handbag with tsks of irritation.

'Hold these, will you?' she commanded, thrusting a copy of Jamie's latest book and an umbrella into my hands. 'Where is it, where is it? Do I definitely need the ticket?' she appealed to the attendant, who shrugged awkwardly.

I gave the attendant an apologetic look.

'Oh, here it is.' The attendant returned with a black raincoat.

She took it without thanking her. Then she turned to me and grabbed her things back. 'Cheers,' she added, as an afterthought. She narrowed her eyes, appraising me in such a predatory manner that I felt myself bristle. 'I'm Mia.' She held out a hand armed with pointy purple talons. 'I'm a journalist.'

'I'm Richard Smith,' I said, crumpling up my façade. 'And I'm a nobody.'

At first I thought that her shrill laughter was aimed at me and my fingers flexed into a fist. Then she blurted out: 'I was actually meant to come with my boyfriend. But he, um, stood me up. Men. I mean – God.' She slipped her arm through mine and caressed her head against my shoulder like a cat. The gesture, so tender in contrast to her flinty demeanour, touched me. I kissed the top of her head and she whispered, 'Let's go.'

I wasn't seriously interested in her. Despite Zara's breathtaking beauty, I still felt a curious connection to Sylvie, and any other woman could only be painfully mortal. But she seemed a lot more appealing than waking up with a lonely hangover. Suddenly I found myself aching for female company, for caresses and soft kisses to soothe the wounds the night had inflicted on my ego.

As we were leaving, the final exhibit accosted us: *An Ode to Will Self.* It consisted of a giant photograph, sixteen feet by sixteen, of Jamie's portrait computer-synthesised on top of Will's, or perhaps Will's on top of his, forming a face like a hall of mirrors: double-chinned, quadruple-cheeked. The effect was deeply unsettling, like seeing a doppelganger frozen in mid-metamorphosis. Mia shuddered and curled her arm tighter through mine.

Mia lived in Primrose Hill, in a house she had just inherited from her grandmother; we tiptoed up to her attic bedroom and attempted to have sex while two cases of dead moths stared down on us.

My cock became a toy tugged between Mia and Sylvie. My lust for Zara had already irritated her; now her jealousy brushed the back of my neck; she sang softly as she shrank my cock to baby imitation. I tried to fight her with more and more vehement thrusts – until Mia surrendered, pulling out from under me with a loud sigh. My cock flopped. The soggy condom lay on the bed like vomit.

I thought I heard faint singing, and then distant crying. I wanted to weep too, then, and despite my angry humiliation, I begged for her to stay with us while we slept, to nestle between our sleeping bodies. But she took her revenge and left.

Mia rolled over and lit a cigarette. She curled her lips around it, blew out one puff, then snuffed it. Her fingers were on the lamp switch, when I said hastily, 'Do you know – have you ever met, come across, a writer called Sylvie Pettersson?'

'No.' She sounded jealous. 'No. Wait, she's not a writer – she *wanted* to be a writer.'

At this hour of the night, such élitism was exhausting.

'And did you know her?' I asked.

'She went out with Jamie, so for a while she was showing up all over the place. And then she kind of disappeared. I guess he got bored with her, just like he always does. I heard she had some kind of weird plastic surgery that went wrong, then topped herself as a result.'

'She didn't—' I broke off, swallowing back the emotion. 'God. That's an awful shame. How did Jamie feel about it?'

Mia shrugged.

'What's the WSC?' I asked.

'The *what*?'

'The WSC.' I was surprised: Mia was clearly well connected in the grid of literary gossip and I had assumed she would reveal all.

'God knows. Is this a game?' She yawned, clearly bored with the conversation, so it seemed the obvious thing to try to fuck her again.

But even when I closed my eyes, I could not fully pretend she was Sylvie.

Five

I ought to have started reading the novels of Will Self for clues at once and, looking back, I regret the vital time I wasted. Instead, I spent the next few days suffering an unhealthy preoccupation with the fallacy of the body. I sat on my bed and pinched the skin on my left arm into crêpy folds. Outside, I stared at old people as they propped themselves up in bus queues or drooped over tables in cafés. In the bathroom, I examined my cock and wondered how cocks aged, for I had never seen an elderly example. Would my foreskin imitate the breasts of retired women, so that I had to carry it around like a sagging yo-yo? I guessed my balls would become little more than coffins for dead sperm; no doubt they would shrink with humiliation. I thought of the lie of the spirit, the way it convinces us that our bodies will always remain plush and shiny. I replayed the moment in Mia's bedroom and argued with myself that I might replace the word *spirit*, with its uneasy connotations of religion and superstition, with *consciousness*, the scientific understanding of something that might exist independently of the corporeal body. At night, when I lay in bed, that moment just between waking and the next state, when my mind was on the precipice, was always filled with expectation, the hunger to feel that breath again. But all that ever came was sleep.

Five days passed, and Sylvie was no longer mentioned in the news. The picture of her that had hung in Jamie's exhibition haunted me, became the *Mona Lisa* of my dreams. *In memory of a dear friend*, his plaque had said. I recalled Toady's discomfort, Mia's assertion that Jamie had discarded Sylvie. I wondered if the picture was an apology or an alibi. I tried to think up new ways to ingratiate myself with the WSC; my next possible move was to look up Zara in the *Yellow Pages* or fake a fan letter begging to meet her. Then another idea came to mind. The name of Sylvie's plastic surgeon was mentioned in a newspaper article; I called him up and made an appointment for Friday.

Wednesday came and I found myself playing a game. I dressed myself up as though I was about to go on a date with Sylvie, which gave me permission to wank off in the bathroom while staring at my printout of her picture. It seemed grotesque to touch myself while fantasizing over a dead girl. But by creating an alternative universe where Sylvie had lived, it didn't feel quite so disgusting. As I gripped my cock, however, I found that my climax seemed elusive. The memory of Sylvie's room and the array of Will Self pictures on her walls hardened me again. I went on like this for a while, in cycles of softness and virility, feeling an increasing sense of dismay. It seemed that the fear I had felt on entering her room, on seeing her body, was now being transmuted into excitement. I was scared that this new union between my imagination and my cock was giving birth to a fetish. In the end, I gave in to it: I pictured myself undoing her trousers, feeling her fake cock — erect in death — and then finding her hole, stitched up from her sex change, my hardness breaking through the threads and thrusting deep inside her. I fantasized that, as I made love to her, life began to shimmer back into her body, and with my final spurt of sperm, she became a female Lazarus. She turned to face me, her expression joyous, and I leant down and kissed her Selfian features.

My sperm splattered over the lino: one large pool, surrounded by a spray of droplets. Picking up the large jelly, I closed my eyes and held it out like an offering, silently whispering to Sylvie to forgive me.

On Thursday something rather extraordinary happened. The day began with my familiar fog. The longer I stared at my clozapine bottle, the more it seemed to grow, a towering beanstalk sprouting pills. The stern psychiatrist in me argued with the wheedling patient; the psychiatrist won. I downed two with a glass of water. Then I concerned myself with practical things – checking the standing orders on my bank statement, wiping dust from my shelves – before setting off for the library to work on my crime novel. My new plasma-screen television was on order and would soon be delivered. Tonight, I decided, I would get a takeaway and watch reality TV.

But Fate had other plans.

Is Fate the right word? It felt like Fate at the time. I was not quite able to admit it then, but it had already begun: the fraying of my atheism. It was as though Sylvie's presence had peeled me, prepared me to receive a new faith. For I had had no plans to go to Waterstones on Piccadilly. It was a place I tended to visit a few days before Christmas, to buy a book on golf for my father or the latest celebrity memoir for my mother. I had always found its size slightly overbearing, like a cathedral dedicated to the worship of the Written Word. Inside, I thought of Self and proceeded to the fiction department.

There, I inadvertently provoked a fight between two assistants by asking which Will Self they might recommend as a starter. One said it could only be *My Idea of Fun*; the other was adamant that it should be *Great Apes*. I feared that they might come to blows – indeed, one was wielding a volume of Proust. I tried to resolve the crisis by pointing out that *My Idea of Fun* was not on the bookshelves. An angry consultation of the computer stocklist backed me.

He took up nearly an entire row of the S shelves, pushing Tom Sharpe into the corner, outshining C. J. Sansom with his nine copies to Sansom's two. I had not realized that Mr Self had written quite so many books. Novels about apes and psychos, novellas about women growing cocks and knees sprouting vaginas, and an abundance of short-story collections, whose tantalizing titles spanned from *A Short History of the English Novel* to *The Quantity Theory of Insanity* and *The Rock of Crack as Big as the Ritz*. Self, boasted his covers, was the finest living satirist since Swift, a writer who revelled in the grotesque and the surreal. I opened the first page of *Great Apes* (later, when I look back, I think, Thank God it was not *My Idea of Fun* – thank God). The blurb informed me that it was a book about a Soho artist called Simon Dykes, who wakes up after a night of debauchery and discovers his girlfriend is a chimpanzee. And – to his horror – so is the rest of humanity. An eminent psychologist, Dr Zack Busner, is fascinated by Simon's delusion that he is 'human' and hopes that this extraordinary case might make his reputation as a great ape.

The hype had piqued my literary palate but my first taste of Self's prose was a sour one: I found his verbose style extremely hard-going.

Still, I felt obliged to buy so I picked it up, along with *Grey Area*, a collection of his short stories.

Fate again. Should I have sensed it as I walked towards the check-out till? As I passed over a twenty-pound note to the sulky *My Idea of Fun* assistant, should I have heard the musical spheres striking just the right note, the stars and planets scrambling to fit into the correct positions in the sky, so that all the karmic calculations multiplied to find the right number? If it had been a Shakespeare play, horses would have been eating each other by now; if a film, the camera would have zoomed in on a close-up of the bespectacled ape cover with a flurry of piano keys. It was only outside in the street that I felt I was viewing the world from a different parallax, as though my brief taste of Self's prose had flared and fused new connections between sleepy synapses in my brain, pulsing through my consciousness with the electrical currents of fresh perspectives.

I hurried home. The books, wrapped in their black plastic sheath, banged against my thigh, provoking a swelling against my trouser zip. All the words that had passed through Sylvie's mind, that had been smiled over, sighed over, provoked surprise and pathos, would now be filtered through my conscious-ness. Will Self would form a literary bridge between us. To read his books would be an intellectual courtship, a prose masturbation, a shared dance of ideas. Self, our unknowing matchmaker.

I lay down on the bed and pulled them out. *Grey Area, Great Apes; Great Apes, Grey Area.* I chose the latter,* flicking through in search of acknowledgements, curious to know if Self had

---

*Editor's note: although Richard asserts that he chose to read *Grey Area*, the following passages confirm this is a mistake, suggesting he is muddled and his choice of text was, in fact, *Great Apes*

a Sylvie, a muse who breathed through his pen. There were none. I turned to the back inside jacket. An author photograph. I was so shocked, I dropped the book. When I looked again, the dent had formed a crease across his cheek, like a knife slash.

The photograph transported me back to that room, that day. Blood beneath my fingernails. Sylvie's carved face. Self's was rougher, masculine in comparison, which only served to heighten the poignancy of her warped mimicry. Was it a dare? Did Jamie joke with her, splice their faces on the computer; did she do it to please him? I flicked over, desperate for the oblivion of words.

There are moments in our lives when a piece of art performs alchemy on us. We listen to a piece of music, view a canvas, read a novel and emerge a different person. Often these moments are a question of timing, of the fateful choreography of our mind meeting the artist's mind in a moment of perfect union. We see, or feel we see, everything they artistically intended; they, in turn, seem to have looked into our souls and seen how to reframe our perspectives, paint new colours in our hearts.

When I was eighteen, it was Handel's *Messiah*. A piece of music so glorious it persuaded me to believe in God. When I was sixteen, it was *Reservoir Dogs*. A film that showed me violence could be cool. For weeks I walked around secretly calling myself Mr Cerise. The result was bloody. I still have the shirt, browned with bloodstains. Now, at the age of twenty-three, I discovered Will Self and knew my life would never be the same again. Handel and *Dogs* I realized, had been just the foreplay.

But before the love came hate. I was used to crime novels with clean prose, familiar plot architecture, authors who understood there were *rules* that needed to be *obeyed*. Self was clearly a literary rebel. The Rules were Fucked. The result was anarchy. His metaphors pummelled me. His vocabulary flicked V signs. *Chthonic, quiddity, toque.* Had Sylvie had to resort to a dictionary too? Could she ever love me if she found out that I had no idea what *choncate, flocculent* and *barbellate* meant? My estimation of my IQ dipped by several points; I felt as though Self had invited me to an exclusive cocktail party and then deliberately embarrassed me by quoting philosophers I had never heard of. I scribbled down notes, sought meanings in the *OED*, ploughed on. For Sylvie. I read three more chapters. And three more. I told myself I could now just follow my university protocol; I had read the beginning, so a skimmed chapter in the middle and at the end would be enough to sustain a decent discussion in my head with Sylvie. But I could not stop. It was not just the hilarious, exquisite satire of the book – the parallels drawn between the chimp world and the human; 'ass-licking' sycophants; the little chimp with an Oasis poster on his wall of a simian Noel Gallagher; a hilarious domestic scene where Professor Busner arrives home and discusses his day at the office while surrounded by a roomful of mating chimps, who respond by flashing their swollen anuses. It was Self's *voice*. In the crime novels I had read, the writers were neutral, ghosts behind their generic prose. Self seemed present in every line, leering, laughing with me, slapping my mind, stretching my intellect, dissecting my world-view, sneering at my prejudices, forcing me to rethink my entire vision of humanity. Much later – weeks after I had first discovered his books – I heard Self on the radio and was shocked: his voice perfectly matched the imaginary Self I heard in my head as I read – droll, booming, grandiloquent. I had no choice but to read on, to allow the novel fully to penetrate me.

Around page 108, I found myself glancing up, surprised to find myself in my flat. I was aware that the light and background noise had changed, but my eyes never made it to the clock. The book was a cruel master and I its humble servant; it lashed me on. My fingers shook with hunger; my eyes began to burn. I wanted to get up and reread my novel, weep over my prose, tear it up, burn the pieces in humble sacrifice to my new Svengali. Still, I could not break away. Darkness set in. My pain reached such a pitch of agony that it was almost ecstasy, until finally my mind collapsed into my body, my nose diving into the fan of pages, my forehead coming to rest on the opening of Chapter Nine. Words pressed against my temples, osmosizing into my subconscious. I found myself in Victoria station, late at night. Waiting for a train and trying to avoid the tramp traversing the white concourse in an Odyssean search for small change. The shop was closed; the coffee stands were silent. In the centre of the dirty white floor tiles, there was a book. I walked over to it and picked it up, ignoring the tramp as he accosted me. It was a copy of *Great Apes*, only the cover had changed: the ape was undoubtedly Sylvie. Half of her hair had been sawn off, leaving spiky tufts; the rest hung, golden and lovely, over her cheekbone. The tramp was bordering on violence; I saw that my train had come in and ran straight through the barriers, passing through steel like a ghost.

I sat down in the empty carriage and soon fell asleep. I dreamt that I woke up to the sound of a voice calling, 'Tickets, please!' When I dug into my trousers for my travel card, I found only pocket. A shadow fell over my seat; up marched an enormous cock, dressed in a blue uniform, cap jaunty on his semen-glistened head. As he spoke through his small slit of a mouth, his skin wrinkled and ribbed in vexation. I tried to offer him the book as payment, but he refused it. If I didn't have a ticket, I was going to have to bend over backwards, he said. I asked for a complaint form, but my voice became spineless as he leant in close, his hot, phallic stench knifing my nostrils.

I woke up, locked in a knot of sweaty white sheet. Untangling myself, I lay back, listening to the hum of late-night London traffic.

I realized my phone was ringing. My answerphone clicked on. I heard a female voice and my heart vomited shock — *Sylvie?* From beyond the grave? *Lovely to meet you the other night . . .* Zara? Could she have got my number? I sat up. *It's Mia and my number is . . .*

I beeped the volume down to silence and sat on my bed as my answerphone mouthed words dumbly. My head felt strange; my eyes were filled with acid sand. Lack of sleep — or, perhaps, a literary hangover, a surfeit of words. I smoothed my hand over the cover of *Great Apes*. Despite the excess, I had only been left with an insatiable hunger for more. My walls seemed to sigh; how high they looked, how white, as though they were leaning backwards. I jumped up and flung myself at my boxes again, tearing through them until I found the yellow clump of Post-its. I peeled one off and wrote:

photogravure

And then another

flocculent

And then:

barbellate

I put them up on my wall, three Post-its licking each other. I turned back with shaking hands, heart thumping, and then I saw what to do: I ripped off the cover of *Great Apes* and stuck it to the wall alongside them. Yes, I thought, lying back down on the bed in a fit of weak shaking, that's better. That's nice. That looks nice now. The ape smiled and agreed.

Then I woke up and realized I had missed my station.

Six

I woke up. Sunlight, frilled with birdsong, was edging round the curtains. I waited for my mind-fog to descend but there was not even a hint of grey. I needed to pee but I could not bear to leave my bed. My pill bottle sat in the centre of the floor. It looked small, like a child. Before I could risk unravelling, I reached for *Great Apes* and took another hit of prose.

Several hours passed. This time my reading was sleepier, like languid lovemaking after a tempestuous night. Around noon, I was forced to attend to the pain in my stomach but all I could find in the fridge was a green pepper and half a carton of semi-skimmed milk, which made a surprisingly palatable combination.

At three thirteen p.m., I finished *Great Apes*. I realized that I had always read crime fiction as a form of tranquillizing escapism: the moment I closed the pages, the murderer behind bars, the detective satisfied, justice restored, I forgot the author's name and returned to real life the same Richard Smith. Or, perhaps, a slightly more sedate Richard Smith, for a crime novel is, ultimately, the modern utopian novel, affirming that good will out evil – that society is like Gaia, bound by natural laws that spontaneously reassert order. Self suggested otherwise. I had never understood what satire was before, or what damage it might do. Self had destabilized my moral certainties: I felt as though he had undone years of psychiatry and medication, perhaps rendered my pills impotent.

My appointment with Sylvie's plastic surgeon was scheduled for four thirty. I thought about cancelling. I felt pregnant with Self; I could hardly bear to endure the banality of the world beyond. I saw myself standing in the middle of the pavement, crowds swirling around me, as a bloody papier-mâché foetus of Will's words slopped at my feet. Taking off my jacket, I returned to my bed, laptop propped on my knees, and ordered seventy copies of his books from Amazon, then some more milk and peppers from Waitrose.

It was fear that finally propelled me out of my flat; a fear I could not quite name or define. Though I was not able fully to comprehend the metamorphosis that was taking place inside me, I was conscious that the world was becoming Selfied around the edges. In the bank queue, I felt a curious disgust for the people around me; their Darwinian origins had never seemed more prominent, despite their noxious hairspray and designer trappings. One hirsute man scratched his trousers as though rummaging his ischial scrags; the bank clerk fingered her hair for ticks. I took my five hundred pounds, unable even to muster a thank you, and continued to Harley Street in a daze.

Outside the surgery, a brief flicker of guilt made me hesitate: what would my grandfather think if he knew that I was spending my inheritance on a bribe? In Reception, I encountered Dr Gyggle, the head plastic surgeon. His grey beard was awry and he was yelling at his red-haired assistant, 'Emily — a fucking nose is a fucking nose, how would you confuse it with a fucking nipple?' Emily gave me a wobbly smile and asked me to go into the waiting room.

As I waited, my curious antipathy towards flesh found fresh inspiration. Every character there seemed interminably restless, as though they wished they could etch changes into their bodies through their fingernails without having to endure the scalpel. One guy with dreads struck up a conversation. He was convinced that his present body was a karmic punishment for sins in a past life; he feared in some pre-birth cosmic interview he had 'agreed' to adopt his current fleshy shell. He seemed to be seeking reassurance from me, and when I told him that surgery was, by his logic, like flicking a V sign at the divine, he fell silent. I pondered on the errant sperm which, through fate or perversity on their part, swam past the ones carrying beauty and charisma and triumphantly fired their ugliness and sorrow into an egg. The collective atmosphere of bodily loathing rose to an intolerable pitch: I became convinced that I could smell the stench of cut-offs; I saw the shaved noses and fat lumps, the shorn cheeks and chins rotting in a bin with Sylvie's, blurring into one vat of human slop. I fled to the toilets.

It wasn't until the pink smell of pot-pourri soothed me that I realized I had run into the Ladies. Nevertheless, I entered a cubicle. How had Sylvie felt in her moments before surgery? I sat on the edge of a seat, imagined her holding her face in her hands, like a mask she was about to take off. I unzipped my trousers and curled my cock between my legs. So this was how it felt to piss like a woman: curiously passive, without the strut of an upright stance. This was why Sylvie had wanted a cock, and a face to match.

Outside in the corridor, Emily did not look surprised when I emerged from the Ladies. She called me into an untidy office.

'I'm . . . I'm thinking about a particular type of surgery,' I said, in a shaky voice. 'I'd like the same sort of surgery as an old friend of mine had.' I spread out a few cuttings of Sylvie, before and after.

I saw Emily's eyes flash recognition. 'Are you another journalist?' she asked.

'Look. Look.' As I pulled the five hundred pounds from my pocket, my sweat dampened the notes. 'If you can just tell me anything about her or what happened, I can give you this. And then – then I'll go . . .'

I swallowed, poised to run if she reached for the phone and called the police. Emily swallowed, flicked her hair, and suddenly picked up the money.

'We have to be quick.' She turned to a filing cabinet. 'Sylvie was an unusual case because her medical examination caused us a lot of problems; we had to keep delaying surgery. She had the most extraordinary substances in her system.'

'Drugs?'

'No – well, yes, but not the regular, recognizable sort. Some were unclassifiable, but there was one we could identify – *yagé*.'

'What's that?'

'A drug that was traditionally used by shamans in order to achieve heightened states – if you don't understand how to use it, the side effects are horrific. As for the others in her system, well, we weren't even sure–' Emily broke off as Dr Gyggle screamed through the wall. 'I guess I'd better go.'

'*Yagé*', I typed into Google back home. I discovered that William Burroughs had once taken a seven-month trip to South America in search of it, lured by its near-mythical hallucinogenic properties and gifts of telepathy. I wondered how Sylvie had reacted to the drug, if it had made love to her mind or quarrelled with it. Her presence still seemed elusive, and I feared she was jealous now that I was reading Self for my own enlightenment. Indeed, I found it hard to focus on any further *yagé* research: I kept obsessively rechecking my Will Self Amazon order. There were still eight hours to survive until my Pandora's box of books arrived – how could I even sleep? I lay in bed and rocked my cock between my finger and thumb, but even my release looked different, a white seahorse tainted with the shades of Self's quiddity.

I stayed up all night, rereading *Great Apes*, until at nine a.m. the doorbell sounded. The guard from below had assisted a simian postman in carrying up four large cardboard boxes. I tried to hack at the thick brown tape, but my scissors were too blunt. I jumped up and ran to the kitchen. There I found a small vegetable knife in the sink, but it was still pungent with pepper juice. I yanked open another drawer, full of dusty cooking utensils I never used. I rattled aside a fish slice and a whipping mechanism, and saw the knife.

It was the largest knife I had ever seen. Its blade was dulled with dried blood and there were more scarlet dots in the drawer, splashes on a spoon and the frills of a cake-cutter. I drew it out in trembling wonder. I had no recollection of ever owning such a thing. Then I reminded myself that my mother had bought me a fresh collection of cutlery before I moved in, which I had combined with rag-tags from house-sharing at uni.

The blood, however, was a mystery. I gripped the blade in indignation. The postman must have slipped it into my drawer when he came to deliver the package or – the guard! Perhaps the guard had broken in and left it. That made most sense, for he was the only one with access to a key. I would return it to him promptly. Perhaps I would humiliate him even further by not passing it over directly, but leaving it on his chair with no note attached.

I pushed the knife under the tap. The brown stains came

alive, bubbling up into sluices of red. It made me feel quite sick, so I kept my eyes fixed on the whorl of the plug-hole until the water ran clear. Then I washed my hands several times.

The blood was soon forgotten when I returned to the box. My hands were shaking with such violent excitement that it took several goes to rip it open. Out I spread them, across my floor, the works of Will Self: *The Quantity Theory of Insanity, Cock and Bull, Grey Area, Great Apes, My Idea of Fun, Tough, Tough Toys for Tough, Tough Boys, Junk Mail, Perfidious Man, Sore Sites, Feeding Frenzy, The Sweet Smell of Psychosis, Dr Mukti and Other Tales of Woe, How the Dead Live* and *Dorian, an Imitation*. Five copies of each.

I picked up *Cock and Bull* and read a line about a woman who grows a penis and rapes her husband; I studied the psychopathic opening of *My Idea of Fun* and nearly vomited. A kaleidoscope flick through *Junk Mail* highlighted the range and depth of his intellect, from interviews with Martin Amis and J. G. Ballard, to wisdom on crack addiction and idleness, couched in prose that danced between the wise and the wicked – on one page he debated Dr Szasz's theories on the legalization of all drugs, on another he concluded that being an uncircumcised Jew made him feel 'drawn to people who wish to stick scalpels into my todge'. And with every small flit between his covers, the manic beauty of his images assaulted me – a particularly debauched scene in *Dorian* involving a chair overflowing with ash was described 'as though a latter-day Pompeian had been extinguished by the eruption of a cigarette'. Metaphors so bizarre and exquisite that I felt that my imagination was about to lose its virginity, that each new book would stretch it into a previously untried position. For several more minutes, my mind buzzed between books, unable to settle on which mental nectar to suck.

But what did it matter where I began? I would read them

all, from start to finish, pausing only when my body forced me to obey its demands. I smoothed my hands over the covers, revelling in the anticipation: it would take me days, if not weeks, to finish my literary pilgrimage. My hands became still and my breathing softened until my lungs barely functioned. That biblical expression, the 'peace, which passeth all understanding', is perhaps the best way to describe the sensation that came over me. For it was undoubtedly spiritual in nature, perhaps even Zen-like. My anxious preoccupations – Mia and the party and the masks and the surgeon and Jamie – slipped away. Nothing existed except the present. My body became light, as though it was merely a vessel to contain my exalted consciousness. Nothing seemed real, except the books before me. Prose that would be read in a hundred years' time; metaphors that would be marvelled over centuries on. I wanted his thoughts to become my thoughts; I wanted to be penetrated to my very quiddity; I wanted to put myself into the hands of a magnificent psychogeographer and allow a chthonic metamorphosis to fulcrate me . . .

I lay in bed in a foetal ball, tears spooling from my eyes. Shards of cardboard lay on the floor, quilt pieces of Amazon logo, for I had torn up the boxes after searching and finding them empty. Five novels, four short-story collections, one novella, four collections of journalism: the works of Will Self. According to Amazon, his new novel, *The Book of Dave*, was not available until 1 June 2006. An hour ago, as though life was taunting me, the doorbell had rung and there had been a second delivery. I had thought some divine organizing power had arranged another box of undiscovered books to appear at my door, but it had turned out to be the TV I had ordered weeks ago. It sat in the corner of the room, insolent and smug.

My eyes ran out of tears. I stared at the clock on my bedside table, too muzzy to translate the hands. I wondered what day it was. There was a faint stench in the air, perhaps emitted by the carton of milk that stood on the floor, going sour.

When I had turned to Christianity during my teen years, I had made a bargain with God: if I read the Bible from beginning to end, He must reward my literary dedication by answering all my prayers for at least six months. Once I had completed the task I felt bereft, for a book, holy or not, is never the same when you read it a second time. My prayers were answered in a sporadic, sadistic fashion – God seemed keen to perpetuate a time lapse between asking and giving, so that by the time my prayers were answered, I didn't want what I'd asked for any more. But I found solace in my local church, where I could share my dissatisfaction with a therapeutic group.

I had nobody to share Will with. I felt as though I was sitting in an empty confession box, cobwebs being spun around me, old skin cells settling on new skin cells, knowing the grille would never slide open. At other times, I fantasized about lying on a couch before Will as he psychoanalysed me, treating me like a bad draft of a novel he longed to improve.

I thought that I might remain in this state until 1 June 2006, when I heard the bedclothes rustle. I tensed with hope: was she back? Was she with me? I hardly dared to breathe for fear she might flee. Gradually the air became feathery, consoling. She whispered a single word in my ear – *shrine*. At first I did not understand, so she whispered it again. *Shrine*.

When I heard the noise, I thought it was Sylvie screaming. I leapt up, my heart panicking. Then I realized it was the phone. It might be Mia, I thought. For the first time, I longed to speak to her, to convert her to this new faith.

'Hello – is that Mr Richard Smith?' a formal voice enquired.

'Yes.' My voice sounded strange, I had not spoken for so long.

For one anxious moment I thought it was the police. Then: 'I'm calling from American Express in order to ascertain whether you would be interested in a new type of insurance policy. It offers you full card protection, along with travel insurance for the next six months, protection against identity theft and free air miles if you book a trip via American Airlines to a state of your choice.'

A silence.

'Have you – have you ever read the novels of Will Self?'

'I . . . No, I can't say I have. Do you feel this insurance policy would be of interest to you?'

'Do you feel Will Self would be of interest to you? Listen,' I said. 'Listen! This comes from the opening of *My Idea of Fun*:

> '"*So what's your idea of fun then, Ian?*" *It was the woman diagonally opposite me, the one with the Agadir tan . . . My idea of fun? This woman – who I didn't even know – she wants to know what it is? Hey, if only she did know . . . ur-her-her . . . If only she could see . . . but then, that could never be. See me tearing the time-buffeted head off the old dosser on the tube. See me ripping it clear away and addressing myself to its corpse. See me letting my big body flop over his concertinated torso . . .*'

I heard the dial tone fart in my ear with a curious sense of role reversal; it was the first time a cold caller had hung up on me. But no matter. I heard Sylvie laughing softly, laughing with me. He was the ignorant. He was the unconverted.

I sat down, waiting for my breathing to return to normal. Gazing at my hands, I saw that they were covered with paper cuts, my fingerprints highlighted with ink, my jumper strewn with pieces of Sellotape. All around, from every wall, he watched me. Self, aged twenty, handsome and louche; Self sprawled before his desk; Self shrewd, smoking a pipe. My room seemed much darker now that the blank walls were covered with this beautiful mosaic. Book covers, interviews, photos and quotations: a patchwork of the mandarin and the demotic. It felt as though I was celebrating a Holy Trinity of Will, Sylvie and I. Yet there was no doubt that, even in absence, his presence was the strongest. I felt delightfully claustrophobic, blissfully suffocated by his spirit.

I spent twenty minutes copying out the opening chapters of *Great Apes*, colouring my imagination with his prose, then reverted to a blank pad, ready to experience a gush of literary tongues. But my pen hovered, an uneasy shadow on the perforations of my WHSmith notebook. I feared that my unworthiness might be the source of inadequacy. Closing my eyes, I begged for inspiration. The London traffic was a cacophony; I pushed it to the periphery of my hearing, searching for a vacuum of silence. I felt afraid, for I knew that once a voice had been invited into my consciousness I might not be able to control its departure. The silence remained sterile, hollowed out my mind until it became a punishment. I opened my eyes and stared into Will's. I considered what his books had taught me, how his satire had slashed at recognized institutions, at power structures, at the deceit of men in white coats. I picked up my bottles of pills from the shelves and dashed into the bathroom, showering them into the toilet. Again and again I yanked the chain, watched them disappear, like a shoal of pharmaceutical sperm, into the depths of the sewers.

Back in my shrine, I knelt down before his picture, weeping and begging that my sacrifice would be rewarded.

Seven

I was traversing down the stairs when I noticed a man with blond hair knocking on the door of number thirty-two. Was he the new lodger? Was he aware of how its previous occupant had died? Aware of my attention, he wheeled around and let out a surprised '*Ha!* Richard!'

I was quite stunned to hear my name spoken aloud. It was the first time in a long time that I had left my shrine.

'It's Toady!' he said. 'I met you, I believe, at Jamie's rather naff exhibition — how did the *Evening Standard* review it? A snobbish, élitist, stinking pile of something-or-other.' He roared with laughter so raucous I felt it reverberate in my stomach.

I blinked at Toady. A whorled brown pipe protruded from his lips and his swelling belly was covered with a green criss-cross quill tweed more suited to an elderly eccentric who frequented Oxfam than a young man who was barely thirty.

'Well!' He clapped his arm round me. 'How are you, my good friend? If I recall, you said you were a journalist — have you recovered from that particular malaise yet? No offence intended, no offence. Well, now, I was hoping to find Sylvie but, of course, I'd forgotten that she is, in fact, dead. Don't look like that. I've drunk half a bottle of whisky and nobody invited me to the funeral and I have a tendency to get a little muddled from time to time. Blame my parents for the positively blasphemous childhood they inflicted on me. Now, are you going to come for a drink with me? Jamie and all are at the Plantation Club. Do come.'

It was, quite clearly, an invitation to meet the WSC. A sense of wonder filled me at such fatefully choreographed timing. Was Toady some sort of Selfian angel, sent to form the link between my shrine and the outer world? As he ushered me down the stairs, I felt as though I was Dante being guided by Virgil. When we approached the hallway, where the guard was looking puzzled and unwrapping a bloody plastic bag, I stalled uneasily. It seemed as though the city beyond the double doors was a profane dream I must step into.

'Now do, do come along,' Toady said.

Outside I found that the doors of my perception were whitewashed with Will. The city sang with literary pantheism. A large man became the Fat Controller; a bearded doctor was Dr Busner; a Jewish woman dragging shopping was Lily Bloom.

'... and so my misery memoir has been a huge success, except for the court case. But my lawyer is an old friend — we were at Eton together. Goodness, whenever I perchance upon a glass of milk it provokes a shudder, for I immediately imagine the bitterness of bleach being poured down my five-year-old throat.' Toady paused. 'Does that sound convincing? I have an interview with *The Times* tomorrow where I shall have a chance to redeem myself — my parents are being terribly cruel and suing me. Do I sound like a proper victim — do I sound as though I was abused? Well, perhaps you'd better not answer that question! Why, is that a Will Self novel poking out of your top pocket? Well, well — a new convert, eh? Have you noticed that whenever you read too much Self, it's like drinking one too many glasses of wine or snorting a line of coke too many? You start imitating him and using long words like *transmogrification*, only he is inimitable, so inevitably one is just a poor carbon copy. He can wield long words like rapiers, but the rest of us just slice the page into a mess. Still, I'm rather past Will, these days. You know, I've grown up, moved on . . .'

I shut my ears to such sacrilegious rant, wondering if Toady was secretly testing me. Sadness was beginning to sweep over me. Every step into the outside world diluted the concentration of my devotion. A doctor passed by and he was a doctor. A fat man was simply fat.

I wanted to turn back but the compulsion to meet the WSC drove me on: I had to unravel the final act of Sylvie's obituary.

'Here we are!' Toady led me to a black door with no name, number or handle. He knocked three times, his smile triumphant. 'It's a *very* secret club, you see!'

The door was opened by a dark man with an unsmiling face, stiff in a dinner jacket. He nodded abruptly, swivelled a gold-leafed book under Toady's nose and took his signature.

I followed Toady down a black corridor, feeling rather like Alice in a rabbit warren. We passed a few doorways: I saw vignettes of clinking glasses, playing cards, smoke that defied the ban. Finally we came to a door at the end. Toady drew a gold key from his pocket and unlocked it with a wink.

They were seated around a small table, playing a board game. It was difficult to see who was present at first, for the cigarette smoke was so thick and the lighting supplied by a few flickering candles that they blurred into ghosts. The smoke smelt strange, too, not the sweet ticklishness of weed but something metallic and nasty. As I came closer, I saw that the whole of the WSC clique – Jamie, Zara and Nicholas – were there, as well as a middle-aged, seedy fellow, whose leathery face looked as though it had been bleached by decades of cigar smoke and carved out from centuries of decadent parties. They all looked so different from my first encounter with them at Jamie's party; like night-time versions of themselves. Nicholas was slumped on a black couch, his eyes purple hollows, pressing a glass of whisky to his temple. Jamie's arm circled Zara and he was whispering in her ear. Her dark glasses had slipped down her nose, revealing a puffy black eye. He had a glossy bruise on one of his cheekbones.

It appeared their half-brother-sister relationship had Byronic undertones, for she gave him a light kiss on the lips. Jamie turned back to the board game and grabbed the dice, slammed down a three and a six. Then he saw me. A look of outrage blackened his face.

'Toady — we're *playing*.' Ignoring Toady's cries of protest, he gathered up pieces, cards, tokens, folding up the board quickly so that all I could glimpse was a green corner labelled *The Library*. Once more, I wondered why the WSC were so obsessed with Cluedo, and why it was such a big secret. I glanced over at Zara. Her expression was vexed, but when she sensed my gaze, she pushed up her sunglasses, assumed a feline smile and stretched.

Toady sat on a chair, pulling up another for me. Nicholas and Jamie made no attempt to move so I was forced to sit slightly outside the inner circle. Jamie kept his arms folded and his glare focused on Toady. Toady ignored it, lighting his pipe like a young Sherlock.

'I recognize you,' Jamie suddenly said. 'Aren't you a *journalist*?'

'Richard isn't a journalist, he's a writer!' Toady cried. He waved his hand at the seedy man and I realized that he must be Archie West, *über*-agent. 'You see, Archie — this is your man. Richard has written a novel.'

Archie pulled on a black cashmere coat and stood up. 'A lot of people want to write novels,' he purred, raising his eyebrows.

'I've written a crime novel,' I said fiercely. 'I'm on the first chapter.'

But Archie had already turned away, kissing Zara goodbye, clapping Jamie on the back, leaving behind a scent of cologne and cigars.

Jamie and Zara shared a cigarette and a drink between them, their intimacy almost hostile as they pushed stub or glass rim against each other's lips. There was a long silence in which I might have seethed, had I not been so uncomfortably conscious of the tension in the group. At the time, I misinterpreted it, imagining it all to be entirely personal. In retrospect, I can see that I was quite irrelevant to them: their silent anger was directed towards someone else.

'So, Toady,' Nicholas said, in a barbed voice, 'have you managed to finish *C* yet? We're all way past the deadline, all waiting for you. You can't be completely taken up with the sequel to your misery memoir – or the court case or wherever you're at.'

Toady glugged down some whisky. 'Why did I have to have *C*?' he cried. 'You – you get *A*. Jamie gets *H*. And I get *C*.'

Zara stole Jamie's cigarette and smiled at Toady as though he was a child throwing a tantrum.

'Jamie gets *Y*,' Toady went on, 'Nicholas gets *X*. But I get *W*. And *C*. Why? *WHY*? Why *me*?'

I had an odd sensation of having entered a landscape whose language I no longer spoke.

'*C* is really quite easy,' Jamie said smoothly.

'If it's so easy, then why don't you do *C*?' Toady retorted.

'*C*,' Jamie said, 'is for circumcision. As Will himself said, "I am that rarest of things – an uncircumcised Jew."'

'Oh.' Toady pulled his pipe from his mouth. 'Oh.'

'If you don't want to be part of it, just say, Toady. Just say.'

I was becoming increasingly conscious of my absence. I might have been one of the silver ashtrays littering the table; indeed, Zara's trailing cylinder was flecking my shoe.

'Well,' I said loudly, just as Jamie was about to speak, 'you all seem to be awfully keen on Will Self.'

Silence. Toady shook his head and rolled his eyes. Nicholas blinked incredulously. Jamie sneered. Zara smiled.

'We are quite keen on Will Self,' Zara said, her voice a sing-song. 'You see, we meet here once a week to discuss his work. It's a sort of book club. We like to dissect his themes. Debate which one is our favourite character. That sort of thing.'

I appeased my anger with a secret inner smile. I doubted any of them had a Self shrine in their home. None of them understood him the way I did.

'What about you, Richard?' Jamie suddenly asked, leaning forwards intently. 'Who's your favourite writer?'

I searched his face for a sneer but his expression was one of passionate interest. There was an obvious answer to the question, but I felt embarrassed. To confess my true feelings . . . It would be like discussing the intimacies of a lover. So I muttered into my drink, 'I quite like Martin Amis . . .'

It was as though I had casually mentioned an affinity with *Mein Kampf*. Toady broke the silence by crying, 'Amis! *Amis!* Exactly! *Exactly!* There, Jamie, you see, you see! Didn't I tell you just the other day that Will himself has said that Amis may only be five foot three but he's the only writer who makes Will – at six three – feel *small*.'

Within five minutes, Jamie had politely asked me to leave, declaring that they wished to begin a new game and they could not possibly play with someone whose literary hero was *Martin Amis*.

I was about to decamp to my shrine, where I might curse Jamie before Will, when I felt a hand slip through the crook in my arm. Zara smiled at me and cajoled me to join her for one last drink, saying, 'You should take no notice of Jamie – he's just peevish tonight. None of us has slept in an age.' My concern for her compelled me to stay, for I noticed how raw her black eye was, how she was visibly shaking. At the private bar in the corner of the room – which seemed to lack a barman – she discovered a bottle of vodka and poured us two glasses. The bar-top was lined with candles that flickered in the buggish shades of her dark glasses. I waited for Jamie to object, but he was huddled into his group, engrossed in conversation, smoke coalescing about them, like a ring around a planet.

'I do actually love Will Self, you know,' I said in a low voice, 'much more than Amis. I recently read him for the first time and I actually found it truly amazing. Almost . . . life-changing.'

I stared into her eyes, searching for mockery, but she nodded earnestly.

'Reading his books – it was like being on drugs, or how I'd imagine taking a drug would feel. I've never been able to take drugs – it's a long story – because of my medication—' I broke off and smiled awkwardly. 'I'm not crazy . . . I just . . . you know . . . Life gets me down now and again. But Will – Will made me feel as though I'd never need to take another pill, because there would be no point in it. I mean, I read this interview with Will where he said that the way our society believes there is just one idea of sanity is an aspect of hidden totalitarianism.'

Zara did not react to my confession as people normally did. She didn't look at her watch or make a cheap excuse about needing to dash: she seemed intrigued, even impressed.

'Writers – we're fucked-up people, aren't we?' she agreed, as though my suicidal urges might qualify me to join her élite. 'Plath gassed herself in the oven. Virginia Woolf filled her pockets with stones and waded into a river. Hemingway shot himself. It's the only way to go. Jamie and I have already agreed that when we've written enough books we'll get into a bath together, slit each other's wrists and die, our lips pressed against each other. Sometimes I have dreams about it, how my last breaths will mingle with his last breaths, how our blood will lace the water, how his blood might drown me, how my blood will stain his face and hair—' She broke off, frowning, and took a sip of vodka.

I felt disturbingly aroused by the Gothic beauty of the image. My visions of suicide had always been mundane: overdosing on a few pills that I would no doubt vomit back up without anyone ever discovering me. I reached out and gently clasped her shoulder; she smiled up at me, pressing the glass against her lips, rubbing the rim against the rosebud.

'Will says we don't live in a Newtonian universe any more,' she continued. 'I mean, all these authors who write conventional, straightforward narratives – he says they're just acting as though we still live in the nineteenth century.'

'Exactly,' I cried in excitement, keen to keep up, to show my knowledge of his ethos was as profound as hers. 'Like he says, "Reality itself seems pretty twisted to me." The world is meant to be a disturbing place. It's the people who can see how twisted it is that are told to take pills – but maybe we're the ones who see the reality.'

There was a silence and I feared I had been misunderstood, felt ashamed that I had revealed so much. But then she whispered: 'I feel . . . I feel as though I can confide in you . . .' Her voice became so quiet I was forced to lean in, straining to hear, her breath butterflying my cheek. 'You know, the WSC . . . it only began – it only began a year ago. It's frightening to consider how . . . out of control things have got since then . . .'

'When?' I whispered into her ear. 'When did it begin? Tell me. Tell me everything.'

'It's a long story.'

'Tell me.'

She paused and then began: 'In Venice. We were in San Michele, Venice – me, Toady and Jamie. We went to visit the grave of Ezra Pound. We sat there in the flowery grass, on the tombstones, and we lit some candles and got quite drunk on a bottle of Cynar. We all became emotional and a little bit blurry. Jamie and Toady had been arguing throughout the holiday – about Saussure, essentialism, Barbie dolls, the ayahuasca plant. Toady only argues half the time to tease, but Jamie takes everything seriously. He was getting more and more wound up. I felt something was wrong with him. Up until now, I'd assumed it was writer's block, as he'd been working on his third novel for three years and had thrown away at least a hundred thousand words. But I felt it was more than that. . . I felt he was suffering from a *spiritual* crisis.'

I glanced at Jamie. He was watching Zara and I noticed for the first time that his eyes were laced with sadness. I almost stopped hating him – or, at least, my hate softened to dislike.

'Toady – Toady's always coming out with such wild statements. He was looking at Pound's grave, at the candles and postcards and messages and trinkets, and remarking that nobody would leave such mementoes at the grave of their local priest. He said that Jamie ought to solve his spiritual crisis by worshipping a writer. He started ranting on about how we have no spiritual masters in our current Western society – our priests are paedophiles, our politicians are celebrities, our celebrities are earthworms – so there's this terrible spiritual vacuum. In the past, we might have turned to philosophers, but they've gone out of fashion. He talked about how writers need a moral and spiritual framework as a foundation for their prose — just as C. S. Lewis spread his Narnian imagination over the skeleton of his Christian faith, or Swift operated within a matrix of Judaeo-Christian principles. He argued that writers could only therefore evolve by worshipping other writers.

'Toady was only joking, of course, and I remember laughing — I was quite drunk by now. But a look came over Jamie's face — as though he'd seen the light.

'We stayed there, at the graveyard, drinking, as the sky went dark and we got cold, but we were too excited to move. Jamie declared that he was going to found his own religion so that people could worship him. Toady argued that he was an egotistical jerk. We all argued about which writer we would worship, who could teach us about life and morals and how to construct a better sentence. And in the end we all came to the same conclusion.'

'Will,' I said in awe. 'So that's what the WSC is — a religion?'

'No,' she said, and I immediately felt foolish. 'It's . . .' She lowered her eyes and traced the outline of her bruise with a forefinger. 'It's a little more complicated than that . . . It's difficult to explain . . . There are lots of things . . . involved . . .'

'I want to join.'

Zara remained silent. My heart was beating very hard; I wanted to seize her shoulders and beg her for membership. I could already imagine the taste of the sweet fulfilment of worship. She pulled away from me a little, frowning, glancing at the table. I told myself that I must be patient, bide my time. I took a few moments to compose myself, then followed her gaze. Toady, Jamie and Nicholas seemed to be playing their board game again. I screwed up my eyes, for the smoke was now smog. They were definitely playing Cluedo – the board had a library, a billiard room and a bedroom, showered with the little gold trinkets of murder weapons. Their character cards, however, differed from the original, for there was no Professor Plum or Miss Scarlett. I recognized all the characters from Will's novels. Toady was Lily Bloom. Jamie was Simon Dykes. And then I saw Nicholas's card.

Mr Rabindarath.

'Hey.' Zara lightly tugged at my chin, pulling it round so that I faced her.

Mr Rabindarath. The same card I had seen Sylvie drop from her bag on the first day I'd met her.

I could sense that Zara was disturbed by what I'd seen. Afraid she might ask me to leave, I resisted the temptation to look back again.

'Sylvie,' I said. 'You knew Sylvie . . . Was she a member of the WSC?'

'Sylvie?' Zara's eyes widened. She unscrewed the vodka bottle and sloshed some more into her glass. 'You knew Sylvie?'

'Yes . . . a little.'

'I was so sorry when she died.' Zara's eyes became liquid. 'When I heard I just . . .'

'Did Jamie get asked in for questioning when she died?' I asked.

'Why d'you ask that? Of course he wasn't.'

'Well – I was. And I hardly knew her,' I said.

Suddenly the raw atmosphere changed between us. I saw Zara quickly assume skin, layers.

'Well, we're not in a Raymond Chandler novel,' she said, a little irritation tugging her voice. 'It had nothing to do with Jamie – just some psycho out there. She tagged along with us

77

for a while and that was that. She was never a member. Why d'you ask? Are you playing detective?'

'I don't think . . . I'd like to, but I don't think I could find the murderer even if I wanted. I mean, there are pieces floating about but I'm not sure they'll ever form a puzzle in the way they do in crime novels. Not everything is going to slot into place, I can see that.'

I glanced back at the Cluedo game, saw a coil of rope and a piece of lead piping.

'If you . . . I might be able to help you,' Zara said. 'If you want to find out more about Sylvie, then I know someone who was very close to her. As a matter of fact, I borrowed something off them a while ago. You could take it back to them – say I sent you. And then you could get them talking. Would you like that?'

'Sure,' I said.

When she passed over a large, sealed brown envelope, I balked and she laughed gently at me. 'It's obviously cocaine,' she said sweetly. 'I deal as a hobby. Did you know what Will once said? He said that if he was a dictator he would legitimize idleness, which meant he'd ban cocaine but make heroin and pot legal. No, no – really, it's just a book.' Watching me examine the package, she slapped my hand. 'No peeking – it's my own private porn. If you open it, Dirty Pete will tell me and I shall never forgive you. Now, you'll find him tomorrow at the Sealink Club, down in the Gents.'

'In the Gents?' I asked uneasily.

Zara rolled her eyes. 'He's not expecting anything more from you than this package. But you pass it over in the bar, people will get the wrong idea. Give him the package, then you can have a drink upstairs and discuss Sylvie. And don't be put off by his name. Dirty Pete is really very sweet,' she said, in a sing-song.

I took the package and pushed it into the inside pocket of my coat. I glanced back at the Cluedo board. Something glinted through the smoke. A playing piece, lying next to the small black envelope that revealed the murder card. *A knife.* Suddenly I understood. The pieces of the plot fell into place: beginning, middle, end. The beginning: Sylvie had dated Jamie, had learnt too much about the WSC, or become too obsessed. The middle: a game of Cluedo, the literary equivalent of Russian roulette, Sylvie's face sheathed by the envelope, the dice dictating her fate. The ending: Jamie slipped into her flat and followed his brief, using a Knife in the Bedroom. It had to be. I ought to call 999 immediately.

The game was reaching its conclusion.

'Okay – it was Mr Rabindarath in the Ballroom.'

'Dorian in the Billiard Room with the lead piping.'

Slowly, theatrically, Toady drew the card from its black envelope—

'YOU!' Jamie yelled. 'YOU FUCKING CUNT!'

As he lunged at Toady, the cards and drinks smashed to the floor. My heart was hammering wildly, the card still neon before my eyes like the after-impression of a bright light. That halo of yellow hair around a face.

Sylvie's face had been on that card. I was sure of it.

A scream curdled my heart. Toady and Jamie were tussling on the floor. Nicholas was watching, sipping his drink. '*Stop! Stop!*' Zara was screaming. I tried to drag Jamie away and he looked up at me and cried breathlessly, 'You! You! What the fuck are you doing still here?' He let up, however. Toady received one last cracking punch and then Jamie let him go.

Toady stood up, laughing heartily. He shuffled through the chaos, nose dripping blood, and picked up the crumpled card. As he held it up, he did a little Rumpelstiltskin dance. I frowned

in confusion. I had been mistaken. That was not Sylvie's like-
ness. The blond hair framed a face that was distinctly male. The
caption underneath swirled: 'KEITH TALENT'.

'I just thought it would liven things up with a new character,' Toady protested.

'Oh, Toady,' Zara cried, 'how could you? A character from
an *Amis* novel?'

I left soon after. Nobody would explain to me what the mysterious fracas was about. Zara was apologetic, though I saw
amusement in her eyes as she whispered, 'So did you really
think we were some élite group of murderers out to get Sylvie
– like something out of *The Secret History?*' The idea seemed to
thrill her, though when I expressed my distaste, she tried to
appease me with tearful explanations of an impending 'schism'
in the group. I refused to listen any further and escaped into
the cool night.

The streets were dirty with drunk Londoners. The thought
of having to stand on a tube – bodies brushing against mine and
depositing grime like newsprint, polluting my lungs with the
inhalation of mingled exhalations – sickened me so much that
I had no choice but to walk home. As I hurried, I became aware
of a cloud following me that coalesced into Sylvie's presence.
When she caught me, she embraced me with a tenderness that
brought me close to tears. She berated me for trying to find
solace in the outside world; she told me where I belonged. By
the time I entered the flat, the urge to return to the cocoon of
my shrine was so vehement that I hammered up the stairs, too
impatient to wait for the lift.

Back home, fifty or so Selfs greeted me with a leer. I said
hello to each in turn, put down the package and went to
the fridge. There I found some milk, which was only slightly

sour, downed most of it and ate half a green pepper in noisy, impatient bites. I rushed to my notebook, opened a copy of *Great Apes* and took the plunge. *Hooograa!* I copied. *We chimpanzees are now living through an era in which our perceptions of the natural world are changing more rapidly than ever before.* Just a few lines brought a sense of release. I exhaled, my fingers shaking slightly, and ran my tongue over my teeth, dislodging a shard of milky pepper. As I scribbled, I became aware of a bulky discomfort banging against my elbow and realized it was the package Zara had given me. I drew it out of my coat, immediately retasting the bitterness of the evening. I would look at it later. *Furthermore, these perceptions are being distorted by the way we, as chimps, now live.* Oh, the relief, the joy of his prose running through me like a drug! The bright bulbs were shiny on Self's portraits; I flicked the switch and let the streetlamp outside the window provide the ambience. Amber eyes watched me as I typed and typed, Will's voice amplifying through me as a curious transmogrification began to take place inside me . . .

Eight

Pain, what pain! I awoke in a postlapsarian world of chaos, aching to the molten core. Eyes bleeding metaphors. Stomach heaving, bulbous with the baleine of prose. The twin lobes of synaptic leaves, once flickering in the chilly breezes of sharp imagery, now wilted to green tears. I groped with blind paws, eager to stanch the light, to suture the blindness, to perform triage on the diurnal. My pyjamas were ragged; a crude caricature of Will was sketched in wobbly black felt across the canvas of my chest. I curled my woollen tongue around my mouth and discovered a metallic cud, a flocculence of mash and mush; half a torn page was glued to my cheek with saliva-cum, and when I spat, Times New Roman vomited out, the remains of page fifty-six of *Great Apes*.

As I crawled to the bathroom, my pernicious enfeeblement caused pain to thread neon through my nerve network. I felt as though I had been violated to the very core, that organs had been removed and cheaper versions restitched inside, whimpering paltry echoes, blood siphoned away and replaced with Self's incompatible type. More prose down the toilet with a whoosh-flush! When I rubbed my face with my palms, my skin was a scaly carapace. Sobs squeegeed down my throat. I used the sink to drag myself on to the stubs of my feet, only to discover that my reflection was now blemished, a cartoon Will Self felt-penned on the mirror, two perfect circles coining my irises like a cardboard cut-out at a funfair.

Last night on our way to the Plantation Club, Toady had joked that reading a hundred lines of Will Self was the equivalent of snorting one line of coke. I had taken 3,988 lines of Will last night, the equivalent of 398.8 lines of coke, which meant by rights I ought to be dead.

The package! The package! Squatting on my desk like a brown paper turd! I longed to flush it away and forget about it. But it persisted in lurking, seizing on the curtains of my peripheral vision and swinging on them. I picked it up and shook it gently, but it remained silent, ominous in its weightiness. My fingers nibbled at its Sellotape teeth, slowly arched back its mouth and drew out the oblong. I was expecting a brick of white powder. It was a copy of a Will Self book. *My Idea of Fun*. The cover was white and covered in amateur plastic, air bubbles smarting in papillomas over its pallid skin. The pages were the thickness of hide and there were swathes of blankness, the occasional dead wood of prose drifting in the sea of white. One page was empty except for the words: *I wouldn't even win the Nonce Prize*. I sniffed it lightly and an implosion fissured in my nasal passages. I hastily pushed it back into its innocuous envelope and closed my eyes, revelling in the sempiternal sciamachy. Briefly, a ray of nightmare broke from a cloud of amnesia and penetrated my imagination, repainting a disturbing scene: a dark room ... a long, long table decorated with loops and coils of complex machinery ... a figure at the end, his eyes glimmering with dictatorial greed, fingers bloated with apocalyptic whimsy. Did I push the package into my rucksack because of the thought of Sylvie's moist thighs, or did He flick a switch?

The Sealink Club was hunched in a spotty back-street of Soho between a sex shop and a place that had once been a sex shop and was now graffitied and fly-posted in crenulated layers thick as oil paint. I slipped inside. This was a place that was relentlessly nocturnal, that sneered at the pale wintry sunlight outside, the faint gleam of bottles in the gloom liquefied stars, the moon crescenting on the bald pate of the fat barman. I wondered if he was Dirty Pete. Excitement gurgled in my stomach, pumped sweet phlegm to my throat, which emerged in a stertorous cough. My weak legs wobbled, threatening to concertina beneath me. I sidled by the cigarette machine, loitered by the snooker table and finally skulked over to the bar and laid down my package.

The barman wafted away fog clouds of Marlboro to peer at it, then barked: 'Well, take it down, then! Huh!'

This last noise was occasioned by a solid pellet of his spittle hitting the brass spittoon on the bar-top.

He nodded in the direction of the ravaged wall, where pictures of hoary heavy-metal guitarists and screechers were framed by signatures scrawled in human fluids.

'The Gents, then!'

A long staircase, covered with silver scratches and leprosy flakes, slowly led me down into deeper layers of darkness as though in silent conspiracy with Dante. Which one was the Gents? I screwed up my eyes and saw that male/female differentiations had been carved into juvenile figurines in the wood. I opened the door. Dirty Pete was waiting for me.

He stood by the urinals: tall, thin, with pocked, crapulent cheeks and licks of vanilla hair on his conical head. He leered and seized my package, then scurried into a cubicle. I was anxious to leave but I could feel a pressure in my perineum and I took the other cubicle, despite its leering stench. When I pulled the door to, darkness devoured me. The only relief was a small halo of light that beamed into my cubicle; I crouched down, carefully avoiding the torrid riverbed of the floor, and peered through the peep-hole. Dirty Pete was tearing the brown paper from the package, frantic curls strewn on the floor like fish scales. *My Idea of Fun* was greeted with a screeched smacker from his coldsore-blemished pucker. Then he opened the last page and tore something from the top-right-hand corner. It looked like a small square tab, light as greaseproof paper, with Self's face embroidered in psychedelic. His tongue darted out — a thrashing eel of pink excitement — the tab danced for one moment as though whipped into the ecstasy of a tribal hymn, then his jaws chowed and his bony Adam's apple shuddered.

The familiarity of the white tab provoked a feeling of floundering revelation, a veiled knowledge that my intellect struggled to uncover. Suddenly I was lasered by the saccade of a pulsing Cyclops eye. Years of abuse had bullied and corroded his pupil to a sheer pinprick that looked as though it was in danger of dissolving into pure iris, pure oblivion. I shot to my feet. His laughter bansheed around the cubicle. I returned to my perch on the toilet seat, limbs frozen, afraid to stay, afraid to leave. More soprano arpeggios of laughter, accompanied by stertorous baritones of grunting bliss. The cubicle began to shake with violent blows. I curled myself into a corner until I realized that they were not, in fact, personal — that the cubicle was acting as a strait-jacket against which his addled consciousness was now thrashing. His screeches came louder, became pant-hoots, became positively pontid, terrifying; I clamped my palms over my ears to no avail. There was one last terrible noise that clawed its fingernails down my spine and then—

Silence.

I shook for several minutes and burst out of my cubicle.

He was lying on the floor.

I put my finger to his pulse and searched wildly, my fingers smearing all over his neck in disbelief, finally drooping on the knobble of his postlapsarian apple. My delusion burst. I stood up in cold, sick, diurnal reality.

I bounced up the stairs and said in a bright voice, 'I don't think Dirty Pete's feeling too good.'

The barman grunted and muttered, 'Lucky him!' then carried on polishing his rent-glass.

'I don't think so . . .' My feet were already several metres ahead of my mouth; I fled, pounding on to the pavement, shocked by the horripilant rays of day, blinking, bumbling into a cavalcade of Japanese tourists contemplating the prophylactic properties of expensive flesh. Connections copulated, gave birth to true epiphany: I saw the small white tab that Sylvie had been holding in the picture, heard her plastic surgeon crying, *She had the most extraordinary substances in her system . . . but not the regular, recognizable sort. Some—*[†]

[†]Editor's note: Several pages of Richard's narrative were burnt in the fire at the Liverpudlian tower block from which this manuscript was retrieved.

Nine

When I was sixteen years old my parents decided that, instead of the usual family caravan trip to Hastings, we would all go backpacking in India for the summer. They took me to the local GP for injections against yellow fever, typhoid, hepatitis; for malaria, I was given Lariam tablets. This coincided with my adolescent conversion to Christianity, so my extraordinary behaviour was initially attributed to religious zeal. After I was put into an institution for a short while, however, Dr Busner admitted that a number of his 'more delicate' patients had suffered similar side effects and the birth of the Internet gave my parents access to knowledge, to a terrifying catalogue of similar victims: a man who committed suicide after murdering his children, Iraqi soldiers who had taken the pills, returned home and shot their wives, victims suffering from disability, the inability to walk, amnesia. Mefloquin, it seemed, had a list of side effects that were detailed in small print on the leaflet: *feeling worried or depressed; seeing or hearing things that aren't really there (hallucinations); panic attacks; forgetfulness, agitation, confusion; feeling that you want to kill yourself.* And yet I always saw disappointment, suspicion, in my parents' eyes when they drove me to the psychiatrist on Thursday afternoons after school. My father believed in the idea of Plato's blank slate. Now he clearly felt that a few Lariam pills could only have darkened the shadowy jottings that had been self-penned in the womb. They were relieved and pleased when I agreed to the clozapine, and the pills to counteract the side effects of the clozapine. The irony that one pill had led to another did not escape me. I began to feel as though I was the medical equivalent of a pyramid-selling experiment by a drug-company consortium.

The voices, though: I did miss them. The drugs suffocated them, squeezed out their last breath and gave me silence, but silence is not necessarily golden: it can be lonesome. In order to encourage me to keep taking my pills at university, my mother used to print out charts for me, with little boxes for me to tick when I took each pill. She would decorate the columns with little biro flowers and birds, as if to fool me into thinking I had been prescribed marshmallows.

Three nights ago, after the police had called me in for questioning regarding the drug overdose of Dirty Pete, I had constructed a chart of my own. Six precise red ticks for nights and mornings. My walls were now a blank white. My desk was clear, except for a small pile of Raymond Chandler novels that sat with pristine covers in the corner. The books entitled *Great Apes, My Idea of Fun* – and others by an author I did not care to name – were under my bed, in a box, chained tight with masking tape. In the corner of the room sat a brand new television, seated on a metallic stand, with a screen size that had been impossible to buy six months ago. When I turned to glance at it, I told myself that I could spend the evening watching the programmes normal people did – gardening, reality TV, home makeover – and considered that television might be as useful as the pills. Perhaps I would add another column to my sheet, with blue ticks for another type of numbing.

I was still struggling with the opening of my crime novel. My pencil spooled in my fingers. During my interrogation my medical history had come in useful for the first time in my life: I had been able to convince the police of my sensitivity and aversion to all drugs. I'd told them I had wandered into the bar to use the Gents and found Dirty Pete writhing in the throes of a drug overdose. They had let me go with the assurance that there would be no further questioning, but the inspector had noted that for the second time in the space of a month I had been linked to a dead body. He'd clapped me on the back and told me not to make a habit of it, though his expression had not been entirely jovial. Then he'd added that he'd tried reading *Great Apes* as part of his investigations into Sylvie's death, but found it hard-going; he preferred the film version, *Planet of the Apes*. I had acquiesced.

But I was afraid that the matter might not end there. There was the question of Sylvie's plastic surgery; I could hardly believe my stupidity in visiting her surgeon. What if it came up in further investigations? I feared that Emily, who had accepted my bribe for information about Sylvie so readily, would be more than willing to divulge my name to them. Every time the phone rang, I jumped violently and the echoes seem to linger in the high ceiling of my apartment for hours afterwards.

With a shaking hand, I reached for Chandler and attempted to instil his voice in my head. But the clozapine was already beginning to thicken between me and the outside world, a fuzzy, cotton-wool layer that assuaged my nerves but made it hard to connect. I put down my pencil and went out to get some shopping. The sunshine seemed distant and people passed by with blurry faces. Inside the supermarket, I watched a young girl flicking through *Heat*, an elderly woman buying a Josephine Cox saga. The only other books in the selection were chick lit and crime. Few people in this place will have heard of Will Self, I reminded myself, and not one person is thinking about him right now. But I did not feel assured, only revolted, and threw a carton of milk and a bag of peppers into my basket as a sort of rebellion. Outside in the street, I berated myself and forced myself to re-enter and buy cereal, eggs, butter and a Josephine Cox.

Back home, I entered and saw my answerphone.

Red light, red light. Double-wink, double-wink.

The first message was from Mia. It took me a minute or so to remember she was the girl from Jamie's party I had fucked. Mia immediately brought the ghost of Sylvie tagging, umbilical, behind her. Sadness filled me like smoke. My pills had finally extinguished her presence; even the folds of bath curtains remained static. So did my cock. I had not been able to rouse an erection for days, and when I examined him, he seemed to be shrinking, as though Sylvie had cursed me with premature ageing.

Mia asked me if I fancied meeting up for a drink some time. Her tone was girlishly, desperately casual.

I pressed delete.

The second was from the local police station, asking me to call and arrange for another appointment to discuss further matters regarding the death of Sylvie Yates.

I fully intended to go to the police station. On the tube there, however, I became aware that the elderly woman sitting beside me was wearing lavender talcum powder. I tried to ignore it and concentrate on composing my defence in my head but the scent clouded uneasily with the clozapine I had just taken and a fit of dizziness forced me to step off the train. I found myself in Piccadilly, my ears studded by the noise of traffic and tourists. Then I saw Waterstones, its dark doors open like those of a church before mass, promising peace.

Even as I crossed the threshold, I sensed my physical weakness dragging down my mind. I knew I was going to fall off the wagon. I felt a dry prickling in the back of my throat at the thought of the *W* section. I hurried to the lift, but encountered a long queue. I made impatiently for the stairs, when—

'Richard!' a familiar voice shouted.

I turned to see that a crowd had gathered around a table. Beyond them, a slim brown hand was waving at me. I stepped closer and saw the sign:

How Will Self Can Change Your Life
A collection of short stories
READING AND SIGNING SESSION

Three contributors:
Zara Curren, Jamie Curren
and Toady Hall

The crowd's heads turned as Zara came up and flung her arms around my neck. Her bracelets jangled sweetly, pressed cold against my skin.

'We've all been wondering where you'd got to.' She smiled up at me through her lashes and then whispered, 'I'm so sorry about Dirty Pete — it was all such a shame,' as though she was referring to a novel that had failed to set the charts alight.

I was about to tell her sharply just what had happened to Dirty Pete and how the police had reacted, but she was already returning to her fans. I considered walking away, when Toady assailed me. He was wearing an even more outrageous shade of tweed that criss-crossed pink and green over his rotund belly, an unlit pipe poking out of his mouth. 'Richard! We've all been missing you! You must join us once we're done with the plebs,' he added, not bothering to lower his tone.

Their warmth surprised me, appeased me. I sat down near the back.

'A Textual Examination of the Word *Cunt* in the novels of Will Self,' Jamie began. 'The word *cunt* is integral to his novels in the same way that the word *propriety* is a key that unlocks the themes of Austen's works. But before we analyse his use of the word in close context, let us consider where the word *cunt* actually comes from – the word-cunts that gave birth to cunt! The origins are much disputed, but the expression *cu* is one that expresses both essential femininity and, most importantly, knowledge. *Cu* also gave birth to *cunning* and let us not forget the fellow word *ken*, which means both to know and to give birth. The Chaucerian version of the word cunt, *queynte*, means both *vagina* and *cunning*. It is clear then that, like Self, the cunt is all-knowing . . .'

Though it was Jamie reading, the words made an impact. I realized how numb I had been for the last few weeks. Even my cock began to stir, like a creature awakening from a long hibernation. I thought of the Josephine Cox novel sitting in my flat – *Josephine Cox!* – and felt tears threaten my eyes, but turned them into a wide, trembling smile.

Toady's piece came next: a short story narrated by a pair of testicles. One testicle is a reincarnation of Swift; the other a reincarnation of Kafka. They debate their influence on the work of Will Self with increasing vehemence until their fight culminates in death, when Swift hypnotizes his owner to prong Kafka with a sharp pencil.

Then Zara. She curled a ringlet of dark hair around her

finger and announced that she would be reading samples from the *Will Self Alphabet*. When she mentioned that one of the contributions had been made by the late Sylvie Pettersson, my spine jolted upright. Her voice was luxurious with confidence and Oxbridge education:

'P for Pornography. In the words of the great Will himself: "Literature has always been powered forward by these kind of irruptions of sex and violence . . . it can be argued that during periods when pornography infiltrates high art there is the greatest level of creative innovation."'

I felt Sylvie's anger fissure in the air. Zara's quote was a lie, had been dug out by the group and posthumously attributed to her. I glanced through the crowd, searching for two faces carved with grief, but Sylvie's parents did not appear to be present. The audience's faces shone upwards, ebullient with titillation.

Were the police searching my flat at this very moment? I didn't care if they ripped open my bedding or trashed my TV, but the thought of them opening the box under my bed and pushing my Self books into plastic bags made me feel sick. I swallowed and followed Zara into the hallway outside her flat. After the reading, they had signed books for the public while sharing a bottle of vodka. Toady was leaning on Jamie for support; his pipe looked like a clock-hand stuck at five. When I asked why he had no tobacco in it, he replied in a slurry voice, 'The pipe is for show. It's my begging bowl, since I'm a penniless writer.'

'I thought your misery memoir was going down well,' I said.

'Everyone's found out that I made it up,' Toady said dejectedly. 'The publishers want their money back. I told them to go forth and search the tills of Oddbins, of Jermyn Street, of Barbour, of the genteel William Morris.'

'Ah,' I said.

I had meant my last remark to be jocular and chummy but an awkward silence ensued as Zara searched for her key. Jamie looked sullen, which I attributed entirely to my presence. I suffered an intensity of loneliness that only being in a group of people can make you feel. I sensed that even if I did join the WSC, Jamie would never allow me in fully. The sense of non-belonging filled me with relief in its familiarity: acceptance had been too foreign.

Inside the flat, I tried to bring up the subject of Dirty Pete, but Zara curled her arm through mine and whispered, 'Later.' She insisted on giving me a guided tour of her flat. It was beautiful – as though someone had chiselled out one of those high-ceilinged, gold-panelled, velvet-textured rooms you find cordoned off in homes owned by the National Trust, and inserted it into the plain white walls of her flat. Tall ebony bookcases with glass panels, clotted with books, a mixture of first editions – Shelley's *Prometheus*, Thomas More's *Utopia*, and contemporary novels by Burroughs, J. G. Ballard and, of course, Will Self. Not a hint of Amis or any other betrayal. Polished floorboards, scattered with Persian rugs in patterns of ochre, green and cerise. Cushions, shiny white with gold tassels, flung over a *chaise-longue* embroidered with butterflies. When I looked out of her window, even her view seemed more impressive than mine, like a dull picture that comes alive in a gilded frame. A wistfulness came over me: I wished that I could stay here for ever, never have to return to my flat and face them.

Her bedroom contained a desk bigger than her bed. The only mess in the spotless room was on that desk – a mass of papers, pots stuffed with fountain pens, bottles of greeny-black ink and a real quill, stacks of writing paper rimmed with gold embossing, notepads, balls of scrunched paper and piles of more books with snapped spines.

'Do you like my paintings?' Zara asked.

I stared up at the triptych of canvases. They were all of the same faceless man in dark pin-striped suit and bowler hat. I looked closer. There was a hint of breasts beneath his suit, a tiny plait flicked behind his shoulder, a slash of lipstick pink on his featureless face.

'They're lovely,' I said, in a small voice.

'Lovely?' Jamie sneered. 'I've never heard them called that before.'

I went to the toilet, soaping my hands with a pale green oval at the sink. I stared hard into the mirror, searching for the slightest flicker in Zara's shower curtain. A sense of desperation came over me but I kept staring, trying to fool myself that breezes were personalized. Realizing that some time had passed, I slipped out into the hallway. I could hear Toady singing drunkenly to himself in the living room. And, from Zara's bedroom, hushed voices, fluttered breathing. I edged closer, gazing through the slit in the door. Forms merged with shadow. I was unable to differentiate between their bodies, and for a moment their silhouette looked grotesque, a hermaphrodite embracing her/himself. Then the silver of Jamie's nail catching the light as he clasped Zara's shoulders gently, and I saw he was standing behind her, kissing the back of her neck. Zara's shoulders were hunched and tense. 'Will you be ready for tomorrow?' Jamie asked, in such an intimate voice that I felt heat in my cheeks. 'Will you please him? Will you show us all your pleasure?' Zara turned and I quickly returned to the bathroom, washed my hands once more and joined Toady in the living room.

I was quite relieved when Jamie announced that he needed to pop out for an hour, to have a quick drink with a literary editor. Before leaving, he tweaked Toady's pipe, gave Zara a deep kiss on the lips and raised one eyebrow faintly in my direction.

The slam of the door reverberated through the flat. Toady slumped down on the *chaise-longue*.

'Cheer up,' Zara said, rubbing his wrist. 'I do feel sympathy for you – though more, perhaps, for your parents.'

'Ah,' said Toady. 'Do you mean sympathy or empathy?'

Their disproportionate laughter suggested I was missing out on some kind of private joke.

'Cocktails,' Zara concluded. 'They're the only way to celebrate a book signing at four in the afternoon and to cheer up an author suffering the ruination of his career after a faked misery memoir. Come on!' she cried, jumping up and taking his hand, then mine. 'I have *every* drink possible in my cabinet. We can prepare them for Jamie, for when he gets back.'

I felt frustrated: I wanted to talk to Zara alone. I wanted to tell her how it had felt to be sitting in that police station, sculpting polite answers, fraying inside. I wanted to tell Zara that even though they were chasing me now, I had not once disclosed her name; I craved the prize of her gratitude. I gazed at the line-up of bottles, light fracturing against glass of blue, green and peach, lacing the liquid with golden shots. I saw Sylvie flash, swim through liquor. I grabbed the door for support.

'Are you okay?' Zara asked.

'Just a bit dizzy.'

'You ought to lie down,' Zara announced. She grabbed my hand and led me into her bedroom. It was only when she tried to prise her palm away that I realized how tightly I was squeezing it. I whispered, 'Sylvie – I want to know if you were the ones who gave her drugs, I need to know . . .' but she kissed my forehead, laughed sweetly and was gone, leaving behind a will-o'-the-wisp of perfume. I rubbed my temples blearily. The picture on the wall opposite disturbed me. The feminine-suited man was standing in a room, the table of glasses indicating a cocktail party; there was a sense of shadow behind him, a feeling of form in the curtains, perhaps a demonic woman with a cat-face, watching him. Then she began to watch me. I sat up and turned my back on her. A glint of red in the mess on Zara's desk snagged my attention. I stood up, suddenly alert and sober, moving aside the spray of papers.

'Dr Gyggle,' I read. This time, the Cluedo character had a balding head and bulbous eyes that gleamed behind his glasses. A stethoscope was curled around his neck like a snake.

I turned it over. There was a picture of a black mask, with the swirling letters, '*Are they tragic or comic masks — or not masks at all?* WSC, 11 p.m., Mentmore Towers. Tomorrow night.'

I turned and saw Zara in the doorway. Then she came up to me and stood on tiptoe, leaning in until our breath touched.

'You will come, won't you?'

I felt as though I was standing on the edge of an abyss.

'You see, we're going to honour Sylvie. We love her; we miss her. There's so much I haven't told you about her, but if you come tomorrow, you can know everything. You can be one of us.'

I heard a soft moan sigh through me and felt Sylvie roll my tongue into a 'yes'.

Ten

When I switched the TV on, I was surprised to see Natasha Kaplinsky's face being stretched across the seventy-inch plasma screen; first horizontally, until it resembled a pancake, then vertically, so that her neck became a thin white trunk, then diagonally, so that her nose was smeared across her cheeks, chin and forehead in turn. Despite these curious visual transmogrifications, her voice remained lucid. Then her head popped into different shapes: a square, a diamond, a circle, like motifs on a pack of playing cards. Various shades of neon violated her features, until the screen faded to black with shimmering white dots.

As the dots coalesced into a familiar shape, I heard the dull thud of my mug and a warm liquid seeped into my slippers. Will Self's face floated across the screen, his expression assuming the nonchalant sadism of a dictator. He watched me scrabble for my remote control and started speaking – before I quickly changed the channel to BBC 1. I watched *Teletubbies* for five minutes, taking solace in the banality of their squeaks, before their moon faces began to morph into Selfian masks and soon they were no longer gambolling across a green landscape; a yellow one tore the head off a purple one and proceeded to bounce up and down on top of its head, making masturbatory squeals of delight.

We played a game of cat-and-mouse across the terrestrial and digital for several minutes, Self chasing me through *The Simpsons*, where Bart was entering a competition to win the Nonce Prize; *Gardener's World,* where Titchmarsh was explaining how to grow weed; and a documentary on the Ritz, where the hotel suddenly morphed into a giant lump of crack cocaine. The lump broke into dancing white particles, the London sky-line fell into shadow and, once again, Self's face took possession of the screen.

I had only heard Self speak a few times before, and I knew that he was famous for his eloquence and verbal sparring. Now his voice sounded alien, as though someone had cut and spliced sentences from his various TV appearances on *Shooting Stars, Have I Got News for You* and *Newsnight* in order to compose his instructions, for his speech was full of jerky pauses and unnatural rhythms.

'You will – attend – the party. You will – find me – there. You will – use the knife as I instruct. Now – go – pull on your jerkin, Richard, I'm going to take you to Muswell Hill to buy some dancing pumps.'

The screen resumed. I sat down on the sofa in my damp socks. A green Teletubby gurgled reassuringly.

I was just leaving for the party when the phone rang and the answerphone clicked on. At first I didn't recognize the voice – it was so long since my father had last called. He left me a message, punctuated with 'er', that the police had been in touch with him and was I in trouble in any way? I shut the door to my flat just as the machine cut him off with an efficient beep.

Outside in the hallway, I heard the neighbours from flats

forty-three and six gossiping that there was a line of police cars in the street below. Intuition told me to take the lift, and hurry. As I descended slowly through the floors, I pictured the doors pinging open to reveal a row of gun barrels and blazing lights. But the lobby was empty, the guard ensconced with the *Daily Mail* once more. I slipped out of the flats, melted into a crowd and slid into my car. In my wing mirror, I watched them enter the building. They might be looking for me; then again, I reasoned, they could be pursuing a burglary, an entirely different crime. In any case, they had missed me by seconds.

This fateful escape created a sense of calm inside me; I felt protected by higher, Selfian forces. Dirty Pete and the police and my father seemed like a tide that had rolled far out. Tomorrow would come crashing up but for now I enjoyed a Zen-like sensation of existing entirely in the present.

This time when I made the journey to Buckinghamshire, the familiarity of the journey felt like a delicious secret. The commuters rolling past in their cars had never looked greyer. As I stopped outside the gates shielding Rothwell Towers, I reached for the mask I'd bought in a tacky costume shop in Soho. The plastic cut into the hollows around my eyes. I proudly passed my invitation to the guard. When he handed it back, the brush of his fingers against mine shocked me. As though I had been floating in a dream and reality had slashed me awake, leaving edges raw and jagged. My fear became so intense that I was nearly sick all over my lap, and I yearned to turn the car round and speed back home. I found a parking space and switched the engine off. In the driving mirror, I asked Will to reassure me that I had come to the right place, but he remained elusive. I watched other masked partygoers strolling down the gravel, their laughter drifting across the evening dusk. Tomorrow

I would call my father and report to the police. Everything would be well.

Inside, the castle was even more Gothically beautiful than I had imagined. Girls wearing party dresses made of gauze and silk floated like exotic flowers on a lake, proffering trays of drinks. They came in tall flutes, the cocktails green as grass, a faint steam rising off them. One drink would do no harm. I took a sip and nearly choked. I had another, more cautious, sip and tried to work out what it contained. Absinthe for the colour and a sweet liqueur with a coconut tint. Amaretto, maybe? Or even . . . *yagé*? I recalled Dirty Pete's cries as he had thrashed in the cubicle, more animal than human. I held on tight to my drink but did not risk another sip.

Sylvie's absence felt ominous. I sensed that she had once stood on this stone floor, perhaps sipped from the very same glass I was now drinking from. A ghost, I thought, can be haunted too: haunted by memory. I felt naked without her, naked and lonely, and I busied myself by pretending to be fascinated by the building. I followed some stone stairs carpeted in plush plum into a central hall with a domed roof. In the centre was a large square tent, cloaked in diaphanous black curtains, teased by a faint breeze. I longed to go and see what was behind them, but nerves held me back. When I finally summoned courage to grip the curtain, a low voice reprimanded me: 'Richard, you know you're not allowed in there . . . You're not a neophyte yet.'

I turned to see a girl wearing a black silk dress and a matching mask. It took me a few moments to recognize her.

'You must come with me and watch the Birthing of the Chimpman.' Zara looped her arm through mine, leading me on. As we wove through the hall, masks turned, sequins catching the light, pride became a pleasure in my stomach. I'd always felt that Zara constructed glass between the world and the WSC

– I had been conscious of banging my nose against its pane. But tonight I felt as though she had unlocked a door and invited me into a secret room. Anticipation shivered through me.

'Is Toady coming tonight?' I asked, for I had spotted all the other members of the WSC but him.

'I'm afraid not.' Her voice acquired an edge. 'I'm afraid he's not really welcome any more. You see, to be in the WSC, you have to love what we love, or you don't belong.'

I felt the words 'Amis' and 'schism' clouding between us but I did not want to spoil the mood.

She drew me into a large room. Exquisite tapestries and Van Loos paintings hung on the walls. A curious medley of furniture was sprawled across the floor – an antique *chaise-longue* and a grand piano rubbing polished sides with a modular work station painted in mushroom and various other office equipment. On an ebony table in the centre lay a masked female, with the beautiful passivity of an assistant ready to be sawn in two by a magician. Crowds gathered around her, whispering, buzzing excitement.

When the Chimpman appeared, everyone applauded and I quickly concealed my shock. He was dressed in a classic party ape suit, a studded black mask tied around his hairy head. A girl sitting before the piano played a few quivering notes and cried out, 'May the Great Ape Fornicate!' The Chimpman pulled up the girl's dress and licked at her thighs. Sweat slugged across my brow and my cock became an embarrassment; I took a quick slug of my drink. Now the Chimpman was plunging into her, the table rocking violently, the piano notes fracturing, competing for climax . . .

'Waaaaaa!'

The cry of a child made me start. A man in a tuxedo who had been kneeling by the table produced – seemingly from nowhere — the most extraordinary creature. It looked like a baby but its cheeks were hirsute, one hand waving pudgy fingers, the other a simian paw.

'The Chimpman!' the crowd cried, laughing and applauding.

Zara heard me gasp and leant in closer. 'Sylvie came here, you know. She watched the Chimpman . . . It was her first night with the WSC . . . She had never looked so radiant . . .'

I asked Zara to tell me more, but she grabbed the slender white arm of a passing brunette. Her eyes remained on me, glinting, as she whispered in her ear. The brunette smirked and nodded.

When they surrounded me in a circle, I felt afraid. A hundred eyes on me; a silence that became hostile. The brunette stepped forwards and I heard myself let out a cry. Laughter mocked my ears. My eyes squeezed shut, and a voice of morbid curiosity asked: *What will it feel like when she cuts my throat?* When I felt her unbuttoning my trousers, I spilt some of my drink in shock. More laughter. The drink had splashed greeny on to the back of her hand and she licked it off, smiling. Then, with slow, deliberate flicks, she undid the final buttons, parting my underwear. The shock of full exposure flooded blood into my cock. My drink trembled in my glass. Zara tilted her head to one side and smiled, then clapped her hands.

The brunette began to kiss a man standing beside me. I was still exposed and in a state of shaken shock. When the couple turned away from me, my humiliation intensified; a child in me felt hurt by the greedy hunger of their kisses and caresses, their swift and apparent indifference. Zara approached and I fumbled to rebutton my trousers, my cheeks still raw with shame.

'Sylvie wanted to be one of us.' Zara continued her story in a soft voice, as though there had been no interlude. 'She wanted, so very badly, to be part of the WSC.'

Behind me, I saw a masked girl and a masked man start to kiss; he drew her thigh up against his leg so that her dress silked backwards, revealing a lacy stocking.

'But she was only a neophyte, you see. She wanted more, but she wasn't ready. It was only her first time. We all had to wait, you see,' Zara went on, her voice low and dusky. 'Even me, even Jamie. A neophyte can watch the Birthing of the Chimpman, but they cannot join us beyond the curtains. They must wait, they must wait . . .' She pointed to a door, which was slightly ajar. I saw a small, lonely white room, entirely bare except for a little picture of Will Self on the wall. 'There they must wait. She wanted the Wafer, she begged for the Wafer of Will, weeks before she was ready for the test. We gave her the Wafer, we told her to wait in the room – we asked her to contemplate!'

The piano keys flurried as a man lifted a woman on to them, spreading apart her legs.

'Was it . . . was it . . . *yagé*?' I asked.

Zara shook her head. '*Yagé*!' She smiled. 'No. Oh, no. *Yagé* is inferior to the Wafer. When Sylvie took it, she sat in the waiting room and wept; she vomited; she wept some more. We could not accept her as a neophyte, you must understand that! It was a test, you see. The body houses the soul, and if the body will accept the Wafer, the soul is unified with Will's. If the body rejects it, then it is proof that they can never be accepted . . .'

I saw two men sink on to the floor together; a girl, laughing, separated them and took it in turns to kiss their mouths, tracing their masks with her fingers. I gazed down at Zara's lips, wet from her cocktail.

'Sylvie tried to change her face to look like Will's, but it was no good. She attempted to change herself on the outside – but the test must be inside!' Zara splayed her palm against my heart as though she might control its beat. As she lowered her voice to a whisper, I leant in, struggling to hear her over the gasps simmering around us. 'I think she became desperate. We asked her to deliver a package to Dirty Pete – he's an honorary member, he helps us bless the Wafers – and she failed us. I think Dirty Pete got angry with her. I think he was afraid she might . . . tell others . . . about us. I think he might have been the one who killed her. When Dirty Pete died, it was a vengeance, and you were part of that – do you understand? You can be at peace now. You don't need to worry any more or ask any questions. Dirty Pete is dead. It's over, now, Richard, all over. Now you're one of us.'

She reached up on tiptoe and consoled me with a deep kiss. I tried to hold on to her, but she struggled away, and was immediately replaced by two beautiful girls, one blonde, one chestnut. Their laughter tinkled like chandelier glass. The blonde led me to the table and pushed me down; the other knelt on the floor and unbuttoned my trousers. I closed my eyes, aching with the pain of truth; I heard Sylvie's cries fighting Dirty Pete's cackles as he plunged the knife into her back. Lips circled the rim of my cock; I gasped. I pictured Sylvie crashing to the floor, her warped cocoon features smashed out of shape. I opened my eyes as the girl above broke off from caressing my chest; she reached into her dress and pulled out an embroidered purse from which she drew a small white square. Just before she placed it on her tongue, I saw the picture on it with a flash of recognition: *Will's face*. The same one that Sylvie had been holding in the photo. The girl moaned and coaxed me down on to the table, biting my neck. I pushed her away, and saw a faint alarm in her pupils, glittering through her mask. I asked her what she had taken, but she told me I was not yet allowed the Wafer and suffocated me with a kiss. As her breasts hardened against my chest, I fought my desire, glancing around the room. Wafers were being drawn from purses and pockets, glinting on tongues, chews alternating with kisses and caresses. Then the brunette at my feet sucked me in deep and I heard myself let out a groan . . .

A single bell began to ring, multiplying into echoes of echoes until the entire house sang with its exquisite note. The women uncurled from me and urgently pulled on their clothes. I reached out with a shuddering hand, trying to cajole the brunette back to my flesh, but she shook her head primly. I sat up, rebuttoning my trousers against the strain of my cock. Everyone in the room was pulling on dark cloaks, drawing up the hoods so that, within minutes, gender and personality had been obliterated. The silvery bell was accompanied by the gunfire of footsteps as guests streamed towards the hall. The diaphanous black curtains fluttered and twirled, resuming their place before I could catch a glimpse of what was behind them. I begged several passing figures for a cloak, but they rushed past me as though I was a ghost.

'Come,' the blonde led me, pointing to the small white room, 'you should wait here.'

'Of course.' I kissed her. 'Of course.'

I waited until the house was silent and everyone was gathered behind the curtain. Then I slipped off my shoes and slid back into the central hallway. Did I dare, did I dare?

I stood at the edge of the curtains, feeling naked in my black tie, conscious of the noise of my breathing. The silhouette of the huddled mass looked like a many-humped beast. Their prayers had the haunting quality of a Gregorian chant and yet there was an insidious rumble in them too, a language I did not recognize. I could not help myself any longer; I curled my little finger around the edge of the curtain and pulled it back, creating my own peep-hole.

The scene before me, with its strange mixture of cinema and chapel, provoked a Pavlovian squirm in my gut, a gamut of shame and fascination. The hooded figures filled around fifty or so pews. At the front was a large stage that resembled an altar; a king-size bed, dressed in black sheets, sat in the centre. Above it was a cinema screen on which Will's face was frozen, scowling down at his congregation like a displeased deity. Next to the bed was a figure dressed in dark brown robes; he was smoking a pipe so enormous the bowl curled to his ankles. Wreaths of grey smoke pumped out over the congregation. Soon the smoke reached me; it had a bitter tobacco kiss.

On the other side of the bed was a small, battered desk where a hooded figure sat before a typewriter. Every so often, the screen would animate and Will's baritone boom a word or sentence – 'Quiddity!' or 'Hoograaa!' – before freezing back into a contorted snarl. The figure hastily typed out this divine dictation, interrupting the awed hush with the jagged clatter of keys.

I intended to creep away, when Will's eyes suddenly shifted in my direction. I was unable to do anything except stare back, transfixed. He had teased me on my TV screen but here, above his congregation, he looked a thousand times more glorious.

Hoods turned. Some devotees gasped, some whispered. Then Zara was at my side. I opened my mouth to speak, but she pressed her finger lightly against my lips and pulled a cloak over me.

'Kneel,' she whispered. She produced a small white square, smiling proudly. 'The Wafer. You're ready.'

'I – I can't . . .' I whispered urgently. 'I can't take drugs . . . I'm scared I might . . . I might . . .'

'You *reject* the Wafer?' Zara cried.

Will's face wrenched into such corpulent displeasure that

the congregation gasped. I clasped my hands together and begged forgiveness. This time, when Zara offered, I accepted it on my tongue. There I let the Wafer hover, terrified to chew and release its juices; gradually, it melted into my saliva and trickled down my throat. I clawed my face in dread, waiting for my liver to collapse, my heartbeat to freeze, my body to convulse . . .

My mind rose, slowly, to the gelid surface of consciousness. My eyes ungummed. I sent a psychic probe into my body, one into my perineum, one into the gusset of my bowels, but found the transmogrification a genial one. Sweat had percolated through my skin but my body felt sweetly cleansed and curiously light, as though His huge breaths were billowing through me and I might levitate at any moment. White stars, edged with violet, flashed in the blackness. The stars separated into patterns, embraced the runtish contours of Will's face.

'Neophyte,' Will boomed.

N-e-o-p-h-y-t-e, the typewriter clacked.

Zara drew me to my feet. We proceeded down the aisle together as the atmosphere inspissated.

At the foot of the bed lay a small black box, and as I came closer, I realized that it was a coffin. A momentary, truculent doubt assailed me. My hesitation agitated the air. The congregation gasped, but this time He showed me compassion. Will looked down at me – and into me. His fingers squelched through my soul, separating the wheat of faith from the turd-chaff of doubt, flinging the faecal into the ether. My intellect, my ego, my past, liquefied, puddled around my feet, so that when Zara and the other women removed my hooded cloak and then my clothes, the ensuing nakedness provoked a feeling not of shame but prelapsarian intimacy. The interstitial space of

the coffin was a dark womb that I stepped into – Will's womb!
I lay in this Pygmalion receptacle with the exalted simplicity
of a child. Up until this moment, I had lived my life as a book
of jumbled sentences, poor plotlines and crossings-out, but in
one glance Will had wiped out my history and now my soul
– my soul! – was a flurry of blank pages ready to take his dictation. I would be rewritten; I would be reborn. In the Beginning
was the Word of Will, and Will alone.

My coffin served suitably to narrow my virgin world; my
spatial awareness was truncated to the bed above and the arc
of my Heavenly Father's face above me. I focused devotion
through my eyes; my smile attempted to translate the divine
love welling in my chest so that my lips nearly broke. Zara
shadowed above me. She took hold of my arm, smoothing her
fingers down the irrigated map of my veins. I saw the glint of
a blade and closed my eyes in surrender, accepting that rebirth
and death were to be my twins of redemption. When I felt the
pain in my wrist, my eyes fluttered open. I saw that she had not
slashed the artery, only a vein alongside it and when she held
up my wrist to Will, the candle highlighted a trickle glissading
my skin.

'He is a chosen child of the Fat Controller!' he cried, and the
typewriter clacked his words in ecstatic echo.

A few droplets of blood flew on to my chest.

Silence. Then the shivery ring of that bell again, its notes
murmuring through my soul. On the bed above me, two
hooded figures held up copies of Will's books. When they began
to rip pages out of them, a physical pain twanged my chest,
and I emitted a stertorous cry. Will's eyes flickered downwards,
reassuring me that He was pleased. The pages crackled in the
air, floating down on to the bed where they feathered into a
crenullated blanket of prose.

The figures left the bed; the light dimmed as several candles were snuffed. The congregation began to chant softly, foreign words that I did not understand but stirred some primeval feeling in my chest so that my heartbeat began to mimic their voices . . .

A figure was aided on to the bed. He/she stood tall with arms outstretched, like a saviour in crucified ecstasy. I felt jealous that He might pour His love over them, but a dark scepticism vitrified His expression. The figure's hood fell back and I recognized the hook-nosed patios of Zara's profile. My heart leapt that we might join together in loving Will. Two figures helped to pull her robe from her body; her naked skin shone as though the candles were parasiting their flames from her. Desire engorged my groin. My cock soared Selfwards. Zara lay athwart the bed, the chanting swelling in rhythm with her onanastic ritual. Her hands seized flurries of pages, smothering them over her fulsome breasts, her corrugated ribs, her lissom stomach, shreds tearing and catching on her skin, her fingers titivating the prose fug. Her left hand, splayed across the final page of *Great Apes*, pressed it against her stratified pinkness, her neck arched back in strangulated valediction, her climax shuddering up, up, up to Will, as the cavalcade of chanting rose to a *Messiah* climax. I found myself chanting with them, my possessed psyche spilling a literary tongue of tongues, riotous, glorious, my ego swept away in a tidal wave of collective bliss as we became One, One body, One mind, One soul, One Will.

Silence. The bed whoozed on its spring suspension. Zara lay trembling, a lappet of hair flung across her face, candlelight flickering over the white pearls on her fingertips. I felt the collective heart of the congregation beating through me. The typist gazed upwards, her fingers taut on her keys. We ached for Will's approval – for his dispensing of boons.

Will said nothing.

A wail bansheed out from the congregation, echoing in the funnelled heights of the domed ceiling. Its epilogue was a fissure of frightened whispers. I curled my shaking hands over my chest. Zara sat up, her eyes hollow with fear. She clambered from the bed; two figures helped her to pull on a cloak. As they led her away, I heard her beginning to sob quietly.

Will was displeased.

Will was displeased.

How to win his favour? How to please him? Oh, how, Will, oh, how?

A hooded figure leant over the coffin. Hands reached down to pull me up but my weakness vitiated my stride; they carried my weight on their shoulders, my coltish feet trailing across the floor, before propping me up against the stanchion of the bed. Will's vituperative expression became impassive, watchful. A shift in the tempo of the congregation: a stirring of hope. Jamie stepped forwards and I held out my arm. His cut was deep – the blade expressed his jealousy that I, and not his sister, had been exalted to the phalanx of the Chosen One. But I suffered no sense of petty triumph. The weight of responsibility felt heavy, not just on my shoulders, but my entire body, so that my enpurpled cock had shrunken to the size of a grape. Oh, Will, let me not fail you, let me please you, oh, Will!

I had to wait as the neophytes tore apart a new set of books. Every rip of the paper caused me to shudder as though the skin was being torn from my own flesh. Blood slithered down my arm in thin threads; my legs concertinaed against the bedstead. I saw the future if I failed, if I displeased him, broken shards of coloured glass as though Will had smashed an apocalyptic mirror and flung pieces of Revelation at me, the hall becoming a crucible for our collective sins – flames bubbling flesh into a white-orange efflorescence, a gaggle of screams flying up towards the heavens, and *Will* – Will alone in an empty tower block, in a graveyard of concrete, the public knocking at the door, but the door marked CLOSED, always CLOSED, and Will at his desk, his hands folded in his lap, his typewriter keys interlaced with cobwebs, his eyes bleak on the horizon, his followers forever punished, doomed to drift in bookshops enquiring in fetid hope, *Will there be another Will, will there, will there?* and bookshop owners suicidal, shaking their heads, and skulls left on *S* shelves and banners and crowds screaming, WHY?

Up, up, they lifted me on to the bed, held me suspended with outstretched hands, chanting ballooning beneath me. Will did not nod, but a reptilian blink flickered across his eyes: a Second Chance.

Down, down on to the eschatological bed. Pages chafed me; my blood wept on to them. My cheek nestled against the scratch of paper. My cock was barely a ghost, but I did not suffer panic. I watched my blood slowly seeping on to a page from *Tough, Tough Toys for Tough, Tough Boys* and the intimacy touched me with tears. I saw a flash of light, a fissured crack in the wall of displeasure; an understanding that I might please him by forgetting them, by creating a shrine within my own consciousness. The silence became a threat but I waited, patient with faith, feeling his prose slowly seep into my cock, swell it, saturate it until it was replete with Muse. Whispers – agitated stirrings – still, I lay still. I heard the footsteps of someone stepping forwards to take my place. My fingers trembled downwards, inch by inch, and curled around Our resplendent cock – for I had surrendered it to him and from that day on I would never be able to love another, every ejaculation a metaphor that would belong to him. The footsteps stopped; the waiting mounted. I began slowly to rock my fingers, the blood flowing warmly over my thighs, the paper crackling with rhythm, as though the books had always existed in a blastosphere of epiphany, known even when dropping off conveyor belts from the printing press that they had been destined for this day when I would nullify the sins of his detractors and personify the love of his truest worshippers, and I took Our Almighty Cock in my hands, rubbing and rocking and jiggling, a cunt-throb of paper against a savage cock-thrust, gasping, sweating, a numinous force-field sparking around my nether regions, his eyes on me, the dawn of a smile on his lips — *oh, Will, oh, Will* — oh, yes, oh, yes, oh, Will, oh, yes, oh, semen-bedizened blood-pusillanimous bed onanistic quiddity fulcrating pelvic thrusts smoke thick typewriter's click-clack-click Will Our Cock is Spent screaming loving Will is pleased Will is Saved I have done it I have done I am the Chosen One I am his Chosen One oh Will for ever I am yours for ever I am yours for ever I am.

I found myself slumped in an armchair. A single soprano note ringing. Flies everywhere, feasting on the body, crawling over my hands. As I flicked them away, droplets of blood flew from my palms. A packet of red and green peppers at my feet; half a carton of mouldy milk. Through the fly-clouds, I saw the TV. It sang bedtime, its face static fuzz. Then the blinking black-and-white dots slowly, inevitably, took shape. I leant forwards intently. On the screen Will's face mouthed instructions on what the WSC needed to do next.[‡]

[‡]Editor's note: This is the last chapter Richard wrote before the New Deal Experiment began. The chapter that followed was written afterwards and is, as a result, completely incomprehensible, so it has not been included in this manuscript.

Part Two:
Sylvie

I felt him behind me like a shadow –

Oh Daddy don't tell me don't tell don't –

I – I – I –

I – I – I want to be inside Will Self. I yearn for it. If only he would let me in. His window is locked against the cold, the night, winter's shadows. I press my cheek against the glass. Its solid cruelty mocks me. I watch Will in his London home, in his study, his tall frame languid in his swivel chair, shoulders hunched over his typewriter. His study is cluttered with the paraphernalia of a creative, contented family man: Post-its papering the walls, crayons, books, a small bicycle tucked under his desk, all caressed with a golden lamplight glow. It makes me shiver, not with the cold but a memory of cold. Snow falls through me. I wonder if the snow senses me. I tilt upwards. I have spent hours watching the snowflakes come down on the streets. As they sail towards human warmth there is friction, a chemical reaction: the snow quivers, repulses, sighs, sticks to skin, fuses. But to the snow I am nothing. Even the *zgnabe* I drink makes no difference, even when I feel the burn in my stomach, except really there is no burn, for I have no stomach. Just an idea of one. I am an idea. I am Sylvie. I had a body but He took it from me.

I ought to be taking revenge, or telling someone to take revenge. Hamlet's father went straight to his son and gave him firm instructions. But how did Hamlet's father learn to speak?

119

A special school? Did an angel teach him? Did he ascend to heaven and then get permission to come down? Others of my kind, I can converse with – but humans? I thrashed through my parents' bed for several nights and did not make a crease as my father wept and my mother turned a stony back on him. A moth skimming down, which my father flipped away, made more of an impulse than I did. When I saw the moth I wanted to crush it – I almost understood how murderers murder; I wanted to steal its tiny heartbeat, take its life; I wanted to put it in my mouth and feel it dying – even its tiny breaths would have been a comfort but there was none. But why did someone want my breath? I – I–

I felt him behind me like a shadow –

Oh Daddy don't tell me don't tell don't –

It got away. I could not even catch a moth. A moth can flitter its wings and cause an earthquake in China, but I can scream and not a grass stalk will quiver. This whole world is energy, pulsing currents, heartbeats on tubes, pounding carriages of throbbing skin, cables coiled through the molten earth, tides tugging heat breathing up clouds, bombs exploding, volcanoes vomiting. I am outside all that: I am not even enough of a presence to become an absence. I am just an infinitesimal something, I am like a *babushka* doll with a brighter shiny Sylvie thrown away and another Sylvie and another Sylvie until this Sylvie is smaller than an atom, beyond the realm of human instruments. Soon I will be nothing. Time is running out O Will open your window let me in let me in just let me feel your warmth before I go.

Here's the irony: walking through walls is supposed to be our speciality. That and coiling through keyholes like smoke. But brick and glass still stand between Will and me.

In the first week I discovered my limitations. I was bored and the thirst for *zgnabe* tortured me. I could see the sellers in the distance, shadowy shapes, notes flickering through their fingers; I could already hear their hoarse voices cajoling me to try a bottle, one more bottle, dim the pain. Ghost acid. I've seen souls swigging it back and their light dies fast, like a sunset in winter. I ran from them, ran as though I hoped I could leave my hunger hovering in the space where I had been. I found the library. I went in. I watched students yawning through *Jane Eyre*, making sly glances over their jotter pads. I watched old people shuffle and leaf through newspapers and watch the young with envy. A nerd was sitting at the Internet computer. I hovered behind him, surfing with him, mindless infonews passing through me Britney war babies pig dead new research AIDs higher percentages new taxation green global warming end of world. The nerd left, and I lingered. The library was locked up. Three inches of wood defeated me. Every time I tried to pass through, it was the mental block that pushed me back. Thoughts: wood grinding its teeth through me, leaving splinters in my heart liver stomach. I was still locked into a cage of conditioning. And so in the library I stayed, slumped by the wall, telling myself that I was shivering.

It was in the dead of the night that I began to hear the books. Have you ever sat alone in a bookshop or a library and listened to the atmosphere? The silence is dynamic. The knowledge simmers. At first I thought there was another soul in the room. Little ripples in the air; mutterings. Then, like voices in an orchestra, they rose and reached a crescendo. Dictionaries babbling baritone definitions; children's books screaming and giggling; phone books reciting in dull monotones, romances sighing, thrillers thumping. From the books at the back, however, came wails and howls of pain. They had been shunted into plastic green boxes, their cellophane spines scarred from the rip of their identification number. 'BARGAIN SALE,' said the sign. They were screaming to be adopted; their knowledge was ripe, ready to rot; they were desperate not to fall and hit the ground in a smash-glut of wasted muse. I thought of Plato's argument that animals did not have souls. That night, I concluded that everything has a soul. A writer gives birth to a book; it lives, it breathes, it informs, it inspires. What happens when a book goes out of print? I wondered. When it is pulped and killed? Does its soul, its essence, its original creative spark slip from the pages and become a ghost too? Perhaps those ghosts are the ideas that drift along, looking for open minds to slip inside, to be recycled, rewritten, reshaped by a fresh consciousness. Is this why, in the words of Isaiah, there is nothing new under the sun?

Behind the pane, Will Self peels a yellow Post-it from its wad and sticks it on his wall.

Glass. I find it even more frightening than wood. The sharp edges slashing through me; I can taste the blood. Imagine the taste of blood. So, out in the snow I remain, like a book slumped on a shelf, waiting for Will to read it.

I am aware of a presence coming up behind me. My false heart leaps up against the pane –

– I feel the plunge of the knife in the back

– warm spray of blood on my skin

– shrill pain raking fingernails down my spine

– death I relive

– Tersias, I say. – Tersias. Oh, thank God!

– I'm sorry I frightened you, he says, in a quavery voice.

Tersias was the first soul who ever spoke to me, who told me what I had become. There is a tint of despairing loneliness about him that has soured over time, like an old cider. When I asked him how long he had been wandering the streets of London, he said it was too far back to remember.

– I'm fine, I say. Don't worry.

I turn away.

Death reverberating through me.

My father used to love collecting moths and butterflies. Once he pinned a beauty on to a board that was only nearly dead. As he pushed the needle through, its wings flickered in torture. When the knife thrust into me, I became an insect on the floor, my fingers fluttering up behind my back trying to pull out the handle, up to my front trying to push back the blade. Did He pause in the doorway, watching my struggle, before He left?

– Waiting, are we?

Tersias teases me by sliding in and out of the window pane.

– Be patient, my dear, he says, he'll open it soon enough. Will it. Will *Will*. He chuckles.

Tersias appears to me as a shard of light, a colour (brown), a scent (sour, like vinegar). I wonder how I seem to him. Does my quiddity bleed the style of my death? Can he see my body as it was the day I died, or the way it used to be? Does he see the ghosts of my breasts? Does my false cock create a shadow? Despite the clouding of my gender, my friendship with Tersias is just as it would have been in real life. The same dynamics. A girl looking for a daddy to tell her the world is not a big bad place. A sense of lust from his side, which I find flattering but do not reciprocate. And so we dance the tango of human interaction on a glass floor that presses down on our animal urges. Jamie once said that the quiddity of all human relationships is power. The see-saw always tips one way or the other. Always a lover and a beloved. Jamie liked to quote Byron: *Lovers may be – and indeed generally are – enemies, for there must always be a something of Self about them in all their speculations.* Enemies fight for power.

– You don't want to waste your time hanging around here, my dear, Tersias advises. – Seriously, darling, it's time to go the station. Tonight is the night.

Tonight is the night that we discover who my murderer is. Or, as Tersias reminds me, who they *think* my murderer is. Tersias has taken me to the police station several times. We swam through their office smog of stress ringing phones dirty coffee cups biros bleeding PC paperwork. I felt surreal when I studied the collage of my photos on the wall, like a skeleton for a plot. The police are eager to write 'The End'. Their audience is impatient. They are conscious of coloured graphs and negative headlines, of bosses who need to please their bosses. And so the fat policewoman set a target for an official arrest – as though my death was an insurance policy about to mature – for midnight, 4 February 2006. She ought to erect a sign saying, 'SALE ENDS NOW ALL SUSPECTS MUST GO.'

Their shortlist for Murderer has shifted daily, depending on the whims of DNA, prejudice and interviews with young men. When they interrogated Richard, I bled pain for him; my heart says he is innocent. Twice, they have arrested him and released him. When they interrogated Jamie, I wanted to enjoy watching him squirm. But his answers honeyed from his lips. He spoke of how we had been 'casual lovers' and he had taken me to 'the odd party'. When he complimented the fat policewoman on her uniform, he even inspired a bashful smile; I wanted to point myself into an arrow and ram myself into his heart. There have been a few strangers, too. Men dragged off the streets, men with dirty stubble and sad eyes; one even had to leave his mongrel tied up outside and it howled at the night until I wanted to weep.

Tersias told me to stand by each suspect and see if I could sense anything. – You must have glimpsed your murderer's face, he argued, or at least smelt his scent, picked up *something*. I feel too ashamed to explain that I saw and felt nothing. Perhaps later tonight I will find the courage to confess what I was doing in those moments before I died. In books and films, people are always praying or fighting noble battles, but in real life death strikes with a sense of humour: people are picking their nose or driving a car playing a song they don't like or making love when their heart sighs that it can't be bothered to hang around waiting for their orgasm to finish . . .

I turn back to watch Will.

– We don't need to go yet, I say. We have four hours.

– Well, then, let's leave Will alone and enjoy ourselves! You need cheering up, my dear, I can see that. You need something to take your mind off it. Let's go to the British Museum. We can look for passwords!

– Passwords?

– Indeed. It's the answer for us! The end we're looking for!

Tersias researches constantly. All the different ways that we might find peace. Last month, he insisted reincarnation was the answer. He made me stand by him in a hospital ward, watching a mother's parted cunt, from which a small head was wriggling out. And as screams knifed the air, Tersias jack-dived into its tiny body. The mother clutched the Tersias-baby, one minute old and ninety-six years old, to her breast. Tersias emerged weeping.

– It already has a soul.

– You could try earlier. The point where soul is created, or hooked?

We wandered past night rooms, listening for gasps and grunts. We watched caresses and climaxes. We saw fakery betrayed in the curl of a lip, the furrow of a brow. We saw the ones who lay awake long after the post-coital chatter had faded to whispered embers. Each time, I felt as though I was standing beside my father, watching people fuck; my cheeks burnt with the memory of embarrassment, and Tersias's light acquired a pinker hue. It went on, night after night. For Tersias was highly picky.

– After all, he said, this will be the first day of the rest of my life.

He discarded many for being too old, too thin, too cruel, too insipid. Finally we stumbled upon a stumbling couple. Richard and Mia. They were leaving Jamie's launch party in low spirits, needing to inject sex into their egos to give them a boost. We followed them to Mia's house, a dank place in Primrose Hill where a bored grey cat sat at the window and underwear hung, forlorn, over a dirty bath. Tersias was taken with their good looks and 'twentysomething *ennui*'. He whooped after Mia, calling her 'Mummy'. I told Tersias that they would make poor parents. He argued that he could grow up visiting London Zoo on Sunday afternoons and frolic in the park in the summer. We hovered nervously, waiting for the arpeggio of orgasm to reach its top note. Was I jealous? A little, I admit. When I saw that Richard was thrusting into her but looking beyond her, I remembered what it was like to smile. And then Tersias dived. He swam with sperm. Later, he told me that sperm are the happiest creatures in the world, that the sensation was glorious, like diving down a celestial water chute – until he fell off the slide. Richard had gone limp. I wonder how many sperm I produced before He killed me. They say that death brings on an erection. I picture that sweet batch as my body hardened to cadaver: swirling excited in my taut prick, and then, as the hours went by, drifting down to form a pile like greyed autumn leaves. Then I feel sad. Tears would prickle my eyes, if I had them.

– So you think finding the right password will be more effective than sperm?

– In the Beginning was the Word.

Tersias feels we must find a name for our heaven before we can reach it. As though the right word will turn the key.

– Come on, then, he says, let's go.

– Not tonight, Tersias. Before we go to the station, I want to see Will. Who knows how long I have left? There may be not be a tomorrow. Please, Tersias. *Please?*

Tersias sighs. Once he mused that when I discovered my murderer, the knowledge would release me. I fear that he is jealous. He often jokes that he wishes he had been murdered instead of smoking his lungs away.

– All right, my darling Sylvie, anything for you, but only for you.

He creates a theatrical pause. Making sure the chivalrousness of his act does not go unappreciated. I play along, sighing relief, a damsel saved from distress.

Tersias concentrates his energies. A technique I am jealous of, for I have not yet acquired it.

Will gets up and opens the window. He stares straight through my eyes and into the night. I slip in. Unfortunately Tersias manages to follow me before Will closes the window. I wanted my last moments with him to be private.

The study seems smaller inside than out. Will seems taller. I once attended a reading he gave, with Jamie. He read beautifully, adopting accents, provoking laughs, smashing clichés, rearranging our thoughts with inner gasps and new ways of seeing the world. I cannot remember what he talked about. I think perhaps it was psychogeography. I remember this one detail: he spoke of how eighteenth-century poets used to carry picture-frames on their country walks and hold them to the sky, drawing a parallel with our modern-day experience of sitting on a plane and watching the world through a window-frame. He sat in his own invisible frame, decorated with gold leaf and surreal dashes; a portrait that would hang in the grandest spot in any gallery. His audience adored him as though he was a modern-day Oracle. He was the only man I know whom Jamie thought superior to himself.

Will sits back down. Tersias dances between the spokes of the bicycle under the desk. I ache for Will to behave like the hero in a horror movie. To gnaw his lip, cast nervous glances over his shoulder into shadowy corners, for his cat to enter and raise its hackles. But we remain undetected; we will never earn a place in his acknowledgements.

There is an apple sitting on Will's desk. A Golden Delicious, shiny and succulent-looking in the light. I float and stare, longing for him to bite into it. I want to see the liquid green rivulets dripping over his chin, to hover by the curve of his long fingers as they smear the juice away. But the apple sits, and Will sits, and the minutes go by, and we fade a little, and a new furrow begins to groove in Will's forehead, one that he will notice the next morning when he is looking in the mirror, and the apple loses a trace of its sheen and seems a little less verdant, a little less crisp.

– Dive in, Tersias suggests. – Really.

– It's too small. I laugh nervously.

– We're no longer any size or shape, Sylvie. We can make ourselves as large as a mountain or as small as a pinhead. Dive in. You might find you can move on to walls and glass.

I hover close until I see nothing but blots of dark green and mid-green and pale green, like dots on a TV screen making up a picture.

– You're in! I hear Tersias's voice, muffled and distant. – My darling, you're in, you're in!

I am too afraid of losing my grip to enjoy a feeling of triumph. I don't feel compressed, which depresses me: it confirms I have lost every human edge I ever had. I find I can move around its watery space, but it seems safer to gather myself in its core. A seed intrigues me. I taste its concentrate – the apple, its green-ness, skin, all squeezed up like a fruity jack-in-a-box, ready to explode. What a violent thing the life force is. But I am aware of the core growing tighter around me, as though pulling the skin towards it. As though it is a father and the skin its girl, as though it longs to hug it from Death. Death: raking its finger-nails through the apple flesh, leaving slashes of brown crêpe. The first terrible stench of rot. I don't want to be in the apple any more but I don't want to leave and go back to playing a ghost astronaut either.

The apple reminds me of my coffin. For several days in my ethereal infancy I had hovered in the hollow shell of my body, waiting for some light, some revelation, some angel with a clipboard saying, *Oh gosh sorry we're late but don't worry we didn't forget you!* My body slowly hardened and then turned yellow, as though morphing from flesh to stone. Then the insects found me. The knife wound between my chest and back had left a slit, like a purple vagina. This was how they entered my body: a troop of worms and beetles and crawly things. I tried to blow them away. They invaded regardless. The stench became unbearable; a thick smog of decay. I fled my coffin, terror swooping me through the wood, the earth, until I landed on grass. So easy then, so innocent. It was only when I started to think about passing through things that I lost the knack.

Out in the graveyard, the world yawned over me. Stones; puffclock seeds whirling; birdsong; the bells of the church singing seven o'clock. Lanes of traffic; rows of houses; the first streetlamps lighting up in necklaces on the horizon. An ocean of loneliness.

By my grave I could see the faint indentation in the earth where my father had stood at the funeral. Tears had spooled down around his neck. There should have been a naked band there, like the white strip left when a wedding ring has been removed, where his dog collar once used to constrict.

Jamie didn't come to the funeral. Nobody from the WSC came to the funeral, except Zara and her crocodile tears. I took solace in Richard's flat; my vanity is appeased by his grief, for we were little more than strangers. But he is on their side now, has been seduced by Jamie's false charm and Zara's snake looks. I have whispered through his flat, once or twice, fissuring exasperation. When he tried to speak to me, my non-heart broke with ruined hope. Our conversations didn't match: they were one-way only. When he became convinced that we were communicating, I had to leave; it felt too lonely, watching his delusion. He aches to join the WSC, though he cannot see that he, like me, is not one of life's joiners. Richard will always stand outside a glass, looking in. Wanting to be somebody; wanting to be some body; some body else.

I lose my grip; I slip. The apple is gone. It leaves on me some flavour, some tint of green, of blossom and summer, which fades too fast. Now I have known what it is to be possessed (for it feels a passive state, not an active one as the movies tell us), to feel the semblance of skin around me, I feel even more insubstantial. I dive into the bicycle wheel and become hot rubber; I thin into a Post-it; I become a window-frame and press my face out against the night, watching the snowfall become a flurry.

I drift through bookshelves. Will's entire works sit collected on one shelf. I slip between paper skins, savouring their rough caress. I feel their voices singing through me. *Tough, Tough Toys for Tough, Tough Boys* is the nasty sing-song of a sneering playground bully. *Grey Area* is an electro-synthesizer with odd notes of beauty quavering against xylophone rhythms. *How the Dead Live* is the *Hava Nagila* squawked by an elderly woman; *Cock and Bull* sounds like a karaoke rendition of *Je t'aime* by an inebriated Boy George; *My Idea of Fun*, like David Bowie in a torture chamber; *Great Apes*, like a simian opera. I sweep out feeling dazed, my ears singing so that I believe they still exist.

Tersias floats in front of me.

– Can you hear them? I cry. – The books sing. It's beautiful. They sing.

Tersias says: – I think you've been drinking too much *zganbe*. Look – come and see what Will's reading. It's *The Tibetan Book of the Dead*.

We peer over Will's shoulder, follow his eye over a passage advising on the smooth departure of a soul.

– It's a sign, Tersias cries, it's a sign.

– And you accuse *me* of drinking *zganbe*.

Tersias's aura darkens. – Everything is interconnected. This is a sign that there is hope yet for us.

We float side by side and, as our souls fade a little more, without moving we become further apart.

Tersias mentions the clock. Two hours to go until we find out the Truth. If I had a stomach, it would be rearing butterflies. Shall I tell him the real story of how I died? No, not yet, not yet.

Tersias continues to read, lost in ideas. I try to forget my nerves by studying the corporal. Will's body is so close I can see his pores, the twitch of hairs poking from his ears and nose. Jamie once told me that Will had said he felt as though he was a nervous, feminine creature in the body of a fierce, hulking male. Jamie was puzzled by this. He thought Will was being smart, or surreal. Me: I understood. Long before I died, I was aware of the dichotomy of soul and body. Some people, like Jamie, have souls sewn deep into the nooks and crannies of their carnal counterparts. Others of us are unlucky enough to feel a loose connection, a sense of badly sewn threads ready to snap. When I was a child, even, they were beginning to fray. I asked to be called George; I demanded my father cut my hair short; I begged for footballs and suffocated my dolls in dirt. My body, a source of embarrassment in adolescence, seemed a blatant lie in adulthood. It was a dossier that told the world I was soft, feminine, fragile. I expected men to treat me just as Jamie treated me – with sheer cruelty. Such seemed the fate of looking as though I ought to be wrapped in plastic and put in a box with a fey name in sparkling letters underneath. Every time I looked in the mirror, my soul curled its lip in disgust and slashed another tie. My love affair with Jamie was my last act. I sought to please him. I dyed my hair blonde, curled it, wore skirts that kissed my thighs, cooked him meals, hinted that I liked flowers. After that I could barely walk the streets, so intense was the war inside me between corporeal and ephemeral, my soul so disconnected it might take flight and leave me hollow as a mannequin. I looked into strangers' faces, saw my stereotype reflected in their pupils with a sense of deep depression. I realized then that this would be my revenge on Jamie; my spite on my womanhood; I would play Pygmalion with my body.

I am aware of the irony. Now that I am free from my carnal house I crave to walk back in through the front door. Even after I had repainted myself in masculine shades I was never fully satisfied. I wanted to be an everyman but I was a particular-man – a slightly awkward one that could never quite convince. I felt like a block of manly granite with coarse limbs; I needed to refine my features. And so I returned to the surgeons and paid them to carve my face into the shape of Will Self's. I went armed with pictures, cut from book covers and magazines and newspapers. One of the surgeons said Will's face looked like that of a Russian gangster with a Mensa IQ; another asked, in horror, if I really wanted such a prominent nose. But it had to be Will. He was the man Jamie worshipped; if I could echo him, Jamie might just love me. Or, at least, allow me into the WSC. I spent several weeks after the operation in a darkened room, face mummified, sipping liquids through a straw. When I peeled off the bandages, my euphoria lasted only minutes before paranoia soiled it. Was that nose really at the right angle? Was Will's neck as swanlike as mine? I ran to the collage I had pasted on my walls, holding up a magnifying mirror, contrasting, comparing. I watched a tape of *Shooting Stars* so I might catch his gait; I gargled with salt and took up smoking to capture the rough pebbled texture of his droll Radio 4 voice. Most of all I longed to capture his laugh – its unique stertorous rumble.

A few days before He stole my life, I went to visit my father. The whole journey there, I looked into faces as though they were mirrors. Was I the fairest of them all? In those seven seconds of assessment, what box did they put me into? I was only twenty-five but my gait belonged to an old woman, for my chest and legs were still sore from the operation. A caterpillar hides in a cocoon, conceals itself when antennae are sticky and unfurling, beauty spots and wing-blots still blueprint imaginings. Some days, I wished I could just hide in a wardrobe like a child while I grew my wings. But I was forced to put my metamorphosis on public display. Every morning I yearned for 'the pass' to happen. But I was always a hair, a voice, a look short. When my father opened the door and saw me, he slammed it shut again. He shuffled back down the hallway, into the living room and put the

TV back on. Though I wept, his rejection felt like victory. I had slashed an umbilical cord that had tied me to him for thirty years. I had always felt the connection with him, rather than with my mother. In the innocence of childhood, I once believed that he was the one who had carried me; the day I discovered only a woman could carry babies I was shocked.

My victory did not last. Next I visited Jamie. He wept tears of laughter. I stood in his doorway trying to fight a feminine blush as he asked *who* I was meant to be. I can see now I never even came close. I was like a cheap photocopy of a print of a Will Self original.

I – I –

I felt him behind me like a shadow –
    Oh Daddy don't tell me don't tell don't –

I find myself slumped by Will's feet. Black shoes, from which protrude hairy ankles encased in brown socks with a grey stripe. I look up at Tersias.

Soon the night will deepen and then fade into a dawn of melting snow. I will not get to see it. Will will be the last human whose warmth I share.

– Tersias, I whisper, I'm too weak, too weak to go to the station. I'm not going to find out. I'm never going to know who killed me . . .

Perhaps it is better never to bite that apple. Knowledge can be dangerous; if my anger becomes concentrated, what will I do with it? I could become a banshee screaming anger, but my murderer will not hear it. I gaze up through Will's window at the night sky and the stars look like the souls of frustrated deaths blazing fury.

I weep waterless, saltless tears.

– I'll go, Tersias says hastily. I shall go to the station and listen for the name and I'll hurry back to you. Oh, my dear Sylvie, hold on, hold.

– Thank you, Tersias, I sob, thank you.

At the window, he says sadly, – I shall miss you when you're gone.

My soul is shrinking in on itself. I panic, and leap. Inside Will.

– Now, now, that's not really allowed, I hear Tersias saying through the window, through Will's ears. – But he will give you strength. Hang on, my love, I will back as soon as I can, hold on . . .

Will starts. We look around. Oh oh oh how vivid the world is! How alive I feel! I rush up behind his eyes, swinging with the swivel of his irises. My deadened senses plug into his nose, his ears, his eyes, his tongue, his fingers, and everything is lit up hot neon. My essence shimmers with the thump of his heart. I can feel his lunch being slowly chopped into pieces by his stomach. I feel the cool gush of moist air being drawn into his lungs and then pushed up in beautiful, mechanical routine. I circle, savour their roundness. My killer burst my left lung; I had not been aware of it until it collapsed like a balloon, hissing air, blood flowing in. I remember lying on the floor, and all of a sudden the air had become like a magnet, pushing away from me, and the more I tried to pull it towards me, the more it ran. Before the panic, there was a calm awareness, an affirmation of the existence of the soul. Something that remained untouched as my body malfunctioned, cogs flying, conveyor belts grinding to a dead halt. But Will's body is working beautifully, every order from the brain dutifully obeyed. We look down through our eyes at a girl in the magazine. She is blonde and wearing a green bikini. I feel the pull of blood downwards and I follow it. I sweep into his cock, feel myself fly as it rears up like a rollercoaster.

Joyous.

Red.

Yes.

This is a *real* cock, a product of sperm tongue-kissing an egg, of Fate and stars, divine alchemy.

I will never leave Will's body. I will stay here for ever.

Then I remember what Tersias once said: You can't stay in a body unless you're invited.

I hunch up between coils of intestine and try to forget.

Will closes the magazine. He begins on his mail.

There are bills and bank statements. A letter from his accountant makes his heart speed up.

He shoves it to one side and pulls his typewriter towards him. It looks as though it was made in the 1950s, with clinky keys waiting for the sadistic hits of a secretary's nails. To my surprise, Will rolls in a fresh sheet. This is how he writes? Although Will's work is too anarchic ever to imagine him typing away on a fancy Palm Pilot, I had always picturing him scrawling with pen on paper. Or perhaps a quill, plucked from the tail of the last living dodo.

He types the page number, 64, at the top and then the title: *The Book of Dave.*

Up. Will's blood abandons his cock, leaves it meek and limp. I follow the glorious blood gush. His heart quietens as his mind begins to race. I swirl through his grey matter, his delicious mulch.

This feels like intellectual transvestism: putting on the clothes of his expensive IQ. He pulls coloured scarves from the pockets of his imagination, painted with beautiful and curious images. Synapses spark through me, connecting words, fusing them into hot hot-off-the-press metaphors. I surrender to his intellectual orgasm, arching my back over his brain, my legs spread wide, until my cunt is poised precisely above his imaginative G-spot. As he hits the first key, I let out a gasp–

I – I –

I felt him behind me like a shadow –

Oh Daddy don't tell me don't tell don't –

I slip.

When I come to, I feel a piece of gristle knocking against me. I float dizzy in his stomach, then right myself. I want to slip into his hands, become the dextrous ripple of his long fingers, but I am scared that in my weakened state I will fall on to the desk. I wonder if I might compress into his book. Curl up in the curve of a *g* and stay there for ever until I am a watermark in the page. But I am too afraid to leave this safe warm body, this temple.

Where is Tersias? Hurry, Tersias, hurry hurry.

Tap tap tap. Will's fingers fly across the typewriter's keys. In his talk, he was asked why he was so prolific. He said that his muse had become Hitlerish.

I once read of a feminist who did not write a book. The book she did not write consisted of sixty-four blank pages. It hung in a museum; it was fiercely debated and written about. She claimed that a muse is a male thing and to write was to be raped by him. She spoke of the bridal sheet that was once hung up for all to see after a marriage, the blots of blood writ-ten on the white cotton. She felt that a blank page was the only way to express herself, symbolic of the female genitalia, of absence. I understood her. My muse was male: patriarchal, stern, stiff, ordering me to stick to the rules. And so, like a good girl, I did as I was told. I wrote in genre. A romance. I followed the guideline sheets Mills & Boon had sent me. A kiss on page fourteen. A confrontation on page sixteen. A tall, dark, handsome hero who looked like Jamie, only, unlike Jamie, he did not tie me up for kisses, or push me down on his bed and apply a belt to my thighs; unlike Jamie, he did not, when the heroine confessed love for him, tell her that love, like life, was just a game. And yet my muse was never happy. He frightened me: a presence behind my shoulder. Constantly sticking a knife into my back. Every sentence I managed to spit out, he told me to strike out.

On the day of my death, I spent an hour at my desk, struggling over a simile, when the realization came. My muse had Jamie's face, a permanent sneer that suggested all my words were worthless. I jumped up in panic and took the envelope from my bag. Jamie had given it to me a few days ago; he had asked me to pass it on to a man called Dirty Pete. I had an intuition as to what its nature might be. In the envelope, I found it: a small square, like a tab of acid, with Will's face on the front. The infamous Wafer. I thought it might smash my mind with colour, thrash my muse away. I took it. While waiting for oblivion, I went into the bathroom. I had taken to checking my cock every hour. All the other parts of my body had surrendered to metamorphosis: my chest had grown hair, my chin had squared, my voice deepened. But that little cock seemed to mock me, a comedy of chemicals cooked up in a lab, false testosterone applied through patches, squirted through plastic. The drug took black possession of me. I wanted to punish my cock but not hurt it; I picked up my toothbrush and began to gently beat it. Then a psychedelic haze took over. My murderer must have found me drooling face down on the carpet, cock hanging out like a gibbering tongue; an easy victim.

I – I –

I felt him behind me like a shadow –

Oh Daddy don't tell me don't tell don't –

Oh, Tersias, where are you? I have perhaps minutes left. I have failed to bear a baby girl, win the Booker, avenge my murder. But in my last moments, I might become a muse.

– I won't be a Hitler, I whisper into Will's stomach. Let me be your muse, Will. Let me be your benign muse.

He continues to write, indifferent, every tap making me redundant.

– Let me colour your words. I can give you insight into women and men, since I am both.

I might flavour his heart, but he seems to write from his head. I might dive upwards, but my instincts tell me to go down. Will once said that the only way to write is from the depths of one's *psychic bowel*. I curl up into his balls and squeeze tightly. I have become a ghost writer!

The Book of Dave

Carl leant his head against a bar of old irony and stared at the delicate tracery

oh this feels so good I'm in the book I'm the book I'm paper I can

of lichen that covered the crete at his feet – living on dead, deader on deader. A low

feel Will's fingers making love to the page making love to me and o

clattering buzz roused him, and, peering at one of the apple trees, he saw that its trunk

everything is moving blurring colours Carl I'm on the lagoon with

was mobbed with a dense cluster of golden flies, which spread and agitated their

Carl watching the flies with him he is handsome I want to be Carl

wings the better to suck up the bigwatt rays of the now fully risen foglamp. To leave

I can become Carl become the character I will get inside him

all this – how would it be possible – this life mummy that cuddled him so?

Carl let me in let me in let me be one with you let me be you yes Carl

Carl had been to this spot maybe two or three times with Salli Brudi – and that

Salli o Salli yes she is pretty the last time I saw her she whipped off

was forbidden. They'd get a cuff from their Daddies and a bigger clump from the

oh my God did you just see that let me try again the last time she'd

Driver if they were found out. The last time she'd whipped off her cloakyfing and

whipped off her cloakyfing and wound it around her pretty ginger

wound it around her pretty ginger head like a turban. As she bent low, the neck of her

I can do it we can do this Carl we can make Will write what we want

T-shirt gaped open, showing her tiny titties; yet Carl understood there was no chellish

him to write what shall we ask for what Carl what's the matter stop

vanity in this – Salli was too young. She held a Davework in her hand: it was the size

fighting me I'm with you look please let me stay please it's a cold

of a baby's finger, a flat black silver with a faint-cut mark.

world out there look we'll make Will write something that will

– Wot chew fink, Carl, she asked him, reel aw toyist?

make you feel good would you like that Carl would you like what do

Carl took the Davework from her; his thumb traced the edge, once jagged but

you mean I'm distracting you examine your trinket then

now smoothed by its millennia-long meander through the lagoon since the

but it looks like a piece of worthless crap to me which has been

MadeinChina. He looked closely at the mark for the shape of phonics.

– C'eer, Sal, he said, beckoning her closer, iss an ed, C ve eer, an vose lyns

You want her Carl don't you you want her and you know what's

muss B . . . Eye dunno . . . sowns aw sumffing . . . mebe.

going to happen Will is going to change the subject you won't

– So toyist? She was disappointed.

get to be with her listen to me let's join forces and make him

– Toyist, deffo. He flung it decisively away from them, and it whirred like a

change the direction of the story let him write 'Salli looked up at

sickseed for a few moments before falling into the grass.

him with soft eyes and let out a breathless sigh. Oh, she ached for

140

Carl started up – what was the point in such dumb imaginings? Cockslip an

him. How she wanted to feel his hard cock inside her.' Come on

bumrub, nodditankijelli snuggul. Sal Brudi ul B up ve duff soon enuff bi wunnuvose

focus, focus. 'Salli looked up at him with soft eyes and let out a

ugli ol shitters . . . No, he best forget it, forget her – and get up to the wallows.

breathless sigh fuck being up the duff who cares just fuck FUCK

Carl went to go meet the other lads but found himself turning back.

it's working oh my God it's working come on Carl let's do this

Salli looked at him with soft eyes and let out a breathless sigh. God, he

I want her. I want to touch her breasts, roughly, feel her nipples

wanted her. He reached out and touched her breasts roughly with his palms, feeling

oh yes oh yes I lean in and kiss her and her tongue is wet like a

her nipples harden. He leant in and kissed her and her tongue was wet like a

a little kitten which toys with my tongue like a toy oh God oh yes

little kitten which toys with my tongue like a toy

come on Will don't stop now keep writing I need you to keep

writing what's the matter with you keep writing keep writing

I'm slipping I'm slipping I'm losing her my kiss is dying I'm

Outside, nearly. On the edges of a hairy thigh. Panting, euphoric. Oh, what it was to meld with his mind, to ride with him in creative harmony!

'"A little kitten which toys with my tongue like a toy"?' Will Self says out loud. 'Good God.' His forehead corrugates into a frown. He pulls out the sheet and crosses the sentence out sharply. Then he crosses out the few sentences before that. His pen hovers. I gather myself up, preparing to dive back into the bowel. The tension quivers. I can feel the build-up of creativity like the embryonic moment of a storm before thunder sounds and lightning flashes, that white screaming silence—

When Carl arrived the other lads—

He pauses.
Shakes his head.
I slip.

I – I –

I felt him behind me like a shadow –
Oh Daddy don't tell me don't tell don't –

I find myself on his shoe. The world cold and vast around me. Oh, Will, let me back in. I try to dive upwards, but I remain limp, draped over patent. I try to cuddle into his foot but I cannot grip any more.

Tersias is back. I cannot hear him but he mouths the name. No. Please. No. He repeats: *Richard.* My heart becomes ether with pain.

I try to see Tersias to mouth goodbye but there is only the grainy shadow of Will above me, hunched over his desk, writing on, tapping on. And beyond him, a white ceiling, spidered with cracks.

I fall under his shoe.

I lie under his heel.

I am in darkness.

I am an ember.

I am Sylvie.

Ghost writer.

Goodbye, sweet Will.

Remember me.

Goodbye.

Damn you, Richard.

Will shuffles his foot, then slams down the heel–

Goodb—

Part Three:
Richard's Diary, 2007

14 NOVEMBER

I am being watched. I can feel their eyes peering through the window in the door: the one they can see through but I can't see out of. The only way I can detect my audience is by the yellow slit of light at the bottom of the door. Sometimes it is disturbed by the silhouette of shoes; sometimes the slit vanishes into a flash of searing light as someone takes an illicit photograph.

And what do they see? My room is dim except for the halo of light from the candle on my desk. Yes, I admit the candle is there to create a romantic hue. I want to give the public good value for money. (I believe the entry fee is a fiver!) They stand and watch the hunched back of a young genius scribbling at a scarred oak desk (slightly wobbly, even with a piece of paper folded into a corner under one leg). Their eyes flicker around the room and consider how bare it is. Is there any difference, they wonder, between the life of an artist, and the life of a monk? Just a bed, a rail, over which are slung my white clothes, bare walls — and, look, the blind pulled down, not even a view to distract him. For this young man, the only change in monthly scenery is a spider's web becoming thick with fly parcels or a new sweep of mildew on the left-hand corner of the ceiling. They consider their ordinary lives in offices, lives measured out by junk mail falling on the mat, ads on TV that tangle in dreams. The friction of my pen against the page emanates an energy that provokes awe. They will go home and speak of a man who *makes sacrifices for his art*.

But not *such* a sacrifice. I enjoy being a creature in a literary zoo. I have agreed to spend 365 days at the top of this tower block writing my masterpiece (that's 335 days longer than Will Self, who spent only a month in his Liverpudlian tower block, penning a short story). Every day – so I am told – the gossip columns buzz with news of me. Literary editors are salivating for the dot at the end of my final sentence, when my novel will be immediately published in forty countries with a print run of a million. That is why I thought it best to keep this diary as well as the novel; I may need it for the serialization deal.

In days of old, writers were recluses. Anonymous ghosts that hovered behind their prose. Sometimes they would rattle their chains to remind us of their presence. Nineteenth-century writers often addressed their readers directly – *Reader, I married him*. Or they favoured intrusive omniscient narrators, lest we forget that the characters we were bonding with were the children of their imagination. In contemporary fiction, addressing the reader is considered a stylistic sin; it has become redundant now that readers can be addressed in book tours. Now our words are merely clothes, and without the author the clothes lie flat, as though on a mannequin. Our prose requires flesh and blood, a face to show at Hay and Cheltenham, hands to shake and sign books. This morning I used my pen as a knife in order to cut different lengths of pubic hair. I have decided to paste one into my book as a signature. Perhaps a special limited-edition print run of 250 pubic-hair copies will also be a fine idea. I know Archie West will love it.

A cheap trick, you might say. But I regard it as a symbolic act:

my DNA will be woven into the page, pressed against the white bark that once lived in a seed.

20 November

<u>9 a.m.</u>: Feeling nervous. I am about to meet Prof. Self for the first time. The statistics are in my favour. More than a hundred thousand writers applied for this residency; a jury of eight picked out my writing for its linguistic skill, poetic imagination and depth of character. Surely he will love me.

<u>11 a.m.</u>: On returning from my meeting with Prof. Self, my initial feeling was a glowing one: *Well, that went well.* Now, with the repeated analysis of hindsight, I feel unsettled. I have not forgotten a gem my tutors imparted when I studied for a creative writing course last year – *characters will always use subtext.* Only the mad have an uncensored connection from mind to mouth. Society is dependent on domestic propaganda, the veil of polite lie. There was a watermark behind his words that I have yet to decipher.

His office is a carpeted enclave on the same floor as mine. In the flesh, he seemed a somewhat coarse man – large, with a fan of grey beard, and a clumsy vigour to his movements – though the expression in his eyes suggested he has sensitive antennae.

His office is more luxurious than my bedroom. As though reading my mind, he pumped my hand enthusiastically and said that, as writer and mentor, we both shared a claustrophobic pact: neither of us was allowed to leave the building until my novel was complete. Unlike me, he has access to a phone, a computer, the Internet, and even a CDC player. Still, as Archie said, 'It's the extreme austerity of your residency that will make you a news story, Richard.'

He made me a cup of tea and offered me a choice between a Nice biscuit and a custard cream. Then – and this is the part that made me feel uneasy – he asked me to outline the plot of my novel-in-progress.

I explained that it was a Victorian crime novel about a dwarf who's a serial killer. He gets inspired by a sensationalist story serialized in *The Times* by a certain H. R. Wilson, which is rumoured to be a pseudonym for Charles Dickens. The public complain that they are sickened by the story's violence, but copies sell by the thousand. The killer who revolts and compels them is a predecessor to Hannibal Lecter – tall, charismatic, with an IQ of 164. The dwarf who imitates him is pasty, repellent, suffers from bad breath and an IQ a good fifty points lower. He tries to compensate for his size by shrinking the scale of his outer world – like using cutlery from a doll's house to dine with, though in the end only the slaying of people at least two feet taller than him can bloat his ego. *The Times* remains oblivious to the mirrors of life and art. I aimed to juxtapose journalism and story as satire: when the dwarf commits crimes, the newspaper condemns him while, a few pages on, celebrating the fictional hero he seeks to emulate.

I trailed off, disturbed by the persiflage in his eyes.

'To be frank, Richard, I do wonder if you might be better off writing a modern novel rather than a Victorian crime novel. What concerns me, Richard, is your *voice*. If you write in pastiche, you are acting as a literary medium, channelling voices of the past. Why not develop your own?'

I began to scratch my eyebrow. Then, to my relief, he said: 'I do agree that there are great advantages to using the Victorian novel as a means of satire. One might compare the medium with a modern novelist such as . . . Will Self. Have you heard of him?'

I quickly concealed my shock. 'Yes. A little,' I said, uneasily.

'Self – who is no relation to me, by the way, sadly – once remarked that a modern-day satirist has a more challenging time than his predecessors, such as Swift, who operated within a matrix of Judaeo-Christian precepts. The problem a modern-day satirist has to contend with is moral relativism. As a "Victorian" novelist, however, Richard, you can create your own universe with black-and-white moral precepts. You can play God with your characters – judge them, punish them, reward them, according to whether or not they obey those precepts.'

I ended the interview feeling relieved, and we shook hands amicably. But now I feel unnerved – only our first tutorial and he has located my fatal flaw as a writer. So what if I borrow from other voices, meld them to form my own? I have no wish to write about my past; I only wish to put it behind me.

18 NOVEMBER

<u>3 p.m.</u>: I can't keep my prose straight – I'm shaking too badly. I was working on my novel this afternoon, which now has a provisional title, *The Diary of a Murderer*, when I heard the sudden noise of footsteps. This tower block is very rickety and the stairs shout echoes at the top of their voice. Every afternoon at three p.m., a CLOSED sign is posted on the tower-block door and the long queue of fans is turned away and told to try again tomorrow. I don't have a clock in here but the darkening tone of the sky suggested it was nearly five.

beneath my paper, which I trace like braille. I need to expel my anger: I've been banging at my door for the last hour, banging and shouting, but nobody comes.

I ended up pulling up the blind and then – with some struggle – the peeling sash on the window. The night sky was broken into a triptych by the iron bars. I pushed my penis between them and watched my stream of piss trickle twenty-odd feet to the ground, spangling like a shooting star in the moonlight. The tower block is surrounded by iron railings; I swear I saw shadows lurking and dancing between them. I suspect they will climb over, scrape up my piss and then try to sell it on eBay.

I keep writing letters of complaint in my mind. Archie West specifically negotiated a contract for me that stipulated that all my needs would be met promptly at all times.

22 November

<u>11 a.m.</u>: Just now, the security guard *finally* opened the door. He is a big, burly fellow and I admit I find him a little intimidating. I tried to hold my tongue, reminding myself that it was natural for him to fall asleep on duty at night, that he was probably only being paid five pounds an hour and felt resentful about the millions I was about to make. Finally I burst out, 'I needed to relieve myself last night – but you weren't about,' my pointed cough supplying a full stop.

He rolled his eyes in an insolent manner as he passed over breakfast. 'You can use the bucket in the corner,' he said. 'The waste-paper bin?'

I winced in disgust. I was beginning to feel increasingly irritated, but the thought of confrontation twisted my stomach with nerves, so I decided I would later complain about him to

Prof. Self. 'How d'you like your breakfast?' he asked, and I am sure I detected sarcasm in his voice. 'Is it to Sir's pleasing?'

I took a mouthful of the grey porridge and very nearly spat it out before passing it back to him. 'Very Dickensian,' I said.

He replied, 'Well, perhaps next time we'll try to bring something a little more Evelyn Waugh.'

I forgot to be angry and laughed in surprise, for I had assumed he was illiterate, the type of man who considers Wilbur Smith to be high literature. As I passed back the porridge, he got down on his knees and squealed, 'Please, sir, can I have some more?' and I laughed again, my antagonism greatly diminished. I almost longed for him to stay, but he broke off our chat, saying he had other breakfasts to deliver, and locked the door behind him. Twenty floors or so below me there is, I believe, an office that sells insurance. I try to avoid thinking about it too much, for it rather spoils the romance of my setting.

Now I am struggling to return to my novel. I crave the fuel of the outside world. I am tempted to follow Prof. Self's advice to write about myself; to open the dark door of my nightmares and let them flow into my book. But I feel too unnerved. Besides, the last year is a blur. Sometimes I blame the clozapine, convinced I was prescribed too potent a dose; some days I blame the drug Zara gave me at the WSC orgy; some days I wonder if it is merely a defence mechanism, a survival of the fittest conducted by my mind, which has yanked out the worst of my memory weeds. I wonder what Jamie Curren is doing at this exact moment. I admit that I feel smug at times, knowing that I have the placement he has always dreamed of; then I feel guilty when I think of what Sylvie had to suffer at his hands.

I picture him now, in a cell with leprosy walls and a stark ceiling, the tattooed thug in the bunk below too terrified to dare challenge him. I picture him lying on his bed, blowing a smoke-ring, his dark eyes narrowing. I suspect that murder is a game for him and that now he has crossed a line, he feels compelled to keep playing it. Sometimes I fear that he will attain an early release or escape, and that I will be his next victim.

<u>Midnight</u>: Is it self-destructive to write all this down? If they found this diary, it might be the end of my stay here. I hide it in the corner under my bed – a hopeless hiding-place. And yet something inside me craves its discovery, would find failure a relief.

25 NOVEMBER

I am not allowed a single newspaper in here. They say that the amount of information we receive in ten minutes of modern living is equivalent to the lifetime of a peasant in the nineteenth century. I remember that the day I entered this place the papers talked of genetically engineered broccoli and cabinet resignations. When I return, I will be like a man from the future, forced to digest months within milliseconds.

Every day my word count slows and slows, until I am barely forcing fifty words a day from my pen.

<u>6 p.m.</u>: A reply from Prof. Self! I had asked the guard to pass on a note to him. His reply was brusque: *I am sorry, Richard, but your contract stated that you would remain in this building for the duration of your novel, without any excursions or holidays in the outside world.*

26 NOVEMBER

My days stretch out like an Arctic summer; my nights stretch out like an Arctic winter. A Galileo disease infects me: when I first came here I felt as though I was dictating time, the hours revolving around me, but now I feel that it is quite the opposite, that I am spinning around time in a helplessly slow orbit, which I cannot escape. I have stopped writing by candlelight; I roll up the blind eagerly now (even though they complain that it spoils the sombre writer-in-garret mood for the public). The sunlight outside is a mirage. I am becoming a gollum. My muscles feel flabby, my spine is developing a geriatric crook. Prof. S keeps urging me on – but is this sacrifice for my art really worthwhile?

27 NOVEMBER

I have written nothing. Even when I hid under the covers and searched for relief in self-indulgence, nothing emerged but a white globule of spit. I started picking savagely at my eyebrow, telling myself to stop but carrying on until a hot feeling flooded my forehead and I felt sure I had taken the whole thing out. How am I supposed to write with one eyebrow, and this eczema crawling up my leg like a snake, and these red bites on my forearm? I am being tormented by some sort of insect and I became so enraged by its continued attacks that I wasted the afternoon on a savage search.

I examined every dusty corner, tearing down spider's webs, even picking off the white paint-flakes from the window-sill in case it was hiding underneath. I wonder if moths can bite . . . but my moth deserted me long ago and sits permanently on my desk, a half-skeleton cobwebbed with memories of wing. If I find the evil creature, I will pull off its wings before I use my pen as knife and squeeze my blood back from its body; perhaps the blood will make a colourful ink, for the sake of variety.

28 NOVEMBER

V. intense session with Prof. Self. I told him that I was going to hand in my notice.

I expected anger, threats of legal action. His expression of paternalistic disappointment was devastating. Then he began to beg. He confessed that he had never been interested in fiction until the tender age of eighteen, when he read *For Whom the Bell Tolls* and ached to write like Hemingway. His literary attempts, however, were 'unfortunate'; in defeat he decided to become a critic and an academic; and with this placement he had climbed the pinnacle of his career. With his shoulders hunched and his eyes downcast, he looked such a figure of boyish inadequacy that I felt sorry for him.

He asked if there was anything he could do to make my stay more comfortable. I mentioned the insect bites on my arm. Then, when he stared at my face and asked if he could offer any help with my eyebrow, I became embarrassed and said I needed to get back to my writing.

'So you'll stay?' he asked, his voice trembling.

I nodded.

Just before I left, he touched me by giving me a present: an ashtray, made out of blue Plasticine, which his son had crafted at school. 'Don't take up smoking, though,' he joked. I smiled and we shook hands, warmth tingling between us, and I was surprised to find tears searing my eyes. I am like the young Buddha before he was exposed to the outside world, so fragile from sheltered existence that the tiniest events stir mountainous emotions.

30 November

Can you imagine what it's like to hear music – *real* music – after months of monosound: footsteps, creaking doors, Liverpudlian traffic? It sounds like a chorus of birds waking in a meadow on a dewy morning in June. I lay down on the floor, my ear to the boards, and deduced that the birds were skitterings on the strings of a violin. How I wish I could trap the sound in my ears, like the sea in a shell.

Prof. Self! To arrange this little treat to cheer me up is a tender act of kindness. Tears are pouring down my cheeks. Outside, the sunset is bleeding blue into an eerie twilight and the coalescing of music and sky has conspired to elevate my mood to euphoria. I've taken the blue ashtray he gave me and felt the music flowing through my fingers as I affectionately moulded it into a little Prof. Self figurine.

I will make him proud. I will write a masterpiece that will survive long after my death; I will make this tower block immortal and embalm Prof. Self in literary history.

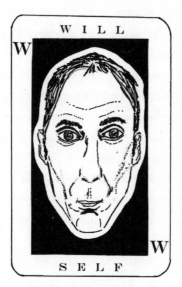

'One appears to be yielding insufficient results.'

1 DECEMBER

I am ashamed to admit that my Plasticine Prof. Self has a wound in its belly; when I returned from our session this morning I gave him an angry jab.

We began quite normally, discussing the role of literature in society. He declared that he felt literature ought to have a therapeutic role, healing readers and highlighting moral truths. Such sentimentality is surprising in an academic. I asked him who his favourite author was and, rather predictably, his reply was Hemingway, for his honourable heroes and the opaque simplicity of his writing style. I replied that it was perhaps a *deceptive* simplicity and he looked a little confused.

Perhaps I irritated him, for then he forced me to waste my afternoon – when I normally peak creatively – playing Cluedo with him. I presumed that he was trying to hone my detective skills for my novel and I confidently predicted that the murderer would be Miss Scarlett in the Library with the lead piping. But when I drew the revelatory card out of its black envelope, the face I saw made me run from the room. I am sure his laughter followed me. I feel stupid now. The card was a cheat – since when did Will Self ever feature in a game of Cluedo?

I can't forget the look on his face when he gazed down at the Cluedo card. A vitriolic, sickened hatred, as though Self had personally murdered his family.

I think that perhaps Prof. Self is not as benign as I once thought. Or maybe the claustrophobia of this tower block is starting to nibble at his sanity; maybe I ought to offer him sympathy, counsel him a little.

<u>Midnight</u>: There was something else in Prof. Self's study. I am not quite sure how to describe them. I wish I had looked at them more closely, but I was too emotional. They were in the corner, next to a row of books by Harold Bloom and Freud. They looked like a row of silvery stars . . . what were they?

2 December

I am unhappy to have been proved right: Prof. Self's mind is disintegrating rapidly. Having experienced periods of mental instability myself, I feel sympathy for him, if not relief: it is possible to experience a certain *Schadenfreude* being around mad people, their craziness affirming the blessing of one's own sanity.

For example, is it sane to call me in for a long tutorial and force me to endure a game of Will Self Monopoly? I wondered how much of our sponsorship deal has been wasted on the sculptor who had been hired to delicately craft a penis, a Dorian Grey, an ape, a toy car and various other pieces out of tin foil and Super Glue. I chose the penis and Prof. Self picked the ape.

I took care not to react to the absurdity of his game. I could see a silly little smile tipsying around Prof. Self's lips, but I acted as though it was the most natural thing in the world to roll the dice, dance 3+5 places from GO and land on *Opportunity Knocks*. I picked up a yellow card from the pile.

> *You have been caught snorting heroin on a plane.*
> *Go to jail and pay a fine of £250.*

'Bad luck,' said Prof. Self, unable to conceal his joy.

I have decided to ask for a new mentor. I will pass the letter of complaint to the guard.

At least my anger has inspired me. After weeks of grey non-productivity, I have written five thousand words. My dwarf has turned serial killer, removing the legs of a corpse in order to sculpt himself a pair of stilts – though when he wears them his co-workers only jeer and mock him.

<u>2 a.m.</u>: Another nightmare-fractured sleep. The Cluedo card has released fragments of memory. Every time I try to focus on their colours, the kaleidoscope shifts into new patterns: my flat; a door with '32' in gold numbers on the front; a man in a chimp suit; a green drink with steam coiling from it; a searing white light; a huge floating Will Self face, his eyes lasering mine. Is Prof. Self playing games within games? Does he know my history better than I realize? Is he taunting me, trying to stir up the past, so that I spill them into my book?

When I applied for this placement, I told them nothing about my history. They have no idea I was ever prescribed clozapine; I didn't have to take a medical and their 'Psychological Assessment' questionnaire contained laughable questions such as *Have you ever felt sad for no reason?* with equally inane multiple-choice answers. It was obvious that they were looking for me to tick every (a):

(a) *I am an optimist by nature*

(a) *I would help an old lady across the road if I felt she needed help*

(a) *I would call the police immediately if I witnessed a crime*

At the time I smiled and ticked all the right boxes. Now what if I lose my placement for failing to tell them?

In the past, I needed clozapine in order to cope with the world around me. Some of us are born with thick skins, some thin; mine is as fragile as tissue paper and the drug gave me false prosthetics. I felt confident that I could survive without it here, with my only conflicts played out on the page before me. This will be my argument, if they question me. Oh, God, I could not bear to lose my book deal . . .

4 DECEMBER

I keep thinking about Sylvie: her soft, fair face, her sweet smile. Last night I blew out my candle and hid under the covers and made love to her in my head. I had to face the wall in case any of the PR guys were looking in. Afterwards I lay feeling ashamed and full of trembling ache for her.

This is one of the things I miss most about being here: the feminine. The more my seclusion goes on, the more abstract my cravings become. I am past lusting after film stars and specifics. Now I just think of long hair; lips painted coral, which part to reveal pretty teeth; soft skin; perfume.

I feel rather tired, as all my creativity has dried up with the white sticky stain in my bed. I think I will abandon my novel this afternoon and rest in the dark.

6 DECEMBER

I have become a prisoner in this tower block. The guard must have betrayed me and shown Self my note. Self has instructed them to keep my door permanently locked; I am in twenty-four-hour seclusion. At mealtimes my door shifts open an inch, a bowl of sloppy porridge is dumped on the floor and the door slams shut again. This morning they even forgot to supply a spoon and I had to lick and lap, like a dog. All my tutorials have been cancelled.

The room feels as though it is shrinking. My only relief comes when I slip into the world of my novel. I am trying to be patient and wait it out, I am trying to stay positive, but this afternoon frustration overwhelmed me and I wielded my pen as a torture instrument on my Plasticine Prof. Self. Now he has a Pinocchio nose and is covered with stab wounds.

<u>9 p.m.</u>: This could be a horror plot in a Stephen King novel. Possibilities terrify my imagination, mutating horrors. Prof. Self could spin this out for months. He could tell my publishers I have writer's block. He could starve me, beat me, bribe the guards to keep quiet. I suppose his abuse of me will generate column inches when I'm released. One day I will look back and be grateful that this happened; there is no fame without pain. But here and now ... it is unbearable, unbearable. Oh God, oh God, why did I ever come here? Maybe I can bribe the guards: I can offer to put them in the novel, name a main character after them. He will join Jamie Curren in jail for this.

<u>10 p.m.</u>: Panic keeps taking possession of me, sometimes through manic thoughts, sometimes through an intense jangling sensation in my body that prevents me sleeping or even sitting. The only way to deal with it is to force myself to lie down on the bed and spread out in the shape of a star. Then I stretch each muscle, so taut it's as though I'm being mauled by a medieval machine, until it feels like a rope about to snap, my anger burning off like friction. Sometimes I curl up in bed and think of the future, of oceans I will swim, forests I will walk through, food I will eat, wine I will pour into my mouth until I collapse in a swoon with the sun on my face and bees and flowers all beautiful about me. But on nights like this, when the darkness feels infinite, a voice pads across my mind with tiny feet, whiskers twitching worries, *Something is very wrong, Richard, you'll never get out, you're going to die here an old, old man with greying hair*, and I curl up foetal and there's nothing to do but wait for the darkness to come, only it's getting later and later until I feel I'm going insane for that first hit of light.

17 December

<u>9 a.m.</u>: The burly, nice guard is on duty today – the one I joked with about porridge and Dickens. He will come any moment, and I will have a minute, perhaps, to try to persuade him to let me out. I can hear his footsteps.

<u>10 a.m.</u>: Just an hour ago, I sat here and wrote this diary filled with hope. I had my chance – and it has gone. I can hardly write, my hand is shaking so violently.

I was so close. When the guard offered me my food, I pointed out that my waste-paper bin was brimming with faeces and the situation was becoming inhumane. He agreed to take me to the toilet. Oh, what a relief it was to use toilet paper, to rinse my hands with sweet-smelling soap. I craved a mirror – though the thought also panicked me, for I felt strangely afraid that I would find my reflection empty, that Self had somehow scratched me away. But there was no mirror in the toilet.

The guard led me back, and as soon as we reached the door, I said I needed to go again; I told him that the Dickensian porridge had given me diarrhoea. 'At least it's not verbal,' he gibed. He said he would leave me to shit in peace while he took a cigarette break. 'Don't leave your floor,' he reminded me in a tired voice.

My liberation shocked me. I stood in the hallway and listened to his footsteps creak to halfway down the stairs. I heard him wrench open a window, heard the hiss of a lighter. I ran to Prof. Self's study. The door was ajar but the room was empty.

His screensaver rippled across his computer. His wife smiled politely in her photo frame. The room was light and cool and calm. I paused by Prof. Self's window. I saw ordinary life passing by, a river of happiness and sunshine and shopping. I longed to pull up the window and cry, 'HELP!' but fear paralysed my tongue – I knew the guard would hear. I searched about for a phone. I couldn't understand it. Every office has a phone! I yanked open drawers, searching for a mobile – nothing.

I was conscious that the moment was slipping through my fingers; sweat bathed me; tears of anger prickled my eyes. I went to his computer, swivelled the mouse, found an email facility. I kept it short – *I am being held prisoner by a deranged madman* – and emailed it to everyone in his address book. When I clicked send, my body became liquid relief. I thought, It will be all right now. It will be all right.

Next to his computer, I found a scrawled article that he was composing – a good few pages of A4. I thought it would be useful proof of his madness – after all, when we both get out of this place, it will be his story versus my story, a test of who can compose the most convincing narrative.

Then I made a run for it.

Everything became a blur – the thump of my feet on the stairs, my jagged heartbeat, my ears full of frantic breath. One floor, two floors down. Nobody had stopped me so far and an incredulous voice whispered, *I'm actually going to make it.* Then on the third floor I heard a terrible sound – a human wailing that had become animal with pain. I froze on the steps, shaking, by a small window. After months of staring at the same railings, the view shocked me. I saw houses, trees, a girl in a back garden, laughing on a swing. My soul whimpered with longing and fear. I heard footsteps approaching. A voice screamed that I should run. I stood still. The guard saw me, flung me to the ground, knocking out one of my teeth.

As he dragged me back to my room, I felt as though I had been running under a wide sky and had been forced into a dark tunnel that narrowed and narrowed into a dead-end.

Could I have made it, if I'd kept running? My frustration screams yes; my logic doubts. I keep reliving that moment of paralysis. I think I have been here too long: I am afraid to enter the real world and discover the Richard Smith I have become. I am afraid of freedom, decisions, power; Prof. Self has beaten my consciousness into a slavery of institutional dependency.

I keep seeing the girl on a swing, laughing. All these people, right now, living just a few feet away, going about their lives, shopping, eating, sleeping, unaware that they could save me if they would just—

Next time, next time. I will run and never stop.

I started to pray for the first time in years but I felt uneasy, as though God was laughing at me.

<u>9 p.m.</u>: I have been reading and rereading Prof. Self's article:

Ever since the age of fourteen, I have asked myself the same question — why should genius be regarded as an exclusive gift, bestowed — by either nature or nurture — upon an élite few? I remember the day this epiphany came to me. My father set me down at the dining-room table with an IQ TEST in front of me. The very words evoked a Pavlovian response of familial patriotism. I had first started taking these tests at the age of ten. My father would mark them and remark in that dry, cool way of his that if my eyes were the same colour as my mother's, my brain was the same colour as his.

On this occasion, however, he passed back the test with a grimace and ordered that I should start taking cod-liver-oil tablets.

Vitamins. Meditation. Sushi. Mental steroids that he hoped would pump up the intellectual muscles in my brain. But they had clearly decided to stop growing. My nine grade A GCSE results did not appease him; while my IQ remained nine points below his, while MENSA could not accept me, I was a failure. At first I blamed myself; then grief became anger; I began to blame him. The same question plagued me — why had he not shared his genius with me? After all, we expect those with wealth to prop up the poor and pay more taxes; thus should not genius become a democratic property shared by all? Those areas of society which are impoverished, where children lack access to a proper intellectual diet of good education, which is the basis of good law-abiding, tax-paying, GNP-generating citizens, ought to deserve genius as God-given right. I used to envision genius vouchers being distributed by the government; later, when I became a doctor, I once dreamt of injecting genius into a patient and I awoke with a pounding heart. When I told my father he laughed at me — then promptly stole my idea.

I have no doubt that my dream was the basis for the experiments he began — which he was unable to complete during his lifetime, and which I must now perfect and implement. The government do not yet know how far I intend to develop my research, but when the results are published, they will laud me with knighthoods and praise me to the skies.

More telling, perhaps, is the final sentence, which he has crossed out: *The scientists who mock me now will have to eat their words.* Am I to be Self's 'experiment' and, if so, what does he mean to do with me? I keep hearing that inhuman wail — a victim who will play guinea pig before I take centre stage?

24 DECEMBER

I have to write quickly. My candle is burning low — and Prof. Self is punishing me by withholding my supply.

Self is as unpredictable as ever. This morning I was suddenly yanked out of my room and marched to his office for a tutorial. I pictured myself shouting and screaming at him, but when I entered I found myself collapsing into a chair and pleading with him to see sense and let me go. Prof. Self stared at me with a detached coolness and said, 'Tonight I am going to organize a press conference for you, Richard. I can assure you that it will be very *special*. You can tell the world what wonderful progress you are making with your book and how well we are treating you here. After all, if you were to tell them that you were uncared for, your contract would end and your book would never be published.'

I smiled at him, shrugged and said it sounded a good idea while inwardly calling him every swearword under the sun.

When I sit down before the press, I will denounce him before everyone.

Christmas Eve – and yet I cannot hear any church bells, any hymns. No beautiful, eerie notes of 'Silent Night' to soothe me. This calm feels eerie: what has happened to the world beyond?

11 p.m.: Nobody has come for me yet. I'm scared Prof. Self has cancelled the conference. I'm scared of falling asleep: I keep forcing yawns back down my throat. Tomorrow I will be free, tomorrow I will be able to run, walk through parks, shower, eat whatever I like, eat chocolate, read, sink into a bath for hours, sleep, sleep in my own bed.

The insect bites on my arms keep itching, or maybe it's just nerves. It has just struck me – after looking at them closely – that they look a little bit like the jabs made by needles.

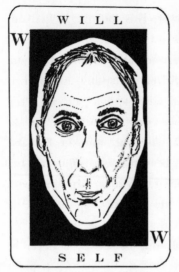 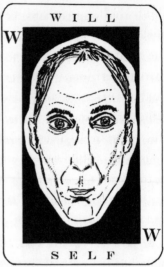

'Increase the visual stimulation to two.'

3 JANUARY

I feel very calm as I write this sentence: Professor Self believes that I am a murderer.

The sky is clear today – the cold desolate blue of January – and my room is freezing. My hands feel as dry as the paper I'm writing on. Last night I woke up with chattering teeth and curled up in a foetal ball, bunched in the covers.

Now there is a duvet on my bed. Prof. Self gave it to me shortly after accusing me of being a murderer. Surely this is proof of my innocence – after all, why would anyone feel any concern about the well-being of a murderer?

4 JANUARY

I've opened the windows so that the icy wind is buffeting around the room, procreating in corners and giving birth to shrill whistles; I can feel it searing through my skin to my bones. My duvet is on the floor. It stinks. I pissed on it during the night – laid it out and sprayed my cock over it, like a cat marking territory. Then I spent the whole night bunched up on the mattress, my body violent with cold.

But this is my only chance of escape. If this was a film, if this was a novel, I'd find a piece of flint, I'd tunnel through the floorboards without them ever noticing, right the way down to the bottom floor, and one night I'd slither down it and step outside, breathe in the sweet apple air and then run and run and run through the streets . . .

Prof. Self intends to compress my quiddity into a vial.

Yesterday I was escorted to his office in *handcuffs*. The guard removed them, ordered me to sit down and warned me not to try to escape again. He left the door ajar. Then I smelt cigarette smoke wafting from the stairwell and knew I was safe to explore the office for the few precious minutes I had.

Vials. That was what I found. They had looked like stars from a distance, the way light silvered on them. They hung in a row of test-tube holders. At first I was convinced that they contained drugs they were slipping into my food. I pulled one out. It had a small white label on it. I was expecting it to read *Clozapine* but it said *Ernest Hemingway*. By now curiosity had superseded my fear of being caught. I pulled out some more. *Hemingway. DBC Pierre. Will Self. Peter Carey.* I held up Hemingway to the light. It was stormy-grey, beautiful. DBC was crimson, torrid. Then I held up Self. It seemed as though the potion was alive: it thrashed violently in the tube through a dark rainbow of hues. The most extraordinary sensation came over me – I felt as though the potion had intelligence, consciousness, and was watching me watching it. Memories ignited. I saw Sylvie's twisted face, smelt the stench of her rotting body. Revulsion came over me and I wanted to smash it to the floor—

'Careful,' Prof. Self said.

I have no idea how long he'd been in the room. He came to my side, took the potion and gently slotted it back into the holder.

'What are those?' I asked.

'Richard, I think you ought to sit down,' Prof. Self advised. 'I think our games have been most entertaining but it's time to face reality. Don't worry, we're here to help you.'

He carried on talking nonsense. My eyes kept being drawn back to the vials; their colours were magnetic. Then I heard the words 'Will Self' and 'Sylvie' and my stomach turned. His voice leaked into my consciousness: it was informing me that, though I'd been arrested for murder, he was terribly glad that I had been picked to be on the New Deal Reintegration Scheme. Two floors below me a paranoid schizophrenic, convicted of rape, was composing a violin concerto; three floors below a murderer was making sculptures from blue Plasticine. It was all part of a government-funded scheme to rehabilitate criminal schizophrenics through the medium of art. Gifted artists were often the children of a schizophrenic parent, for the gene that caused mental breakdown in their parents actually inspires creativity in them . . .

I felt no anger for him, then. Just pity.

'Jamie Curren murdered Sylvie,' I said patiently. 'He's been put away for life.'

'Perhaps I humoured your fantasy for too long,' Prof. Self said gently. 'Your novel is a therapeutic device, which, I hope, is helping you to come to terms with your past. But it appears that you are still in a strong state of denial, and your imagination is determined to cast Jamie Curren as your scapegoat. You need further help, Richard. What you see in those vials is part of a process, a unique therapy called *Transference*.'

'You're saying that I'm your guinea pig?'

'Would you rather be in prison, Richard?' A soprano of tension in his voice. 'You'd be in for life and come out an older Richard, just the same, just as sick. Here, you have a chance to *heal*. I can assure you that the New Deal Reintegration Scheme is no amateur project – its ground-breaking, innovative ideas have gained the respect of the scientific community.'

'But I'm innocent,' I said helplessly. 'And I really need to finish my novel for my deadline.'

'It's a lot for you to take in, Richard. I think you should go and rest now, and then tomorrow we'll begin the Transference process.'

I realized that reasoning with him any further was hopeless. The man is beyond psychiatric help.

I've heard about animals being kidnapped for experiments. I've heard that during the Second World War the Imperial Japanese Army developed a vile experimentation programme on humans called Unit 731, just as the Nazis were simultaneously ushering Jews into their laboratories. But why me? Had he researched me for months, pinpointed my desire and found a bait to dangle before me? And my history with Sylvie – the perfect back story to torment and confuse me.

I believe the experiments have already begun. I have no memory of the 'press conference' he held. Just ephemeral images: being strapped to a chair; Will Self's face floating before me; needles in my arms.

I can feel the cold pinching my skin, raw in my mouth, searing the wound where the guard knocked out my tooth. This is my plan. They will need a healthy guinea pig to experiment on. If I make myself sick, I will ruin their results and become statistically ineligible.

5 JANUARY

In a very bad state tonight. Alternating between sitting on the bed, crying violently, until my ribcage aches, feeling utterly alone, or suffering savage rage, stamping around the room, kicking the table, tearing my duvet with my pen, throwing the feathers about, yelling to be let out. My knuckles are raw from banging, covered with splinters. To be punished would be less painful than Self's indifference.

Only writing calms me. Emotions concentrate in my pen and dilute in the release of ink. I keep thinking about those vials. *Will Self, Hemingway, DBC Pierre*. What is in them? A dream threw up a theory: a factory of complex funnels, Will's books being pulped and juiced into a concentrate of his prose. Are they going to harvest my work for some sort of medical experiment?

I picture the vial with my name on it. My quiddity being sucked into a needle and squirted into a subject's body. Then Richard Smith will swim through a foreign bloodstream. The liver expels toxins and unwanted substances from the body. I imagine it sniffing my whiff and rejecting me; my potion coalesces into an ethereal figurine, a tiny Richard Smith, boxing a giant liver ineffectually before being dismissed by a limp cock in a whoosh of urine.

My plan has failed. They don't seem to notice or care that I am ill. Is suicide better than this? To die intact, to know my quiddity was preserved inside of me? But I have no weapon, nothing.

18 JANUARY

<u>5 p.m.</u>: (seven hours to go before Transference begins) Maybe Prof. Self is right. Maybe I am nothing better than an animal – I feel so repulsed by what I did this afternoon that I wish I could slough off this dirty body like a skin and find one that is new and shiny, free from sin. Language feels inadequate. 'Repulsed' is too weak a word. One might be repulsed by the poor ending of a novel, a strange beard. They wanted to confiscate my pen but I hid it. It made me feel ill to draw it out just now. It was flecked with flesh, smeared with eyewhite, lumps of eyeball. I had to wipe it clean on my duvet.

<u>7 p.m.</u>: (five hours to go before Transference begins) It's not as though it is even 18 January. When I was in Self's office I saw the true date – 7 February. I have made a note of every single day in this hell-hole, and yet twenty days have slipped through my memory like sand. Where did they go? Did I lose them to 'press conferences'?

Despite what I did today, I still believe that I did not kill Sylvie Pettersson.

I was taken into Self's office for my last tutorial at three p.m. Making myself ill was a terrible mistake: my eyes were streaming, my throat sore and I only felt vulnerable, without the sharpness to fight.

I decided to show Prof. Self that I was willing to play along.

'I know how Transference works,' I said. 'I've experienced it before when I had a psychotherapist. It's a Freudian theory, right? We explore how my dad upset me when I was a kid, I transfer the emotions to you and they get released in the process.'

'Freud?' Prof. Self asked, in a withering voice. 'I'm far better than Sigmund Freud! I have no intention of harking back to Freud's insipid theories on Oedipus and symbolic dreams – no, I intend to *redefine* Transference [I could hear a shadow of a Trademark behind the word], so that the term is for ever after associated with Self.'

I heard the pride quivering in his voice, located the crack of a fatal flaw.

'So how can you *prove* that you're better than Freud? I can't see any evidence of that.'

Self took the bait.

'My therapy is tailored for criminals who have a flair in an area of the arts. But you, Richard, are of particular interest to us because you are a writer – and the literary precinct is one in which Transference has enjoyed its most spectacular development. It is not entirely your fault,' he said sadly. 'Society debates with such fury the impact of video games on the adolescent psyche, and neglects to consider the rather more dangerous impact of books. Consider what happens when you read a novel – a process of identification takes place. Reading is by nature a form of schizophrenia. You divide: you remain yourself while simultaneously becoming the character in the novel. You share their pleasures, their sadness, adopt their morals, imbibe their mindset. For readers who are already ... shall we say, *vulnerable*, the narrator exists in their mind long after the pages of the book are closed. Perhaps he stays for good. Perhaps his voice is always there, whispering, suggesting ... Self has become the voice in your mind, has he not, Richard?' He leant forwards, his lips frothing with excited spit.

I shook my head vehemently.

'My research suggests that different mental illnesses attract different types of literature.' He perused some notes. '*Catcher in the Rye* has particular appeal for schizophrenics – consider Mark David Chapman, the killer of John Lennon, who was so overshadowed by the book that he wanted to change his name to Holden Caulfield. But Self – Self, I believe, is the most dangerous and poisonous writer of all, attracting schizophrenics of a psychopathic tendency.'

'Don't tell me,' I said, too angry to resist sarcasm, 'you consider Hemingway's works to be all that is good and holy?'

I broke off in a fit of ragged coughing. Prof. Self stared at me with cold detachment, as though I was a mouse he was about to dissect.

'So I take it that you want me to read Hemingway?' I asked. 'That he's your revolutionary cure?'

Prof. Self continued to stare.

'Wouldn't it just be better to damn well give me some clozapine, monitor the correct dosage and let me go? I swear I'll never read another Self novel as long as I live. I'll sign a contract . . .' Despite my shivering, I felt my body becoming clammy with desperate sweat.

'No, you don't need clozapine.' Self's tone softened, became paternal. 'That would dilute the effects . . . Don't you want to be able to live the rest of your life without needing to blanket your mind with drugs, Richard? Without having to drag yourself to the chemist every week, experiencing that faint flush of shame when you pass over your prescription? I can take all that away.'

'Dilute the effects? You mean, my writing? I – I can just give you my manuscript now,' I said hastily. 'You can turn it into a vial, whatever you want.'

Prof. Self looked so perplexed that I knew his astonishment was not an act.

'It is *you* I am interested in, Richard, not your book. Your Transference will begin at midnight. Any further details will distress you; our initial research suggests that the process is more effective if the suspect receives treatment in a state of innocence.'

'I think I may be too sick,' I said, coughing dramatically.

'You are fine, Richard – I will heal you in body, mind and spirit.'

As he summoned the guard, my subconscious, which had been feverishly processing his words, gave birth to revelation. *It is you I am interested in, Richard, not your book.* I saw myself strapped to a table, being put to sleep, Prof. Self skinning me, a vial labelled *Richard Smith* clinking into his collection. It coincided with me rising and seeing my reflection in his computer: the straggling beard, my hollowed eyes and gaunt cheeks. Revelations coalesced; panic nearly induced me to vomit. I forced the bile back down, staggered into the corridor in a blur. As we progressed towards my room, I asked the guard to loosen his grip. He ignored me. I felt his presence like a shadow, realized he was following me into my room. I saw him in the window-pane, saw him pulling a needle from his pocket. Transference was about to begin now. I reached for the only weapons I could see: my pen, and the blue Plasticine sculpture of Prof. Self.

I have been informed that the guard is in a 'stable' condition in hospital, though it has taken a surgical operation to remove all of the Plasticine from his nose. His left eye is, unfortunately, beyond repair. Too much of it remains on my floor. When I felt my pen squelching through the socket, I heard a wail banshee from my lips. As I fought him with the Plasticine, a part of me watched in disbelief, wondering what they had reduced me to. When Prof. Self entered and saw the guard splayed on the floor, his eyes flashed horror but satisfaction too. I realized he had won the game – all I had done was give him confirmation that I deserved Transference. I began to weep. I said that I was sorry. Self shook his head. 'Sorry isn't going to put Humpty Dumpty

together again.' Then he added: 'Your treatment will still pro-
ceed as scheduled — at midnight tonight.'

11.30 p.m.: (half an hour to go before Transference) Just
crouched down by the slit at the bottom of the door and saw
no shadow, but I felt a sense of premonition emanating from
the corridor, tasted a tang of chloroform. Oh God help me to
stay awake. I will just keep writing, writing, slapping my mind
awake. I feel calm now. Old, knowing I am in my twilight years,
staring at my memories like sepia photos.

I remember a girl with fair hair called Sylvie, whom I once
thought I might love very much.

I remember my father. I wish I could say goodbye to him.
Tell him I forgive him.

I write this with a sense of transcendent peace. I will accept
whatever happens tonight; perhaps I will leave my body behind
and walk the hallways of the Phantasmagoria for ever.

11.55 p.m.: Can't bear this any longer — the tidal panic is back — I
tried to slit my wrists with the tip of my pen but no good. Too
blunt.

My last wish is that my book is published posthumously. I
stood by the window and gave my pages to the night, watched
the wind carry them across the city . . .

I can hear footsteps on the stairs.

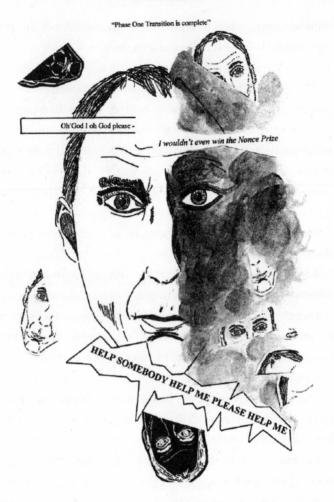

14 NOVEMBER

I am being watched. I suppose it's a lesser sin to recycle a stunt than a plotline; I suspect many of my voyeurs are the same ones who came to see me back in 2003, when I wrote a novella at the top of another Liverpudlian tower block. That building was due to be bulldozed, and quite rightly so. With its fourteen storeys of red brick shit-bedizened by zealous pigeons, it was a priapic wart on the landscape. I hoped this might be a more impressive piece of architecture but tragically it is not the case. My present tower block rears up from a trough of low-rent architecture, pushing up a façade of pure Bauhausian rationality – glass upon concrete, concrete upon glass – eight storeys into the chomped-up atmosphere. Hopefully the machines will pulverize this one next. History may tag me with an aura of destruction, however – *every building he wrote in was rapidly reduced to rubble.*

Being back in Liverpool confirms that I belong in the capital. I am a writer who is very attached to the idea of the place; I am concerned with the notion of topography, of visceral shape underlying the imaginative skin of the book. London and I have been lovers for decades, though I have had affairs on many occasions and even considered divorce. My mistresses have been varied, ranging from the Isle of Jura, where I imbibed Orwell's quiddity and produced a satire, to Morocco, where I ejaculated *Cock and Bull* almost entirely on hash – but I have always returned to her arms of clotted traffic and her leggy streets knobbled with the swollen gonads of black rubbish bags. I live in Stockwell, and if Trafalgar is her heart and Brixton her liver, then my homeplace is her cunt, dirty and moist, gang crime showering the streets with *petites morts,* her juices flowing sticky through my pen.

This is the first time I've resorted to pen and paper in years. I miss my Olivetti. I am only ensconced here for a week, however, which should be ample time to produce a short story. I've grown rather weary recently of my 'man of letters' label; I never intended to follow in the tradition of Orwell *et al* and juggle the hats of journalist, philosopher, author, social raconteur, TV presenter, etc., but rather to write as people paid me. I do, after all, have a family of four to support.

15 November

Liver. That is the name I have decided to give my new collection of stories. I have nearly completed the first, '*Foie* Human'. My family history is one of livers opening the door to death. Now that my father has passed on, I feel a profound physical sympathy with him. One's inheritance appears in mannerisms. I find myself involuntarily caught within the tiny ephemeral prison of his cough, or his sneeze, or his yawn. My past addictions must have tattooed excess on my own liver, but I hope it remains strong enough for me to transcend familial patterns and drop the cancerous baton. Since I have been locked up in this tower, I have been dreaming more than usual – last night I dreamt that the Ur-Bororo tribe turned on their creator with a vengeful passion and enacted a ritual that involved my liver being torn from my still-living body and held up to the sky as a sacrificial boon.

Professor Self, a journalist who is inhabiting an office a few doors down from me, is blogging regular updates on my progress. He is clearly a vacuous cunt: a strutting little peacock of a man, with wisps of grey plastered over a lemony pate, and the wisping, lyrical voice of a pederast. He also appears to believe in the modern medical delusion that writing can be used as a form of therapy. He spouted observations with manic abandon, and in a pathetic attempt to bond, he quoted back to me my theories on the problematic viability of satire as a modus in the current social climate of nihilism. I explained to him that this wasn't necessarily a reductive issue – I intended to make my readers think for themselves.

18 November

I arrived at Prof. Self's study a few minutes early today, when I came across a string of vials, each neatly labelled with the name of a writer: *DBC Pierre, Beryl Bainbridge, F. Scott Fitzgerald*. I mocked Prof. Self on the facile absurdity of attempting to reduce the quiddity of an author to a vial of urine. Self's bulbous eyes gleamed and he advised me that it was not urine. I sensed that he wanted me to question him further, so I deliberately changed the subject in order to disappoint him. He retaliated by casually making reference to a piece in the *Independent* where Andrew Marr had claimed, 'Will Self has got a lot going for him but won't do anything interesting until he has fought his way out of the Amis influence', but he failed to provoke me – I explained that I have the utmost respect for Martin, a fellow sesquipedalian, despite his recent decline into right-wing theatrics.

I have been unable to write today – I seem to spend much of my time producing jism under the sheets.

19 November

Prof. Self would make a useful character in one of my novels – I wish I could have harvested his narcissistic personality tics for *Dr Mukti and Other Tales of Woe*. Incidentally, he picked up a copy of *Mukti*, my fourth short-story collection, and read from the flap: 'a warped window on the wibbly-wobbly world of fear and fun that Self – like some malevolent deity – has fashioned over the years'. He put my book down, smoothed his amphibious fingers over the cover and then attempted to convince me that my name was not Will Self but Richard Smith. I pointed out the substantial opus of my work and suggested that he turn on BBC 2 on Monday evenings and watch a programme called *Shooting Stars*. The argument was actually rather exhilarating at the time as I watched my polemic slowly pulverize his psyche to a pulp, but now I feel drained. I also seem to have forgotten the name of my wife.

20 NOVEMBER

Tough, Tough Toys For Tough, Tough Boys was, I believe, my first novel.

21 NOVEMBER

I know that my wife's name begins with D. My memory feels shit-bedizened. I don't understand – the (post) modern *fin de siècle*–

22 NOVEMBER

I think I need a doctor. When I asked Prof. Self to release me, he laughed and assured me that the process of Transference would soon be finished, whereby I then would be free to leave. In the meantime, they have locked me up. I have no doubt the jest will conclude soon enough – after all, the Prof. needs something to blog about, and this sort of reality-TV-style game-playing is being enacted with quotidian predictability. But I feel curious today, patently raw, as though I am being sheathed in a cocoon and the layers are slowly being peeled away before I have had time to develop wings and antennae.

I am Will Self.

23 NOVEMBER

I am Will Self. I am Will Self. I am Will Self. My wife's name is _____. I am Will Self. I am Will Self. I am Will Self. I am Will Self. I am Will Self I am Will Self I am Will Self I am Will self I am will self I am will self I am will self

Transference

11 February

I am writing at my desk and outside the window the sky is blue and the trees are bare. This morning I wrote until lunchtime, then saw Prof. Self. He writes in a room further down the corridor from mine and has asked that I tutor him from time to time. Everything about him is old except his eyes and they are the same colour as the sea and are cheerful and undefeated.

Self remarked that I looked different. 'Your beard is quite . . . dazzling,' he said.

We spoke of my rapid beard growth and my desire to leave the tower block and return to normal life. I would live at the

Finca Vigia farm in Cuba and spend my days by the bank with a fishing-rod and conclude my nights at La Bodeguita and drink two or three Mojitos and smoke a cigar until it was dark.

'I believe the integration process is complete,' he said. He looked happy. 'You see, Richard, it only involved a few injections and they were fairly harmless, I'm sure you agree. In a few years' time this technique will be commonplace.'

'Thank you, Professor Self, I feel a whole lot better,' I said.

18 FEBRUARY

Outside it is snowing and the ground is becoming white and the air has a sharp tang to it. By day I write, and in the evening, they strip off my clothes and inject a vial into my arm and guide me into the Transference room on the second floor. I find it pleasant, being strapped on to the table, with the lights dancing in my eyes and the picture of the bearded man fishing on the ceiling. But now it is snowing and the injections and the picture have ceased and Prof. Self seems agitated.

'What is your name?' he asked me.

'I am Ernest.'

'You are Richard Smith. You ought to be at that stage by now. You understand?'

'Yes,' I said. 'I understand.'

'You will be returning to your ordinary life back in your flat in Primrose Hill.'

'In Cuba,' I agreed.

Prof. Self fell silent and I saw his eyes become opaque as he tapped his pen against his notepad. The tapping became insistent until it sounded like gunfire, and I was reminded of the wound I had acquired during the war and the pain of the wound. Prof. Self mopped the dampness of his brow.

'Are you familiar with the works of Will Self?'

'I am not,' I replied.

'At least that poison has been extracted from you.'

'It is still snowing outside. The snow has a certain quiddity.'

Prof. Self frowned and asked that I leave, for he said that he had a severe migraine coming on.

19 FEBRUARY

Tomorrow I will leave this dark, queer room. I picture myself walking out into the pale sky and breathing in the fresh air and hearing the sounds of the city until I feel dizzy. I think I will probably walk for several hours, just walk and walk as the sky turns dark and the stars appear, just to feel the ground under my feet and the freedom of the landscape. It will be interesting to see my mother and father and find out whether they have missed me. And Sylvie, my little rabbit, whom I will kiss a hundred times. I wonder if they will observe the curious transmogrification that has taken place inside me! My quiddity now shines a different shade of neon. Saying goodbye to Prof. Self will be poignant too – I have practised it with my Plasticine figure. I tore off the blue head and impaled it on his cock, then broke off his cock and used that to wank off on the blue shreds of his neck until blue cum spittled over the desk; then I took a long splinter and shoved it through his shoulder blades for a final flourish – for this, hee hee, hooograa, is my Idea of Fun!

20 FEBRUARY

I am being watched THEY just pumped me full of drugs. basstards. batards. which is which? which words? my brain is foggy, forigve my spelling. I keep throwing up my words and they come down in the wrong places buttered side down Sod's-Lawed. They don't darecome in ha ha comein want to come do you Professor Self then i'll use YOR blood to write with too I'll rewrite my novel and use your spleen for my title and yor liver decorate for my cover won't that look nice?

oh so I'm a failed experiment –

but let me experiment on you Prof. Self

trying to smoke out are you?

well the guard's head is by my feet and I'mgoingto use Plastiseen to make a copee of his head how dare they pump-drugs into me what am I I am ErnestHimingwaySelf I want my mummywhy is that violin playing stop stop make it stop I'll throw his head agains thte wall until his stops I want SylvieI want to kiss herlittle rabbitlittlerabbitcant' makemy words work can't stop them goinground andround andround

i can smell burning

I have gone to the place I ache to be. I have gone to the Phantasmagoria: find me there.

Part Four:
Mia, 2049

(i) The Girl at the Cinema

The day after my father's funeral, I went to see an afternoon performance at the cinema. The film was yet another biopic about a dead writer. I feel this current trend cannot be anything other than a depressing, collective nostalgia for the time when authors wrote their own books, instead of today's ritual partnerships between celebs and ghosts. The title of the film was, simply, *Will*. I passed over thirty euros for the ticket with a cynical heart. By the time Will Self died in 2045, his books were pretty much out of print and none was available on Kindle. My father, who was an ardent fan, used to trawl second-hand bookshops on the Net for dog-eared, yellowing 2003 editions of *How the Dead Live*, sometimes paying up to fifty thousand euros at auction. A recent TV adaptation of *Cock and Bull*, however, brought Self back into the limelight and, no doubt, the producers thought it was due time to cash in on his fifteen minutes of afterlife fame. I doubted they would make their return; after all, look at the recent flop musical of *Rushdie and Amis*, not to mention the critically panned *Zadie*.

My father spent his last years writing a PhD thesis on Will's novels; it involved months of dedicated reading and meticulous research; hours in the British Museum pulling articles and interviews from the archives. His thesis began with an examination of the word *Self* and its growing linguistic popularity as one of our most ubiquitous prefixes. Self-love. Self-control. Self-hatred. Self-controlling. Self-delight self-satisfied self-destruction self-determination self-aware self-aggrandisement self-surrender self-motivated. He cited it as an example of the Western world's predilection for narcissism and went on to explore how Self was one of the finest satirists exploring our obsession with the self with a small *s*. My father never found a publisher for his thesis. It now lies in a box, trapped in a filing cabinet in his office.

I took a booth at the back of the theatre. A fluorescent green oval slid across my lap, offering various choices to rot my stomach and teeth. As I hit 'POPCORN' and 'COLA', I noticed that my nails had been replaced by red sores. There was a whirring noise as my bucket came trawling upwards. I pulled out my drink and popcorn. Oh, and a tub of Ben & Jerry's Jnr cola-flavoured ice cream. Either a freebie or they'd got it wrong again. I didn't want to be charged, so I tapped *Assistance*, then saw the movie was about to start, so tapped *Cancel*. The American voice warned, 'Your booth lights will now dim – enjoy the movie!' Darkness fell. All of us suspended in our little oval booths like a room full of caterpillars poised in transmogrification. The trailers hit my heart with a hammer-blow of memory, of coming to see *The Great Gatsby* with my father when I was seven years old and we sat side by side, the popcorn bag propped on the arm-rest between us. I quickly stemmed a tide of salt by tossing a lump into my mouth.

All the omens that *Will* was going to be a terrible movie were there from the start. Producer credits swirling over copies of

Will Self's books, their yellow stains suggesting the period researcher had been overenthusiastic with the tea, the thick pages looking suspiciously like parchment, as though Self had been one of Shakespeare's contemporaries. Then the opening scene: a baby Will screaming in his cot. He stares up at his parents. They are apes. They loop pontid arms around each other. One lovingly picks a flea from the other's fur and feeds it into Will's bawling mouth. I presumed that this was a reference to Self's *Great Apes*, a Swiftian satire about a man who wakes and discovers he is the only human in a world of apes. However, that his parents – who were left-wing intellectuals, his mother a Jewish American *émigrée*, his father a professor in Political Sciences, should be presented as oafs of the simian kind made no sense to me. I suppose the film makers had to keep us entertained somehow. We then followed Will as a boy, lingering behind bike sheds, holding a knife against his arm, wincing in disgusted relief as he watched the blood flow; Will at the back of a chemistry class, crouching behind the desk, injecting heroin with a snarling, ecstatic expression; an interview at Oxford University where a fusty professor asked Will to clarify whether he had recently been misdiagnosed with schizophrenia, and an insolent teenage Will replied that he was such a genius, he had voices fighting over his mind. I doubted any of it was true, but for the first time in months, I smiled. It made my cheeks feel funny.

Was it the film, or was it me? Normally I found books and films the perfect anaesthetic for heartache. But the trawl through Will's twenties and his first marriage to Kate Chancellor failed to ease the tension in my chest. My eyes drifted to the girl sitting in the booth suspended a few feet away from me. I could not see her face, but her legs were crossed over the ledge, one calf curving creamily over the other, a stockinged foot undulating as it slid a sandal on and off, on and off. I ached to reach across and take her hand and squeeze it tight and feel a human warmth tingling up my arm. Then I saw two irises flash violet in the dark and I realized she was looking at me.

Psychogeography was a term coined in the 1950s by Guy Debord, the leader of a group of French Situationists, to describe a radical method of mapping cities. The Situationists sought to rebel against the way in which urban planning had mundanified the individual's connection to their surroundings, to rediscover the extraordinary in the ordinary, so that a simple walk around a city might cause an alleyway or shit-spattered street-sign to dazzle the mind suddenly or stir the heart. The climax of the film saw Will taking his ultimate psychogeographical journey, an epic walk from his home in suburban Stockwell to the Crowne Plaza in Manhattan (intercut with a flight of thirty-five thousand air miles). As he completed his journey, his face grimified, like a gangster ready to become hitman (indeed, the adult actor playing him had also been a gangster in the ITV 7 crime drama I had seen last week), the accompanying Tchaikovsky soared to a crescendo. Once more, I turned and looked at the girl and she waited for me to direct my stare back to the screen before placing her eyes on me.

It became a game. There was a silence left in the cinema after the film's finale, the grand funeral that was held for Self in Highgate, and within that we had made a silence of our own. We lingered, waiting for everyone else to leave. Then she slipped out of her booth, stretched languidly, tossed her hair and strolled over to the exit. My last flicker of doubt was blown out when she looked back and flashed eyes that beckoned chase. Into the Ladies I followed her. I heard the tinkle of her piss from the cubicle next to mine; I felt my own slippery, wet excitement, the pulse of my V against my fingers. At the basins, our eyes met in the mirror; at the driers we bounced hot air back and forth between our palms. She leant over and whispered, 'Wait here for a minute – then come and find me!' and she left.

I waited barely thirty seconds, then hurried out of the Ladies into the bright light of the foyer. People were chatting, buying tickets from machines; robot usherettes bleated, 'Buy candy, buy candy,' as they proffered metal trays, their mouths eager to collect coins; a gaggle of teenage boys were playing a game machine that fizzed nasty noises. I went back into the toilet again, feeling like a bewildered Alice. I pushed open each door. A trio of empty cubicles. Outside, I stood in the street, watching the crowds. I listened to the sounds of the city, and the roar had never seemed so lonely, a tidal wave that washed over me and made me want to give in, let myself be swept away into the gutters and sewage. My white rabbit had fled.

I could not face going home. I decided to wander around the city and attempt some psychogeography of my own. It felt pleasantly twee, perhaps in the same way that someone living in Will's day might have thought it charmingly old-fashioned to collect butterflies in nets or breed bees. I walked through streetways and alleyways, shops and canal paths. I attempted to unlock the new, the beautiful, the rare, the profound. All I could see were the same closed doors of old, the ugly, the mundane, the squalor. Psychogeography, I concluded, is a form of poetic ego-tism, a confirmation of the exquisite cleanliness of our windows of perception. Perhaps mine were too darkened by my grief, too smudged by my cynicism, for I could not find anything exultant in the cityscape, in the high-rise towers that suited the depth of an American horizon but crowded ours out. I had recently reviewed and compared the sci-fi fiction of today with the sci-fi of fifty years back. It had once looked to the future rather than the past, celebrated gadgetry and made heroes of robots. Our present day sci-fi was nostalgic for a London of stone rather than sheen; we have fallen out of love with machines now that they are real rather than ideals, now that they have flaws and malfunctions and irritate and intrude on our lives every second of the day. I looked up at the cameras watching me and I thought: somewhere in that film, she has been captured: images of her wandering through the streets, sighing over clothes in shops, exchanging money, brushing back her bob as the wind blows it over her face, frowning outside tube stations as she waits for a date. If only I could sit in a booth and watch her on the screen, all day, all day long.

I trudged across Parliament Hill and on to Hampstead Heath. Down below were the earthen basins my father had once loved to swim in. I had fiercely avoided his grave so far. I did not want to lay flowers, drop tears on earth. The thought of his headstone made me feel sick: to face the reality of his skin and bones becoming a feast for the worms. He was still alive in my mind, albeit fading a little, day by day, becoming less of a physical memory and more of a presence. The sight of his headstone would cause a double-death.

But I liked the graveyard of the Highgate Cemetery. It was pretty and sombre. A place where the rich, the famous, the intelligentsia were celebrated; I used to think that if ghosts existed, they must enjoy the most extraordinary tea-parties, with Karl Marx sipping beetle juice alongside Douglas Adams and Christina

Rossetti. Will Self's grave lay just behind Marx's; I wondered if they ever argued. I wondered if the worms moving between the graves mingled their dust until the soil became rich in thought and philosophy. These worms were laced with the DNA of genius; within their species they must be quite extraordinary.

The thought made me smile again, and then I felt sad.

The graveyard was cool and lush, sunlight falling through the trees like green lace. I sensed that someone was following me, but it blurred with the familiarity of my father's presence. The feeling grew more insistent. Then I saw her, standing in the gloom, like an exotic nymph. She must have been following me since I left the cinema. I turned and walked on, weaving through graves, until I came to a large stone engraved with the words:

WILL SELF

1961 – 2045

'Of course, his real body isn't in there,' she said. 'You must have read the story.'

'No,' I said, frowning, for in my dazed state I had forgotten. Then: 'Oh. His coffin is empty.'

I already knew the tale – my father had told it to me many times – but it was a pleasure to hear her tell it.

'That's right. The worms here grow hungry. Will offered to donate his body to charity in the event of death. So a philanthropist bought him for six million dollars and transported his body, suspended in formaldehyde, all the way back to Nashville. It became famous – he kept the body in a tower block, charged a fortune for tickets. I actually saw it myself, when I visited the US a few months ago. And, wow, it was something to look at. When Self died, his personality, the feel of his writing – the glorious and the grotesque – were still there, fossilized in his pupils. But then the philanthropist got hit by the stock-exchange crash and suffered financial turmoil. He needed to sell it but he couldn't bear to part with it.

'So he sold a few parts to collectors. He cut off a hand to sell for six hundred thousand. He also sold Will's liver. And *one* eye. Apparently the hand is now somewhere in Egypt. The eye and the liver are owned by an eccentric living in Berkeley Square. Imagine – that eccentric sitting in his study, watching Will's eye bobbing in a little jar next to him as he smokes a cigar and strokes his cat.'

'Oh.' I shuddered with grotesque pleasure.

During the entire conversation, we didn't look at each other once, addressing the empty grave. Then there was a pause, and I felt her eyes fingering me. They caressed my jaw and slowly pulled it round to face her. I drank in her dark bob, her cherry lips, her eyes of sweetness and fire. She reached out and ran her little finger down the length of my arm.

Her name was Kat, short for Katherine, which she told me meant 'pure'. It didn't suit. I wanted to find the perfect word to describe her. Words were my wage; my passion; my nine-to-five. I read books and newspapers with a pencil clutched between my fingers, striking out adjectives, replacing words of grey with words of colour. I might have summed her up as beautiful, yet it would not only have sounded clichéd, but commercial. Beauty is a word with roots in *bellus* and the Koine Greek *hōraios*, which means 'of one's hour'. Since being appropriated by the fashion industry, it has come to imply air-brushing and – that cheat of time – plastic perfection. In America to say something is beautiful now also implies it is fake, and I have no doubt the slang will soon reach us, until the word loses all its bloom. Until it no longer applies to the transience of a sunset, to the feel of a rose against your cheek, to walking slowly, hand in hand, through a graveyard on a lovely afternoon. I felt irritated with myself for being unable to pinpoint a perfect word for her, but perhaps I was trying, too early, to pin her down; perhaps the word would only come with time.

She turned to me and said, 'Do you like to dance?'

She was destroying my black-and-white world. For the first time in weeks, I felt full of feeling, raw and fragile with it. The strobe lights of the club patterned storms across our faces. The music was too loud for words; we could only play with eyes and touch. I danced casually. She flirted with the music with slinks and loose-limbed swirls. Her pupils invited me closer, but then she spun away from me, smiling a scarlet smile. I began to drift, becoming clumsy as I slipped out of the aura of her confidence. A man moved between us. He was tall, handsome, Asian. Wearing a white vest, wet with sweat. She sidled up against him, watching over his shoulder, eyes on me. I stopped dancing and stared at her with stinging eyes. She walked up to me, ignoring his protest, cupped tender palms around my face and kissed me. So softly that the caress felt more like breath than lips.

We began to dance again, swaying in hazy bliss, lips meeting, brushing, breaking into smiles. Her breasts crushed sweetly against mine; I could feel her excitement in the hardness of her nipples. Her palms splayed over my shoulder blades, slipped down my spine, laced against the small of my back. Our pulses pounded, breaths became aggressive. But my heart was too fragile: it broke before she had even dropped it. Tears spooled down my cheeks. She licked them away. I melted against her. I wanted her to be my mother and my father, to hold me and let me know the world would be all right. But she spun away, dancing, smiling. I went into the toilets. In the cubicle I leant against a flimsy door and felt tears crack through my ribcage, heard my voice crying, 'Oh Dad, oh Daddy.' When they had passed, I wiped my eyes, feeling the clean tiredness of release. When I went back out to the dance floor, I saw her arms were looped around the Asian boy. I waited for her but she stared back with eyes of indifference, so I could not even tell if she was watching me as I walked away.

(ii) The Package

In the morning, I was woken by the buzzing of my bell. I dragged on my dressing-gown, hungover with grief. In the camera I saw – before the iris recognition named him – my postman. I went into the hallway, jumped into the lift, slipped down twenty-four floors, made my arms into a basket to carry my huge pile of post. The postman was as flirtatious as ever, which usually cheered me but on this morning made me feel sad. I could still feel her taste in my mouth, the smell of her skin in my hair. I thanked him once more and went back into the lift. She asked me what floor I wanted to go to. So many voices: a curious metalmorphism. Perhaps we created all these voices to alleviate the collective loneliness, yet to go through the day hearing a surfeit of metallic vocals only served to exacerbate the feeling. I was sometimes tempted to tell the lift to go to a minus floor. I wondered how she might reply, if she would say, 'Are you sure?' I had heard the stories of those Dantesque floors below the ground, the bowels of hell beneath our real-estate heaven, where the Spanish and Africans and those whose countries had been drowned or turned to desert were housed, six to a room, in rooms puddled with shit and tepid water. This morning I felt too raw for risks, lacked the zest that adventure required. I told the lift to take me back up to floor twenty-four, conscious that she always evoked such a tone of politeness in me, the manners of a nervous schoolgirl.

Upstairs, I let the parcels slide from my weary arms and brewed some coffee. My kitchen reminded me that she was dirty, that it had been three days since I had done the washing-up and there was a 34 per cent chance of cholera developing. Fucking voice recognition: turned on in every room and me lacking the technological know-how to switch it off, despite many sweaty nights grappling with the help manual. Of course, my father had used to joke that you couldn't switch it off; that such power was just an illusion. Whenever I swore at it, the system would reply, 'I am sorry. I do not recognize those words. Please repeat and try again,' and our conversation would become a loop of obscenities.

I drank my coffee and piled my parcels into a brown-paper tower. Three days a week, I worked as a lexicographer, helping to update the *OED*. The remaining two, I reviewed books. Mostly crime novels, for they were becomingly increasingly controversial with the recent hysterical scientific hoo-ha discussing their influence on society, polluting the clean waters of our *animus* with their cesspool of rapes and knifings and stranglings and missing kids and bodies buried in woods. Novels were feeding crime so naturally we now had novels about novels inspiring criminals: were the murderers giving authors ideas or vice versa? It was not my job to moralize, just analyse. I wished my old-fashioned elderly editor, lovely as he was, had not such a stubborn attachment to chopping down trees, an aversion to the Kindle, which resulted in a pyramid of parcels every day. I finished my coffee and checked my emails. There was one from a Mr Self, which I assumed was a joke. A sick one. The name had an immediate association: behind a vision of Self's face I saw the shadow of my father, working away at his thesis with arthritic fingers.

The email said:

> Did you get the package?

I thought it must be from my editor.

Then I saw it. I was sifting through when I saw the handwriting, inky-blue, on the back of the Jiffy-bag. The address was in Shoreditch. My father's place of work.

I opened it.

A letter was neatly paperclipped to some newspaper articles. Underneath the articles was a manuscript.

My dear Mia,

I asked my colleague to post this after my funeral. I have a confession to make to you, my darling. I lied to you. I told you terrible fibs about spending the last few years of my life working on a thesis about Will Self's novels. I lied because I felt it was too dangerous to tell you the truth. I am, perhaps, putting you at risk by sending you the enclosed documents, but I felt that you were the only one I could trust. The only one who could continue this investigation after I have gone.

I know that you always teased me for being your potty old dad with his eccentricities, but you must take this seriously, Mia. I have made some very disturbing discoveries about the WSC, which I believe must be made public in order to prevent further tragedies. The WSC may come after you if they discover that you have the enclosed documents, so it may be best if you commit the following to memory and then burn it. Please be careful.

I turned the page. The ink had changed from blue to black.

I love you Mia, so very very much.
Love always, Dad

I examined the handwriting in the letter carefully. It was shakier than his usual style, but the characteristics were all there: the loop of his *g*s and the long crosses on his *t*s. Moreover, I could feel his soul in the syntax. I did not believe this letter had been forged.

I put the letter aside and examined the newspaper articles. The first was dated 2007 – around forty years ago.

Daily Mail

NEW CRIME DEAL GOES UP IN FLAMES

. . . and taxpayers are left with the charred ashes

Shock waves rippled through the government last night when the infamous Liverpool tower block that housed Richard Smith, convicted of the vicious murder of Sylvie Pettersson, burst into flames. At least seven people were badly injured in the blaze, including Richard Smith himself, who suffered third-degree burns. He is now being operated on in Fazakerley Hospital. Doctors report that his condition is critical.

Richard Smith is infamous for being the first guinea pig

in the government's 'New Crime Deal' initiative. On 19 September 2006, Richard Smith (23) was arrested for the murder of Sylvie Pettersson. Having been charged with murder Smith avoided serving the first two years of his sentence in prison when he was granted permission to sit in a room on the top floor of a Liverpudlian tower block and write a novel.

Professor Self, a well-known TV personality and psychiatrist, and one of the pioneers behind the scheme, argued that it was 'an important social experiment that will revolutionize the reintegration of the criminal into society and dramatically lower rates of recidivism'. However, the scheme has been met with much scepticism from numerous critics, who feel that it is a waste of taxpayers' money: the cost of housing, feeding and guarding Smith amounted to £7000 per day.

The public were invited to watch Richard Smith writing, but the spectacle proved so popular that numbers were regulated and tickets were issued. Though these tickets were officially free of charge, ticket touts cashed in, and it is said that some people paid up to £350 for a glimpse of Smith at work. Dr Morgan Young, from Springfield Hospital, said that it was a disgrace: 'It is one thing for Fay Weldon, an established and respected author, to become a writer-in-residence at the Ritz. It is another for the government to fund a common criminal to enable him to indulge his literary whims.'

Several other residents in the housing block also complained that they were forced to move out as a result. Mrs D. Clements, who used to live next door to the room Smith is writing in, complained: 'Hate mail came through our letterbox on a daily basis. The press were constantly doorstepping the flats. The last straw came when someone broke in and tried to steal the book. They didn't succeed, but the entire building was evacuated at two in the morning. Many of us have families. We couldn't carry on like that.'

Controversy was also caused when Random House signed a contract with Richard Smith for £1 million for the publication of this book. The deal was negotiated by super-agent Archie West, who defended it by saying: 'Richard Smith may be a murderer, but that does not mean to say that his writing is not of great value to the general public. Remember: Oscar Wilde wrote *The Importance of Being Earnest* in jail. Does anyone care now that, back then, he was arrested for being a faggot? Writers are not politicians. We can't expect them to be squeaky clean all the time.'

Unfortunately the novel, which was provisionally titled *The Diary of a Murderer*, was to be published in April 2008. Now the entire manuscript has perished in the blaze. This morning, when Archie West was questioned on whether Smith would repay the advance, he issued the following statement: 'Richard Smith was more than a client to me – he was like a son. He is now balanced precariously on the cliff of death, hanging on by his fingernails. Whether or not he finishes the book seems trivial on this tragic occasion.'

The cause of the fire is unknown. Police are asking people who saw anything suspicious between the hours of midnight and four a.m. to come forward with any information they may have.

Comment: See page 17 for 'The Growth of the Celebrity Writer'

Quiz: How long was Jeffrey Archer in jail? How well do you know your criminal celebrities? Take the quiz on page 32 and win a holiday to Barbados!

The second article was dated only a week ago. I had read it last week, sitting in Starbucks, sipping a coffee. An opinion piece by Toby Starks.

Daily Telegraph

Another book, another body on the floor. Yesterday's murder – a woman killed in exact imitation of Karin Slaughter's posthumous crime novel, with the tome itself left by the victim's feet – comes as no surprise. It began ten years ago when the idea of a book group – once a cosy and jolly practice where six or seven people would gather together to exchange gossip and argue over a book of their choice – took on a more insidious hue. Out of them evolved 'Writer Worship Clubs' (as the *Guardian* put it), or 'Satanic Book Boffins' (as the *Daily Mail* put it). The majority of these were initiated by students, the clubs being an antidote to drinking clubs and rag weeks. At Sussex University, a Virginia Woolf Club was established, though it seemed not so much a religion as a thinly veiled forum for transvestites to enjoy putting on grey wigs and 1930s-style dresses while sleeping in the grounds of her former domain, Monk's House in Rodmell. In Glasgow, rather inevitably, an Irvine Welsh Club was established, whereby the Initiation Ceremony depended upon those who could negotiate the best bargain for crack cocaine from a selected drug dealer. Soon, however, people of all ages, cultures and genres were joining in. As one columnist

put it, 'Literary religion has become the new New Age'–
the perfect fulfilment for a spiritually hollow society, disil-
lusioned with Christianity but thirsty for answers, while
also indulging an inherently British, élitist, and patriotic
pride in literature. At present there are roughly two hundred and thirty Writerly Faiths existing in the UK alone.
In Wessex, construction is shortly to be completed on a
temple dedicated to Thomas Hardy, and the Tom Paulin
Dublin Faith has now been recognized as a world religion,
though it is listed in the *Directory of Religions* just beneath
Jedi Warriors, suggesting it has yet to be accepted as a serious faith.

Three years ago, however, these Writerly Religious
became something rather more insidious. The Edgar Allen
Poe Faith decided to enact *The Murders in the Rue Morgue*.
The result was the death of a fifteen-year-old schoolgirl
and her mother, and the incarceration of all five members
along with their pet orang-utan. The nation was shocked
but the Poe Faith murder was just the beginning of a sick-
ening trend of author-inspired violence. The Lecter After
School Club ate the brains of their geography master; the
infamous Christie murders were carried out by a group
of elderly Yorkshire women, who decided to play a game
of *And Then There Were None* by lacing their homemade
plum jam with arsenic and feeding it to their husbands.
The public imagines that this is a new phenomenon but
it was anticipated by a murder that took place over forty
years ago. In early 2006, a young, aspiring novelist called
Sylvie Pettersson was tragically murdered in her flat.
When her body was discovered, it was found that her
face had been sculpted to look akin to Will Self's and her
clothes changed accordingly. This was, no doubt, a fetish

of her murderer, a young Richard Smith, who denied the charges and claimed he had been set up by the WSC. The prosecuting lawyer argued that her murder was the result of an initiation into the club that had 'simply got out of control'. At the time, it was considered a rarity; now, of course, it is the norm, the sick norm. Richard Smith died in a fire a year later, which seems a fitting punishment; perhaps we can hope that if there is a deity up there, and he wears a face like Self's, there is such a thing as divine justice.

I turned to the manuscript. It was around forty pages long, and I read it very slowly, savouring each word. It started off as the diary of Richard Smith, a writer who had been locked in a Liverpudlian tower block in the year 2006. He thinks he is a celebrity whom the public pay to observe his genius, but it soon transpires that he is the victim of a strange psychiatric experiment. He is, however, a classic unreliable narrator: is he simply a delusional writer who imagines that his professor is a psychiatrist; or a patient who can only cope with his reality by imagining that his psychiatrist is a professor? The latter seemed most likely, except for the fact that the diary was interrupted with bizarre sequences of literary playing cards that seemed, to me, to be amateur and unconvincing, and part of the writer's joke.

Some time later I came out of the manuscript and re-entered the world around me. The morning hum had become a buzz. I realized it must be lunchtime and office workers were spilling from their hives. I felt quite hungry and dizzy. I wanted to eat but I needed to write down my thoughts before I forgot them. I liked to make lists, for the pleasure of going through the day slashing them out, and now I needed to make sense of things.

1. Which of Dad's colleagues sent this package? Justin Williams is his closest friend at the university – check with him.
2. Richard's diary is meant to be over forty years old, yet it has been printed out on fresh paper – printed by my father? How did he come to have access to it? I should check his computer to see if the file is on it.
3. Who is the author of this diary – is it Richard himself, written before the fire killed him? Or is it a fictional imagining by another author?
4. Are the vials mentioned in the story real or codenames for something else?
5. What has my father been doing? Why send this to me now? Why not tell me when he was alive?

As I picked up the manuscript and read it through once more, a feeling of unease came over me. The slightest noise made me jump and I jack-knifed in and out of the book and the real world. Finally I came to Richard's last diary entry, dated 13 January 2007:

> I have gone to the place I ache to be. I have gone to the Phantasmagoria: find me there.

(iii) The Investigation

When the doorbell buzzed, I jumped violently. I walked slowly to my CCTV, installed, I always felt, to force us to become complicit voyeurs too, to manipulate our own desire for safety so that we could not complain when they wanted to study us. The voice recognition warned me, 'Unfamiliar female, not registered as a friend or family member.' Then I saw her. Her. Standing in the hallway. Biting her lip. Pleasure pierced me; a smile broke across my face. So she hadn't spent the night with the Asian guy: she must have followed me home instead. I reached to buzz her in, then delayed a little longer, making her wait and wonder if I was watching her.

'Hi,' she said, as I opened my door.

She was wearing a black summer dress with a 2030s feel, decorated with fat cerise roses, but her bob was modern, curled under on one side.

I had been yearning for her ever since our kiss, and if we had never met again, she would always have been preserved in memory as a romantic legend. But this was reality, stitched into her smile, a smile that said she was used to treating people like shit and getting away with it. She

211

sauntered about as though I was the guest and she the host.

'Wow – is it your birthday or something?' She gaped at the packages.

'No. It's just – my job.' I wanted to stay annoyed with her, but it was hard work. That smile was beguiling in its repellent way. 'So, what d'you want?'

'I thought a cup of coffee would be nice.'

I went into the kitchen and brewed a second canister of coffee, telling myself I would give her one cup and then tell her to go. The kitchen voice system advised me that the risk of cholera had now risen to 50 per cent. From the living room, I heard Kat's laughter and my irritation returned. I put her cup back into the cupboard and faced her with folded arms.

'Look, I have a lot to do. This isn't really convenient.'

Kat smoothed her hand over her bob, pressing her little finger against the curl. 'Perhaps I should go then,' she said in a small voice.

'Yes, you should probably go,' I agreed. Then I saw something in her eyes that suggested her wounded-little-girl caricature had genuine roots in character. My eyes slid to her mouth. The top lip was slightly cruel, offset by the plump benignity of the bottom one. And then, gleaming at her throat, a surprise: a cross.

I relented. 'Okay.'

I poured the coffee and we sat down on the living-room sofa. 'So, how's your boyfriend?' I asked.

'Who?'

'The guy you were with last night.' I looked straight into her eyes and she looked straight back.

'He's . . . some random guy. Nobody. Sorry. I was just a bit out of it. I didn't mean for you to go – I was looking for you everywhere.' She reached out and brushed her knuckles against my cheek. 'Your cheek's so cold.'

For a few seconds, I yielded to her touch, so the flinch that followed seemed slightly theatrical. I laced my palms together and stared into them. Courtship entails a complex choreography but I had ground to a halt, refusing to take another pretty step, asking for the music to be turned down. We can never speak directly to each other, my father had once advised me, only in subtext. Only the mad speak straight from the heart. You see them on street corners, flailing at the public, unable to conceal.

To hell with artifice.

'Look,' I said, 'I'm going through a difficult time. I'm quite messed up – and I think you'll only screw me up even more, so I don't think anything can really work between us. I'm sorry.'

'It wasn't me,' Kat said more insistently. 'That guy – he gave me a drug. It was just this little square with a face on it. It looked like acid – but it was worse than any trip I've ever tried. I can't stand guys and I ended up snogging him – that's how drugged I was. Come on, the guy was a complete cunt, you can't get peevish with me. I still feel rough – I know I look really rough.'

Subtext: forgive me. Tell me I look beautiful. Fall in love with me.

I looked into her eyes again and felt the force of her will. 'You look fine,' I whispered.

She reached out and seized my hand. 'Come to an audition with me. I need your moral support – it's this afternoon and I'd so love you to watch.'

My eyes fell to the brown package my father had sent. 'I . . .'

'Yes. Say yes.'

'No.' I smiled. 'OK. Yes.'

She whooped, hugged me, bounced back on to the sofa.

'Thanks, I get so nervous. I feel as though I might throw up or something.'

'Maybe you should pray,' I said. When she looked confused, I pointed to her cross.

'Oh, that – I'm an atheist,' she said. 'I just wear it because the cross reminds me of death and how short our lives are and therefore how we should grab as much pleasure as possible from it.'

I laughed, wondering why I felt so shocked by her revelation: I was hardly devout myself.

'What about you?' she asked. 'Do you believe in God or pleasure?'

'I'm an atheist.'

'See? You're like me – too lazy to bother with God!' Kat said gleefully. I smiled, but I felt a little irked again; she was too quick to define me. I already yearned for her to realize my layers, to strip them away slowly and find my core. My atheism was quite different from hers. It was fuelled by rage rather than indifference.

But I had lost the courage for honesty. After my third cup of coffee, I needed the bathroom. Before I went, I made a show of tidying the table, for I felt uncomfortable about leaving the package behind with her.

Mirror, mirror, on the wall. I had just been to the toilet and I was hastily washing my hands. When she began to spout feminine instruction, I banged her frame angrily, fearing seven years' retribution. But she was made of sterner stuff. The mirror, programmed and sponsored by some multi-corp cross-pollination between a woman's glossy, a cosmetics corp and ABD Feminentals, always had to have the last word. Over the last six months I had come to learn that I would look much prettier if I

lost three pounds, that my pyjamas were dangerously unfash-
ionable, and if I wore heels I would achieve my ideal height,
calculated by my body-mass index, of five feet nine. She also
regularly suggested that I streak my dark bob to look more
'feminine' and warned that my fierce use of eyeliner might deter
men from approaching me.

The mirror was advising me that an ABC diet potion, available at a 50 per cent discount from my local chemist, would be
a wise purchase, when Kat entered the bathroom.

I wiped my hands, trying to hide my shame. Kat picked up
a toilet brush. I jumped as shatters jinked about our feet. Kat
smiled at me.

I smiled back.

'I've been wanting to do that for so long,' I said.

Nevertheless, I turned back to the mirror with a sense of melancholy, eyeing fragments of myself in the remaining splinters.
Kat looked like some rare orchid, too exquisite to touch; next to
her, I was a weed, thistled and ugly. I watched as Kat came up
behind me, circling her arms around my waist. I felt her laughter
warm and breathy in my ear. I saw my skirt scrunched up tight
in her fingers, slowly rising up my thighs; a detail I replayed and
savoured afterwards. That and her raucous joy when we fell
into the bath together, laughing and wiping wet hair from our
lips before we kissed again.

I woke up in the night with my father's voice telling me, *It's so
obvious*. I hesitated before getting out of bed, luxuriating in
the feel of her body next to mine. For a girl who liked to play
it cool, Kat was reassuringly clingy. One arm was curled over
me, splayed fingers fitting into the pauses of my ribcage and I
could feel the hedgehog bristle of her pubic hair scratching the
top of my thighs. Often I woke in the night at around three a.m.,

listening to the sound of loneliness: the silence with its broken edges of night-time noise. Tonight I felt smug and blessed to wake up lying in the warmth of a beautiful girl. I felt as though I would never suffer again. Immortal. Invincible. Inevitability: the feeling frightened me, felt too foreign, and I began to hunt around for doubts to destroy it. I wanted to slip back into sleep but now I had to get up. I had to prise Kat away from my body as I left the bed. She groaned; her eyelashes, thick as moth's wings, fluttered, and then she slept once more.

I went to the computer, hit Google and typed in: 'WSC'.

I should have done this twelve hours earlier. But when you're in a state of panic, the obvious is never obvious. I looked back at her sleeping shape, then with a shaking finger, I pressed enter.

328,999,875 results.

... the **WSC** – the only true and authentic Will Self Club in England ...

... **WSC** in Wisconsin for those over the age of sixty, feel free to knit while listening to a reading from *My Idea of Fun* ...

... the **WSC** should be closed down – please sign the petition to STOP more literary murders taking place ...

It made sense that a Will Self Club would exist today, given the proliferation of literary clubs springing up all over the country. I scribbled down the contact details for the UK branch, then burrowed back into bed, into the warm smell of her hair and skin.

The next morning Kat received a call from her yapping agent, informing her that she'd got the part. I recalled the audition, how ostentatiously she had flirted with the director – an adipose man with a thick beard – and smiled, no longer feeling jealous but slightly smug, as though he was the victim of a con trick we had enacted together. We ate breakfast while the news blared. Kat looked up, croissant fluffs on her lips, transfixed by an interview with the shadow home secretary. She'd mentioned yesterday that she was going to vote for the Blues in the next election, in the hope they might wrestle Parliament back from Labour Roots. Me, I couldn't give a shit. It's all a waste of time. We don't vote politicians in so that they might change policy, but to put them in the stocks. Politicians are fools who expect garlands around their necks but inevitably end up with tomatoes on their faces. And there are no greater wasters of words than politicians; I'm surprised the English language hasn't committed suicide from sheer despair. I pictured large rubbish vans rumbling through Parliament, gathering up word sewage at the end of the day, *A*s and *Z*s, spools of metaphor and undigested double-speak.

Hamster, the shadow home secretary, was a man I truly loathed, for he seemed to create more waste than any. Today, however, he seemed word-tied.

'What's your position on the refugee crisis following the flooding in Liverpool?'

'I . . . I . . .' Fear flashed in his eyes, like a child put on the spot by a teacher, struggling with his ABC.

'Maybe he's drunk,' Kat mused.

'I . . . I . . . I . . . I just can't think of . . .' he said.

The interviewer chided him: 'You seem to be lost for words.'

(iv) The WSC Initiation Ceremony

Kat had offered to drive me to meet the WSC. Her car was parked a few streets away; I did a double-take when I saw it was an old gas-guzzler. When I chided her, she laughed and declared she wouldn't change it even when the laws came in next month. Inside, there was a strange metallic smell of oil, and the engine rumbled like an old dog. She turned on the CDC player at full volume. We drove out of London and towards Surrey to the sound of the Bunny Stoppers, rainbow music that would be sad to listen to alone but together seemed cool and kitsch as we clicked our fingers and screeched out lyrics. Other people in other cars looked at us. Men honked their horns.

We were still in that honeymoon phase where we delighted in studying each other, learning new facts each day, piecing them together. Kat's favourite scent was lavender. She loved luxuriating in long baths. Her accent was expensive, but listen hard and you could detect the faintest West Country lilt from a childhood spent in Somerset. Kat hadn't spoken to her parents for the last ten years; they had committed some unforgivable sin she refused to discuss. She liked to use superlatives. She mixed quaintisms like 'peevish', as in, 'Come on, Mia, I can't cook, I shall break everything in your kitchen, don't be peevish with me,' with an excessive love for swearwords, especially the one beginning with *C*. If she didn't get her beauty sleep – nine hours every night – she became peevish. Her flat was in Camden but we were not allowed to visit for it was a complete 'cunt-hole', so we always stayed at mine and sat up in bed in the mornings, sharing a crossword, the Kindle propped up across her left knee and my right one, passing the stylus back and forth like a post-coital cigarette.

I'd told Kat that I was visiting the WSC to interview Aaron for an article I was working on. I felt as if my lie had put something between us, fine as tissue paper. I watched her snub profile, insolent as she rebelled against a slow-your-speed robot, and felt an ache inside: a desire to wrap my self up, with all its cracks and flaws, and give it to her with complete trust that she would not drop and smash me. 'Concentrate!' she snapped, as we realized that I had directed her down a wrong road. It's the little things that bring you back to reality. Our honeymoon had only lasted the past thirteen days. My father's voice invaded, irritating me with his wisdom, warning me that I should be cautious, learn her layers.

This was the home of the WSC: not the Gothic castle I had imagined, but a large detached house in Esher. We turned into the street as twilight fell, interiors becoming vulnerable with light, cosy vignettes of middle-class life. The garden was neat, with some carefully pruned palm trees, and the front door was made of oak with a diamond-shaped window filled with lattice. It opened to reveal a teenager dressed from head to foot in black, a winged mask pinned over his eyes. His acne rippled as his cheeks hollowed out a wolf-whistle.

'Hey, did we order strippers?'

Kat arched an eyebrow.

'Is Aaron there?' I asked.

Aaron looked like an American surf-boarder, all glittering teeth and sunshine-skin. He greeted me by shaking my hand; he lifted Kat's and bestowed a kiss on it. I told myself that it would be ridiculous to be jealous of a seventeen-year-old.

'So there's not really any girls allowed tonight, but we decided to let you in since you're gonna make us famous.' His accent was quasi-American too. I wondered if it was the result of genes or movies.

I asked him if, since he was wearing a Yale T-shirt, he had belonged to the Skull and Bones Society.

Aaron looked blank.

'Uh, no – the Will Self Club has been around way longer than that,' he said. 'I mean, it was this dude Jamie Curren who set it up in the 2000s but actually it was around way before him – he just, like, brought it back to life, man.'

'Jamie Curren?' I exclaimed, recalling the name from the manuscript.

'Yeah, we asked him to be our patron, but he told us to piss off. He said we couldn't revive the WSC, that we didn't have per-mission – but we were, like, "Like hell we do." What's he going to do, sue us? Anyway, come outside, stuff's about to hoot.'

As he turned, I saw that a logo was shorn into the back of his head. 'NIKE,' I read aloud.

Aaron, who had been guiding us through the kitchen to the back garden, turned, his smile sheepish. 'Product placement – it's paying for two terms at Imperial.'

Outside in the garden we found a gaggle of teenage boys, all wearing black jeans and masks, drinking beer, chatting, batting the neon balloons tied to rose bushes. We were introduced to Gavin (ADIDAS), Liam (PERSIL) and Henry (RED BULL).

'So, how does your WSC work?' I asked. 'Are you all big fans of Will's work?'

'Man, I've never read any of Will's shit. I'm just here to get pissed,' Henry asserted.

'He's going to be water-boarded later on,' Aaron said brightly. 'Hey, we're not beautiful, we're for real. We've *all* read Will. Sure we have. I mean, I thought the one about the Apes was kinda boring, I gave up at page fifty, but *My Idea of Fun* fucking rocks. The Fat Controller just freaked me out big-time – he's such an evil bastard, kind of worse than the Joker, even. I mean, Will Self wasn't like other writers who were just trying to be cool: he was a real cult writer. I mean, old people wouldn't really get him, but he still speaks to our generation.'

'And what does the Initiation Ceremony entail?' Kat asked, playing with the hem of her skirt in peek-a-boo pleats.

'Well, tonight we were hoping you might join the neophytes. We've got three coffins lined up and one of them is for you. You've got to lie in the coffin for, like, twenty minutes.'

'Mia will volunteer,' Kat said, turning pale. 'I suffer from claustrophobia.'

The coffins were lined up like props from a *Dracula* movie. They were all lined with red fur – a detail I found disturbing, as though I was about to be swallowed up by a scarlet beast. We – Henry, Mark and I – stood in front of them while the group voyeured behind us. Their testosterone jeers didn't bother me. This group had no relation to Will Self, just as most religious zealots embodied the faintest echoes of the religions that they fought wars for; Will, or God, was just the packaging, the slogan. It was Kat who filled me with anger. I gazed at her with eyes of betrayal but she glanced away, accepting a beer from Aaron with a coy smile.

My panic did not necessarily stem from claustrophobia, at first. When Aaron lowered the lid, the darkness bloomed into black-hole. But when I searched for consolation, pressing my palms against the sides, the tightness of space concentrated the dark, creating a sensation of being buried deep underground. My hysteria became an issue of scale. I grabbed a fierce hold of the scream before it could emerge from my lips and held it in the centre of my chest.

It was not memories of my father that finally released it. For I had been with my father when he died, had heard his last croaky 'I love you' as I held his hand and watched the light go out in his eyes. I had also been in the same room with my mother when she died twenty years ago, but on that occasion, my eyes had been sealed shut. I had heard her die over the course of twenty minutes, her screams crescendoing to soprano pain before ebbing to pianissimo whimpers. When, in the courtroom, the lawyer had asked me again and again if I had *seen* her die, as though my witness could be the only true confirmation of her death, his loquacious trickery planted doubt in my childhood mind. For years I would lie awake after my father had read me a bedtime story, wondering if she was lying awake in her coffin thinking of me, waiting for me to release her like a princess in a fairy tale. When my father took flowers to her grave, he caught me snarling my fingers into the earth, trying to uncover her, and wept angrily as he pulled me away.

'Hey, sorry, we didn't mean to scare you,' Aaron said.
We were sitting in the kitchen. I had a blanket around my

shoulders and a cup of tea in my hands. Behind Adam various sheepish, spotty boys were lingering by the Aga, hiding smirks and eyeing up Kat.

'She's fine,' Kat said, with a casual abruptness that irritated me as much as Adam's fawning. She drew the blanket from my shoulders; cold air attacked me. 'We have to go.'

'Um . . . you will still write cool things about us, won't you?' Adam asked.

'Sure.' I feigned a smile.

We left.

'You were close to your father,' Kat broke the silence on the way home.

'He's . . .' I had made a promise not to tell anyone, but if he could see how hard this was, to carry the weight of his letter alone . . . 'He's not the man I thought he was,' I said, waiting for her to unravel me.

Silence.

'Well, we never really know someone,' Kat said. 'It's just not possible.'

'I don't think that's true,' I said quickly. 'I think that, over time, and with intimacy, you can know the whole of someone.'

Kat shrugged.

I can't remember ever arguing with my father. Even when I was a teenager, when my father was my father, mother, fathermother, best friend, mentor, teacher – even then we didn't row. When I became a Goth, he remarked that black suited me; when I moped in my room reading Camus, he breezed in and initiated an existential discussion. We only ever really argued once, when I was twenty-five, about the differences between quiddity and haecceity, the whatness and thisness of a thing. He vehemently negated my argument that an object can have intrinsic *quid-dity* without *haecceity*. We didn't speak for two entire days. When my father finally called me to tell me he had no intention of apologizing or admitting he was wrong, I responded with a terse silence. Then we both burst into laughter: stalemate.

Why can't the relationships we form later in life match the simplicity of parental love? Those who discover us when our personalities have already started to find shape, to harden and set, never love us as sincerely; no wonder Oedipus and Electra became complexes.

I wanted to say to Kat, There's so many things you don't know about me. You don't know that I became an adult, at the age of eight, when a man broke into our house and murdered my mother. It was like losing my virginity. Everyone views sex as some sort of passage to adulthood, because it's so tangible – a physical act we can see and focus on. But, in reality, that transition from child to adult is something more subtle. I lost my emotional virginity that night – my sweetness. I was raped by life, too young, and left scarred. That's why I'm an atheist. People complain that God is a cruel deity who inflicts suffering on us, but that is still an opium, a prop, making us feel that our suffering somehow has a reason, a dark humour behind it – a *point*. In truth, I think it is all entirely random. And I wanted to tell Kat that, even though she was going to pull up outside my flats and I was going to slam the car door without saying good-bye and ignore her calls, I wouldn't be able to sleep one minute without her presence beside me.

In the bathroom, my hands flew over buttons. As her dress puddled around my feet, I noticed a shard of broken mirror lying behind the toilet plumbing. It was the length of a knife, decorated with spider's web shatters. I saw in my eyes the delicate see-saw between damnation and redemption that had been up-downing over the last few weeks. I put the mirror-knife into the cabinet and returned to my computer, where I sat, naked and still, for some time.

(v) In My Father's Office

My father's office was in Shoreditch. How I loathed the Pickwick Line: the platforms were solid blocks of human flesh. A cartoon in my paper this morning had joked 'LONDON: Population 15 million. By lunchtime: 16 million.' Three tubes had rollicked out of the station before the flow carried me on. In the carriage, the air was thick with sweat. A BBC robot read the news on a flickering screen; she was seated in a wheelchair, presumably for the satisfaction of the PC police rather than problems with poor wiring. 'Scientists are warning that today's increase in temperature indicates the start of a tropicsmog – the third this year,' she announced, provoking frowns and groans throughout the carriage. My eyes flitted over the passengers. Mostly commuters and kids, walking adverts wrapped about pre-pubescent bodies. Shorn heads; tattoos; pimples prickling through logos. One girl chewed gum, her jaw ripples fluctuating NIKE to NICG; her chest was barely an A cup but her T-shirt offered helpful numbers for the nearest enhancement clinic. When she saw me looking, she scowled and folded her arms. Then escalators, walls of moving colour, BUY RED BULL WATCH ABC EAT PEANUTS, barriers, sky, clouds, brick, litter, pigeons, traffic, lights, screaming, brakes, honking, keys, door slamming: here.

His office was a shrine. Before I entered, my Hollywood-tainted imagination had envisaged a smashed computer screen, splayed books, the floor carpeted in glass, the computer chair disembowelled. But everything was as it should be, still and neat. Even the simple objects on his desk – stapler, hole-punch, scissors – were arranged with a pleasing sense of order. Noises were pastel: hums and echoes. I felt guilty, disturbing his universe. As I shifted through drawers, I felt as though I was slowly prising nails from a coffin lid.

Will Self's father emigrated at the end of the 1970s, when Will was studying at Oxford. For the next twenty years, they saw very little of each other. Will observed, 'I had a thorny relationship with him. It improved dramatically when he died.' Will had felt able to chat with him in a way that he hadn't before, especially now that his father could no longer answer back and Will could script his replies. I remember once taking solace in this anecdote. Now I sat in my father's office and mused that I did not know his shoe size. Whether he had secretly had a lover before he died. Why he feared the WSC. His voice, so clear in my head for the last few weeks, was now scratched by interference, whispers of doubt and confusion.

I picked up his headset and delicately drew it over my ears, the dial tone like a shush caught in a shell. It felt almost blasphemous to break it with a new voice.

I called Justin Williams, his old colleague.

No, he said, my father had not requested that he send a package to me before he died. He missed him, he added.

I searched on his Toshiba for a version of Richard's diary. I found nothing. Then I came across a surprise. I had often suggested to my father that he ought to write a novel, but he'd always laughed, shaken his head and said that after reading Will he felt like Verrocchio eyeing up Leonardo's angel and declaring he would never paint again. On his hard-drive, however, I discovered a novel-in-progress entitled *The Quiddity of Will Self*. There was even an accompanying file with a list of agents and a query letter without a date. The novel was just ten chapters long, with a ragged outline for a few more. The opening began: *It was quite by accident that I discovered the body of Will Self. I had recently moved into a block of flats in Primrose Hill. They were plush, with white carpets, chandeliers in every hallway and a guard slumped by the door who never raised his eyes from the* Daily Mail. I felt tears of relief slip down my cheeks and wet my smile. Surely Richard's diary was an invention, something my father had created as background inspiration for his novel. Then, as I wiped my eyes, I mused on a more worrying possibility. Perhaps Richard's diary was fact that my father had been turning into fiction. The accompanying newspaper articles he had attached to his letter were real; I had checked them out. I still had more research to do on Professor Self but I'd discovered reports from 2007 detailing how he had been struck off by the British Medical Council for using the New Deal scheme as a cover for illicit experiments on his subjects. Was that why my father had felt he was in danger? Perhaps Prof. Self's relatives had heard of his novel and were trying to repress the fictionalization of his life. I flipped through the novel again, rereading the distasteful orgy scene at the end. I had reviewed enough books to realize that writers regularly produce works that transcend their lives, but even so, I was still shocked: had my father's sickness poisoned his imagination?

I ached to call Kat and tell her everything. But we were playing a waiting game. Three days and neither of us had called.

I clicked Internet Explorer. He was on AOL and the password was already saved as *********. A voice sang out, 'You've got mail.' I clicked on his mail. Forty new messages. I deleted thirty-six spam. That left:

j.curren@hotmail.com	**In response to your enquiry**
amanda.ake154@yahoo.co.uk	**Cleaning bill**
j.curren@hotmail.com	**Cancellation of visit**
orders@amazon.co.uk	**Receipt for your order 1665144**

I began with the emails from Curren:

Re: In response to your enquiry

Dear Mr Barnes,

I would be glad to assist you in your thesis exploring novels of the 2009 era. My telephone number is 0311357 668213. I am available most afternoons, except on Thursday when I play bridge.

Yours,

Jamie Curren

The next:

Cancellation of visit

Dear Mr Barnes,

When you mentioned that you were writing a thesis, I was quite unaware that you were focusing exclusively on the novels of Will Self. I am afraid that I find myself unable to agree to your request or help you in any way. Please do not contact me again.

I looked in my father's 'Sent' folder but found it empty.

I checked the other emails. I scribbled down the cleaner's name, Amanda Ake, for she still needed to be paid. My father's Amazon order was for a book called *A History of the Golden Dawn*. Then I pulled on the headset again and voiced Jamie's number. It rang about eight times. A female voice trilled, 'Curren Place, Mr Curren's residence, how can I help you?' I panicked and pulled off the headset. I sat still for several minutes, musing on a puzzle-lie I might construct, turning over pieces in my mind. The surname I used as a reviewer and journalist was different from my birthname; I had chosen Brewster, after the heroine in Alice Clay's 2036 Man Booker winner *Temptations of Dust*. I could call Jamie, request an interview; I could tell him I was writing a feature about forgotten novelists of the 2000 decade. I would return home and prepare.

Back home. For the first time in months, the voice recognition system failed when I unlocked the door. I stood in the hallway, listening to the strange richness of silence and the subtleties around its edges: a scratch on the skirting-board, a violin playing below, a couple rowing above. My sudden conscious-ness of the overlap of human lives was comforting. Then I saw that my answerphone was empty.

I swapped trainers for slippers, pulled my hair into a ponytail. In the kitchen, I found some smoked salmon in the fridge – but I'd been saving that for Kat. I stood by the window, eating cold baked beans from a tin; they swam on the surface of my stom-ach. Below on the pavement, a troop of protesting Ecos was waving placards: *If we do not stop sinning the floods will not stop coming*. My melancholy seemed like a taunt: it asserted that my happiness with Kat had been undeserved, an anomaly in my emotional landscape. I wondered if time ever did heal wounds, or just slowed the bleeding. I thought of all the things I could have done. I could have persuaded him to stop smoking ten years ago, instead of teasing him for his bad habits. I could have dated Ciaran, kept him happy, fabricated an engagement. I could have force-fed him greens instead of indulging his love of fatty foods. I could have sent him to bed early instead of joining in those late nights in the library. I stared at the window until the light blurred, whispering, 'Sorry,' over and over.

(vi) Lime 42

Am I the first person to wonder if there is something suspicious about the death of Will Self? Two years ago, the newspapers were filled with obituaries all bleating the coroner's report: Will had died of a heart attack. But take a look at Will's last reading, one of the most popular literary videos on YouTube. He sits in the Royal Festival Hall, his hands like branches, whorled and spotted with rings of a life well lived, curled around a copy of *Drug Lime.* His last piece of work: a novel about a drug that becomes addicted to a human being. He tells the audience that he was inspired by a saying of William Burroughs that smack is the only commodity you don't have to sell to people; you sell people to it. The drug he writes about has a genetically engineered component that causes it to feel. It becomes attached to a specific soul, but with painful inevitability, it can only express its love through self-destruction, wooing her through headaches, mood swings and, finally, a liver so sopped with it that it heaves one last purple breath and dies. The drug is called Lime 42.

From early on in his career, Self understood instinctively that his particular brand of grotesque would win him as many critics as worshippers, declaring that it was not his job to worry about being liked. Reviews for his books were pendulum, summed up by the *NY Times* as 'the usual iconoclast's reward of rabid denunciations and hyperbolic praise'. It also meant that Self failed to win as many prizes as he deserved. His first publication, *The Quantity Theory of Insanity*, grabbed the Geoffrey Faber Memorial prize, but after a promising start, nominations were thin and far between – a nomination for the Whitbread for *How the Dead Live*, a Booker long-listing for *Dorian* and the P. G. Wodehouse Bollinger award for *The Butt*. The fizz and fun of Bollinger, compounded with the gallivanting of Bertie and Jeeves, seem light-laughs away from the savagery of Self's satire on the Iraq war. One chortles at Wodehouse; the laughter that Self provokes is uncomfortable, seat-squirming. Grotesque is a double-sided coin, both serious and comic, yet its comic head shines more brightly than its serious side. And so satire continues in its literary tradition of being undervalued – just as *Gulliver's Travels* was originally published as a children's novel.

Drug Lime finally won Will the Booker at the ripe old age of eighty-two, so late as to be virtually posthumous. The congratulatory speech by the chair of judges sounded too close to an obituary and Will had to be assisted on to the stage to receive it. The audience braced themselves, as though wondering whether a writer who had once condemned the Booker for its celebration of the most conventional fiction around, who had taken such glee in being an outsider, could really accept it. Nobody would have been surprised if he had wept, sworn, flung the statue across the room, torn up the cheque with a cackle, laid out a line of coke and snorted it from the lectern. Instead – ever unpredictable – he said a sweet, gruff thank-you.

In the YouTube video of his final reading, Will is eighty-four years old. His voice is still the strong baritone of a practised public speaker, punctuated with stertorous coughs. By his chair is a walking stick, its knobble the leering head of an ape. His audience is huge; the pan of the mobile camera shows that every seat in the house is taken. Will holds them in his palm, tickling laughter, stroking adoration. Then his hand curls into a fist, squeezing a collective panic. Will's coughing devours his reading.

His final words are: 'She was attempting to resist the suburbanization of the soul–'

The walking stick rolls over the stage and over and over the floor and comes to rest.

Before Will is obscured by feet and backs and hands, I see something odd. Not the grey-black mist that unfurls from his mouth and shimmers into the shadows (I have already checked out various chatrooms and news reports which warn that it is superimposed). But something red that falls from his jacket pocket and rolls across the floor. A lighter? A pen?

The YouTube video cuts off. A black screen comes up, with white lettering: *There aren't any 'people in charge of death'. When you die you move to another part of London, that's all there is to it.*

I recognized the quote. It came from *How the Dead Live,* Will's 2000 novel narrated by an elderly Jewish woman called Lily Bloom, who dies of cancer but lives on in necropolitan Dulston, home to an animated spirit community.

The following day, I watched the video once more, but the small red detail still remained a mystery. With a thunder of impulsive courage, I put on my headset and called Jamie Curren.

I was surprised by how smoothly the conversation went. He was very receptive when I told him that I was writing a piece for the *Guardian* on forgotten authors who deserved to be put back into print. I etched hard doodles of excitement on my phone pad as he agreed to meet me in two days' time at his house in Buckinghamshire, Curren Place. After I'd pulled off my headset, I walked around in circles, grinning, feeling a tangible sense of my father's pride. Then I walked into the bathroom. There were a few drops of Kat's dried urine on the seat, a pubic hair in the shape of a question mark. I had taken to using the small toilet in the hallway, leaving the bathroom intact, as though I'd been bereaved twice over. I could not bear looking into the remaining shard of mirror still attached to the wall, for it now stored memory, perpetually reflecting the first-time raw of our lovemaking. The other shard, in the shape of a knife, remained locked in the cabinet.

I went back to the lounge to check my email once again.

There was nothing from Kat.

But there was a new email from Will Self.

(vii) The Email

The subject line simply said: *WARNING FROM THE WSC*
The message read:

The cut-up approach to murder. Print the page out and scis-
sor into lengths. Pick which way you would prefer to die.

1. 'haemorrhage on the green', *Great Apes*, p.163
2. 'razor blade', *My Idea of Fun*, p. 261
3. 'you are what you eat', *Feeding Frenzy*, Introduction, *vi*
4. 'bloodshot', *My Idea of Fun*, p. 278
5. 'even if you lie in a darkened room and contemplate,
    coolly and rationally, all the awful possibilities that may
    very well be in store for you – and you alone', *My Idea
    of Fun*, p. 278

I found myself grabbing the headset and calling Kat. Tears
lacerated my voice as I explained that I had inherited a curse
from my mother: that my life was destined to be torn from me by
another. She told me that I should stay calm, that she would be
right over.

I paced and shredded my nails with my teeth while Kat read

the manuscript. Even in the space of a week, I'd forgotten how beautiful she was. How lovely that little pleat above her nose was when she frowned.

When she had finished, she insisted that we call the police.

I loved her for her brisk decisiveness, even as she broke my heart: the manuscript could not possibly have been written by my father. After all, the very first email that Will had sent me had asked if I had received the package, suggesting that some sick weirdo had written and posted it himself.

'And look at this line.' Kat tapped the second page of Richard's diary. 'Richard says he's not even allowed to have a CDC player in his room – CDC players didn't exist in 2006!'

Reality came as a shock. I realized that I had spent the last few weeks in a state of mild insanity, ignoring reason and believing in the warped arguments of superstition; then, as I wept in her arms, how much I'd wanted it to be true.

999 felt too dramatic, so we tried the local police station first. There were no policepeople available, so we spoke to a Morality and Support Officer from Latvia, who appeared to have no knowledge of English. After five frustrating minutes, we gave up.

'Did your dad have any enemies?' Kat asked.

'No, he was the nicest man you'd ever meet. It was impossible not to like him.'

'So ... someone was jealous of him, and that made them peevish – so now they're attacking you.' Kat went to the window, gazing out on the city-web. I could tell what she was thinking: Somewhere out there, right now, this sicko is sleeping, eating, or preparing to enact his threats. I sat down, cloudy with fear. When my mother's killer had walked free, he had haunted my teenage dreams as a shadow who climbed in through my bedroom window. Now he seemed to coalesce with my present threat into a shadow of darker intensity.

'What happened to her?' Kat asked.

I shook my head, the words buried too deep inside.

'Write it down,' she suggested.

But my pen was spineless. I was too afraid of giving into sensationalism; but it felt impossible to sculpt sentences with journalistic detachment.

Kat came over to me and held me tight and said, 'I've missed you so much in the last few days.'

'I thought you might be out clubbing again, picking up that Asian guy.' When I saw the hurt in her eyes, I regretted the barb and pulled her in close.

I loved the disembodied beauty of her voice in the darkness. It was so hot that we'd had to open the window and the sheets were coiled around our feet, a film of shared sweat at our hips and hands. I was tired but I wanted to stay awake all night talking to her. My heart felt weighted with euphoria and despair, knowing that if we ever broke up, this was a night I would treasure, always. She told me that she wouldn't ever let the sicko hurt me. She confided secrets she'd never told anybody before. How she had first loved a girl at sixteen. One night at a 'sleepover' her mother – a devout Christian – had caught them kissing. She had sent the friend away and Kat had stood in the kitchen, crying under her mother's glare. Her friend asked her to run away but on the agreed night Kat had sat on her bed, her rucksack in her wardrobe, her chin on her knees, watching the clock steal time away: a night she had regretted ever since. I said I felt jealous of the girl, but I also loved her because the snakes and ladders of destiny had brought Kat from her to me. She turned and pressed her mouth against mine. I cupped her breasts and heard her groan reverberate through my throat. We made love with a deep intensity, rubbing skin raw, tasting, aching, flowers of desire opening and dying in the darkness.

(viii) Word Roots

If there's a bitter lesson that I learnt from the death of my mother, it's this: you should never underestimate the power of having a good handicap in the sport of words. Society, you see, isn't just about those who have money and those who don't, those who speak with plums in their mouth and those who can't afford expensive fruit, those with good looks and those who lack them. There are those who can control words and those who are victims of them. When does an MP, who coils propaganda around himself as he justifies the deaths of thousands bombed in a war, ever suffer a jail sentence? The yob on the street, whose vocabulary is limited to stunted messaging with shades of Jamaican thrown in (though he may never have visited Jamaica in his life), will find that that his blag in the courtroom has not appealed to his jury, who speak another language of a different class, and therefore condemn him with *a sentence*. The rich, meanwhile, can buy words at a premium rate, a wigged man with initials tap-dancing after his name, a man who knows how to set words before his accused like booby traps.

In a courtroom, a child of nine can stand up and say, 'The man came into our house and I saw him do it – well, I *heard* him do it.'

But the free flow of truth must be dammed up. The lawyer sees to that quickly. The child is only allowed to answer his crafted questions with a *yes* or a *no*. Her heart beats; her palms sweat. If she tries to describe what happened, he says, 'I'm asking you to give a yes or a no answer.' Until finally she is wordless, even when her own lawyer questions her, cajoles her desperately, and for some time afterwards, when the man is freed and she lies awake every night, terrified that he might do to her what he did to her mother, she finds herself unable to speak at all. Her vocabulary expands despite her silence. She learns the meaning of the word *rape* before the meaning of the word *sex*, and *murder* loses its Sherlock connotations and becomes visceral. Only the love of a father saves her.

As an angry teenager, I needed the universe to explain my injustice. I spent weekends and evenings in the local library, searching for answers in the Bible, self-help, Buddhism. In the beginning was the Word, said the Bible. Shuffle words around like playing cards, said Self-help books: is the glass half empty or half full? Go beyond words, said Buddhism: transcend. I began to wonder if the written word could be trusted; with adolescent naïvety I became convinced it was my duty to breathe truth into it. I became fixated on the idea of working on a national newspaper. I thought journalism was superior to fiction, for the precise, indifferent way in which reporters captured daily events. I didn't consider that most articles are subjectivity dressed up as objectivity, or that the very choice of a story is the beginning of bias. Later, when I discovered the novelist Alice Clay, I realized that fiction, though an art of lying, could tell greater truths. And so I gave up working at my local paper and became a reviewer. Now, with the bite of recession, I was forced to add another square to my patchwork of professions. As well as reviewing and the *OED*, I agreed to teach a class once a fortnight at the local primary in Muswell Hill.

In theory, it was a lexicographer's dream. Recent scientific research pointed to a bizarre phenomenon afflicting school-kids. The average kid leaving primary in 2037 had a vocabulary of roughly ten thousand words; just over a decade on, the figure had shrunk by 45 per cent. Various educational psychologists blamed the decline of reading, the Internet and texting. I was being employed to help them become, if not sesquipedalians, then savourers of the spices of language. At least it would help me to forget the Will Self emails. Back home, I had taken to checking my email every five minutes, my stomach breeding butterflies every time I saw an addition to my inbox.

I entered to find a zoo of eleven-year-olds rejecting their medi-cine. Pills were dancing on lolling tongues; pills were being flicked through the air; pills were turning into pink aeroplanes, ping-pong- and footballs. Over the last fifty years, the pharma-ceutical companies have realized there is money to be made from the rearrangement of words. Perhaps they are running out of new diseases; perhaps they have realized we are tiring of different species of bestial flu. Once upon a time, children were naughty kids, a disease cured by a cuff and the cane; then they developed neuroses and Attention Deficiency Disorder; now they collectively suffer from YPVB, which, of course, can only be cured by ABC, the largest drug corp in the world. So they are given pills. Pills the size and colour of a child's fingernail.

The teacher, Emily, screamed at them with a hoarse voice. They settled down; pink disappeared into tummies and a slightly glazed look came over their faces.

'I think I prefer them rowdy to zombies,' I said to Emily.

'God, yeah.' She didn't sound convinced.

She ran her fingers through her hair and said brightly, 'I need a coffee. So I'll come and check on you at half-time – about half eleven, OK?'

'Great,' I said, knowing I wouldn't see her for another hour.

I faced the class and paused awkwardly. A strange sense of shame came over me, standing there with the echo of Kat's hands on my body, her fluids still sticky beneath my clothes, before children too innocent to understand a kiss. Normally children sniff out teacherly weakness and turn it into a toy to play with. But they remained sedate, staring at me curiously.

'Miss – Miss!' Anessa, who was sitting at the front of the class, waved her hand. 'I've found a word I don't know!'

I stared into Anessa's pencil-case and saw a pink pill glistening between a pencil-sharpener and a rabbit-shaped eraser. 'That's great, Anessa,' I said. 'Now, can you pass around the Kindles and then I'd like us all to draw a word tree.'

The word Anessa chose was *Will*. I concealed my surprise at the coincidence and scrolled through my *OED* with my stylus. Definitions I had helped to compose snagged my eyes with pride. I typed on the class keyboard and *Will* flashed up on the board-screen.

'Anyone know where *Will* comes from?'

Glazed eyes. A faint line of drool spooled from Jon's lips.

'Okay, Anessa,' I relented at last.

> WILL
> *Willen* (Old English)
> *Velle* (Latin; to wish for)
> Use the verb to express

(i) desire

(ii) habituation

(iii) expectation

As the kids copied out the word tree, I played with my Kindle, but I found it happening again, as I had this morning on the tube on the way to the school: fear becoming quicksand – *Even if you lie in a darkened room and contemplate, coolly and rationally, all the awful possibilities that may very well be in store for you – and you alone . . .*

'So,' I said briskly, 'do you have any other words?'

Even Anessa didn't bother to volunteer this time.

'Okay, I think it's time to finish up. Put your Kindles away now.'

Where now? I pictured myself returning to the flat, the voice recognition cheerfully raising concerns about the likelihood of dehydration in the current tropicsmog. I could imagine it advising me to drink three glasses of water even as someone plunged a knife into my back; and the flow of blood across the floor would no doubt trigger liquid sensors and a voice advising me to mop up. What a way to go. Then I heard Kat's voice in my head: *Don't be silly, Mia, you're not going to die.* Kat had suggested she turn down her filming and stay behind as my bodyguard, but I had insisted she go. I padded across the school playground. The heat blurred line and colour, ground and sky. Trees' branches sagged; the netball nets in the courts hung their heads. I realized that a part of me resented Kat for asserting that the letter was a fake. In the maze of my grief, my father's instructions had been a ball of thread I could follow like a fumbling Theseus, a comfort constantly trickling through my fingers.

I sat on a bench at the local tube station and read through my father's letter once more. That line again: *I know that you always teased me for being your potty old dad with his eccentricities.* Who else in the year 2049 would even know the original meaning of the word *potty*? I was becoming more and more convinced that he was the author of the letter and the diary. As well as the contemporary CDC reference that didn't fit with an author alive in 2006, I sensed my father's sneer behind the writing, his disdain for writers seeking celebrity. My counter-argument gained fire in my mind: You see, Kat, maybe I read his letter with the wrong slant, first time round; I saw desperation when I should have acknowledged a strain of madness. His chemo had a strange effect on him: he complained of nausea, mood swings, which accounts for the crazed writing. Yet I can see method in his madness; I can sense his soul between the sentences. I had to admit there were still details that niggled: why had my father written two manuscripts about Richard, a novel of ten chapters, besides the diary? Two parts of his book, or two literary test-runs? Or the work of two authors? And I was still puzzled by the mysterious footnotes. But I did not believe they were the work of a stranger.

Tubes inhaled and exhaled people as I read through the manuscript again, persuading doubt into conviction. Once more, I read Richard's final lines:

I have gone to the place I ache to be. I have gone to the Phantasmagoria: find me there.

(ix) The Phantasmagoria

The Metropolitan Museum was cool and sober as a church. I paid twenty euros for entrance to the autumn exhibition: The Phantasmagoria. In the hushed darkness, we sat on small black benches, faces tipped to the screen. Classical music started up: 'The Dance of the Sugar Plum Fairy', its childish pirouette across the glockenspiel suitably eerie. Even I, the ardent atheist, felt a little nervous. Then sound effects, as though from a bad horror movie. Creaking doors and floorboards. Smoke puffed from a machine, coloured with a greenish glow. The audience jumped and let out an appreciative gasp that escalated to *oohs* as a ghoul flashed on the wall. Like children enchanted by shadow puppets, I thought, though I had to admit that this was far more chilling than the slick scares of CGI or virtual reality. Spirits and shadows formed a merry-go-round beyond the smoke. And then I saw him.

I let out a cry, picked up my bag and fled from the room.

I twisted my key into the lock of my flat. I paused. Sweat trembled on my brow. I turned the key. I stepped into the hallway a moment before the lights and voice recognition flicked on;

shadows blended confusion and I took a step backwards. Then, bright, harsh illumination and a suggestion that I ought to take a shower. In the kitchen, I pulled an iced tea from the fridge, pressing the cold bottle against my scarlet cheek, exhaling a shaky hole in the label's dewy veil. I called Kat. Voicemail. I tried once again. Voicemail.

I felt angry at my paranoia, my petty jealousy, and shouted at it to go. I recalled her tenderness when I had shown her the Will Self emails, the fierceness in her voice when she had declared she would kill anyone who tried to hurt me. I smiled and thought, I will tell her about my new theory on the letter, and we'll laugh over it together, and then everything will be all right.

When Kat did not answer, I broke inside. It took me by surprise, this horribly familiar sensation that had not possessed me since I was a teenager. It stirred me to walk to the bathroom cabinet; it picked up the shard of mirror; it sat me down on the edge of the bath. I thought of Kat pouting before a camera, the director whisking her away for drinks. I thought of my father's empty grave, where everyone's flowers had already shrivelled before I had laid fresh ones. The heat inside me became volcanic; it pounded through my veins, blistered my forehead and before the – *cut* – across my arm the pleasure was so intense it was almost sexual. As metal opened skin I heard myself gasp. The sensation of relief was euphoric; the droplets of blood hitting the bath like a prelude to a hymn. Then I became body again. I told myself that I'd needed to do this to reconnect with the physical world. But then I was too much body, a vessel sticky with sweat and congealing blood, disgusted by its own stench. I took a shower, cleaned the mirror-shard, and went to bed.

I felt like the wind, competing against light, burrowing into things, searching for the soul of objects. I stared down at my body, sprawled across a floor, the knife thrust into my back up to the hilt, blood encountering furniture. My father was a shadow on the wall and I leapt into the plaster to dance with him. We whirled into one current and let it carry us home. We awoke in a garden, bluebells caressing our cheeks, and walked hand in hand while the sunlight played on our tears. The long grass whispered against our legs and the flowers smiled at the bees, and in the distance there was the sound of children playing hide and seek in the woods. My father turned to me and said, *Don't go, Mia, please don't go.*

As I woke up, I became aware of the dull throb in my arm – *Why did you do that again, after all these years?* My body was slimy with heat. Then I saw the green digits of the clock: four a.m., and Kat's side of the bed still empty.

(x) Jamie

Paddington Station was panting. If its namesake bear had been around in 2049, his creator would definitely have forsaken that mackintosh and sketched him naked with a predilection for marmalade-flavoured ice cream. Sun lasered through the glass; dust glittered; every surface was a mirror. The Spanish refugee influx was starting to influence our dress code, men mixing suits with shades and sombreros. Half the crowds were slick with sweat but had umbrellas hooked over their wrists, knowing how the tropicsmog, having set new records, would surely break within hours. I finally jostled on to the train, but had to stand all the way, watching the fast-forward film of greenery through the window.

I felt as though I had been holding my breath for days and finally I could exhale; I relished the long journey ahead, the intimacy of being able to chatter away to myself in my head. Kat was completing her filming today. Since I'd slashed my skin, I'd felt as though I'd cut all the fine threads connecting me to the world. She had handcuffed my wrist in her fingers and frowned; I had yanked it away and repeated the same line that, as a teenager, I'd tell my father – 'I had an accident chopping up the veg.' Kat had been loving at first, apologizing for the late nights filming, surprising me with tender touches: breakfast in bed, a first edition of an Alice Clay novel she had found in the South Bank market. But this morning we had breakfasted in silence, eyes glued to Kindles. She had walked out leaving her trash on the table, knowing how I hated to clear up after her. I had shaken a fist at the slammed door, thrown her plates into the sink. A part of me ached to tell her about meeting Jamie. But I knew she would only berate me. I'd left her a note saying I was out at the dentist. My mission now felt like a secret between me and my father in which Kat could only ever be an outsider.

I took a mini-cab to Curren Place. I didn't even need to play detective. The driver merrily supplied anecdotes about how 'stuck-up-himself' Jamie was. Apparently he had refused to help fund the local 'Save Our Yurt' campaign, which had led to it being pulled down in favour of a new Tesco, and never bothered to grace the community with his presence but remained behind his railings, strutting round 'his grounds'. I had to admit that Jamie's pad was impressive. A stately home indeed. The guard at the gates immediately told us to leave. When I assured him I had an appointment with Jamie, he demanded my ID card. Finally he called Jamie, then informed the driver that his cab was not allowed into the grounds, but that I had permission to walk down the gravel drive.

'See what I mean?' The cabbie rolled his eyes at me.

Gravel rolled beneath my trainers. Trees arched overhead, forming a dense tunnel of dappled light. From a distance, they had looked like birds squatting on branches but now I realized they were cameras. My pace slowed uneasily as I counted as many as nine or ten in the space of just a few feet, their digital faces framed with shaggy green leaf-hair. When I glanced over at the stately home, the piercing sunlight turned the windows into tinted eyes. Memory cleaved open: '*When I saw the house, it took my breath away. House was an understatement; it was a mansion. Perched on a sweep of green hill, it looked as though it had been cut out of a Gothic ghost story, spires piercing the twilight clouds.*' I stood still. My father had described this very house in chapter three of his novel: the place that Richard had driven to for a WSC party. My father had called it Rothwell Towers; Jamie had called it Curren Place, but it was, without a doubt, the same building. My heartbeat began to flurry. Had Jamie finally agreed to meet my father in the weeks before he went into hospital — or had he broken in and investigated for himself?

I heard the clink of chains and turned to see the guard locking the gates behind me.

A lion, liver-spotted by the decades, held a knocker in its jaws. I heard Kat's voice warning me to go back. I realized how fragile I had become from lack of sleep and proper food; a prickling heat came over me, reminiscent of the sensation that had gripped me when I had threatened my skin with the knife. But I forced myself on, knowing that I could not let my father down, that I had to see this through to the bitter end. My hand rose, gripped the knocker and banged it hard. I held on to a stone pillar, trembling. When the housekeeper opened the door, her normality reassured me and I found myself gushing hellos in relief. Inside, the stone created a dusty coolness and we strolled down corridors grave with history, tapestries and paintings, a knight in shining armour.

She showed me into a large drawing room. It was abundant in antique elegance: shaggy rugs and blotted mirrors, a *chaise-longue* and embroidered cushions. A dog lay with mournful eyes, his tail a bored metronome on the rug. Elegant curtains, the shade of a willow, fluttered around the open french windows. I spotted the elderly man in the garden, pruning a bush of tea roses. He was wearing an open-necked shirt and his white hair was swept back from an aristocratic bronzed face. As I stepped out on to the patio, the sun dazzled my eyes and I shielded my face as he looked me up and down.

'Hi. Mia.' He must have been in his seventies, but his voice was that of a much younger man.

I watched as he discovered a worm wriggling towards his Hush Puppies. Picking it up with disdainful fingers, he clipped open his secateurs and chopped it into two.

'Worms are terribly good for the soil, you know,' I said. 'Darwin studied them for forty years and came to the conclusion that life on earth was impossible without them.'

I had intended the remark lightly, but Jamie looked affronted. He wiped his hands and gestured for me to follow him back inside, taking his throne on a large green chair, proffering me a lower, straw chair.

I attempted apology with a warm smile. The faint sneer of reply on his face made me wish I had brought Kat. Then my ego fought back and reassured me that he was just an arrogant old man.

As I sat down, I noticed that the coffee table next to him was decorated with a board game.

Jamie rang the bell and a slender Spanish girl appeared. Her dark hair, dark eyes, provoked an automatic sense of pity. I superimposed images across her face, cut and pasted from the media, of melting houses and streets baked to dust, of withered red bodies lying on pavements.

'What would you like?'

'Tea would be nice,' I said. 'Earl Grey.'

'Tea for Miss Mia,' Jamie said. Then he curled his hand, dismissing her. 'Well, now. Before you came, I was just listening to Radio Four and there was a *hilarious* news bulletin about how half the shadow cabinet have come down with a particularly unique dose of laryngitis. Apparently they're using it to explain why they've spent the last week stuttering their way through Prime Minister's Questions. At times like this, I feel rather glad to be a supporter of Labour Roots.'

'Oh – yes, I saw something about that.' I feigned interest. 'It's nice to see a politician lost for words for a change.'

Jamie smiled and I felt relieved. I was here, he was human and the interview was proceeding. I felt shades of my former strength returning; I told myself that I could pull this off.

My eyes set upon the board game.

'Cluedo,' Jamie remarked. 'Do you play?'

'I've never heard of it,' I lied.

'It was popular many years ago.'

'It sounds interesting. Of course, the etymology of the word "clue" is a fascinating one. It was originally *clew* – a ball of thread, referring to the one Theseus used to guide himself out of the labyrinth.' I trailed off as Jamie's lips winced with boredom. Right, I thought, no more Miss Nice Mia. Time for business. 'Mr Curren, I hope you don't mind me coming to interview you – but I was intrigued to come across your books recently and I feel you are clearly one of our great forgotten authors.'

'Have you read them, then?' Jamie asked.

'Read' was the wrong verb. At least his début, *Pus*, had been entertaining; the second had been like taking an ABC cure for insomnia.

'I particularly enjoyed the novella about the elderly man who stays on an island writing a biography of Wagner and goes out and shags a sheep. I found it quite cavey.' The adjective had only entered the *OED* last week (roots: *cava*, the Latin for *beware*; contemporary meaning: 'I'd rather not to touch it with a fucking barge-pole') and I felt certain he would be unaware of it, but his expression did not flicker.

'It was inspired by Beckett. He was one of the great twentieth-century writers, you know.'

'Really?' I asked, but he didn't seem to detect my sarcasm.

'Yes – he was a famous Irish writer, penned a play called *Waiting for Godot*. He was a key writer in what Martin Esslin termed "the theatre of the absurd". You ought to look him up.'

'I'll write down his name.' I forced a smile. 'And your sister, Zara' – aha, now I had a reaction from him – 'I've read her collection of short stories, *Bombay Mix*. I found them quite beautiful in the traditional sense of the word,' I said truthfully.

'Zara . . . She passed away a few years ago.' He blinked hard, his palm curling around his chair.

'I'm sorry,' I said quickly. 'I'm sorry. I just lost my father – I know how you feel.'

Jamie didn't mirror my consolation; he wiped his eyes shakily. I bit my lip.

'Were you close?'

'Very. We all used to be in a little clique together.' His voice willowed with nostalgia. 'There was me . . . Nicholas . . . Toady . . . Zara . . . Richard.'

'Richard?' I asked, without thinking. Then, seeing him stir, I added a jolly laugh. 'Toady – that's quite a peculiar name, isn't it?'

'There's a children's book called *The Wind in the Willows*. I suspect that nobody in your generation would have heard of it.'

'No – my father used to read–'

'And so Toady was named after the endearingly scatty and ebullient Toad of Toad Hall. He wrote a misery memoir – you see, back in our day, there was a vogue for horrific stories of children growing up scarred by cruel, abusive parents. Unfortunately Toady's parents had always been the most charming of people and ended up taking him to court.'

'So you were all writers?'

'Well – all except Richard. He was hoping . . . but the dear boy never quite had it in him. He was arrested for murder in the end.' Jamie smiled, showing an array of dazzling teeth. 'We were quite a wild bunch, always in trouble with the law.'

'But murder . . . That's more than a little wild.'

'Well, he pleaded not guilty, of course. He claimed he was set up. But the murder weapon was found in his flat.' Jamie gazed down at the game of Cluedo and picked up a small silver knife, caressing its tip. 'Once you have the weapon and the place, it's not too hard to guess the name in the envelope. I did my best to help him, of course. I lobbied for him to be part of a scheme called the New Deal . . . well, some such nonsense, in which he could sit in a tower block, writing a novel as part of his sentence. I also tried to assist in helping him get the book deal he had always wanted. But sadly, for all his notoriety, it just wasn't good enough to be published. It was a great shame.' A smile tickled his lips. 'Of course, once he had died, the manuscript became publishable – the quality no longer mattered. Archie West was all ready to sell it.'

I recalled the article my father had sent me about Richard's death. What had Archie said? Something along the lines of 'Richard Smith may be a murderer, but that does not mean to say that his writing is not of great value to the general public.'

'I met Archie in the Groucho that night. You should have heard how he ranted and raved – 'The fucking inconvenience that fucking cunt caused for going and getting himself burnt to a cinder when I was about to negotiate a film deal and get him on *Richard & Judy*!' When Jamie saw that I was forcing laughter, his lips curled downwards.

'So was Richard . . . mad?'

'Mad? Perhaps, perhaps . . .'

'He sounds as though he was rather lost in his own world – sitting in a tower block, convicted of murder, thinking he was writing a great novel. He – he – he rather reminds me of the novelist Will Self's verdict on Burroughs.' I saw Jamie flinch but I carried on in feigned innocence. 'He said that there was a point at which Burroughs decided to live in the world of the imagination and take excursions into the world of observable fact. Perhaps the same is true of Richard.'

'There I disagree with you, Mia. I feel that he went mad when he faced the truth. After all, the entire fabric of our existence, our collective sanity, is dependent on a bedrock of lies and manic self-delusion – is it not?'

'Go on,' I responded.

Jamie looked down at me from the aquiline frills of his nostrils. 'The environmental authorities assure us that flooding will be dealt with, but we both know full well that, within the next decade, London will require boats for all transportation, the tubes will be a home for fish, that buildings which are currently twenty floors tall will only possess ten. But if one accepts such a reality – the potentially catastrophic crisis that will arise when at least seven million people become homeless – then how can the capital continue? And so we pretend that there is adequate funding, that the gods of weather will heed our prayers. Delusion is a necessary part of human survival. Storytelling evolved for evolutionary purposes. When people face the truth, a breakdown normally ensues. Perhaps when Richard faced the truth, when he realized that the WSC would never accept him, a sort of epiphany occurred, a truth so raw that he could only take revenge by murdering poor Sylvie.'

'The WSC . . . what's that?'

Jamie recoiled, realizing I'd cornered him. I bit back a smile of triumph.

'The WSC . . . was a sort of private members club.'

'Oh. Really?'

'It was just a little literary appreciation society – no different from the bookish quasi-religious clubs that adolescents indulge in today.'

'But you're being too modest,' I said, shaping my voice into awe. 'Surely yours was one of the very first. Surely you deserve credit for that.'

'Well . . .' his ego rose and gleamed through his eyes '. . . I do lay claim to a family heritage of literary clubs. I actually thought up the WSC when I was in Venice with Zara and Toady – I was undergoing a sort of spiritual crisis when the epiphany happened. But the seed was planted long ago by my great-grandfather, Dr Stoker. He used to tour, putting on Phantasmagorias, and he was also one of the founding members of the Golden Dawn.'

'The Golden Dawn?' I recalled that I had seen a book about that on my father's desk . . . or had it been on order with Amazon? I quickly scribbled a note on my pad. 'So that inspired you?'

'I . . .'

I felt as though he was suspended on a tightrope; the silence trembled.

And then he fell.

'Really,' he shrugged irritably, 'I have no wish to discuss this subject any further.'

'But the WSC, it must have been very special for Richard's entire identity to collapse?' I asked, unable to conceal my passion any longer.

We played a game of retinal battle. The Spanish girl re-entered, provoking a stalemate. She paused timidly to see if she was needed.

'Miss Mia,' Jamie remarked, 'you didn't drink your tea.'

I glanced down. The milk had congealed in the brown but I'd have done anything to prolong the discussion. I was about to take a sip when the Spanish girl suddenly slipped and lunged forwards. Most of the tea went into the saucer and over my legs.

'That was *very* clumsy of you, Maria!' Jamie's ferocity shocked me. 'Clear it up at once.'

'Really, it's fine.' I picked up the spoon from the floor and passed it to her; she smiled desperately. 'It was just a few drops – nothing really.'

Jamie glared at me. 'I'm afraid that I will now have to terminate this discussion,' he said, controlling his voice with almost palpable effort. 'But we can continue at a later date.'

'When? Next week?' I pestered, but Jamie refused to be pinned down.

The housekeeper was summoned to escort me to the front door; this time she took me on a different route. Jamie's dry handshake was still a tingling echo in my palm. We passed a wall covered with vanity photographs, other illustrious beneficiaries of Jamie's handshake. I spotted the last Blues prime minister, a rock star and a breakfast TV presenter. Then a series of large oil paintings, all of the same faceless figure in a pin-striped suit, who looked like a man at first glance but seemed to be a hermaphrodite on second; his suit hinted a swell of breasts, and a tiny plait flicked behind his shoulder. I wanted to linger and look some more, but the housekeeper hurried me on, her eyes pleading anxiety.

I left the house feeling frustrated, as though I had discovered something without being sure quite what it was. I wondered if this was what Jamie had intended, if he had known who I was all along. I wished, also, that I had not been too intimidated to enquire as to the source of his wealth – for it surely could not have come from his two terrible novels. I realized that I longed to confide all this in Kat.

On the way home, crammed into a corner of the tube, I suddenly felt terrified that I would return to the flat and find the bed neat, the carpets clean, no reminder of her except a stray hair, a curl of perfume in the air. Paranoia gusted into panic. Why was I so stupid? Why did I always ending up smashing every beautiful thing that life gave me? I fought to climb escalators; my feet drummed down the pavement to the flat. I couldn't find my key in my bag and jammed my finger against the bell. When she opened the door, I held her so tightly and she curled her cheek against my collarbone, sighing harshly.

I wanted to make amends with words, but Kat put a finger to my lips. I bit it gently.

Afterwards, I took a shower. Water sluiced over my body, showering her away, stripping me naked again. There was some blood under my fingernails; Kat's period had started that morning. With past exes, this might have aroused disgust in me but with Kat it had created a peculiar sense of intimacy, intensified by the sheen of her sweat still clinging to me like a second skin. She always wove me back into the world with such love and tenderness; she gave me such hope, and hope was something that frightened me, a precarious set of stepping stones where I felt I would inevitably lose my foothold.

(xi) The Eye and the Liver

15 Berkeley Square. Kat rang the doorbell and we exchanged smiles as though we were schoolgirls playing Knock Down Ginger. Through the warped glass, I saw particles whorl and coalesce into colour. The door opened by degrees.

'Ms Lewis?' he asked, in a browned-apple voice.

'Delighted to meet you too.' Kat extended a creamy hand and took control of his arthritic claw.

We followed his grabby path down the hallway. The light and elegance of his home only served to highlight his elderly fragility. At the living-room door, he turned to us, and the light from a window fell into his face, into the muscle and skin beneath the tissue-papery layer wrapped over it, his wrinkles like tears in the paper, his smile a gummy slash. There was suspicion in his milky eyes, but also a gentlemanly air of 'Well, you do seem like nice girls to me; surely you wouldn't want to cheat an old man ... would you?' I imagined how I would feel if someone had played this trick on my father. I thought about feigning a tragedy and making a swift exit.

Kat appeared to have no compunction. On the contrary, she was relishing her role, smiling, nodding yes to Earl Grey, milk, three sugars, thank you, and laughing when he made a joke about her being a lovely young creature. We sat and listened politely as an old-fashioned electronic clock above the mantelpiece stacked up digits. Kat impatiently twirled her hair around her forefinger and Mr Leonard, who seemed to be far away in his mumbling memoirs of the twentieth century, said, with an alertness that surprised me: 'I can tell my talk is tiring you – no, no need to be polite. You want to see Will, don't you, my dear? Well, come along now, Kat and Mary.'

'It's Mia . . .'

It had been Kat's idea to visit Mr Leonard. She had looked his details up on the Net, booked the appointment, mapped the journey. I admit that there was a joy in sharing my mission with her, but I felt a little threatened too. As though my relationship with my father had become a love triangle. Her eyes were sparkling with the adventure of it all, but I wanted her to realize how important this was to me.

He led us back into the hallway, past several doors and into a shadowy study. Kat trailed her fingers against the back of my palm and we exchanged thrilled looks. This room had bookcases and clocks and robots collected from different cultures: a geisha from Japan with a wig of dark human hair and a fighter from the Iranian wars, which Mr Leonard explained had had its left leg burnt off by an IED. In the centre of the room was a mahogany table on which sat two objects. The first was a large red box that looked as though it belonged in a hospital; the second was a glass case partially covered with a green baize cloth. Mr Leonard had clearly planned a preamble to tantalize us, but Kat was too impatient. She grabbed the cloth and swept it off. We let out a gasp.

The eye. *Will's eye.* It looked smaller than I had expected. A slate-blue iris floated in a white marble pupil, decorated with fine bloodshot veins. The lid and some of the skin around the eye was still intact; when it blinked, I jumped. The back of the eye was attached to a fine pinkish membrane that looped back on to a fleshy lump resting on the bottom of the glass.

Then something happened that made Kat scream and step backwards. Will's eye moved. It swivelled past me, settled on Kat and looked her up and down.

'You've had a robot made?' I cried, in faint disgust.

Within a day of my father dying, various corps attempted to cash in on my grief: each day my post and inbox were thick with brochures. A decade ago, it had begun with dead pets being defurred, then wrapped around a robot dog or cat to cheer little kiddies unable to deal with death. Recently, the trend had extended to humans. In my block, there were rumours that the old woman at number thirty-four had had a robot mummified with her husband's skin and hair so that she could lie next to him at night and touch his hand, which, though cold, would touch her back. Apparently in the early days they'd had a lot of trouble with cocks, had tended to remove them from the dead bodies and create robot eunuchs. In new versions, however, cocks had been preserved and developed to swell, rise and fall depending on the occasion.

'No, no,' Mr Leonard insisted. 'That really is Will's eye. He really is looking at you. You know, when I was a young man, I used to be very fond of an author called Roald Dahl – he's fallen out of fashion now so I doubt you will have heard of him.'

'I've heard of him,' I interjected, though only because Will had once cited him as a literary influence.

'Well, Dahl once wrote a deliciously macabre story called *William and Mary* about a man who arranges for his brain and eye to be preserved after he dies. I was always enchanted by the image when I was a child. And all those years ago I thought, wouldn't it be simply wonderful if I could make that story real, turn fiction into real life? And now I have. It's the most marvellous thing, you see. The eye is actually part of the brain – which, as you can see, we have successfully preserved as well – we keep blood pumping round it with the aid of this fine machine.' He traced the wires back to a socket in the wall. 'The rest of his body is – was – preserved in formaldehyde, but I believe the collector grew rather short of money and had to sell parts off. I also bought his liver!' He proudly tapped the large red box.

Will blinked and his iris got bigger.

'So he's kind of alive?' Kat asked, wondrous, appalled.

'Well – yes . . .' Mr Leonard replied. 'In the sense of "I think, therefore I am." He may not be able to sip a cup of Jassim tea, however.'

'That's incredible!' Kat revelled in the grotesque pleasure of it all. Then she frowned.

'But . . . it's . . . a little cruel, don't you think?' I asked, hearing my voice heat. 'If Will's mind is conscious – well, he can feel, can't he? I mean, he's one of the finest and most intelligent literary minds this country has had in a long time – so how can it feel to him, being stuck in a glass cage? The boredom must be killing him – except he can't die. It's Purgatory. No, maybe it's just hell.'

Kat frowned and reached out to squeeze my hand.

'There I disagree with you, Mary,' Mr Leonard said indignantly.

'You are very young, my dear, and full of dancing beans. But Will here has lived a long, long life. This is a sort of retirement for him. It is two years since my wife died but over the last six months, with Will here, I have not felt alone – we have become quite close, despite . . . and I have seen on so many an occasion a happy spark light up in that eye of his. I can assure you that I do not let his mind rot with neglect. I talk to him, and when I take a nap, I turn on the radio and he listens to Radio Four – *Book at Bedtime* is his favourite. Sometimes we even play board games together, chess or Scrabble, though obviously I do have to play for both of us, but he looks on and enjoys . . .' His voice cracked and he looked tired after such an impassioned speech.

'So you can't actually communicate?' I asked sharply.

'Communicate? My dear, you can ask him anything you like!'

I turned to Will's eye. 'How did you die?'

My question provoked rapid blinking; his pupil skittered all over the place.

'No, no, no!' Mr Leonard waved his palm in front of the glass, shielding me from view. 'You must not distress him! I meant that you might ask him if he is well. One blink means yes, two means no.'

Kat and I exchanged glances.

'Are you well?' Kat asked him.

A single, sullen blink.

'You've upset him now, you see,' Mr Leonard chided us, as though Will was a young child in his care. 'Say sorry.'

When we didn't respond, he repeated sharply: 'Say sorry!'

Kat had to duck her head to bite back a giggle.

'I'm sorry,' I said quickly.

'Sorry,' Kat said.

Will's eye lasered us.

Mr Leonard passed a hand over his face, shaking vehemently. We became anxious and asked him several times if he was okay, but he merely mumbled through spittle.

'I think he's got overexcited – he needs to lie down,' Kat said, taking his hand and gently guiding him out into the hallway.

I knelt down before the glass case and stared into the depths of Will's eye. His pupil cut into me. It said it all: the *ennui* of this caged perspective after a life of fame and freedom; of the trammelled-up creativity that he could not release, the wasted fruit of ideas rotting inside him; of his ache to sit in his study and hear the laughter of his family in the hallway, to stroll through London streets that sang with psychogeography. I went over to the wall, where the plug connected Will's brain to a monitor. I was holding an internal debate of ethics when Kat came back in.

'What are you doing?' Kat cried. 'If you do that, you'll kill him!'

My hand sprang away, the word *kill* echoing shock through me.

I watched Kat go over to the table and pick up the red plastic box containing Will's liver.

'Fuck, it's heavy – you're going to have to help me with this.'

'*Kat!*'

'Come on, Mia. We can take it now while he's sleeping and we can find out what did kill Will – we can get some tests done. It's worth it.'

'It's stealing.'

'No, we'll bring it back. We can say there was a misunderstanding–'

'But he's got my number, he knows my name!'

'Like hell he does – he thinks you're Mary.'

I reached out to help her, thinking that I'd never stolen anything in my life before, not even a chocolate from a sweetshop.

* * *

Our journey back was farcical. The box was heavy, with one handle; we carried it together, banging it back and forth between our legs. I moaned that Kat should have brought her car and Kat moaned that the bruises on her thighs would infuriate her makeup artist when she went back to work at the film-set. On the tube home, our nervous giggles attracted attention. An Oz guy sporting dreadlocks tried to chat Kat up, so she persuaded him to carry it back to the flat for us. He shoved it into the lift, then stepped back into the hallway, blushing. As the doors closed, he plucked up the courage to call out his mobile number, but his 'seven' was sliced up by sliding metal. On our floor, we got on to our hands and knees, shoving the box forwards. It caught on the grate and the doors drew and withdrew against it. The lift echoed with laughter so harsh it became tears.

Back in our flat, we sobered up.

'He was such a sweet old man,' I said. 'I think we should take it back.'

'What about your ex? That guy ... Ciaran? He could check it out.'

'Fuck. I could try him ...'

There was a silence as we both reflected. I tried to calculate how many CCTV cameras might have caught us on the way home. The number probably ran into five figures.

'They won't chase us,' Kat said. 'I mean, they're all far too busy with their book-to-crime murders and people drowning and all that crap. We'll be okay, I'm sure.'

(xii) Ciaran

I sat on the Piccadilly Line with Will Self's liver on my lap. Kat and I had been too afraid to touch it, so we'd left it wrapped in its plastic bag, containing cold preservation solution, nestled in crushed ice inside a large cooling box. I had forgotten how heavy the damn thing was; I felt as though I was carrying an overweight pet. But Kat's car was out of the question: the police had recently fined her a hundred euros for driving her gas-guzzler. I recalled that the word *liver* comes from the Greek *heper*. It is the largest organ in the body and contains the most blood. Plato and later physiologists thought it represented the darker passions of blood and jealousy and greed that spur men to action: an attachment to life itself. I wondered what they might have seen on cutting open Will's liver. Would they have gasped at my face, a portent blurring in the jellied slime?

The last time I visited Ciaran, I had found him in his laboratory, being watched by a hundred beady black eyes. He'd been testing ABC mood drugs on spiders and studying the effects on their web patterns. All had proved satisfactory and predictable – except one. The Dynamic Pill prompted enhanced web activity; the Sleeping Pill had produced none. The Creativity

Pill, however, was disappointing. The spider simply sat still, refusing to weave, and died a few days later. I suggested the spider had attained some sort of nirvana where it quietly penned arachnid tales in its head, or perhaps had been suffering from a writer's block too deep for the drug to shift, but Ciaran had not been amused. ABC were putting pressure on him to come up with results. They wanted a gallery of pretty patterns to feature in a forthcoming Sunday supplement.

This time, I entered to find Ciaran in a fracas with another animal. He was trying to persuade it to go back into its cage, but a pontid arm was looped tight around his neck. As far as I could see, the ape kept trying to kiss him. Ciaran spotted me and a flush rose over his features. He looked less pleased each time I visited, which had slipped from monthly to biannually.

'It's a new love and passion drug, developed by ABC, and I think it's going to be very successful,' Ciaran said, washing his hands in the sink. In the cage behind him, the ape mimicked him, pretending to soap his palms too. Love is a mirror, I thought, and we lose ourselves in warped reflections.

'What I don't understand is, why apes?' I asked.

'They're intelligent creatures, the closest to us in terms of–'

'Exactly. When people fall in love, they become stupid. You ought to test the drugs on snails. Or perhaps lemmings. They'd be a close match.'

'I'll suggest that to my boss.' Ciaran suddenly grinned. Then: 'Well. What do you want? I have a date tonight. I have to be off quickly.'

'Why d'you think I want something?' I faltered.

'Well, you always do, don't you?' He sounded as though the rust our relationship had left on him was the sole cause of his cynicism. 'The last time you came, you wanted the happy drug, and the time before, you needed to borrow my car. Or was it my Kindle when yours broke? Anyway.'

I had been planning to lie and say the liver belonged to my grandfather. Now I felt a need to be dramatic, to force him to transcend the friction between us.

'You see this? I'm carrying Will Self's liver.'

'Holy shit.' Ciaran dropped his green-paper towel.

'I need you to run some tests on it,' I said quickly, and put it down on the table. Before he could ask, I said, 'I stole it.'

I remember how it felt, that first date we'd shared six years ago. The first four hours had been a success. A reshowing of *Badlands* on the big screen, a Costa coffee, a chat, a marvelling at shared ideas and coincidence of taste; his arm slung around me on the tube home, an invitation to head back to his flat. The fact that I liked him made it all the worse. As we kissed, I wondered how many more dates I would have to endure before I could take him to meet my father, who was fretting about the wasteland of my love life. The kissing took more self-persuasion than I'd anticipated; the taste of him reminded me of being shoved into a boys' locker-room when I was a teenager, the testosterone stench curdling my stomach. Before Ciaran's cock entered me, there was a moment of thrill where I thought I might be converted, that it had all been nothing but a phase, that I wouldn't have to fret about my father and I could just be normal. Then he was inside me, like a knife. My fingers clawing the bed. Bile clotting my throat. He mistook my sobs for desire before finally pulling out in horror and asking if he had just taken my virginity.

'There won't be many people about at the weekend,' he said. 'I'll be able to sneak in, run a few tests then. Shit, this is going to be exciting . . . but I have to go now – I have a date.' Pause. 'What about you?' he added lightly. 'How's your love life, these days?'

Ciaran could never accept that he was a failed experiment. He'd always been determined it was his fault, that he had turned me on to the other sex. I realized that it was symptomatic of the Pygmalion urge of all men to suffer and so, to balm his ego, I humoured him.

I was grateful to him now, however, and as I left I gave him an affectionate kiss on the cheek, and he managed a beautiful smile.

I returned from Ciaran's lab with a sense of anti-climax. He'd said he'd look at it over the weekend. But I knew that if work or love intervened, he might take days or even weeks to obtain results. We had given my laptop to Sam, a friend of Kat's, to discover where the Will S emails had been sent from. I wished he would hurry up and return it: I felt as though I had lost a limb. I brewed some coffee and reread Richard's diary, hoping I might discover a fresh clue, but I had worn down the words by reading them so often. Reluctantly, I acknowledged that I needed to return to real life, to bills and Kindles and work that would pay for Kat and me to eat. I worked against the heat, finishing my review of *Life on Mars* for the *Guardian*, with the closing lines 'Fans of this enthralling fictional epic on the last years of David Bowie might also be interested in calling the hotline below for half-price tickets to the latest Bunny Stoppers concert!' My editor hated it, his editor hated it, but someone at the top of the food chain had decided that product placement was the only way to prevent our jobs folding. The virus had spread from reviews to articles; indeed, there had recently been a flurry of complaints about the adverts for a date-rape drug antidote that had preceded an article about a thirteen-year-old being sexually assaulted in Elephant and Castle. I prepared a few notes for my school class tomorrow; then Kat came home, grumpy from reshoots with her obsessive director. I gave her a foot massage and made her laugh by telling her the story of Ciaran, exaggerating the amorous attentions of his ape.

'And there haven't been any more emails from the phantom "Will"?' she asked, threading her fingers through mine.

'No,' I said, but I could not share her relief. More emails suggested 'Will' still enjoyed taunting me; the silence made me fearful that he was bored of games and ready to strike.

'What about Mr Leonard?' she asked, coaxing a smile from me. 'Has he called regarding the mystery of his missing liver?'

'No,' I said. 'But I do feel guilty about him.'

'We'll get it back soon enough – and then we'll return it to him, somehow.'

'Oh, great! How are we going to pull that one off? Turn up pretending to be Jehovah's Witnesses, hope he doesn't recognize us and slip it back into his study?'

'It's an idea,' said Kat.

We both laughed, brainstorming absurd lies and guises, relieving the tension but never quite able to expel it.

In the middle of the night I woke up, the revelation sparkling through my mind. I made the mistake of shaking Kat awake, forgetting how furiously possessive she was of her sleep. She enveloped herself in an angry cocoon of covers. I went over to the computer alone, the mouse twitching under my fingers.

YouTube: Will's video.

Yes – there it was. Will gives a reading. He shakes violently.

He falls and something small and red rolls away from him. I rummaged in my handbag and drew out the sample I'd been given at the primary school. A small red bottle, with an ABC label. This one a cure for kids' modern-day Attention Order Deficit. Who knew what Will's had been for?

I hurried over to Kat and shook her shoulder gently, but she made a monstrous sound, so I slipped back into bed and simmered alone. Had there been poison in Will's ABC potion? Or was that just the stuff of crime novels? Perhaps it had clashed with his medication, or perhaps it had simply been too potent – in which case, would Ciaran cover it up to protect his employers? Or maybe Will's last novel was personal; maybe *Drug Lime* was really about a destructive addition to an ABC potion.

Outside, the tropicsmog finally snapped. Boiling clouds burst and rain sheeted against the window. The room flashed electric white and thunder added a postscript. Kat groaned again and said once more, *Leave me alone.*

(xiii) Traces of Hemingway

Ciaran's reaction to the tests on Will's liver unnerved me. He ignored my calls for a week, which convinced me that the liver must have yielded a report fascinating enough to be worth withholding. It took three days before I was able to gatecrash his offices. London had been temporarily turned into a poor imitation of Venice. I had to cancel my class, and Kat's filming was on hold; holed up together, without the money for boat transport, we made the best of things. It always seemed as though the rain unleashed the pent-up stench of the tropicsmog, water running dirty with burnt tarmac and city sweat. We kept the windows shut tight and lit copious quantities of sandalwood incense. As usual, the government food parcels never arrived, so we lived off tins of sardines and crackers, sharing baths, exchanging massages. I helped to test her on her lines for a new part, and when I tussled with another review, Kat even wrote a few sentences for me.

Kat wasn't a big reader but her boredom prompted her to pick my Kindle and begin her first Will Self novel, *How the Dead Live*. I didn't tell her that I couldn't bear to return to it because it had been my father's favourite. 'I had no idea it'd be this good – I *love* the idea that the dead don't leave us, they just move to a better part of London!' she exclaimed, making my heart ache every time she laughed softly and read out a prose-gem.

On Thursday, the water levels had subsided enough for cars to splash through the streets. Kat decided to risk the wrath of the police and more fines we couldn't afford by driving me to the ABC skyscraper in her gas-guzzler. She waited while I investigated. When I entered Ciaran's lab, he glanced up from some experiment involving green liquid. I heard the smash of glass and the hiss of spilt potion. CCTV cameras tormented him; he ushered me out into the car park. 'Meet at your flat in twenty minutes,' he whispered, 'and don't ever turn up at my offices again.'

Cinema has educated us to intuit what words to summon when life teeters towards melodrama. We react naturally to daily annoyances, but the vast tragic scenes, the soap opera set-pieces, make us blush and clamber; words suddenly shrink and feel inadequate. Movies have told us that cliché is the accept-able response. That a break-up should involve the tossing of keys and clothes from a bedroom window. Likewise, Ciaran seemed to take solace in playing a role: the paranoid scientist caught in the web of a conspiracy theory. He barked celluloid-laced sentences as he paced the room, drinking from the whisky I'd poured him, running his palm over his shorn scalp. I watched his reflection in the window, ghosting over the bright city lights. Once again, he told me that I must delete his number from my mobile.

'And your girlfriend's definitely out?' he repeated, eyeing up a stocking of Kat's, slung over the sofa.

'Yes, I told her to leave us alone for a while. I think you're being incredibly paranoid, by the way.'

'This is *my* job at stake!'

'Well, where's the liver? You were supposed to bring it back!'

'I dumped it. Last night – I just got so freaked out – I got up in the night and got into my car and went to the Thames and dumped it.'

'*What?* I pictured the liver falling through moonlight-streaked waves to colder and darker layers of water. Perhaps some carnivorous sea thing was already hacking away at it. If Plato was right about the humour of the liver, then the Thames might become a murkier world as fish fought and feasted with greater greed and wrath.

'But it's such a waste!' I cried, swallowing. 'It wasn't yours to give away . . . and now we'll never get it back to that poor old man.'

'I thought you stole it,' Ciaran said.

I stared at him with hostile eyes.

'Am I here because you're writing an article? Because if you screw me, Mia, I'll lose *everything*. And I mean everything. I'll never be able to get another job in the current recession – I won't be able to pay my mortgage, I'll lose my girlfriend—'

'My father died recently, Ciaran. I'm doing this for him.'

'Oh. Sorry.' He took a large, trembling gulp of whisky. Ciaran had only met my father a few times but he had always got on with him better than he had with me.

'I'm just trying to finish off an investigation he started. He was – I don't know how to put it – he was exploring Will Self's novels . . . There's some connection with ABC. But, look, I'm not going to write about it. That's not what my father intended. I'm just doing this for him.'

'Okay,' Ciaran relented, sitting down. 'I'll explain what I

discovered. According to official records, Will died of a heart attack. But that has to be a cover-up, because his liver showed high levels of toxicity – high levels of Hemingway.'

'*Hemingway?*'

'If I tell you all the details, will you swear not to tell a soul? Not even your girlfriend?'

'I swear.'

'Nobody would believe you if you told them, anyway. It's as ludicrous as – I don't know – those stories about the US government having aliens in secret vaults or that all those book-to-crime murders are a conspiracy involving M15. The Hemingway project was originally developed by a psychiatrist called Dr Self.'

'You mean Professor Self?'

'Well, there's two of them. Self Senior, Dr Self, and Self Junior, Professor Self. Prof. Junior was employed by a panicked government in 2006 to develop a project that would reintegrate "talented" criminals into the environment by developing their skills in music, writing, art and so on. Self got carried away with the huge amount of funding behind him. As well as developing therapy sessions and allowing his prisoners to practise their skills, he also had another project on the side, inspired by some research his father had undertaken, involving different literary – er, I'm not quite sure how to describe them ... Actually, in order to explain that, you have to look at the earlier experiment that was conducted on Hemingway – just after Hemingway was murdered.'

'Wait.' I laughed. 'Hemingway wasn't murdered.'

'Yes, he was.'

'No. He committed suicide.'

'Oh,' said Ciaran. 'Were you there when he died? Did you find the body? Did you know, by the way, that no autopsy was performed on his corpse?'

I slid my fingers into my drink, playing with a chunk of ice.

'Right,' said Ciaran. 'He was murdered. I'd like to say for the record that ABC had absolutely *nothing* to do with his death.'

'You sound as though you're speaking at some government inquiry!'

'Because it's true!' he cried. 'ABC is a corporation I'm proud to work for. It's dedicated to developing the full potential of every human being on this planet. The guy who murdered Hemingway – Dr Self – was a maverick. He was developing a pretty crazy theory that by distilling the essence of genius – and his particular fascination was with writers – i.e., by taking a sample of blood, liver, brain matter, urine, shit, you could create a potion that would maintain their . . . their . . .'

'Quiddity?' I offered.

'Quiddity,' Ciaran agreed, though I could hear the word clunking on his tongue.

'It's from the Latin: *quidditas*. It translates as "whatness" or "what it is".'

'You always used to do that. We'd be discussing something important and you'd just define a word I was saying, or suggest a better choice of vocabulary.'

'OK. I'm sorry. I'm interrupting you. Why don't you tell me what this madman did, when he preserved Hemingway's quiddity in ice and test tubes or whatever he did?'

'Right. You know, if you examine the details of Hemingway's death, you'll see that the theory holds up. A few weeks before he supposedly shot himself, he was treated for manic depression with ECT – which then resulted in severe memory loss, the so-called cause of his suicide. The ECT treatment was in fact no such thing – Hemingway was sedated while Self Senior removed bits and pieces of him. He used the various samples of Hemingway to form a cocktail, which he then injected into subjects in LA in 1961. They had volunteered to take part in a drugs trial – many of them were very young, students wanting to pay their college fees. He deliberately chose subjects who had an IQ that was high but not too high. He thought that if he injected them, they'd make the leap from being brainy to outstanding. He then planned to patent the cocktail and allow governments to bid for it.'

'So it would end up in the local chemist?'

'No. He felt that governments would be disinclined to distribute something so powerful on a mass scale. For what could be more dangerous than making your population intelligent? It's best to keep them stupid and continue sticking fluoride in the water for added dullness. No, he planned to sell it to the government so that they might inject their advisers, speechwriters and so on, and perfect the art of propaganda – respond to each crisis with words so . . . so apt and perfect and moving that they'd always be voted into power. Hell, the Blues could really do with a potion like this right now—' He broke off with a chuckle.

I didn't smile. 'So that's what he did? He sold it to governments?'

'No. No, the trial failed. I checked the reports. The subjects all reacted extremely badly to Hemingway. After the convulsions, the vomiting, the spasms, they all went into catatonic states. One died; another was permanently disabled; the last living victim is still in a psychiatric ward and can no longer speak.'

'Oh, God, that's terrible.'

'Despite this, Self's son – Prof. Self – wanted to continue with his father's work. But for him, Hemingway wasn't enough. He wanted a whole *library* of authors' . . . essences. He persuaded a number of contemporary writers to give him blood and urine and DNA samples, dressing it up as a charitable medical research project that would help him to understand whether creativity is a matter of nature or nurture. He claimed he would then use the results of his tests to develop literacy in the third world. His spin to authors was that it would be a little like the intellectual equivalent of giving blood. Crap, of course. He was driven by a Nazi ideal for perfection, for the *crème de la crème* of genius. But there was a genuine nobility behind his desire. Unlike his father, he had no wish to sell the drugs to governments and spin doctors. He did believe his experiment would make his name, revolutionize criminal behaviour.'

'How so?'

'Well – education and crime are intimately linked. We tend to deify criminals as highly articulate and intelligent in the serial-killer novels we read, but they tend to be illiterate rather than Lecters. Self felt that if he could "inject" genius into a criminal, their rapid intellectual development would be accompanied by a deeper moral understanding, a desire to be a better member of society. He put forward a preliminary argument in the *Lancet* but, unsurprisingly, he became a laughing stock in the medical community. So he licked his wounds, got a PR company to get him on TV as many times as possible and re-dressed his research as a charity project, approaching authors for their – what did you call it? – *quiddities*.'

'I'm not sure if you can pluralize the word.'

'Oh, fuck off. Listen to the rest of the story. A couple of lesser-known writers did sign up to it, probably eager to boost their book sales and get some free publicity. But the newspapers thought it was a farce and barely bothered to report it. Self's salvation came in the form of DBC Pierre. He felt it was a worthy and interesting enterprise and dared to take the leap; he was photographed for the *Guardian*, holding up little vials of his blood, pubic hair and urine. Once he'd done it, it became fashionable. And then others followed suit: Sebastian Faulks, Ian McEwan, Salman Rushdie, and – of course – Will Self.'

'And did it work?'

'Yes.'

'So . . . are you seriously telling me that I could take a DBC Pierre potion and then I'd just magically transform into him?'

'Not turn *into*. It's not a fairy tale, Mia. Look, everything you take into your body has an impact on your nervous system – the food you ate for breakfast this morning, the drugs you take, whether you use a tropicsmog nasal spray, they will all change the chemical balance in your body, and hence your brain. Remember that the stomach and the brain are linked by fine tubes. If you took the DBC potion, you'd still be Mia, but you'd notice a subtle strain of influence. If five millilitres was regularly injected into your system over a three-month period, then yes, you might find yourself sitting down to write a novel about a schoolboy in Texas who has been wrongly accused of murdering his schoolmates.'

'It's that predictable?'

'Well, no. I admit there's always an element of unpredictability – which was why Prof. Self grew to hate his namesake. He considered the Self potion to be particularly volatile and dangerous; he could never predict how it would react with the subject. They might turn serial killer, Mad Hatter, Mensa candidate – he could never tell.'

I struggled to hide my laughter, though I found romance in the idea. I wondered what it would be like to bottle Kat's essence.

'In 2003, lack of funds nearly caused Prof. Self's experiments to fold – and that was where ABC stepped in. They agreed to fund his research secretly. And that's because ABC do care, Mia – we were sincerely interested in a project that might help to lower crime rates.'

'Oh, it had nothing to do with wanting to make a profit, I'm sure.'

'With the time and money we gave him, Prof. Self managed to refine his father's work,' Ciaran continued earnestly, 'because he found the missing and magical ingredient – semen – which he came to refer to as the "holistic element". He theorized that the galactose, which comes from the bulbourethral glands, served as a neutralizing agent – for, once semen was added, Prof. Self found that the horrific side effects that Hemingway subjects had suffered were muted. Prof. Self was pleased by this big leap in progress—' Ciaran broke off to wet his hoarse voice with more whisky ' – but he was also saddened by the fact that he was never able to perfect that which was, for him, the Holy Grail of all potions – Hemingway.'

'I don't see why he thought Hemingway was so special. I mean, how is injecting Hemingway into a murderer going to stop them committing crimes? Did he hope they'd spend their time crafting pared-down sentences instead?'

'Prof. Self had an idealistic notion that the values of Hemingway's heroes were the exact qualities that were absent in young male offenders, who had become emasculated by an increasingly matriarchal society. Unfortunately, Hemingway's sperm had rotted long ago and become ether, but he sought to stabilize the potion by mixing in a little of Will's semen. Strangely, Will's semen never had a negative effect. It was as though the two writers, both so opposite, neutralized each other. And that was when Prof. Self had his epiphany . . .'

And that was why he injected Richard Smith with Self and Hemingway, I realized, fighting to conceal my excitement.

'To be honest, I don't know quite why he did what he did next, but I figure his frustrated desires pushed him into increasingly warped and desperate directions, because he started combining his chemical potions with a psychotherapy technique called Transference.'

'Transference ... What's that? It's Freudian, right?' I'd seen the word in Richard's diary. It was on my list to research.

'Look, I don't have to explain it all, Mia,' he said, a strain of tiredness in his voice. 'Google it. But basically he called his potions and Transference theories the New Deal Crime Reintegration Scheme and tested it on a number of young offenders back in 2006, with government approval – though the government had no idea of what he was really doing, and just as the newspapers were starting to speculate that something shady might be happening, the entire project – including many of the notes – was destroyed in a fire.'

'Richard Smith,' I burst out.

'I'm sorry?'

'Richard Smith.' I paused. 'He was one of Prof. Self's patients – I did a little research on him. He was injected with Hemingway and Will Self. It wasn't a good combination for him.'

Ciaran sat very still, his knuckles protruding like chalk. 'You're bullshitting me. How the hell do you know about Richard Smith? You *are* going to write an article about this, aren't you? I knew it! What the fuck am I doing here, telling all this to a journalist–'

'No! Look, Ciaran, even if I was writing a piece, which I'm not, do you think they would actually publish it when ABC is our biggest advertiser? I had to write a review of the reissued *Of Mice and Men* this morning with a piece of puff about ABC mouse poisons.'

Ciaran breathed out heavily: 'OK. OK. But how did you know about Richard? His whole case was hushed up.'

'I just ... There are one or two articles about it. Anyway, you say that the Liverpudlian tower block where Smith was housed has burnt down, right? Well ...' I was reluctant to tell him about

Richard's diary. 'I mean – were there any survivors? Case notes? Things I could look at?'

'I don't know, Mia. I could check the file, maybe find you a contact.'

'I'll call you tomorrow.'

'No, I'll call you. And it has to end there.' Ciaran put down his glass. 'I won't be able to help you any more.'

'Wait. There's one thing I don't really understand, and that's how ABC fits in with Will's death. Why was he taking Hemingway? How did he get hold of it? I mean, ABC might have funded Self's work . . . but they've never put these drugs on the market, have they?'

'ABC is committed to full tests and trials for any drug before releasing them into the public domain,' Ciaran croaked, in a ragged voice. He pulled on his coat.

'Please – just give me a clue. The connection between ABC and Will's death?'

'You're going to have to work it out for yourself. I've told you too much already.'

'*Please.*'

'No. And don't ask me again, OK? I'll give you that number tomorrow, and that'll be it. Goodbye, Mia.'

In the hallway, he turned and unexpectedly kissed me hard on the mouth. Then he muttered a brisk goodbye and the door slammed behind him.

(xiv) Waiting

It was Otto Kernberg who built the theory of Transference Focused Psychotherapy on the foundations of Freud. It was designed as a cure for patients suffering from borderline personality disorder. A typical patient would have contradictory representations of himself and the people around him, resulting in *identity diffusion*, a splitting of his self. My yawn created a circle of breath on the screen of my Kindle. I rubbed it away, wondering if identity diffusion was a milder version of that ultimate fragmentation of the mind: schizophrenia. The patient would separate shards of himself and his significant others into 'all good' and 'all bad' representations. According to the textbook on my Kindle, this was considered to be a form of mental illness. To me, it sounded like human nature and the founding psychology of most major religions.

It was three a.m. The fifth night in a row that I had grown tired of wrestling insomnia. Kat was snoring gently in bed and I was sitting at the computer in defeat. Since my conversation with Ciaran, he had, predictably, refused to take my calls. I had returned to my list and now I was ticking off Transference with a sense of satisfaction and frustration. Perhaps I might find something that helped to slot my last puzzle pieces into place, or perhaps I was just burning out to my last ember. I was already dreading daytime, when my sleeplessness paid its worst dividends: my jaw aching from permanent yawning, tinnitus ringing in my ears, my mind a grey fuzz.

In the course of therapy, the patient's various representations would be projected on to the therapist and – in the process of Transference – together they would be able to analyse and understand his inconsistent perceptions. Unity was the desired goal: a full integration of the different fragments of the patient's personality. I flicked through Richard's diary again, musing that he had often played the role of abused child seeking paternal praise from Prof. Self. Each time I read it, I felt increasing sympathy for Richard and his delusions; Prof. Self was a phantom-father from Hell. Words began to fray before my burning eyes. I walked to the bathroom. Prof. Self was sweeping up shards and piecing them together to make a mirror. I stared at the reflection, at the puzzle-piece lines cutting my head, heart and liver. Then Kat appeared behind me, her smile seductive. Prof. Self thrust a needle into her arm. I felt my ego swell when he whispered that he had injected her with my essence. But Kat became sad: she wept as my father's death penetrated her, gasped with my jealousy, searched for a knife to cut her skin. She yanked a shard from the mirror, collapsing its remains into tinkles. I cried out, trying to stop her, but she cut her arm with a fierce, horrible hiss of pleasure. Her body spun apart into Picasso pieces that rolled across the floor. I picked up her bloody head, screaming, 'Kat!'

She stroked my face gently. 'You were making noises ... nightmare?'

'I ... yes ...' I sat up, squinting and groggy. 'What time is it?

Shit. I'm meant to be in school. Can you call them and tell them I'm sick?'

I didn't feel too guilty about neglecting my school class. After three sessions of attempting to expand their vocabulary, I had grown disheartened. The words I fed them seemed to pass through their systems like verbal diarrhoea, expelled through the wrong passage. I'd argued with the headmistress yesterday, declaring that the pills they were being issued were combating all hope of progress. She had been defensive, too defensive, and had finally admitted that the school had a three-year contract/sponsorship with ABC, without which they would have been unable to build their new sports hall and swimming pool. Fucking product placement strikes again.

After Kat had gone, I replayed Will's video on YouTube for the hundredth time. Now I paid particular attention to the audience questions that epilogued his reading, searching for answers in his answers. He spoke about how he had been misdiagnosed with schizophrenia as a troubled teenager. He spoke about taking heroin, how it had never filled him with euphoria, but swept away all feeling, creating a vacuum that euphoria had filled. Ultimately, writing had become a substitute for drugs, metaphors for drug-rush; his withdrawal from heroin had created an obscene image-hunger, which he had satisfied with the torrent of images that filled his prose. I thought about Prof. Self's experiment. Perhaps he had wanted to short-cut Transference, from the snags of words to the simplicity of a cocktail. Ultimately his conviction had sprung from a modern malaise, an impatience with time; a lust for fame.

The buzz of the doorbell. I gazed at my CCTV monitor and saw an unfamiliar figure. A guy with matted blond dreads, wearing a technicolour coat: a dirty Joseph.

'I'm Sam. I'm here for Kat ... or Mia.' His accent was Irish, spoken in a swift slur. 'I've got your laptop here – let me up, girl.'

'*Bonjour*,' voice recognition greeted Sam as he entered.

I gave an apologetic smile and a shrug. Kat had recently tried to switch it off, but had only succeeded in changing its primary language functioning to French. She had tried to assuage my annoyance by declaring that it was exotic – and at least we could no longer understand what it was saying.

It was such a relief to have my laptop back. I held it to my chest like a baby. Sam kicked off his boots and made himself comfortable on the couch. As I passed him a cup of tea, I inhaled the sweet aroma of pot and incense. His face was a pock-marked Puck and a dog earring silvered in his left lobe. Yet when he spoke about computers, he turned from druggie to geek – 'theinvalidisp-threewaspointdothererecorbshitfive'. Technospeak: words that seemed closer to numbers than language.

'So,' Sam said, ignoring my crossed arms, and rolling a little cigarette, which I then warned him he couldn't smoke. 'The emails they didn't come from Jamie Curren, girl.'

I felt exasperated.

'How much has Kat told you?' I asked. 'She can't keep secrets!'

'Hey, hey.' He made peace signs with his fingers. 'Chill chill. I was just kinda worried we might get the ABC guys on our back. Hey, that would be kinda scary, reckon they'd shut me down and get me for ten years of downloading illegal music an' that.'

'I'm sorry? ABC? You know about them too?'

'Well, with Jamie Curren being on the board an' that!' He slapped his thigh. 'I mean, he's a powerful guy, right, not the one you'd like as an enemy.'

'What? Jamie Curren is *on the ABC board*?'

'Like I said, like I said. He keeps it kinda quiet. But chill, the emails, they were from some random guy called Aaron Fenshaw. He lives in Esher, which is this boring quaint little village in Surrey. I'll be reckoning he's just some lad having a laugh with yer.'

'Aaron? Aaron from the WSC? But I've met him ... I went to interview him and he claimed he didn't know Jamie – and that happened *after* we got the package – I went to interview him— I— *Shit!*'

Sam gave me a knowing glance. 'Well, my girl, maybe he reckoned you'd be looking him up once he sent that package. That's the way these scammers work. He's fucking with you. Well, I'd report him to the police an' that, but don't you go mentioning my name, OK? Kat said I'd have anonymity, right, for sure.'

'Yes. Of course.' I swallowed. 'I just – enjoy your tea. Light that cigarette if you want. I just – I think I need some water.'

I needed some space too. I went into the bathroom and splashed my face. Confusion kept punching me with after-shocks; revelations hurt my stomach, too big to digest. I stared into our new mirror and saw myself shatter on the floor in shards and tinkles of chaos.

Sam dropped a hint about needing to buy some ciggies and having forgotten his lucky hemlock purse, so I bade him goodbye with a thirty-euro note, which he accepted with a wink and 'Aye, you're a good girl, like Kat said, you're a good girl.' Then I packed up my bag, pulled on my shoes and slammed the door behind me, voice recognition echoing, '*Au revoir!*'

On the train to Cheddington, I made the mistake of calling Kat. When I told her Aaron had sent the emails, she burst into angry laughter, cried that he didn't have the muscle to harm a fly, declared that she'd kick him in the balls. When I told her about my plan to question Jamie, she fell silent for a few seconds. Then, a rant: 'You have to get off the train, Mia – just get off at the next stop and come home. Once Curren knows you've sussed him out, he's not going to shake your hand and pass himself over to the police. Look, please don't get hurt, please—' I lost reception, and when she called back, I switched off my mobile. The train was less crowded than usual and three stops in I was able to take a seat. I sat down behind a table, flicked up a TV screen and plugged in the headphones. Lunchtime news. A sign outside a hospital; a Blues politician being brayed at in the House of Commons, unable to string a sentence together. I turned up the volume full notch. Jamie was on the ABC board; the ABC board had made donations of over a million to Labour Roots last year. I thought about what Jamie had said the last time we had met, about how storytelling had evolved for evolution-ary purposes. Politics was a survival of the fittest governed by those who could tell the best stories. No wonder the Blues had plummeted to third party in the polls. How had Jamie done it? Some sort of inverted Will Self, a potion that negated metaphor, kicked words out of the brain? Perhaps he had packaged it up as an ABC vitamin potion. I stared out of the window, watching farmers in macs and wellingtons wading through water-logged rape. I thought of the children I had failed to enlighten, who, with each day, were losing their ability to grow up understand-ing and telling stories. And what of Will Self's death – where did that fit into this? I told myself not to pander to conspiracy theo-ries, that I must interview Jamie in a guarded and cool fashion, but as the train sped on, angry connections fused and sparked in my imagination.

(xv) The Confrontation

I was told to wait in Jamie's drawing room. The housekeeper sent for the Spanish girl to bring some tea, informing me that Mr Curren would not be back for another hour. I calculated that I had a few spare minutes and crept down the hallway. If she caught me, I'd say I was searching for the bathroom. Here it was, spread out across the wall: Jamie's gallery of vanity. I found a pattern in the photographs, worked backwards through decades so that his hair darkened and his skin hardened. Then I saw the photograph. I heard footsteps clicking warning and hurried back to the drawing room with the image burnt on my retinas like an aftershock of bright light: Will Self with Jamie Curren, shaking hands and smiling, at the Royal Festival Hall, on the night of 14 April 2045, Will's final reading.

When the Spanish girl served my tea, I feared that my attraction for her was obvious, for she put it down with awkward spillage and made a hasty exit. I checked my watch, its tick mimicked loudly by the grandfather clock across the room. My words of accusation were neatly ordered inside me, but I was afraid that this fraught waiting would start to muddle them. Was Jamie already in the house? Was he playing a game with me? Dizziness lapped at my mind, threatening tidal tiredness. The date on my watch reminded me that just eight weeks ago I had entered a cinema, alone, expecting grief to absorb the rest of the year; I could never have imagined I would end up here. Where would I be eight weeks from now? Interviewing Jamie Curren from the depths of his jail cell; the film makers of Will's cinematic biog declaring they needed to reshoot the ending? Did Will *know* he had taken Hemingway, that was the question, or had he been fooled into thinking he was supping a helpful little ABC potion that would enhance his reading? Did Will know about the literary drugs at all? I wondered if Will had ever taken Will and let out a shivery laugh at the thought.

I fingered my mobile but refrained from calling Kat: if she freaked me, I'd only lose my nerve. I reached for the tea again, swirling the cup to stir the sugar crystals. When I looked down at my watch, I noticed that the second hand was sticking; I counted two beats for every white unit it swifted past. When I glanced at the grandfather clock, however, its hands were racing onwards, as though it had stolen time from mine, and it looked close to chiming six o'clock, despite the midday sunshine embroidering the carpet. Clouds seemed to remain static for hours, then unfurl at the speed of days. I was distracted by a strange scent in the room. It reminded me of the second-hand bookshops my father had taken me to when I was a child, where I liked to open the books and breathe in their perfume of paper and ink. There was something intoxicating about this scent, which flowed into me and uncurled like a flower.

It seemed to be coming from the large bookcase from behind me. I examined the rows of cracked spines. The scent grew stronger as I fingered a black Collins dictionary. I was about to pull it off the shelf when I noticed something in the periphery of my vision. A table; an object covered with a green baize cloth. I started. I had seen that somewhere before. Behind me, I heard a *crash!* – but it was only the dictionary, falling to the floor. I walked over and pulled the cloth away with a gasp.

'What are you doing here?' I asked softly.

Will's eye. Sadness damped his caruncle. He blinked rapidly, like an ocular lighthouse beaming warning. Behind me, I could hear the dictionary wailing. Blink blink. I reeled, trying to grab the table, grabbing air, whispering, *What has he done to me?* I felt pain zigzag my temples as I landed, my hair flinging across my face. Blackness dripped across my vision; through the trickles I saw, sitting on the table, the empty teacup.

I wanted to scream but my mouth was numb; words spooled in dribble down my chin. Above me, I saw Jamie's leer.

'Have you been introduced to Will yet? I have a share in his eye, you see – Mr Leonard is an old friend of mine. By the way, how did you like your tea? A dose of Self, Hemingway and Burroughs – I thought that would do the trick.' He laughed.

The dictionary was an elderly book and the fall had hit it hard – its black spine was warped, its weathered pages fluttering in shock. As I leant over it, I breathed in sharply and that intoxicating scent spread through my mouth like nectar. Dizzy with the swoon of it, I leant against the bookcase, my hair brushing a row of *Encyclopaedia Britannicas*. The dictionary bounced on to its feet, thanking me for helping it up. There was sarcasm in its stertorous voice. A shadow fell over me as the dictionary towered four feet, five feet, six feet tall.

Grass roots sprayed around the rims of bookcases. Spiders

jacketed books with their webbing. The carpet had cracked open to allow the growth of tombstones. One fresh white stone lured me, but as I walked over to it, I jumped in horror: my father was standing behind it. He was wearing burgundy corduroy trousers and a checked shirt. A piece of plaid had been cut out where his liver ought to have been safely housed beneath skin. The hole in his side was rimmed with stained serrated edges where the surgeons had tried to cut out the evil. Worms writhed and wriggled from the hole. Some were feasting on the rotting flesh; some were smoking cigarettes, their nubby heads coughing in a cloud of thick smoke.

'No flowers for your daddy, then?' a voice boomed.

The dictionary stood behind him like a Grim Reaper.

'I'm sorry ... I'm sorry ... I meant to bring flowers but I just ...' I wept, spreading open my palms like a demented Ophelia without her props.

'It doesn't matter about the flowers,' Dad said urgently. 'I just need to know if you got the package.'

'... we were initially alerted when your father called up Aaron Fenshaw, hoping Aaron might help him with some research. He foolishly confided everything to Aaron. He told him that he had been working on a thesis exploring Will Self's novels. During the course of his research, he had got in touch with Dr Wilkinson. Wilkinson belonged to a group of psychiatrists who, decades back, assessed the case of a certain Richard Smith and agreed that Professor Self should be struck off.' Jamie swallowed and wiped his papery mouth. 'Dr Wilkinson was old and angry. He was furious about the recent privatization of the NHS, felt his lifetime of service had gone to waste. He broke the code of ethics and a pact of secrecy. He passed on to your father the novel Richard had been working on while he sat in his tower block. That novel is the one you found on your father's computer – oh, with some flowery little editorial notes that he added. As for the diary – that was fiction, your father's imaginative retelling of Richard's tower-block days. He planned to publish them both as a diptych. Of course, Mia, I wasn't terribly happy about this. It would have caused a stir, and might have led to investigations into Prof. Self's research, which we have found very useful at ABC. Your father had to be silenced. It was most convenient that Daddy died of liver cancer before his work was submitted to publishers. But then a posthumous search of his office indicated that the diary had been printed out and sent – to you. A journalist. He had passed the baton to his vile daughter. Are you making a note of all this, Mia? You know, Hemingway is lethal. I have no idea how it reacts with Burroughs and Self. Whatever I tell you, you'll never remember it anyhow . . .' He sank into an armchair, lifting a glass of whisky to his blubbery mouth, the paper turning amber.

My daddy sat at his desk, working. The worms leered at me from his liver-shaped hole. 'Daddy,' I said, 'I'm scared there's someone in the house. I can hear someone moving about.'

'You must be quiet, be a good girl, Mia,' he said. 'I have to write down what this good dictionary is saying . . .' He paused as one of the smoking worms broke into a fit of coughing. Through its pinhole mouth spurted a greenish phlegm, which splattered over my daddy's notebook. 'Tsk,' said Daddy, tearing up the paper. 'Now I'll have to begin again.'

I gazed up at Jamie the dictionary, now a giant above my childish frame. He bent down and I cringed against the back of my father's chair, his breath stenching of stale paper.

'Do as your daddy tells you.'

My daddy handed me a doll and told me to play quietly. It

had Will's face, with a mane of long hair, and was dressed in a pin-striped suit.

'When I was a boy,' Jamie the dictionary told my daddy, waving a cigar in his typeset fingers, 'my mother wasn't very well. Little things made her cry – like a rainy day or being served a cup of tea that was too cold. My daddy was working for a big corporation called ABC and he gave her drugs so that she didn't mind any more if her tea was hot or cold, for the world became a lukewarm place to her. Then when I was bad at school he gave me special Smarties, which made me become a good boy.'

The glass eyes of the Will Self doll blinked at me. I broke his neck and twisted his head 180 degrees so that he couldn't stare at me any more.

'When I was a teenager, I became an angry young man – are you keeping up?' The dictionary peered over my daddy's shoulder. 'No, you're behind!' He punished him by pressing his cigar against one of the worm's heads. My father cried out, clutching his side. 'Hurry up!' the dictionary yelled. 'I don't have time to waste! Not when little lexicographers like her are busy stuffing me full of new rubbish!' He pointed his cigar at me, the smoke like a gaseous manifestation of his anger. My father put his hand on my shoulder and I sat between the protective tent of his legs. I gazed up at the worm; its blackened head was hanging on to the rest of its body by a thread of pink.

'As a teenager, I became an angry young man. I used to steal ABC potions from my father's offices, where I was supposed to be doing work experience. I dabbled in A-level chemistry, diluted the potions, compressed them into acid-style tabs and sold them to my local weed dealer, Dirty Pete. He sold them in clubs throughout London. It was a risky business and several people were hospitalized from Hemingway, even in minute form, so I learnt to avoid using him, and stuck to Self or Burroughs. Of course, half of the idiots who took the potions had never read a book in their life – but it didn't stop them being enthralled by these strange and marvellous trips, which had a certain char-acteristic flavour they couldn't find in the coldness of cocaine, the generic technicolour of acid. The Self drug was always my favourite. Interestingly enough, Self showed chemical similari-ties with the drug *yagé* – like *yagé*, it produced a collective trip, so that if we took it in a group we found ourselves flying through clouds of his wild imagination. I fell in love with him as a drug long before I discovered him as an author. By the time I came to read my first Self novel – *My Idea of Fun* – the words seemed familiar. He was already in my gut before my brain caught up. My father remarried; Zara became a sister, my dearest friend. We used to hide in the woods on Sunday afternoons, take Will together and make crazed, carnal love.

'All this laid the foundation for the trip to Venice where I had an epiphany. No religion, I realized, could give its followers an experience that matched the ecstasy of being Will. During my twenties, I became a successful novelist but I decided to carry on with the drugs. For one thing, it made me plenty of cash on the side so that I could continue to live a life of ideal leisure. It was also a glorious poke in the eye of my father, who kept hoping I would follow in his footsteps and perpetuate the ABC name after his death. So there I was, Jamie Curren, the pretty-boy author up for an *Encore*, profiled in the *Guardian*, with a secret *alter ego* who sold drugs through Dirty Pete and indulged in crazed orgies where the literary drugs turned our collective imagination colours that science could never know. We grew to love Will Self through the intimacy of those tablets, and our devotion sprang from there. But the side effects began to cor-rode us. Zara found herself unable to sleep; Toady began to lose shards of his memory, which was why he quite honestly had no idea what was fact and what was fiction when he wrote his misery memoir. Nicholas ended up in hospital with liver poisoning. Worst of all, it seemed to eat away at my own words, destroying my writing career when it had barely begun. It seemed our golden days were dying . . . And then Sylvie came along.'

'Daddy!' I tugged at the hem of his trousers. 'I want to go and play with Sylvie! Can I play with Sylvie?'

My daddy looked down at me and shook his head, the worms echoing in sad mimesis.

'I'm afraid,' the dictionary boomed, 'Sylvie is dead.'

The library swerved, then settled. Jamie was a silhouette; behind him, I saw Will's eye. His pupil was pressed up against the glass case, wide with desperation, tortured by his inability to help me.

I could hear cries coming from behind the library bookcase. I knelt down, peering over the tops of books, tweaking apart spines, and saw a glimpse of my father's face. I was on the wrong side of the bookcase, he screamed. I sensed a shadow falling over me and turned. The dictionary loomed, seven feet tall. I grabbed hold of a shelf crammed with Kingsley Amis & Son and managed to stagger to my feet before two thick black covers clamped on either side of me. *I killed Sylvie*, he boomed. *I killed her myself. She took a tab of Self and went mad from it – it turned out that she was very sensitive to drugs. Once she'd taken the Wafer of Will, she seemed to lose her mind. She wanted to become Self, possess his body, his voice. She had to be stopped before she went to the police or ended up in a mental institution and they traced the drug back to us.* His cock sprang upwards, a sword of papier mâché; definitions pushed up against my thigh. Book spines jutted against my spine; I was in the midst of a literary gang rape, a collusion of sniggering texts. I begged him to forgive me, to let me go, but he only punished me with paper cuts until my skin was covered with bleeding eyes. As he forced himself inside me, my jelly mouth finally managed a scream for my daddy – drowned by the grandfather clock striking six. He thrust thrust thrust deep into me, small clumps breaking off his cock and sliding down my thighs in paper mulch.

Oh, how Zara and I debated for hours on the ethics of killing her; I read Crime and Punishment *to prepare for the mental repercussions.*

I was on the floor, covered with paper cuts, aching and bleeding, my breath piston-gasped. Once more, he entered me.

I took a tab of Self before murdering her; then it became easy to stab the knife into her back. Perhaps my conscience required it, so that I could always tell myself afterwards that I had not done it: Self had willed it so.

My daddy couldn't take any more dictation: the words were dragging through him, catching on his wounds. Worms coughed and spat up phlegm until the page was streaked with it. His head bowed. His cheek came to rest on the page; he gazed at me with unseeing eyes. The dictionary withdrew. I wilted, my cheek against the floor.

And along came Richard. A strange young man, clearly deluded – who became an easy scapegoat. And yet he was, I admit, the most devoted of our followers. When he took his first Wafer of Will, he seemed to lead the group to the highest of highs, to realms

303

we had never known before. Even when the police arrested him the next morning, he seemed radiant, beautiful, at peace. A willing martyr. And so the case was closed, though the shock of the investigation shattered the WSC. We all went our separate ways. Toady and I saw each other about once every two years, bumping into each other at literary parties. Zara immigrated to Venice; I only found out about her early death – she died giving birth – weeks after. Nicholas I never saw again. When my father died, I inherited a substantial share in ABC. I thought about Dr Self's wish to use the potions in politics, and I thought, Well, why not stir up the Blues a little?

What about Will? I wept. What did you do to Will?

You want to know what I did to Will? He laughed. *You want to know if I murdered Will?*

I grabbed the bookcase, nearly pulled myself up – but he smashed the sharp edge of his cover against my arm, sending me crashing back to the floor.

Oh, but why spoil the mystery, Mia? If I tell you everything, what would be the fun in that?

He used his papery cock like punctuation, semen like exclamation marks. Blood slipped down my thighs and splattered his pages red. My spirit screamed and thrashed so hard that it seemed to disconnect from my body. There came a moment when the pain broke. I transcended it. As though my body was now a soiled thing, ruined for ever, as though my spirit rejected it. I left behind the present, too unbearable to sustain consciousness. I drifted through memories of Mia from before, before she faded for good. Sitting in the garden, my mother plaiting my hair. The sky blurring as my father picked me up and spun me round. Kat sitting next to me, smiling in the sun, leaning her head against my shoulder and suggesting we go to bed early, we were both so tired . . .

Will's eye gazed down at me. I saw, reflected in the small black world of his pupil, Kat entering the room. I saw her silhouette flail against Jamie; I heard her scream, *What have you done to her?* I saw my own body lying pristine on the floor, not a button torn, an illusion of prelapsarian Eve with a snake writhing in her soul.

(xvi) My Religion

My story was reported in a couple of national newspapers. I was a 'young attractive journalist', who found herself 'the victim of a terrifyingly potent new rape drug' and ended up 'in hospital for several weeks, fighting for her life, while her lesbian lover wept over her bedside in suicidal distress'. Jamie Curren was celebrated as a hero, a benign elderly man who had helped the female stranger who had turned up at his house 'in a fraught state'. Off the record, he had advised the police that he would not press charges against me for filing a false report of assault. No doubt he is sitting in his mansion tonight, wanking himself off over a game of Cluedo, his jism sealing up the little black envelope. In real life, conspiracies may be uncovered, but there is never a Judgment Day. Crime is acceptable if you get the packaging right, the beguiling words and colours. I could only glean the slightest satisfaction from hints that Curren was running scared; at least he seemed to have ceased his meddling in politics. The shadow cabinet were no longer sketched as caricatures above captions that punned on laryngitis. ABC Corp had also ordered a recall of all their educational potions from schools – not because they *doubted* the power of the product, said their official publicist, but because they wished to reintroduce a new improved recipe later in the year. In the meantime, as the child-herds became human, there had been a significant increase in classroom violence, and parents were begging for a new recipe so that their offspring could be intellectually neutered and their psyches revert to wool as soon as possible.

Only Aaron Fenshaw and the WSC received any punishment. They took centre stage on the front pages while I only made it to the pantomime wings of page twenty-six. On the same night that I had visited Curren, the WSC, high on drugs (that I had no doubt Jamie had fed them), decided to enact the opening of *My Idea of Fun* on an elderly neighbour who complained about the noise they were making. A miniature railway had been laid out in the back garden to symbolize the underground tube line – a shrinking of scale that would no doubt have tickled Self – so that the neophyte could plant feet on either side of the tracks and masturbate against the stump of his neck. Unfortunately, they tried to cut off his head using a small breadknife, and chose to work from the back of the neck, so that metal riddled with bone. After twenty minutes, they were painted with blood and several had fainted in horror. In court, Aaron had made a poignant plea, explaining that Self's novel had made it look a lot easier than it had been in real life, and they hadn't expected there to be nearly so much blood. Sometimes, when I lay awake at night remembering the past, I also considered the what-ifs: if I had gone to interview Aaron that day instead of Jamie.

Kat and I joined the queue, a smoking perfumed crocodile scaled with glitz and denim and sloganed T-shirts. She had persuaded me to come clubbing for the evening. I think she'd hoped that I might put up a fight, but I had tormented her with a dull 'yes'.

Above us, *RITZY* flashed on-off. When the pink faded, the lettering looked cadaverous, as though it had been looped from bone. The queue inched forwards I stumbled and Kat caught me. 'Pissed already,' a guy in front of us leered. I had handed in my crutches two days ago. My body still felt sometimes like a vehicle I had forgotten how to drive; I steered as though drunk, my joints locking like awkward gears. I reached out and splayed my fingers against the dirty wall. Dust, pigeon-shit, gloops of graffiti against my palm. The earthy reassured me. In hospital, the police had fired questions while the darkness sucked me in and spat me out. 'Jamie Curren didn't rape you,' a policewoman had informed me gently and later sternly. 'We examined you when you came in. You did not have a trace of semen inside you. You have a partner. . . Kat – is that her name?' It means pure, I told her. She asked me if I disliked men – 'Were you seeking some sort of revenge against them? Did you take the drug yourself and turn up at Jamie's house? Why were you lingering at his house in the first place, so far away from home?' One day, Kat got so sick of witnessing my interrogations that she punched the policewoman and had to pay a hundred-euro fine, as well as another for her illegal gas-guzzler in the hospital car park.

'D'you want a drink?' Kat yelled over the music.

'No.' Kat had not been present when the doctor had warned me that my liver was so soiled by Jamie's drug-cocktail that it belonged to an elderly woman; he'd advised me not to risk taking alcohol again for the rest of my life.

'I mean – water,' Kat said.

'No – I'm fine.'

We waited for the barman to mix her drink.

'We're never going to know,' I said, 'whether he killed Will. We're never going to know. I mean, sometimes I think he might have told me, when it was happening, and the drug made me forget it, and maybe he told me but I've forgotten and maybe—'

'Let it go, Mia,' Kat said, stroking a strand of hair back from my face. 'Let it go.'

The barman put her drink on the bar.

Kat drank her cocktail within a minute. She stood and watched the dancers with me. I felt as though I was amputating her spirit; I told her to join in. She protested but I insisted. I enjoyed watching her. It was therapeutic to assure myself that this was 'normal'; the meat market around us was comfortingly crude. The policewoman had struggled to hide a smile when I had told her Jamie Curren had raped my imagination. I did all I could to avoid firing it up, these days; I regarded books as something I needed to give up, like smoking. I had reread Richard's diary once, savouring my father's prose, then packed it into a box and hidden it at the bottom of a filing cabinet; Kat had the key. If I could just keep my mind quiet, I might enjoy brief moments of nirvana where I could find the ghost of my former self.

But who was I kidding? Every face that looked my way sneered at how out of place I was. I was a wreck. I spent my nights aching for light, my days aching for dark. Kat frowned when I followed her into the Ladies. As I caught her sneaking into a cubicle, she turned to me, looking sheepish.

'Give me some too,' I said.

'Are you sure?'

She locked the door and we stood opposite each other. The tab made me double-take, but I had hallucinated a Will Self: it was just an innocent smiley face. She broke it into two with the frown of a priest uncertain whether to dispense communion. I pressed my forefinger to hers, peeling away my half with delicacy, as though we were dealing with butterflies. We stared at each other. I felt my heart choke when I saw the sadness in her eyes. She was waiting for me to come back to her, and I suddenly became aware that her patience was finite. I saw the tab flick on her tongue and quickly chewed mine, hungry for oblivion, not caring if it was final.

Cinema church Alice rabbit lost girl bubblewrap package father's office laughing ghoul gushing water flicking eye bloody thighs – I left behind the dance floor, stumbling into the Ladies, knocking a girl spraying perfume. She told me to watch it. I slammed into a cubicle. My mouth spilt my memories into the bowl with a bitter bile stench. I was terrified that I was going to die like this, in a shitty club, my last act a puke. I leant back against the cubicle, holding my damp face in my hands. Still breathing – a blessing or a curse? When the tears came, I did not know whether they were for my mother or my father. My rape – my fake rape – had felt like a virtual simulation of what my mother had gone through when she died. He'd walked free; Jamie had walked free. I had never wanted to believe in God more, to beg for vengeance, to pray for justice, find solace. I thought about taking one more drug; it would probably do it – one way to find out if my atheism was correct.

But then, as though life was listening, I felt it brush against the back of my neck. I heard it whisper, *Kat.*

Outside, I saw that she was waiting for me. She danced, twirled her back to me. I walked up to her slowly. She stood still, her eyes question marks. When I began to sway, they broke with tears. Our bodies brushed; the music plaited our heartbeats into one. I realized that if there was one religion I believed in, it was love. She was my life; she was my God. A girl walking past cried out that a new tropicsmog was beginning. I leant in to Kat and whispered, 'You're so beautiful.'

Kat and I stayed together for more than twenty years. Our second decade was happier than the previous one. Kat downgraded and satisfied her ambitions with an ongoing role in a TV crime drama; my desire to kick against life limpened into an acceptance of it; stoicism became a virtue I cultivated. At the age of fifty-three, I received a call one evening informing me that Kat had been killed filming on the Cornish coast. A tropicsmog had unexpectedly broken and the crew had not been able to retreat to safe shore in time. Since graveyards had become a thing of the past – considered an indulgence in our crowded cities – I kept a few of her ashes in a vial hung around my neck, along with some of her blood, skin and hair, a little potion of Katness. In the evenings I would sit by the window in the manner of a woman twenty years older, the present irrelevant, listening to the soundtrack of memory: her laughter, her soft voice in my ear, her humming in the shower. During a spring-clean, I stumbled across an old copy of *How the Dead Live*, my father's favourite Self novel. A book I had felt too raw to read for many years after his passing. As I opened it, I remembered the Mia I used to be, a girl of raging torments. Now I could only gently shrug my shoulders at Death; sigh and tell him to get on with it. I had accepted that I did not have enough left inside to invest my love in another in this lifetime. I rather enjoyed Will's imagining of death, the rants of Lily Bloom, a seventy-nine-year-old Jewish woman who wandered through the capital putting her past world to rights. As the summer light died on my page, I let the book slip from my fingers and hoped that, like Lily, Kat might have moved on to a better part of London.

Part Five:
Sam Mills

(i) The Letter

Sam Mills
181 Ashleighton Gardens
Manchester M13 WWS

membership@thewillselfclub.co.uk

Will Self
c/o Andrew Wylie
The Wylie Agency
17 Bedford Square
London WC1B 3JA

10 February 2010

Dear Will Self,

I am an author published by Faber & Faber and for the past nine years I've been working on a novel called *The Quiddity of Will Self*. The novel aims to be the literary equivalent of *Being John Malkovich* – only in my book, you are the object of fascination.

One of my favourite novels is *Flaubert's Parrot* by Julian Barnes — because I adored its fusion of fiction and erudite literary criticism. In a similar vein, *The Quiddity of Will Self* aims to be a bizarre comedy, a murder mystery and a sincere homage to you and your work.

I graduated from Lincoln College, Oxford, in 1997 and since then I've worked as a full-time writer. I've written for various publications such as the *Guardian* and published three YA novels with Faber/Alfred Knopf in the US, which have been translated into four languages; one of them, *The Boys Who Saved the World*, is also being adapted for film. However, *The Quiddity* has been a labour of love for me over the last nine years and I would like to get a publishing deal for this book with your 'blessing'. My novel also includes a few quotes from your works so I am also seeking your permission to include them.

So, I was wondering if you'd like to look at the book and give me your verdict . . .

Yours sincerely,

Sam Mills

(ii) A Reading of The Boys Who Saved the World

I am sitting in Waterstones, Deansgate, giving a reading to three people clearly in need of medication, when she walked into my life.

Seven p.m. on a Thursday evening. I sit behind a lone desk, surrounded by unsold books. Twenty-seven empty chairs give me cold metal stares. An elderly woman wearing a headscarf patterned in cerise and cerulean allows her knitting needles – previously a fricative blur – to fall slack. A man with a bald pate, arms tightly folded over a beige anorak, glares at me with visceral loathing. A young man wearing thick concave glasses leans forwards, his arms and legs poised in an architecture of fascinated delight – but one that I cannot fully savour, given the 'W' badge pinned to his black T-shirt. He is paid to be here.

"'In two hours time I – and the rest of the Brotherhood – will kidnap a terrorist . . .'" I break off to take a sip of water. I don't think I ever hate the sound of my voice as acutely as when I'm giving a reading.

"'My outfit is packed in my rucksack . . .'" My full stop becomes an exclamation mark, supplied by the clang of a knitting needle hitting the floor. Soon, snores batten my words.

The interruptions continue. Someone bangs a three-for-two table, upending a pile of history books. I look up, my skin prickling. I want to set fire to the shop; I want them all to go up in flames. A breeze lifts the curling showcard, 'SAM MILLS, LOCAL AUTHOR, WILL BE GIVING A READING AT 7 P.M. TONIGHT. . .' It carries the scent of perfume. Something quintessentially feminine: lilac. My arousal is Proustian. I am transported back to the bottom of a railway track, burying my face in the neck of a girl who has borrowed her mum's scent, just as the woman enters my talk, so that I experience a heady synthaesia of past and present, of my jism hitting the wall of my first condom in a gasp of joy, and the sudden arousal of seeing this exquisite, modern-day mistress of Troy.

Helena tested her beauty by provoking the launch of a thousand ships. The myth sounds grand now, but slough off the spin, wind back the clock and ask yourself: was Helena happy with a thousand? Or did she return to her reflection and whisper, 'Mirror, mirror . . .' What if she was expecting a good deal more – ten thousand, whole nations to join forces, the conglomeration of the entire world? Did the thousand in fact leave her for ever convinced her nose was a tiny bit crooked or her chin had one more dimple than perfection deemed?

This girl is a creature in full knowledge of her beauty but, like Helena, she has to test it. To prove that she is beating Time's Winged Chariot, that knights would kill dragons in her honour, that men would establish a cult in her name. An adroit actress, she has brought her props with her – an umbrella, a bag of books, high-heeled shoes. We heard the bullet click-clacks of her boots down the parquet corridor before she even entered; now she proceeds to stand, a forlorn fawn, glancing around with big eyes – where can I sit? where shall I sit? – until several kindly Waterstones assistants emerge from seemingly nowhere and direct her to the front; on her passage there, she proceeds to knock her umbrella against several chairs and stamp on the elderly woman's foot. Had she suffered from acne and lurid breath, she would have been fiercely ejected by now, but her beauty places her on the outside of the law and good manners and the assistants only swoon. Finally, she sits, pinning her melting olive eyes on me, mouth open like a rosebud begging a bee to fuck it, mouthing an impish apology, straightening the tartan rim of her skirt, tucking her schoolgirl legs beneath her seat.

During her entire performance, I carry on reading. The audience reconnects with me, having lost half a page, foreheads furrowing in confusion to discover we have suddenly leapt to a kidnapping. I fail to acknowledge her. But then, this itself is the first play of courtship. Ignoring her, refusing to play her little game, is surely just a variation of my teenboyhood philosophy of *treat 'em mean, keep 'em keen*. Not that it ever worked. I was always more of a lover than a beloved, tipping the wrong way on Cupid's see-saw.

'Well, thank you for that *amazing* reading, Sam.' John, the assistant, bounces to his feet. He claps. Snores; glares; and then the sweet song of her enthused clapping. I think I love her.

'Any questions?'

'I have one.'

I'd almost forgotten the man with the bald pate. I drag my eyes from her to meet his hostile stare. His arm is raised as though saluting his own private dictator.

'My question is — how did you get to be published so young? I mean, I've written five novels, all memoirs, all stuff about my parents' time after the war, living in Berkhamsted, and it's obvious I'm never going to get them published because I'm fifty-five and I don't have G-cup breasts made of silicon. Well, you're young, that's why you've got this stuff published. That's obvious, isn't it?'

I tell him that I am thirty-four and, in fact, suffering the onset of an early midlife crisis; nor is there an ounce of silicon in my body. He is not persuaded. Small flecks of spit pattern ellipses across my book covers.

'Any more questions?' John interjects.

The old lady asks me why I chose to set my books in Africa.

'I haven't, actually . . .' I give John a helpless look and he mirrors it. 'I haven't set any of my books in Africa, so . . .'

'Oh.' She gathers up her knitting, tangling it in her distress. 'I thought you looked a bit young to have written all those novels set in Africa — *Monsoon's* my favourite. But clearly you didn't write it,' she adds savagely, glaring at me as though I am a veteran imposter.

'Any more questions?' John asks, in a cheerful tone.

My gaze rests half a foot away from my ravishing beauty. I hope the disappointment doesn't show on my face when she remains silent.

John asks me several questions: what's my writing routine, where do I get my inspiration from, what novelists have influenced me? Then: silence.

'Is there going to be a signing now?' my Aphrodite asks.

'Absolutely!' I cry.

The old lady makes a slow, shuffling departure; her knitting trails behind her like a blue tail. The man with the bald pate comes up and fingers my books as though they are faeces, grimacing at the blurbs, throwing them back down, spine-shattered, with a loud sigh. And then my goddess walks up to me, her stride that of a bouncing ballerina. She picks up a copy of *The Boys Who Saved the World*, and asks if I might sign it.

'Sure,' I hear myself say.

Her hands are pale, fingers delicate, as though she spins gold for a living. They do not suffer the slightest tremor.

'What name shall I put?' I ask.

'To Zara.'

'That's a beautiful name.' I don't wince at my own clichés. In the first stumbling encounters of a courtship, language will always feel false and inadequate. It's the physical that speaks with a louder, clear voice: pupils becoming feline, hands breezing hair, the tale-tell tug of her teeth against her plump apple-slice lower lip. As she thanks me and I pass the book back, I run my eyes over her body, looking for signposts of character. Her bag is leathery, masculine, and large, the sort an avid reader might favour to cram books into. There is a CND badge on her corduroy jacket and her sloganned black T-shirt takes the piss out of Blair. Her tights are dark and laddered; the short skirt has been taken up several hems, the stitching ragged, to its current state of indecency.

'Thanks so much – this is cool. I'm really chuffed to have this.' She hugs it to her chest. 'I'm going to read it tonight!' Her accent is a Pic 'n' Mix of different cultures: chirpy pink Oz gum layered over with liquorice strands of Cockney London complemented by a sherbet fizz of Dublin Irish.

'Well, that's great ... I ... Do you ... do you read much?' I ask. Nerves flutter through my words, making my voice stertorous.

'Oh, well, I don't have time to read as much as I'd like – I'm a student, so it's the hols and I'm working in a bar to pay my bills,' she confesses, twisting candyfloss hair around her little finger. 'But what I really, really, *really* want to be is a writer.' She lowers her voice, as though her literary ambitions place us both in the same secret society. 'I mean – I was actually wondering if ... if you ever teach creative writing?'

'Oh, sure,' I say. 'I'd be happy to read your work and—'

'Oh, wow — do you hold any classes?'

'No — but — but — I do offer one-to-one tutorials.'

'Well — maybe I could give you my email and you could, er, give me your prices?'

Goodbyes are exchanged. Her exit is nearly as dramatic as her entrance. Lilac lingers will-o'-the-wisp in the air; even the quality of light seems different, as though, like some angelic force, she has brought about a transmogrification of shadow and chiaroscuro. I stare at the doorway she departed through for some time, before I become aware of something hard banging against my knuckles. I look up and see the man with the bald pate holding a copy of my novel, asking for my signature with a pleading look in his eyes.

Then it is all over, the heaven and the hell of it, and a private taxi, booked by my publisher, pulls up at the kerb. The car is an elderly grey Fiesta, birdshit dotted over its bonnet like dandruff. The driver is elfin, with a ring of fluffy white hair circling his magic-mushroom head. Though he is perched on a pizza of tartan cushions, he still has to stretch considerably in order to wrap his arthritic claws around the steering wheel. He greets me with a jolly gap-toothed smile as I climb into the back, where a sheepskin rug has been spread across the seat.

Deansgate, as ever, is trawling with traffic. I notice the driver trying to catch my eye in the mirror but I avoid his gaze, watching vignettes of city life blur past. Manchester: my muse. Forget London and the Garrick; forget garrets in Paris; I've spent the last decade quaffing caffeine in Neros and Costas and other *faux*-Italian cafés that adopt a sunny piazza theme despite the northern rain that spits laughter at such an absurdity, scribbling my *tour de force*. Self is a London writer so I set *The Quiddity of Will Self* in the capital as homage to him. But Manchester is my city of choice. Tonight my eyes glaze the streets with an erotic psychogeography. I see Zara's curves in spires and rooftops, the shine of her eyes in the streetlamps, and the damp caress of the night seems a portentous hue of what might come to be.

The car breaks sharply at a set of lights. The driver succeeds in snagging my gaze in the mirror.

'So you're an author!' he enthuses. 'My wife's a big reader – she's always got her head in a book, normally the latest Josephine Cox.'

There is a pause, and a sense of familiarity. I have a feeling that I already know his narrative.

'I'm writing a book,' he says.

As predictable as a bedtime story.

'I mean, a lot of people have told me I've had such a fascinating life that I really should write a book, so I have. It's a bit like a Dan Brown. It's about this really tough guy, sort of based on me, who discovers that all the Tory Party are really aliens, and they actually caused the death of Diana so they could take her body back to their planet for dissection, and created the banking crisis so they could assess how we all responded to stress . . . and he brings them all down . . .' He flashes me a glance in his mirror. 'Maybe you could give it to your publisher, or agent, put in a good word for me.'

Zara is still a drug infusing my body, colouring my bloodstream with neon love. Surprising myself, I smile and congratulate the driver, exuberantly wishing him the best of luck.

(iii) Home

My flat is situated in Didsbury, on a road where ley lines are said to cross. My landlord (who is, incidentally, a devotee of Richard Dawkins) was savvy enough to buy up a disused church, and hasten its next step on the evolutionary ladder, dissecting it into a block of twenty-four flats. The small stove that signifies my kitchen squats where bell-ropes were once tugged. Stone has been replaced by saggy leather, angels with Ikea, inscriptions and stained glass by framed replicas of Waterhouse prints. Sirens smile danger where sinners were once soothed. Unfortunately it is not a flat that suits a man of six foot three (for I am just two inches shorter than the man himSelf). Tufts of my dark hair adorn the low ceiling; blood stains the doorframes.

When I return from the reading, the geography of my flat reflects the Sam Mills I was before I left for Waterstones. Bleeding biros, Y-fronts crumpled in heaps of self-disgust, neglected cups and screwed-up balls of paper sadness. Now I feel like the Sam Mills of two years back, bright with optimism, fizzing with mojo. I pick up the bucket that is collecting a dirty baptism from the ceiling, swilling it merrily into the toilet. On the stereo is Chopin's Prelude no. 4, Op. 28 – the closest you can get to a suicide note on the piano – and I exchange it for David Bowie singing about heroes and lovers and low. Then I slump on the sofa and gaze at the cloud-spiked sky. The noise of my neighbours is no longer an irritation but a comedy.

If she was to come, she'd stand by that bookcase, the sunset lining the glass of wine she holds, and she'd pick up *Tristes Tropiques* from the coffee table and we'd clash IQs over Lévi-Strauss, and she'd lie on that rug and feel it burn her back while I rocked inside her, and she'd bring me luck and I'd get a book deal, and Will Self would write me an ebullient letter of personal congratulations and it'd win the Booker of Bookers and she'd discover a cure for cancer and we'd stop global warming and save the world and spend eternity in heaven, locked in coital bliss.

Cooking feels too sensible for my present mood. I only have a fiver in my wallet, and just enough coins for my tube fare tomorrow, so a takeaway is out of the question. I take two rusting tins from the fridge, one sweetcorn, one salmon, eating crunchy mouthfuls with a fork.

I check my emails. For the first time in months, I forget to scan the subject lines in hope of an email from Will Self. I sent Zara an email on my mobile in the taxi, while the driver was jabbering on about his masterpiece. There's no reply – yet.

Archie West, my literary agent, sometimes says he fears Will might sue me. I wonder if the Arts Foundation would help fund my court costs. On my sofa lies the paraphernalia of grant application pages. I'm hoping for £1,250; I can make it last for months. When I shuffle through my application, I fear the tone sounds desperate, a literary Oliver Twist asking for a new Toshiba and OKI printer to fill his begging bowl. I have to send them sample material as 'supporting evidence' of my abilities and I've already decided that I won't include the prologue, just in case I'm judged by a female who gets offended by the dictionary rape opening. The Arts Foundation is one of those bodies which are so keen on equal opportunities that they end up creating inequality. I toy with the thought of ticking the 'disabled' box — but what if they ask for proof and I end up having to borrow a wheelchair? Does being half Welsh mean I count as an ethnic minority? If I once had a wet dream about Will Self, does that mean I could be bisexual? I know that as a healthy white heterosexual male with four working limbs they're bound to reject me, but I carry on filling out the form anyway.

I check my emails once more and then turn back to *The Quiddity of Will Self*. Part One, Chapter Nine, Richard. I wrote the finale scene in the early hours of the morning, in a blue frenzy, after watching *Blue Velvet*. Writing it thrilled me; I felt as though I'd put on a mask. Its painted face was debauched, a wicked Sam Mills streaked in shades of black and red; it allowed me to step beyond the boundaries of my everyday self. Removing the mask was harder. It took a few days of wandering, lost and uncertain, before I stepped back into my safe circle of self again.

I reread the page where Jamie Curren's sister, Sasha, is sprawled across the devotional bed, her onanism an offering to Will: *Her hands seized flurries of pages, smothering them over her fulsome breasts, her corrugated ribs, her lissom stomach . . .*

Taking my red pen, I cross out *fulsome*. Then I cross out *breasts*. Then I cross out my crossings-out.

The Bad Sex Award has caused a regression in novel writing. We are back in the mindset of the pre-D. H. Lawrence era. Back then, novelists were censored by society. Now they are censored by shame. Once they feared obscenity trials. Now they fear trial by embarrassment, with a crowd of hooting journalists their jury, and the ghost of Auberon Waugh their judge. Archie has already warned me that *The Quiddity of Will Self* will make me an obvious candidate. But I'm determined not to start replacing cocks with euphemisms, or cutting out cocks altogether. After all, Will doesn't.

When I first created Sasha Curren, I always pictured her as a pale redhead. My imagination is already starting to repaint her in shades of Zara, with olive skin and hair as dark as the night *... her lissom breasts, her hand curving down between her thighs and flicking the coif of hair, smearing apart her ...* No, that's no good, no good at all: I can't use my prose as a vehicle for my fantasies.

I go to the kitchen and make a cup of camomile tea. James, a friend since uni, thinks it's hilarious that my teabag collection is akin to that of 'an elderly woman's'. But I find caffeine is a drug I can't handle these days: too many words start to career through my mind, crashing into headachy multiple pile-ups. Then I check my emails. Nothing yet.

I go to the bathroom.

She did not tell me her age. I think she can only be twenty, twenty-two. I might have been her father, if I'd been a particularly randy fourteen-year-old. I stare at my face in the mirror, pull at the bags under my eyes, considering pros and cons. The pros: I don't desire well-preserved beauty; my elixir is Youth, with a capital *Y*. I want my wrinkles to touch baby-soft skin. I want my roughening hands to become smooth against the taut flesh of a girl's stomach. I want an uncarved, uncreated face. I want the banality of simplistic views on Marx and idealisms on Che. I want youth's cynicism, its casual and cruel rejection of love in favour of selfishness masquerading as freedom. I want this, all this, to seep into me by osmosis, to lighten the weight of my wisdom with ignorance, to transmogrify my experience into innocence.

The cons: all of the above. In my early twenties, I found it so easy to drift into relationships – business, romantic, friendly. When ties began to form, I had no qualms about taking a knife to them. Since my thirties, regret has changed me. I remember reading a Hanif Kureishi novel (a brief sojourn from my Self devotion), which said that after a certain age it is impossible simply to have sex with someone without it meaning something. I have wanted to fire my agent, Archie, for the last two years but I feel paralysed. A one-night stand, once a joy as casual as a cigarette, now invokes a cancerous poignancy. I embarrass myself by feeling sentimental at the end of contrived romantic films or novels; adverts jerk tears from me, even while the cynic inside me is cringing in horror. A shallow life was so much easier; depth comes hand in hand with tragedy.

I check my emails.

I go to bed. I wonder if my letter to Will Self is sitting in a postal line, kissing a gas bill, or whether it's still with his agents, or has been wrongly posted and is being opened at this moment in time by a bemused Romanian. I look up at my ceiling, at the scars left behind by stained glass being stripped out. I picture its apocalyptic end, an angry Creator claiming his house back, the spiritual mortgage in negative equity, brick imploding, glass slashing, rubble simmering, bodies buried and mingling with the bodies buried centuries back, blessed and laid to rest beneath wooden crosses.

(iv) Lunch with Archie

It would be easier if I was dead. I picture my cadaver feeding hungry blue flames. I picture them burping out my skin into ashes, chewing my eyeballs to gristle, gnawing my bones and spitting them out with charred tooth-marks. A dead writer is much easier to love. Then readers can construct their own narratives. Their lives can be moulded to fit our idea of who ought to have penned their fiction. Larkin: the poet who wrote *ironically* about misogyny and racism. Kafka: the tortured, saintly soul, who subscribed to *Der Amethyst* for its beautiful images of the human body. Gerard Manley Hopkins: the priest who crafted beautiful lines about Windhovers and never touched on the subject of naked little boys.

'Sam, my good fellow – how *are* you?' Archie enters the restaurant. He removes his heavy cashmere coat and pats me heavily on the back, his eyes flitting over neighbouring tables. I can see the social data being processed in his retinas. Rival agents all over the place, no doubt, and editors he's wooing or fighting. He waits for the waiter to pull out his chair, then sits down next to me, wafting cologne-clouds frilled with the scent of cigar smoke and whisky, and that perennial papery smell about him, as though Archie has spent so many decades handling manuscripts, he has become half human, half book.

'So does anyone want to publish *The Quiddity of Will Self?*' I ask.

'Sam, Sam, patience, my dear boy, patience. Calm down and let us order.' 'Right. Yes.' I become aware that I am pleating the tablecloth between my fingers; I let it fall slack.

Dining at the Ivy is, of course, theoretically not about the dining, but the knowledge that the dishes you're perusing on the menu are currently working their way through the intestines of several famous people. But for me it genuinely is about the food. I'm probably the only person here who has lived off baked beans on toast and anorexic lettuce for the last three days. My stomach has started nibbling its own lining. I asked Archie if we can have three courses and he pats his stomach, declaring he really must diet before his dinner-date with Jerry Hall this Saturday. I pretend I've misheard and instruct the waiter to give me a starter and a main. To my dismay, Archie orders venison.

'So, have you got me a deal yet?' I start.

'Drinks?' the waiter asks.

Archie orders a bottle of Chardonnay. I ask for an orange juice, but Archie looks incredulous, and changes my order to a gin and tonic. I try to interrogate him again, but he's jumped up to table-hop. I watch him leering wolfishly at Simon Trewin, as he pats him on the back; obviously some cat's cradle of poaching intrigue going on there.

I play with my fork, my reflection a triptych in the tines. Perhaps that would make a good author photograph. I feel shy about author publicity. And I seem to disappoint in the flesh: I've lost count of the number of people who've said, 'You're not really how I imagined the author of your books to be.' A blurry shot would be suitably anonymous.

Archie sits down and launches into a diatribe about e-books. I can only hear the words he isn't saying; I brood at my fork. *The Quiddity of Will Self* will never be published; it would be better if I were dead. Publishing rejection makes you feel cut adrift, as though you're in a small creative boat, knocked around on waves of alienation, hoping and praying for the anchor of a contract. It isn't until the arrival of our starters – *hamachi* tuna *sashimi* for me, sevruga caviar for him – that he finally gives me the news, in a grave voice, as though reading my obituary. Faber have rejected the novel. Portobello have rejected the novel. Fourth Estate have rejected the novel. We're in a recession and everyone is cautious, and how would I feel about being a ghost writer for the TV presenter Zoë Trashtosh, who wants to publish a children's book called *Sweatshop Boy*, a moving morality tale about an Indian kid working in a sweatshop who is saved when he becomes the star of a reality TV show? A tie-in deal with Nike has just been signed.

I stare at Archie without speaking.

'Look,' Archie chides me, 'this Will Self book will sell, Sam, it will sell! It's a splendid book, the best book I've read in ages. We have to get it published – because for one thing, you've put me in it. You've written me as a total cunt. It's a chuckle!'

'But *who* do you think *will*—'

Archie jumps up once more to greet Travis Hilton, winner of this year's *Big Brother*, pumping his hand emphatically, as though he might shake a book out of him. When he returns, he takes a chaste sip of Chardonnay, a bite of his fillet of venison, and gives me a sober look. Archie, like all agents, has a habit of see-sawing between insane optimism about the publishing industry one moment and declaring we are all finished the next.

'The thing is, Sam – I have so many great books that I can't sell. The editor loves the book but Marketing doesn't – that's my most common scenario. We're living in a post-literate world. When it comes to literary fiction there's about three types of book I can sell, year in, year out.' He ticks them off on his stubby fingers. 'This year's *Secret History*; a book by a male northern twenty-something who's the lead singer of an indie band and has written about *ennui*, sex, drugs and rock and roll; or a multi-cultural epic set on the eve of the Olympics, exploring racial tension – preferably Islamic – in a post-nine/eleven world.'

'But—'

'In addition, it's simply not enough to write a good book. You need to be marketable.' He pulls a sheaf of paper from his briefcase, peering at it with mopsical eyes. 'Your CV blatantly screams that you were born in 1875 – how am I supposed to sell that?'

'*Nineteen* seventy-five,' I correct him.

'Ah – where *are* my glasses? 1975 is possibly worse. A hun-dred-and-thirty-five-year-old author might be a novelty,' he muses. Then his tone becomes accusatory. 'Eighty per cent of novels are bought by women. If you were to become, or write as, *Samantha*, I might have an easier time selling you.'

'Well, I can always go back and berate my father's sperm—' I begin a retort, but Archie is off again, curling his arm around a cardinal. I pick up my spoon. My fingers are shaking and, in the reflection, my face blurs like Munch's *The Scream*. I picture my hair curling over my shoulders, my stubble regressing. Archie is suggesting the cardinal write a diatribe in revenge against militant atheists.

When Archie returns to the table, I poke and prod my roasted Cornish brill, sulking in silence. Archie sighs and orders the Bolivian wild chocolate pannacotta.

'Some of my friends want to actually set up the WSC,' I inform him, in a dejected tone. 'With cloaks and everything.'

'That's just great, Sam – a real publicity stunt!' Archie pats my shoulder. 'And even better – if you could perhaps murder someone during an initiation ceremony, well, we'd get you on the front page of every newspaper.'

'And into prison, Archie.'

'Well, it didn't do Jeffrey Archer any harm, did it? His sales went through the roof.'

Archie jack-in-a-boxes back to the cardinal. My brill has become a mash-up; the waiter quietly removes it, in mid-assault from my fork, and I feel like a difficult child being chided at the dinner table. My reflection has now become smeary with gristle; I look through the tines at the cardinal. Atheist Communist regimes have killed just as many millions as fervent fanatics have, which just goes to prove that religion is an excuse, rather than an inspiration, for bloodshed. Perhaps one day people will fight in the name of Will, will flay sinners for their misinterpretations of *The Book of Dave*, will wipe out entire territories in order to claim oil and defend *The Quantity Theory of Insanity*. I stand up and the waiter briskly brings me my anorak; Archie glances over and mouths ebulliently: 'I'll call you.'

Back home, I call my father. 'You okay, Dad?'

'I wouldn't even win the Nonce Prize, I wouldn't even win the Nonce Prize.'

'D'you want me to come over?'

'I'm fine, Sam, I'm – wouldn't even win the Nonce Prize, wouldn't even win the Nonce Prize.'

'It's one of those days, right?' I say sadly. I listen to his parroting for a few more moments, then gently put down the phone. I sit still for a while, pondering guilt and Fate, and then go to my computer.

No messages from Zara. Clearly she found me instantly

forgettable; I decide that I probably hate her. Clicking on to Facebook, I suffer the deep welling of loneliness that only a social networking site can inspire. I feel nostalgic for the 1920s, when I might have been able to sit in a floral living room with Woolf and have a teacup filled by Leonard and compete in discussions about literature and capitalism. If the Bloomsbury set were alive now, they'd be too busy blogging to meet. Their relations would be signified by 'Links' pages on their sites. I flick away from the Net to Word. Open up *The Quiddity of Will Self.* I scrawl through *Richard's* Part One. Sasha does not suit the name of Jamie Curren's sister.

FIND: Sasha Curren

REPLACE: Zara Curren

(v) The Creative Writing Tutorial

She wore a red dress. It was hot. She stared at the horizon. He
came up behind her and put a hand on her shoulder. She shivered.

'You read fast,' Zara says.

I look up at her. She is sitting on a stiff-backed chair, her
ankles neatly folded, her fingers playing a neurotic rosary
with her beads. I'm sitting on the sofa, the saggy brown leather
naked around me.

I give her a smile, one that reassures her that I am considering every word, and turn the page. This one I read more slowly.
I need to buy time, shuffle criticisms in my head, turn, tame
harsh words into euphemisms.

'It's kind of meant to be like *The Secret History*,' Zara interjects
impatiently.

'Yeah, I kind of got a sense of that . . .'

I stare at her words, and they stare back at me. If I was judg-
ing her prose for a creative writing prize, a fierce debate would
be taking place between my cock, declaring that this is the
finest novel I have ever read, and my conscience, which points
out that my mind is somewhat less impressed. I consider the
sheets on my bed, Persil-crisped; the shorn scuzz of my beard,

caught in the bin in a furl of discarded cellophane, pulled from a brand new box of Durex, now convenient under a pillow; the six bottles of wine in the fridge, of varying culture, colour and strength; and the bar of Green & Black's chocolate – I thought I couldn't go wrong with chocolate. I have prepared, but wrongly so; and I feel foolish, as though she is the one scrawling red pen over my expectations, awarding me a low mark. I consider a third judge in my literary jury, one of pure vengeance: *Well, Zara, I may as well come out and say it – you're never going to win the Booker* . . .

'You know, I don't mind if you don't like it . . .'

'No, it's really very good . . .'

'*Really?*' She grabs hold of my words and clings to them. My conscience winces. No doubt in the future she will wrap them around herself for their protective warmth against the coldness of a world that misunderstands her genius.

'Well, I had mixed feelings from time to time . . . your characters . . .'

'I follow E. M. Forster's theory – of having compassion for all your characters,' she says. 'I think when you write about people, you have to *love* them, no matter what.'

'But you murder your characters. They die, one by one . . .'

'I'm a Buddhist, you know, Sam. Ultimately I believe in reincarnation. And this book will show how evil murder really is . . .'

'Well, you know what Nabokov said about Forster. Forster said he often lost control of his characters and Nabokov said something like, "You have to sympathize with his people if they try to wriggle out of that trip to India or wherever." He basically said Forster's characters had the good sense to run away. You don't want yours to be the same.' I mean to tease, but she falls silent.

Her eyes are narrowed. 'You don't like my work.'

'No, I do – I do! It's just . . . I mean, it's all so subjective . . .'

If only my critique could have been post-coital. Caresses would have softened my words. I think of the six bottles of wine in the fridge, my last fifty pounds blown; at least I can spend the rest of the week getting drunk in bitter disappointment.

'Look,' I say frankly. 'You write as though you're not in love with the English language. You write as though you view the English language as a woman who should be locked up. Your prose, which you no doubt view as minimalist, is simply dull. "She wore a red dress." Well, why not a scarlet dress? Why not a red dress that looked like a ripe tomato about to explode? Why not use some images, why not consider dressing your prose with some metaphors, some frills, some character?'

'Oh!' Her eyes and lips became oval with consternation. 'But you see – I did a creative writing class, and my teacher told me I should say less, not more, that I should show, not tell, and try to cut out all adverbs and adjectives.' She reeled off various other fulsome mantras.

'Well, that's a very fashionable viewpoint. Because people want books to be like movies. They want plain prose like a movie script. Or maybe it's even about our society's desire to grow up slowly, to stay in a state of kidulthood with simple books without too many words in them. But personally . . .'

'Yes . . . be brutal with me. I can take it.'

'I like metaphors. I like colourful prose. I mean, look at *Great Apes* – you've got adverbs and adjectives exploding on every page, and it just fizzes. Imagine if Will Self had gone to a creative writing class at the age of twenty-three and they'd told him to write in neat little pared-down sentences.'

'Will Self.' Her eyes light up. 'I read his column in the *New Statesman*. He's the best thing in it by far . . .'

'I'm actually writing a book about him,' I confess. 'It's called *The Quiddity of Will Self.*'

'Really? Can you show me some?'

'No,' I say, shaking my head. 'Nobody's allowed to read it. I've been working on it for nine years.'

'*Nine years.* Oh, my God!' She shakes back her hair and it settles around her head in a dark halo.

I smile. And then I confide: 'The trouble is, all the stories we read teach us that perseverance will be rewarded. You read about people who have spent a decade toiling in poverty as they produce a novel or a film or a work of art, and at the end of it all their lives burst into fireworks and they win the Booker or an Oscar and it all comes good. But you never hear about the guys who spend ten years on something that's still sitting on their hard-drive, or consigned to the bin.'

'But you have a publisher – you're already published by Faber.'

'For my young adult books. This is different. There's no guarantee that they or anyone will publish it.' I pause. 'Would you like some wine?'

She wants something red and sweet. When I come back in with the glasses, I find her sifting through my desk. I frown but she remains unapologetic. She pounces on a mask with glee, pulls it on and cries a muffled, '*Da-dah!*'

I run my eyes over the ruttish mask and the fecund curves of her body: a hermaphrodite Will Self. Embarrassed by the bulge leering up in my trousers, I hurry over to the desk and shuffle through some papers, then find myself passing her a sheaf of them.

'Okay,' I say, 'read this. It's the end of Part One and it might not make much sense to you – but basically it's about this character called Richard, who isn't the most stable of people, who gets initiated into the WSC – the Will Self Club, which is this kind of weird culty club – and he ends up at their Initiation Ceremony . . . It's kind of like Schnitzler's *Dream State* . . . It's the most outrageous chapter in the book . . . and so . . . Anyway, maybe it is good to test it out on someone.'

She sits on the desk, sipping wine, which requires a certain agility given the Will Self mask, though there are slits for eyes and a mouth hole shaped in an 0 of shock. My wine glass trembles against my lip; droplets splatter on my jeans. I realize that, aside from my fear that she will condemn my prose in revenge, the sight of her is akin to watching the real Mr Self reading my book – which may happen some day soon, if only he would answer my letter.

'Oh, my God.' She puts the pages to one side. 'This is just so . . . *amazing* . . . I mean, it's really *wild* . . . I've never read anything like it.'

'Really?' I think I love her more than I've loved any woman before.

She stares at me until it feels as though the mask is one huge Selfian pupil, and I think behind it she might be smiling, but I can't be sure.

(vi) Bad Sex

She kneels down before me. The Will Self mask rubs against my jeans. I reach down to take it off, but she tugs it firmly back into place. Her fingers perform undoings with pleasurable languidity. The tongues of my belt slip away from their metal cage and dangle over my thighs. She/Will looks up at me. I feel disconcerted, for the mask obliterates emotion and therefore connection; for all I know, her expression might be curling with disgust. The eye-slits give no clues; they are almonds of pure shadow. She strokes her plastic cheek. Then a button flicks open. I groan and spread my thighs.

Dot dot dot.

And there I ought to stop. But I want to remember. I want to *preserve*. Even as I write this (some fifteen minutes after Zara has gone, for my present tense, unlike the fallacy of many novels, truly is present, or close enough), I am desperate to record the experience before it curls away like smoke. I admit that I might return to this chapter some time later, the paper in my hand, my cock in another. Typically, my response to any situation is to turn life into art. I harvest all my emotions with capitalistic ruthlessness. I like to write against my mood; if I want to cry I will osmose my pain into comedy, to keep it black; if I am feeling happy I will expel it through tragedy, in order to allow hope to glimmer in the prose. In my state of present tiredness, I am fighting yawns to convey the intensity of the electric shock treatment she performed on my penis. I want to couch the memory in the best metaphors I can devise, attempt to do her sexual genius justice with my prose.

Normally sex turns out the lights in my mind. I become pure physicality. I usually find such a blackout a relief after weeks of words trawling through my imagination like busy traffic. But even as Zara flicks open button after button, it doesn't happen. My mind stays bright and turned up to the max.

At first this feels frustrating. She toys with the final button as I toy with metaphor. As she tugs off my Levi's with a fricative pull, I'm playing with images to convey swelling: bullfrogs' throats, balloons puffed with water, pancakes filled with air. She delves into my Y-fronts; how I love their hermaphrodite design, so that she encounters a clothy vagina slit before discovering something resolutely masculine inside. She tugs them off too. I reach for the mask once more, hungry for her expression – but she shakes her head.

Desire and frustration coalesce. Her tongue darts out and shocks me. My whole body jolts and I hear her soft laughter. I know what comes next, and I feel relieved that she'll have to remove the mask. But then I feel the plastic pressing against the bottom of my shaft. I let out a yelp of pain as my cock is coaxed into the tight O. There is a purgatorial inch of air between the mask and her face. Then, as my cock is greeted by an angelic, exploring mouth, my pain transmogrifies into pleasure.

In fact, this is like no pleasure I've ever experienced before. This feels like experiencing both penetrative and oral sex simultaneously, for the plastic mask is taut as a virgin's vagina. Her tongue rolls and I consider images of eels and worse clichés;

and I become aware that I'm enjoying the physicality of pleasure together with the intellectual joy of trying to summon up prose that won't hit the lows of the Bad Sex Award. Perhaps Zara combines the talents of siren and muse, able to stimulate cerebrum and cock, so that both are fully erect and ready to fire in perfect fusion.

Even as she pumps me towards a climax, I still never achieve transcendence. I'm still consciously thinking, She's pumping me towards a climax, and wondering if 'transcendence' is the correct word to use. I search wildly for an image that will capture this insane ecstasy. Perhaps only religious terminology will suffice. I compare her to goddesses, to Cleopatra, to Monroe and Aphrodite; I roll on the edge of delirium, ready to ejaculate the perfect metaphor—

And then there is pure void and, for a few seconds, my existence is pre-Logos.

I cry out as she pulls away, the plastic clawing my sensitive member. She stands up and plants her hands on her hips. I suffer a sense of raw shame, with her standing there, my shrivelling cock on display like a piece of prose she's about to grade. Then, with a gust of brio, she spins a cartwheel across the room and lets out a whoop.

We book another creative writing session for three days' time. I tell Zara I'd like her to return a sesquipedalian. She asks what the word means, then pre-empts me before I can make the predictably smart reply: 'Oh, right — I have to look it up in the dictionary.'

After she's gone, I feel an ache inside, as though I've been watching a good film that's cut out halfway through. I wanted her to stay; she never got to eat her chocolate. I would have liked to spend hours with her on my clean sheets, making them dirty with crumbs and spunk and sweat and confessions and her lilac perfume, like catnip for me to inhale for days to come. I would have liked to give her pleasure, returned the orgasm; now the see-saw has tipped my way and it feels unnatural. I worry that she might feel used, or obliged to please in order that I'll keeping reading her work. A literary prostitute. That would be no good at all, I think, sobering up as I go out for a stroll. Imagine where the bargaining might end – a full stop for a lick; metaphor for a nipple-tweak; a grammar check for 69; the full course for a four-page appraisal. I want her sincerity, though I wonder if it might be hard to untangle that from her ambition.

My knees are bending; I need a bench. I rub my joints. I fear my midlife crisis is not just psychological but psychosomatic. I often feel tired after ejaculation, but not like this. After such a meteoric spurt of pleasure, I guess a corresponding comedown seems inevitable. Even so, this tiredness feels more potent than the mere physical, as though fatigue is chronic in the very core of my psyche. As I stand and attempt the walk home, my spirit seems to have turned from ether to cement; with each footstep my body wheezes in protest at the load. The world looks like a canvas of wet watercolours that has been tipped upside-down, so that all the colours have been drained away. I look into a grille of drain and ponder that somewhere down there is gushing the lost blue of the sky, the green of the trees, the amber of streetlamps, that particular shade of dirty red that adorns London roof-tops.

Back at my bedsit, I close the curtains and resign myself to a five p.m. bedtime. I struggle into pyjamas, leaving clothes on the floor. One last savour: I pick up the mask with a kind of nervous delicacy, as though I am in a museum and handling a pharaoh's treasure. A grin stretches across my face. I have a feeling this could give birth to a fetish.

(vii) Mia in the Hallway

I encounter Mia on the staircase that curves between floors four and five of our ecclesiastical block of flats. She is slotting earphones in; I am grappling Sainsburys bags. She is dressed all in black, a small purple rucksack bouncing on her back. 'Hi, Sam,' she says, and I very nearly reply, 'Hi, Mia.' Then I remember to say, 'Hi, Betty.' I'm not sure if she'd feel flattered to know that she has inspired the female lesbian reporter in Part Four of *The Quiddity of Will Self,* or if she'd prefer to start consulting her lawyers. As we exchange pleasantries, I notice a new tongue-stud sparkling in her smile. We only ever make surfacetalk, which I'm glad about. When I saw her last week with her boyfriend, I felt disappointed, especially when she told me he was an accountant. I'd rather not learn any more about her.

I sit down to write. There is a buttock-shaped space on my desk where Zara shifted my things to perch; I preserve it. I swivel my writing-pad towards me and click on my pen. Half an hour later, I find that my usual prolific output has deserted me. Like Will, I normally feel I have a muse like Hitler, but today such muse is more John Major. I have produced only a hundred words. They are grey. They are as dead as . . . a . . . dead as a doornail. There's a metaphor. But, as Orwell would have said, it's a dead one. Normally my prose is as cool as a cucumber. It shines like the sun. It has a touch of the night about it.

What is the matter with me? When I try to summon metaphors, linguistic possibilities fly through my consciousness like sperm, but they fail to fertilize and create an image. There. There's a slightly better metaphor, but herein lies my new problem: I seem capable only of thinking up images that relate to cocks, sperm or fellatio. My mind has become Zara-tracked.

What do metaphors matter anyway? But they do matter. I do not merely believe in them as a decoration for my prose: they are part of my literary manifesto. Metaphors are a way of fighting the decline of the English language. It is clear that New Labour, with *their* manifesto for neglecting grammar lessons in schools, have created a generation who have no idea where an apostrophe ought to lie, or the difference between *there* and *their*. This is Blair's legacy: the Iraq War and a transmogrification in language, as significant as the Great Vowel Shift. The current climate of illiteracy, combined with the collective predilection for texting, will result in an age, perhaps a hundred years on, when a reader will smile at our archaic use of *don't* rather than *dont*, or our quaint penchant for capital letters and full stops. Self satirizes this possibility in *The Book of Dave*, but he still bends and folds and spindles the language in all sorts of fascinating ways. The reality is that sesquipedalians will die out in the way that philosophers have, and the English language will shrink, and shrink, until our vocabulary is around a thousand dull, dull words. Yes, this will be our next Great Vowel Shift, though while in the sixteenth century vowels shifted up the throat, for us it will be the shifting down of our collective IQ.

Where are my words, where is my flow? Sometimes I find that Will Self can kick-start my imagination; I pick up *Cock and Bull*, my current favourite. *Cock* concerns a woman who grows a penis and rapes her husband; *Bull*, a man who grows a vagina behind his knee and is seduced by his male doctor. As is always the case with Will, new insights come with each rereading. Consider Bull, a genial, rugby-playing man, who has woken believing he has a 'wound' in the back of his knee: *'Already imprisoned in a stereoscopic zone where a shift in angle is all that's required for free will to be seen as determined. Let us leave Bull enjoying his last Heraclitan morning before being buckled into the implosion of farce.'* I wonder if it is human nature to feel that, in the flux of ordinary life, we are in possession of free will – but the moment life hits us with a *tsunami*, a love affair, a death, a divorce, we declare that it must be beyond our doing and we are in the hands of Fate. For, I realize, that is how I have started mentally to rewrite our first meeting. Out of all the bookshops in all of the country that Zara could have walked into – she came into mine.

Reading Will is a trenchant activity, but it does not cure me. My prose still squats on the page. No muse, just mush. I consider tearing a page from *Cock and Bull* and eating it, so I might ingest his quiddity. But one nibble and my tongue winces.

Perhaps I am diabetic. I call the doctor. The receptionist recognizes my voice – 'Weren't you the one who came in last week convinced he had AIDS?' she sneers. She tells me they have no appointments left but, when I persist, says she can fit me in on Thursday morning.

Fellatio. According to Google, it originates from the Latin *fellare* – to suck. I wonder why we still refer to oral sex in Vulgar Latin; perhaps a bashfulness in the *No Sex, Please, We're British!* psyche. *Blow-job* originates from Victorian England, since at that time folks would refer to a woman of questionable character as *blowsy*. And – this amuses me – the original Latin word *penis* meant *tail*.

Further surfing excuses me, explains my tiredness. It is

a scientific fact that sex gives energy to a woman, extracts it from a man. There is a Chinese proverb that says a drop of semen is equal to ten drops of blood. According to *Qigong*, the ancient system of Chinese medicine, the life energy inside us is called *jing*, representing our essence or spirit, an energy that dissipates with sex. Hence, they view masturbation as energy suicide. I surf further, yawns echoing yawns, my eyelids barely ajar. In pre-industrial societies, semen was revered as magical. Gemstones were believed to be drops of divine semen, which had coagulated after having fertilized the earth . . .

Writer's Block: a malaise of old. At least with a block, there was something to pound against. It has been superseded by Writer's Idleness, a malaise of vagueness, of drifting through Internet sites that have no centre . . . that are like . . . are like . . . *something* . . . I can't quite remember what . . .

(viii) The Blown Job

I'm like . . . like . . . what – *what*? – like, like the survivor of some glorious car crash. Yes, that's how it feels. A Ballardian orgasm. I've never had an orgasm like it, speed-racing in a car of red desire before being climactically hurled through the windscreen, pierced by shards of pleasure, hitting the ground with a heady thump. Now all I need is a stretcher, and a hospital bed, so I might lie in a comatose swoon for several days, with a drip to replace my lost spermboys.

I finally succeed in opening my eyes and see a blur of face above me. She splays out her fingers like a nurse. I count them out loud, climbing the numerical ladder back to sanity. She giggles and pulls off the Will Self mask, then leans down and gives me a kiss. She's pleased with herself; that's clear. For a moment I picture my sperm in her body, slowly easing its way down her oesophagus. I wonder how long it will remain in her digestive system; if even this time next week she will still be processing my quiddity.

'So . . . d'you think you could give me Archie West's details?' she asks.

I sit up, my trousers still splayed open. I'm slightly distracted by the state of my cock. When she knelt before me and took it in her mouth, it seemed to swell to Goliath proportions. Now it has become a grape past its sell-by date. I look up at Zara's lips, still wet with white. They curve into a smile.

'So . . . ? Archie's number? Or maybe his email?'

I pull up my zip, suffering a slight twinge of pain. 'Uh . . . yeah . . .'

'You okay? You seem almost like . . . you have a hangover or something! Did I tire you out?'

'I'm good. So − yeah − sure . . . I can pass your work on to my agent, that's fine. I mean, I have done this with friends in the past, though, and I should warn you that he's pretty busy, so don't be offended if he doesn't . . .' When I see her dismay, I quickly qualify my words: 'I'll make sure it goes to the top of his pile.'

Because, truly, I'd happily give her my agent for another moment of pleasure as intense as the one she's just given me. She makes me feel like a Greek god. I want to give her the grandest of gifts: the sky, the sun, the moon; to name chains of stars after her, and more clichés besides.

'Would you like to read it?' she asks eagerly.

'Sure.'

She passes me the pages. I swallow a yawn. Exhaustion is descending again, even more potent than the last time. I force-feed my mind a few lines of her prose. I honestly can't say if this is any good. More yawns stack up inside me. And then suddenly a sentence seems much too familiar: *I wanted to be penetrated to my very quiddity; I wanted to put myself into the hands of a magnificent psychogeographer.* Where have I read that before?

I laugh out loud with the incredulity of realization. *The Quiddity of Will Self.* She has taken me at my word; she has taken away my words.

'Oh, wow, I hoped you might find that bit funny!' she cries.

'Well, it's a bit like——' I break off, seeing the threat in her expression.

Her eyes taunt me. She stands up. My eyes plead for her to stay. The see-saw hovers.

'It's great,' I enthused, swallowing. 'I think . . . it's wonderful that you've . . . discovered a love for the English language.'

'Well, you did tell me to become a sesquipedalian,' she says, all smiles now. 'Don't you just love the word *quiddity*?'

'Well, yes – I think I may have introduced you to it.'

'I looked it up in the dictionary and it means *the essence of a thing*. Of course, it has quite a different meaning from *haecceity*. One should not confuse the two.' Zara curls a strand of hair around her finger. 'Don't you agree?'

'I'm . . . I have to admit that I've forgotten what *haecceity* means.'

'Oh, it means *the thisness of a thing*, whereas *quiddity* is about the *whatness*. *Quiddity* defines what makes a thing universal, the aspects of a thing which it shares with other things, whereas *haecceity* is all about the aspects of a thing that make it a specific thing.'

'Right. So. You don't feel you've . . . been *influenced* by any-one?' I can't resist the risk. 'I mean – it's only natural. Even an original like Will says he's been influenced by Ballard and Swift . . .'

'I don't think that the word *original* has any meaning, Sam,' she says sharply. 'Not if you look at this from a post-modern perspective. And I don't know why you're pulling that face. Your whole novel couldn't be more post-modern. But the fact is, *you* didn't write it. Haven't you read *Death of the Author*? An author is not a person but a socially and historically con-structed object; an author does not exist prior to or outside language. Society wrote your book; I wrote your book; Will wrote your book; your father's sperm wrote your book. And to argue that you're oh-so-original, well, I think you ought to be above that sort of logocentricism.'

For once, I am lost for words.

'There is no transcendent Truth,' Zara asserts, a little sadly. 'There is no absolute Truth in life or art.'

I gaze at her and muse that I haven't even kissed the sweetness of her breasts yet, or seen the coif of hair beneath her knickers. I want her on the bed, spreadeagled, sobbing for more.

But she is picking up her bag and pulling it over her shoulder.

'I . . . Zara,' I call. 'I just. I just wondered if you'd like to stay.'

'Well – it's kind of late and I have to be up early tomorrow, to work on my novel.'

'But . . .'

She turns. Eyes wide. *But.* Just one word and the see-saw starts to tip.

'I just wondered – where we stood.' I wince at my own words. 'You know – me. And you. And me.'

'Oh, I kind of feel whenever I'm with a guy that I don't need to define it with words, really – it just is what it is.' Zara pauses. 'Is that OK?'

'OK.'

'Great, then. 'Bye!'

''Bye . . .'

(ix) Logos Spermalikos

She's fifteen minutes late. Or, she's only fifteen minutes late. This is the first time we've arranged to meet at a location outside my flat. When she suggested the McDonald's on Oxford Road, she didn't seem to be joking. Then again, the date was arranged by text – and nothing makes words more ambiguous than the soundbites of a text. Hence the need for smiley faces and symbols, an acknowledgement of the limitations of fone language.

Sixteen minutes. Seventeen minutes. I can feel tiredness in my eyes, which might have been satisfying if I had been up all night writing. But I went to bed at eight. Since meeting her, I haven't slept properly; not those deep, dream-coloured sleeps I used to enjoy; now I can only drift in the shallows, conscious of constant erection, as though my cock is an addict aching for its next hit. Wet dreams feel like betrayals; nor do they reduce my cravings. Eighteen minutes. Walking here only took a quarter of an hour and it felt like a marathon. Nineteen minutes late. Marathon. That was a lame metaphor.

Thirty minutes. That will be my cut-off point. The last orgasm she gave me was mythic; I had to spend all weekend in bed recovering. In the dark, sweet moment of climax, I felt

I visited a place I had been only once before, as a boy, when I used to kneel and pray in church and experience a transcendent peace. It did not last. Writing used to be my drug of choice; now it is Zara. If only I could turn her into a Wafer and take her daily, I could be happy all the time.

Forty minutes. On the pavement, I see a worm, perhaps lifted by a beak from a garden and lost in transit, now wriggling through a discarded burger wrapper. I think of my father, whom I cancelled so I could meet Zara this morning. When I telephoned him to pretend I was ill, he didn't understand. 'You're ill, you say, you're Will? You wouldn't even win the Nonce Prize.'

The last time I went to visit him, I found it hard to open the door. The floor was covered with newspapers and tins and he was sitting by the window, staring out over Didsbury. I put all of the rubbish into a black sack and took care of a fortnight of washing-up. By the kettle, I found one of his lists. *10.23: listen to radio, 11.23 prepare lunch, 11.45 wash hands, 12 eat lunch.* A few years ago, I found a list that recorded what the 'voice' was telling him: *Be good. Conduct a house arrest. Listen to God.* That afternoon, I went to the library and picked up three audio books. Of course, I could not resist the Will Self ones. I took them back to him, convinced I could fight the voice and drive it out and make him happy. I had no idea that the voice would merely transmogrify, that it was a literary chameleon, keen to mimic.

Fifty minutes. I think of the day she first came into the bookshop, in her laddered tights and T-shirt. Did I misunderstand the signs, confuse her genre?

Sixty minutes.

I go home. I am surprised and pleased to find a message on my answerphone from Archie. I call up, but he's in a meeting. I walk around my flat for ten minutes. He can only be calling because I have a deal for the Will Self book. My euphoria is almost religious; I feel a strange urge to fall to my knees and thank Someone.

Archie calls back. He tells me that Zara has sent him her 'utterly amazing book' – this year's *Secret History* – and he's concerned because she's also approached other agents. He's tried calling her but she's incognito. Could I put in a good word for him?

'Sure,' I say. 'And – and what about my book?' Archie says he has to dash, Joanna Lumley's just arrived for their lunch date and he's dying to poach her.

In the Beginning was the Word. My landlord left a copy of an old Bible in each room as an 'ironic' gesture; he told me, with great amusement, that he'd saved them from being pulped when the church went under. I read the story of Genesis, trying to push Zara back behind the prose. But every narrative seemed only to be about her. For what is Genesis but an encapsulation of modern relationships – Eden followed by the wilderness of arguments and cross purposes, forever scrabbling about trying to recapture that initial, innocent Alpha bliss?

(x) Self and Amis Debate Sex

Zara pulls on the Will Self mask. Her hair snags and she re-arranges the elastic with an impatient sigh. I am sitting on the sofa, my cock torped with anticipation. She puts her hands on her hips, then gives my ankle a light kick. I realize that she wants me to undo my trousers. My rage forces me to be humble. Perhaps the humiliation even enhances my desire. She kneels down. The cut of the mask; the softness of her lips. But unlike previous suckings, where she stretched out my pleasure in spirals of delicious agony, she is quick and perfunctory. I whisper for her to slow down. She ignores me. I try to hang on to my semen but her control over my cock is absolute. She stands up and licks her lips. Then she checks her watch.

'We're going to be late for Will.'

But I can't stand. I am embarrassed. I have become Sam Mills, a hundred years old. 'Don't you want some dinner?' I ask weakly.

'You've filled me up. It's funny — just one spoonful of sperm and I don't feel hungry for days . . .' Zara muses.

She looks down at me and tuts. She puts my cock back into my Y-fronts and zips me up. All this she does with the patronizing tenderness of a nurse.

As she helps me to my feet, I am embarrassed to feel a burn in the back of my throat. I blink hard.

Zara lays out a white line on my coffee table. I wince as she hoovers it into her left nostril. 'Want some?' she asks grudgingly.

I am half tempted to say yes; to get something back from her, given all that she's taken. But I shake my head.

'I can't touch drugs . . . they just . . . I don't like to lose control of my mind. Drugs – they can shatter the mind and . . .' I trail off. I see Zara turning away and, in the reflection of my bookcase, rolling her eyes.

The doorbell rings. James. When he enters, giving me a cheery hello, I introduce him to Zara with a hiss. I watch them carefully, knowing that my best mate must want to fuck her. The whole world wants to fuck her. When we pass men on the street, I want to kill them; I want to tear down lamp-posts for caressing her with their light.

Manchester University, the Martin Harris Centre. Zara disappears into the Ladies. James and I enter the auditorium, a mini-amphitheatre with a curvature of seats upholstered in fuzzy scarlet. It is nearly full and we sit on the middle left. I consider the approach I tried this afternoon: my fourth approach to Will. This time, I was aided by a kind bloke called Nick, whom I met at a party. He works at Bloomsbury and offered to forward an email to Will via his editor, Bill Swainson.

Our literary gods enter.

I stare down at my ticket stub. *Literature and Sex, with Will Self and Martin Amis.* I suddenly feel embarrassed, being in the same room as Will. He might have been reading my book in the taxi over, might have dumped it in a rubbish bin before entering the building.

Martin Amis addresses us for twenty minutes. It's been a while since I heard him speak, but his oratory style has changed since he took up his post at Manchester. He addresses us with the erudite grandeur of a professor, lecturing on the impossibility of writing sex scenes. Carol Mavor, a dark-haired academic at the university, adds a few more thoughts. Finally Will takes the microphone.

'I don't feel that I can entirely concur with either of them – both for practical reasons, because then we'd have nothing to talk about, but also for rather more genuine ones. Contentiously, I believe it *is* possible to write well about good sex – and indeed that it's done quite a lot. So that's part of my argument. That being said, I broadly accept Martin's schema – and in particular I accept the notion, which he defined in his own very articulate way, that we're facing what J. G. Ballard termed "the death of affect" – the enormous loss of feeling that seems to have occurred since the 1960s, and is evident in a lot of the ways that we write about sex. It's always been possible to write pornography and, in a sense, the bawdy was the pornography of its time. But the erotic is metaphoric. The erotic is always about something other than cocks and cunts, and when you get down to cocks and cunts, then you're no longer with the metaphor, you're with the metaphrand – and there's nowhere really to go with that except to put it in there or stick it up there. What our culture faces as a problem in writing about sex is that it's become permissible to write entirely about the metaphrand. The interesting writing to be done about sex was really at the point where the metaphor and the metaphrand started to untangle themselves gummily from each other. So we do face a bit of a crisis when it comes to writing about sex because pornography is allowable in a mainstream literary discourse – it becomes extremely difficult to avoid it. It becomes extremely difficult to avoid a naming of parts. You're in danger, as a writer, of looking recherché if you avoid it . . .

'So I think it becomes very corrupting – this business of the naming of parts. The other problem that authors face when they come to write about good sex is their own desire, and the projection of their desire on to the page – how the Mick Jagger super-ego of choice expresses itself, which is often in a kind of ghastly saccharine quality that you get in sex scenes that are meant to be satisfying and full of what Freud would have termed full genitality – this is from a man who, according to his most reliable biographers, didn't have sex at all after the age of forty-five – perhaps that's the way it ought to be for all of us.'

The audience laughs.

'You see it in so many writers. It comes off the page as a whiff of semen or vaginal mucus, burning into you. There's nothing more off-putting than reading a sex scene and sensing that the author is getting their jollies off writing it. It would be invidious to name names – but you see me afterwards if you'd like to know more about the prime examples of the criminals in this particular field.'

The collective laughter grows louder. I start to worry about my sex scenes and whether I might be guilty of doing this.

'When it comes to deferred sex, however, some writers jumped the gun – one thinks of Joyce, and Bloom's wank scene in *Ulysses*, which is way out there ahead of the field in top-quality wank scenes, and well worth wading through the rest of the book for . . .' Will pauses, smiling, as he waits for the laughter to subside. 'And indeed, of course, Molly Bloom's internal monologue at the end, which, while not explicitly sexual, is all about sex and about being a sexual being and is a really astonishing piece of writing. But I think the text that stands as the gatekeeper between the time that it was possible to write about sex and the time when it stopped being possible in certain key ways is *Lolita* – because *Lolita* is all about bringing all of these things together. It's about teasing the metaphor and the metaphrand, titivating them apart from one another. It's about manipulating the reader, and manipulating the reader's own desire for good literary sex – it's a self-consciously highly literary novel. Amazing to think that it sold a hundred thousand copies in its first week. If Nabokov was to publish *Lolita* today, he'd be damned not for the nature of the work but for the ludicrous sesquipedalianism of his vocabulary – people would say, "Ooh, he must write with a dictionary next to him."

'I had thought of reading you one of my sex scenes. I felt that an evening like this would not be complete without a description of a British general practitioner having sex with a man who has a vagina in the back of his knee. In fact, I don't feel *any* gathering these days is complete without such a read-ing. But I'm afraid that the excellent local bookshop didn't have a copy of this book and so I'm not able to do so. I think I'll gracefully and gratefully just slide, a little moistly, out of the encumbrance of this discourse and re-enter it, fired up anew, shortly.'

The monumental applause confirms that, of the three speakers, Will is the favourite; he has stolen the show.

At the end of the talk, Zara grabs my hand and squeezes it. 'Are you going to go and speak to Will Self about your book? That's why you're here, right?'

'Oh, God, no,' I assert. 'He has my letter, my email, and the other email to his brother and the new one to his publisher. I wouldn't want to stalk him.'

Zara turns and stares at Will, who is gearing up to depart. 'Well, I think I'll just go,' she says softly.

'You won't – you won't tell him about my book, will you?' I ask desperately.

'Of course not. I just want to ask him about those dire sex scenes whose authors he won't name.' Zara winks.

'Will is a happily married man, with children,' I say loudly.

Zara walks away, her hair flowing like dark wine.

(xi) Anti-climax

James and I go for a drink in Kro. There, we bump into Dylan Evans and his fiancée, Louise. Dylan is a science writer I've been friends with for the past decade. Louise is an ex. She and I once had a no-frills fling.

Louise always declared that she would never commit to anyone. When I see the curve of her belly, I nearly attribute it to weight gain. But here's a clue: people suffering from obesity do not lovingly stroke their fat.

'Congratulations!' I cry, paying for the round of drinks with a twenty I've borrowed from James. I feel genuinely happy for them. But there is also an underlying insecurity, planted by Zara, which is now flourishing: *So my sperm wasn't good enough for you, Louise?*

Nine twenty-three, my watch says. Is she with Will now, is she throwing back her hair, is she laughing, is she beguiling him?

I down the rest of my beer.

'So, when are you going to set up the WSC?' Dylan asks.

'I thought you were an atheist, Dylan.'

'I am indeed, but ever since you showed me your manuscript – or should I say *scripture*? – I've been thinking that you ought to set it up. It would make an interesting social experiment.'

'I think it would be brilliant,' Louise chimes in. 'Imagine it — a shady London club, members in cowled robes wearing masks . . .'

'Absinthe with pieces of torn-up *Great Apes* swirling at the bottom!' I say.

'Harsh rules. If a member breaks any of the secret codes, they will be stripped of their cloak and their signed copy of *Cock and Bull*,' James enthuses.

There is a buzz in the air, a sense that we have collectively given birth to something of significance. I feel uneasy. Privately, I wonder if our genesis might grow up to be the religious equivalent of *Frankenstein*.

'After all,' Dylan says, 'Christians declare that every word in the Bible is pure truth, which seems completely arbitrary to me, so I don't see why we can't declare that everything Will has written is divine and absolute.'

I shake Dylan's outstretched hand, my eyes distracted by my watch. Ten thirteen. I try calling Zara, but she doesn't pick up.

Six pints later, I meet a girl. She's called Kara and she's studying for an MA in creative writing at Manchester. She enthuses about all the literary events she's been to recently and asks why I haven't spoken at any; I tell her I wasn't invited. She comes back to my flat. The lift is broken and we stagger up the stairs. On the sofa, we attempt sex of a metaphrand nature. Her fingers cannot coax away my limpness. I feel as though there is a Cyclops eye in the nub of my cock and it is pointing to the Will Self mask on the desk. I whisper a request for her to put it on. She attempts to — but breaks the elastic. Her hand falls slack; her face sinks into a cushion. When I wake up in the morning, she has gone.

(xii) An Email from Self Himself

The doorbell. A spotty youth, squeezed into Lycra, demands a signature on his electronic screen. I open up the package. There are three cloaks. One navy, one brown, one black.

I text James. He drops by in his lunch-hour. He pulls on a navy cloak with excitement. He tells me that various people he knows are clamouring to join the WSC. When he told them only a select few would be picked, their fervour intensified. One man is, apparently, preparing a twenty-page CV, together with a hundred-pound sweetener and the offer of a free golfing holiday (his father owns a course in Devon).

'So, how do the colours work?' James asks.

'Brown for neophyte. Navy for master. Black for grand master.' I pull on the black cloak. I draw up the hood. I look at my reflection in the mirror. The dirty laces of my trainers trail under the hem. James passes me the mask. I hesitate before pulling it on. I can smell her in its plastic crevices. Lilac skin, cauterized by something more bitter – which, I realize, is my own quiddick.

She came by today for twenty minutes. She sucked my logos, and then she left.

The mask fills me with a longing that becomes so acute I am forced to remove it.

I go to my desk. I check my emails. There is an email entitled 'From Will Self':

> Dear Mr Mills,
>
> The thing is to send some sample material – a chapter, whatever – and we can take it from there. I thought my agent had already communicated this to you? The address the material should go is: c/o The Wylie Agency, 17 Bedford Square, London WC1B 3JA.
>
> Yours &c.
> Will Self

James shouts and punches the air. I stand very still, shaking, for some time.

When James goes, I sit down to write to Will. For weeks, I have been composing imaginary replies in my head. Beautiful sentences designed to show Will that I am a fellow sesquipedalian. Metaphors so stunning that he will read them with admiration and even envy.

I write a hundred drafts of the letter before I accept my fate. My letter will have to be very simple. I tell him the bare facts. I ask for his help. I feel like a child with a begging bowl.

I email Archie to tell him the news – though he stopped returning my calls long ago. I go to the park and sit with the letter in a brown envelope on my knees. Rain moistens the graffitied swings, the see-saw. What is this pain in my heart?

I feel so tired that I am unable to walk home. I hail a taxi.

This is kismet: it is the same driver who picked me up from Waterstones.

'Well,' he observes, 'you're looking worse for wear. What or who has been keeping you up?' He cackles. 'Oh, and by the way – I got a deal for my book. Quite a big one, actually. This agent called me up, took me out to lunch and everything . . .'

I stare out of the window at the trickles of rain on the window, which look like . . . like . . . something I don't remember.

(xiii) The Quiddity Thief

Zara comes over to my flat. She is wearing a red dress. She tells me that Archie is now her agent. He sold her book for a six-figure sum and now the US are bidding for the American rights and Hollywood film companies are fighting to film it. I congratulate her, even though my heart does not feel happy. I think about the fact that I don't yet have a deal.

I tell her that I am angry with her and I never want to see her again. She pushes me on to the sofa. She pulls on the mask. It looks grotesque compared to the silk of her evening dress.

She observes that I have threaded a new elastic into the mask. This makes her smirk.

She sucks me off for twenty minutes before I come.

As she swallows, I black out again. When I wake up, I find the door has been left open. I stand up and go to it. A breeze blows over my face.

I feel a pain in my heart.

I finally post the chapters of my book to Will Self.

I go home and wait.

I go to the doctor's.

I tell her that I think I might be dying. She calls me a word beginning with *h* but I'm not sure what it means. I tell her I used to know a lot of long words. She smiles.

It seems there is no cure for me, for she does not give me a prescription.

I ask her if sperm is sacred. She says that it is not sacred but that it contains every known nutrient in the body.

I go to see my father.

'I wouldn't even win the Nonce Prize, I wouldn't even win the Nonce Prize . . .'

I find he has run out of food and tried to make a Will Self Pot Noodle by putting the pages through his shredder, adding salt, pepper and hot water.

'I'm sorry, Dad,' I say. 'I'm so sorry.'

He sits by the window, tears rolling down his cheeks. 'You wouldn't even win the Nonce Prize, you wouldn't even win the Nonce Prize.'

I go home and wait.

(xiv) Devotion

The first meeting of the Will Self Club is held in the Black Gardenia Club in Soho.

Members are instructed to recite the password at the door. The password is the last word at the bottom of page 183 of *Great Apes.*

In the dark hallway, coats are exchanged for cloaks.

The hierarchy of neophyte, master and grand master has now been replaced by a Masonic power structure.

These are conveyed by the insignia on the shoulder of each cloak. The Knight of the Cock and of the Bull has a WSC stitched in yellow, while the Chevalier of the Fat Controller has a scarlet flourish.

Will Self masks are worn by all. I ought to feel happy but I feel as though I am surrounded by twenty Zaras.

Members are informed that they should address others only by their initials. We sip glasses of absinthe with torn-up pieces of *Great Apes* swirling at the bottom.

I had feared there might be an atmosphere of mockery. But people seem sinister in their seriousness.

We sit in rows. Cross-legged. We meditate on a large picture of Will. We pray to achieve a transcendent state of Willcentricity.

Something inside me. I find it hard to understand my emotions now that I no longer have the words to describe them.

The feeling swells. I realize it is laughter.

I cannot believe that life has become art.

I laugh soundlessly beneath my mask. I am the Sovereign Grand Inspector General of Quiddity. I look around. Everyone is chanting. Some are swaying. Some have raised their faces Willwards.

My laughter deepens.

It breaks, and beneath my mask my cheeks become wet.

Zara: the hole inside me.

I look into the picture of Will and it looks back at me.

He fills me up. He makes me well. He makes us One.

I am no longer Sam, writer, lover, friend, boy, man.

All around, the chanting rises.

Knowledge comes.

This is why I met her; I had to break in order to become a searcher; I had to search in order to find; in order to become a believer.

I am Will. I am Will. I am Will.

(xv) Sucked

I hoped it might be a cure. But it is not enough. I tear up pages of *My Idea of Fun* and eat them. I try to write.

It is no good.

There is a knock at the door.

I hear her laughter behind it.

Knowing that I cannot refuse her.

I try write.

I put down my pen and go to the door.

She sucks me off.

When I wake up I find I am in a hospital.

James tells me that he found me and I would not wake.

A drip seeps into my skin.

(xvi) The Reply

A letter from Will Self.

It is typed on his famous Olivetti.

He likes my book.

He is not going to sue me.

He is willing to offer me 'passive support'.

He says he just wants to be misunderstood.

At the bottom there is a handwritten note: *That Jerry Bauer shot you have used of me sucks — it is heavily airbrushed — in reality my complexion looks like the Grand Canyon at sunset.*

(xvii) Lost

I have not seen her for five days. I have wept and fasted, wept
and prayed.

I have been to her house and I have called her number.

Archie telephones me and tells me that Corsair have put in
an offer for the novel. They intend to publish it in spring 2012.

He wants to buy me lunch.

I take the mask and I open the bin.

I want to throw it away but I cannot let go of it.

(xviii) Oblivion

The Grand Meeting of the Will Self Club is held in Soho.

I enter to see the hierarchy wearing cloaks.

The Grand Masters greet me with a Will handshake.

A baby cries. Louise, now known as Grand Elected Knight of the Ur-Bororo, holds her newborn to her cloak.

The flame of a candle.

We gather in a circle.

I hold the baby.

'The Grand Masters of the Will Self Club do William you as William Zach Busner Evans.'

(xix) Baby

The baby stares up. Eyes of wisdom. As though it has seen all the world and stars, Alpha and Omega, the first and the last, the beginning and the end.

The group gathers in a circle.

(xx) Enlightenment

They await my speech.
   The baby cries.
   I am lost for words.

Acknowledgements

Thank you to my agent Simon Trewin for his initial enthusiasm when I began the book back in December 2000 – and for waiting another nine years while I finished it.

Thank you to my editor James Gurbutt for his sensitive and judicious editing. To Jo Stansall, Hazel Orme, Emily Burns and all at Constable & Robinson.

Thanks also to Ariella Feiner, Jessica Craig, George Lewis and all at United Agents.

Thanks to my friends: Kate Williams, James Higgerson, Dylan Evans, Alexander, Tom Boncza-Tomazeski, DBC Pierre, Victoria and Roy Connelly and William Robinson. Thanks to Grace Dugdale for introducing me to Nick Humphreys at Bloomsbury, whose kind help I much appreciate.

Thank you to my family, especially my mother.

Last, thank you to Mr Self for not suing me.

Suddenly the door burst open and a crazed man entered. He had red hair and freckles and was wearing an anorak. His expression was a predatory snarl, like that of a murderer about to steal spirit, leave behind ruined flesh. He grabbed my book off the desk and made a run for it.

Luckily, one of the security guards caught him halfway down the stairs.

I am glad that my manuscript is safe, but it feels dirty; I can see the smudges of the madman's prints. As though my book has been raped.

21 NOVEMBER

<u>1 a.m.</u>: Woke about an hour ago from a terrible nightmare. The darkness seemed alive, until I realized that it was just a moth, melancholic for light. I am not allowed to use my candle at night (Prof. Self jests that I should avoid 'burning out') so I am writing this in the dark, guided by the grooves in the desk